NEXUS GATE 4037: THE ANIMAL

A Novel

CANDICE COATES

NEXUS GATE 4037: THE ANIMAL
COPYRIGHT © 2018
BY CANDICE COATES

ISBN 978-1-7326714-0-9 (eBook)
ISBN 978-1-7326714-1-6 (Paperback)

This novel is a work of fiction. Names, characters, places, incidents, and dialogues are either the product of the author's imagination or are used fictitiously. Any similarity to actual events, locales, organizations, or real persons, living or dead, is coincidental and not intended by the author.

Cover Design: Candice Coates

Published by Candice Coates
Columbus, OH

Visit candicecoateswrites@gmail.com

DEDICATION

...To all those who have dared to dream and who believed with enough faith to succeed.

ACKNOWLEDGMENTS

I would like to give thanks to everyone who supported me in bringing this piece of fiction to life in a way that I have been able to share it with others. To my childhood friend, Erika Grady, for all the days you stayed on the phone and listened as I read to you my rough drafts of other stories. Thank you for encouraging me to continue to write and showing an interest even in the rough works. To Rachael Ritchey, thank you for walking me through every aspect of indie publication, for giving me your time and your encouragement as a friend and fellow writer. To Mark and Noushi Stouffer, thank you for sowing into this journey. It is by your gift this story finds life on the bookshelves of many readers. To Tricia Lynn Figueroa, thank you for believing in me and encouraging me to pursue my dreams even in the rough seasons, and especially for telling me to write this book! You are the best. To all my beta readers and fellow writers, to those who voted for this to be my debut novel, to those who have read, and to those who have yet to read this piece, thank you. And most importantly, thank You, Jesus for allowing me to live this dream and for giving me the gift of word-weaving and storytelling. Thank You for this moment.

NOTE TO READERS ABOUT CERTAIN 'WORDS' FOUND WITHIN THIS DOCUMENT.

Dear Friend and Reader,

In the following pages, you will meet with several words, epitaphs that you will most likely find very jarring and offensive. These words will be spelled out in plain text while other words, such as curses or profanity are abbreviated.

The reason behind this choice, to abbreviate the profanity while leaving the slurs intact, has to do with the importance of acknowledgment for such words and the damage they cause while also upholding my own personal convictions. While most if not all profanity is easily recognized in an abbreviated form, racial slurs are not. The importance of leaving the slurs as they are is indeed for you, the reader, to empathize with the victim while seeing the victimizer for who they are.

This choice was not taken lightly, but being as I wanted no room for any misunderstanding I again, left these words in plain text.

Now, without further ado, I present to you *Nexus Gate 4037: The Animal.*

~Candice Coates

NEXUS GATE 4037: THE ANIMAL

CHAPTER 1

"You think you can keep me here, stringed up like some nigga' who done run'd off!? I swear 'fo god I'se gon' kill you with my own hands, rip your dark hide clean from them bones, you black b!#@^!"

The broken words of his old southern drawl were so muddied that Vivian had to cut through them to decipher what he was saying. She would have been better off not knowing what he said. Even with the near absence of certain consonants like 'R' and the lengthening of vowels when he spoke, she could clearly hear his hatred and rage for her. She felt it like biting teeth ripping through tender flesh.

She almost thought him justified in his hatred of her. Fear had that effect on the mind, brought out the worst in the powerless.

Three days, it had been three days since the man she held bound had awakened, and she already felt like she was going to break! The familiar sense of ordered control was sifting like sand through her clenched fingers, mocking her attempts to hold everything together.

But she would hold it together. She had to. John Jay's life depended on it.

Fisting her hands as tightly as the man did his bared teeth, she forced herself to remain in place, not retreat. She couldn't give the appearance of weakness. No, she needed him to calm and she needed him to trust her; a near impossible task since she was the one who'd abducted him. But it had been the right thing to do, the only thing she could do to buy herself and John Jay more time, to buy this man more time.

1

The thought of her husband and the raging of her detainee strapped down in her lab, made her shudder.

How the notion had slipped uninvited into her mental rooms of reason that abducting a fully grown man and holding him against his will was an act of control or even a viable option for survival was beyond her. But there were no other options, of this she was certain. She'd made a deadly error within the last ten days. Truth was, she'd made several, but she was trying to rectify them. She was trying to get her and her husband's lives back…and save that of her unwanted guest's in the process.

At least she hadn't been found out. Not yet at least. As far as the Cleric's Office knew, all was well with Team V.Leona-Spruce 4034-44G.US, from timeline 6034. They were in good standing, had been for the three out of ten years of their surveillance, and hadn't made any disruptions in their host timeline in the Field, 4037.

All of that was a lie, but Vivian hadn't meant to hide anything. She'd always been an excellent Team Lead. She held tight to the rules of surveillance steadily and repetitiously breathing them in and out like the very air. By rote, she recited them in her thoughts. *Never give away your cover in the Field. Never reveal anything from future times that could disrupt the threads of history. Blend seamlessly into the host timeline of your assignment. Always keep your Century Cell Group apprised of all activities and findings.*

Yes. She knew every rule, but she'd somehow managed to lose each rule like an apostate their religion the very moment her husband, John Jay, had gotten lost within the Nexus Gate, deeper in time past.

She hadn't meant for any of this to happen! She had come to the 4030's for two reasons, to survey and restore. Time Surveillance, verifying the happenings of history was her lifeblood. She was there to find the root of the Silent Revolution, the crucible that burned through the dross of The New Golden Age and shaped her very world in the 6030's.

She was also there to restore what had begun to dwindle into heatless embers within her marriage.

It seemed like the perfect solution, take a decade-long Field study two millennia in the past, block out every distraction, survey the timeline, and use it all as a way to repair her emaciated relationship. What she and John Jay had built in the 6030's as man and wife would hold in place just as firmly as their decorations for excellent Fieldwork had held in place.

But nothing had held, not even the faulty Nexus Gate that had lost John Jay somewhere in time and had exchanged him for a vile being that too many people referred to as 'The Animal.'

"You hear me, *negress*? I'se gon'—" Blocking out more curses that spewed from the bound man's lips, Vivian let out a deep groan and shuddered away the sickening roil that had assaulted her stomach. The sickness had plagued her for several days all while the world as she knew it crumbled in her hands like sun-dried clay.

Her effort to diligently restore, her dream to build not only a better future in time surveillance but her personal life had been replaced by a nightmare that bore the same name as her husband.

"Please be still, John, *Tucker* John," she quickly added on the other nickname that history had recorded for the bound man. She couldn't call him an animal no matter how much he behaved as one. "You're going to harm yourself," her voice was deceptively tranquil, a great contradiction to the trembling in her hands that she eased toward his restraints. They were still holding, but just like everything else, there were only so many traumas they could take before they too fell apart.

Tucker John snarled when she drew closer to him, his mono-lid eyes closing up to dark slits. His solid frame tensed. Every muscle strained with sharp definition the more he violently struggled against his restraints. "Be concerned for yo' own self, negress! I'se gon' make you pay for each day you done held me here. I'se gon' kill you slow and savor every minute of it! I swear 'fore god I am!"

Vivian withdrew from his side, quickening her pace with each step, pinching back the slicing pain of stress that cut through her temples. His insults bounced loudly off the walls of the corridor as she hurried through from the laboratory where she kept him. Grateful she hadn't locked the door behind her she rushed into the upper-level of her house and slid the hidden wall shut with shallow breaths. Leaning her back against it, she pulled the mask she'd worn from her face and placed it on a nearby shelf before moving away from the wall completely.

Tucker John continued to roar. Vivian moved to the far end of the room, turning away from his low knocking and distant grumbles. "Jesus, *please* make him be quiet!" She needed a moment to collect herself before she had no choice but to tend to the responsibilities that had been thrust at her, the responsibility of *him*. What could she possibly do with him? Dealing with him was like trying to tame flames of fire with her bare hands. She was definitely going to get burned.

A deep breath escaped her lips. She rested her weight against the window sill and stared out into the vastness of the countryside, forcing herself to focus on the silence of her thoughts, completely blocking out Tucker John's muffled sounding-offs from the other side of the wall and the underbelly of the manor house.

Just thinking about him made her wince. Each time he slung his curses at her she had to remind herself that she meant him no harm, would do him no harm, whether he knew it or not, whether she felt it or not. He was just as much a victim as she or John Jay. He wasn't meant to be in that millennia just as she had no option but to hold him bound until she could explain to him why he was there in the first place and why she couldn't send him home…at least not yet.

She was doing this for his own good, even though he seemed as a prisoner and promised her a violent death the moment he got himself free.

She'd managed to keep that one thought on track. This man was not her prisoner, but he was a prisoner of his upbringing and his own doing, and if she set him free it would only mean his death. He had been bred by a culture of ignorance and had not sought out the truth. Most of them didn't, not back then. In 1837, the deep American South, his lashing words, and condemnation of her melanin was the accepted norm. She nearly burst into laughs of hysterics. *If he only knew how much this melanin cost....*

But now twenty-two hundred years into his future, his ideology was deemed an abominable condition—a contagion with no cure, one that only euthanasia could contain. There was no mercy for those cursed with his sickness, no hope of reprieve, no trial, just death.

Vivian wouldn't have his blood on her hands.

She took another deep breath and tried to steady herself. This was 'Tucker' John, John *Josephus* Spruce, slave foreman and bounty hunter from 1837, the one called 'The Animal' by those he hunted and a 'necessary evil' by those who enlisted his skills. He was not John *Joseph* Spruce, beloved husband and Surveillance Tech Engineer from the year 6037.

How in God's name had she mistaken Tucker John for her husband in the first place? She already knew how, yet it still made no sense. This situation made no sense. Her breath caught in her chest, the anxiety choking her like a hand around her throat. She suppressed an urge to scream and weep, and clutched the white obsidian stone pendant—a gift from John Jay—that hung just above her heart, before she offered a quick prayer for forgiveness, and another plea for help.

Thirteen years she had been with the Ministry of Time. She had been a surveillance specialist for thirteen years, started in the Cleric's Office at age eighteen before entering the Field only two years later in 6026. In all that time, in all the places she had been—and she had been to many—she had *never* made a single mistake, or broken a single rule...until now.

Now, in the deceptively pristine, almost sterile backdrop of the Georgian South of 4037, she found herself on the other side of the good, having withheld knowledge from her Cell Group a handful of happenings that were certainly beyond reproach, while completely blowing her cover.

She reasoned that she hadn't broken the first of the rules. Yes, she had blown her cover, but not to any denizen of *that* specific era. Her self-defense within the cusp of the scenario was nothing more than a loophole, one she could narrowly fit through, but it was a hole nonetheless. She also hadn't stepped into her own future even though she'd made a way for Tucker John to step into his.

The nexus gate had gotten it all wrong, or Vivian had gotten it wrong in her haste. She didn't remember. Her nerves were still too raw to recall. Lourdes, her and John Jay's assistant, a local denizen, had tried to help, but it was to no avail. Tucker John was there now in his future, a place forbidden to those of the past, and John Jay was still missing in time.

It was a mess, one that had Vivian on her knees with a guillotine blade threatening to make contact with the back of her quivering neck.

She swung her attention to the lab wall again. Anger, frustration, fear boiled inside of her. The muffled roaring beyond the wall had grown even louder. She had to intervene, face the source of the terrible clamor; make Tucker John stop.

"Lord, please help me. I *need* Your help." She kissed the obsidian pendant and let it fall back to its place by her heart before again slipping on her porcelain mask, walking away from her visual sanctuary and into what she was beginning to think was nothing more than the bowels of hell.

CHAPTER 2

(Ten days earlier)
Vivian burst through the side door of her home racing down the hill some two-hundred yards to the very place the Nexus Gate would open up an Emergency Portal or E.P. She only had three minutes to get there. She would be in place in two.

One last kiss. John Jay's last words to her, his last gesture before he disappeared within the Nexus, drummed in her head, smothering her like the thick humid air that pushed against her. Tears blurred her eyes and her knee-length tunic tangled in between her legs. She fell hard. The impact jarred her joints and grass stains smeared the fabrics, but she pushed on.

One minute.

She ran even faster, slowly picking up momentum, hardly catching her breath. How had he gotten lost? What happened? *One last kiss.* She called out his name as the unfamiliar crackle of the Nexus tearing open an E.P in mid-air surrounded her. She prayed John Jay's words were not true. *One last kiss.*

"JOOHHHHNNNNNN JAAAYYY?!" She sucked in more hot air, tears sliding down the sides of her brown checks burned red from exertion. Circle ripples grew outward before her very eyes like liquid mercury right in the spot the Nexus Gate had indicated the E.P would appear. Vivian stopped only a few yards away, her chest rising and falling against the strain of stress. She needed to catch her breath. "John Jay?" Her voice shook. "JOHNNNN JAAY?!"

"What's going on?" Panic echoed in Lourdes' voice through Vivian's earpiece.

"*Nothing!* I-I don't know! John Jay, please! Come on!" She pulled at the roots of her hair with clenched, nervous fist. The portal quivered ominously but it had ceased to make a sound, taunting her with its silence.

Several seconds passed, hardly a matter of minutes before Vivian could stand it no longer. She called out his name again before reaching out her hand to touch the E.P.

PHOOM!

A rush of wind broke forth from the break in the timeline, knocking her backward with a force that rattled her equilibrium. Lourdes' distorted voice wobbled in her ringing ears. Blinking deeply, Vivian pushed herself up on all fours only to fall back on her stomach, her mouth open in a shocked 'o'. The world seemed to be spinning around her. If it wasn't for the clamor that she heard echoing outward from the portal she might have collapsed completely.

She careened her head in time to see the back of a woman, dressed in tattered antebellum slave attire, run barefoot from the mouth of the portal and out into the expanse of her property, never breaking her stride. The sun-bleached, sweat-stained threads beat against the woman's legs with each pounding pump and push of her swift legs. She hadn't even realized she had leaped two-thousand years ahead in time, out from the grasp of one hateful century deep into a future that could prove far less volatile but far more deadly.

Several dogs barked, taunting male voices, and gunshots echoed outward from the mouth of the E.P. Vivian forced herself upward beyond the veil of terror that had pinned her to the ground. She had to move. She had to contain the breach!

Three men on horseback broke through the ripples of time, screaming curses at the back of the woman they pursued. None of them, not the men, the horses, the dogs or the slave, had noticed the change in time, or Vivian, frozen on the ground.

What was happening? She staggered to her feet, grimacing from the bruises she'd been given from the impact of her fall, and called out to Lourdes from her microphone. "Lourdes!

LOURDES! Power up the perimeter Fence! Close off the property!"

"WHAT? What's happening? Is John Jay alright?"

"Power up the *fence*, Lourdes! We have a time breach," Vivian panted, running back up toward the house. "There is a runaway slave and a posse on horseback! We can't let them leave the property! I need the fence up, and I need a set of intermezzos! Have them at the back door and bring trackers!"

She tore back up the hill to her house. The perimeter fence lit up like a dome around the 6,400 acres of property before fading into invisibility. That was an even ten square miles covered. Still, she needed to move quickly. No one really came out to her manor without announcing themselves first, but she couldn't take the chance. She needed to get the slave and the posse back through the E.P as soon as possible, and she needed to find John Jay.

Lourdes met her at the back door with the items she had demanded; trackers to locate anyone on the property and an intermezzo to suspend them in time once they were located. Lourdes' face was sheet white. Her shoulders kissed her earlobes from the tension and fear that hung thick in the air. She wasn't familiar with such emotions. "What are you going to do? Where is John Jay?"

Vivian cut her eyes at Lourdes. "*We* are going to locate the people who came through the portal and we are going to send them back to their proper time in history."

"But they have guns! Rifles and dogs—"

Vivian hurriedly checked the intermezzos. All she needed was one shot and she could get them all in a time-net, suspended in a single moment in time and then she could send them right back to where they came from. "Stay out of the way of the guns and the dogs and remember to use your intermezzo."

"But John," Lourdes pressed, her face suddenly washing bright pink with tears. "Where is Joh—"

Vivian cut her off, snatching one of the trackers from her hand and biting at her with a clipped answer. "I. DON'T. KNOW!" She felt her chest tensing and her body shaking. How had this happened? John Jay was only supposed to recalibrate the nexus gate, prepare it for the new fittings like he'd done many times before. But something went wrong this time. What went wrong?

Lourdes' mouth clamped pronouncing her quivering chin. Guilt pricked at Vivian. She tried to calm herself as much as her coursing adrenaline would allow before she routed the settings on the tracker and speaking again to Lourdes.

"I don't know where John Jay is, Lourdes." Her voice cracked. "We're going to find him. I'm going to find my husband, but we have to deal with this first."

She stared into her glassy grey-blue eyes and mustered more compassion. Lourdes had never cried before in the three years she'd known her. "We can't let them stay here. This is their future. There is no telling what kind of damage or paradoxes they're causing by being here. The longer they're here," she wiped her glistening brow with the side of her shaking arm. "The longer they stay, the worse things will be. Dogs and rifles will be the very least of our problems."

(Present day)
Vivian flinched as if she'd been slapped straight through the porcelain mask that covered her face. Even though she knew in her mind this was not John Jay, her heart couldn't shake the wicked daggers that Tucker John hurled at her. Each one landed with a knee-buckling thud to her core that spouted rivers of blood, invisible to the eye—soul wounds.

Eyes narrowed, she studied him, quite like she had when he was sedated. Her eyes froze against the curl of his snarling lips. They looked like the lips she used to kiss, his bottom lip twice as full as his top, only these were drawn and hidden within a long bush of pale blond hairs.

His mono-lid eyes were a gun-metal grey, but they were wild, angry, and cold as ice. Apart from his hair being too long—to the bottom of his shoulder blades—and sun-bleached to pale honey, his body being too cut, and muscularly formed from the life he lived off more physical labors, he was the exacting image of John Jay, even down to placement of his scars, and solid stature.

(Ten days earlier)
A half an hour spent and nothing. They hadn't located a single being. Vivian had gone from frantic to outright angry. Why had she gone on this goose chase on foot? She should have gotten a sled. They could reach speeds of up to sixty miles with their tops down, twice that when covered, hovering mere inches from the ground, gliding on the face of the wind. Best of all they made little to no sound while in motion.

Now completely infuriated with anxious frustration, she kept her jaw clamped shut. She had already given Lourdes an undeserved tongue lashing, blaming her for her incompetence. She'd even gone as far as to blame her for the mess that had come through the E.P. Had she not let Lourdes help none of this would have happened. Stubborn from the fear that hardened her heart, she refused to give place to guilt, or remorse for her ill-laid blame. Instead, she stopped talking altogether. She would make peace later.

The tracker recalibrated in her hands startling her to a stumbling stop. It had located the slave-woman.

"She's just north of the creek!" Vivian whispered. "We have to be careful, understand?" She looked back at Lourdes who scowled back at her.

"Listen, save the attitude for later. It's imperative that we get this right. She cannot see us. Our appearance could give her a mental break. If she talks about these things back in her time there is no telling what the consequences could be for her. She could die before her time, be locked away...most likely, she would be put to death. It could throw off an entire timeline."

"We're wearing knee length, linen tunics and trousers I don't think that could break a timeline."

Vivian gave her a warning glare.

Lourdes raised her chin, a tear falling down her cheek. "Fine! I won't let her see me. Believe it or not, Vivian, I'm *just* as stressed out as you are."

Vivian selfishly found that hard to believe. Lourdes' husband hadn't disappeared into only heaven knew where. She didn't even have a husband! Vivian shook her head. She was being unreasonable, still, the bitterness that coated her tongue kept her from saying so. "Let's just take care of this fiasco and, and...let's just go."

The sun had already begun to set by the time they located the slave-woman. She'd hidden nearly an hour north of the creek and had somehow managed to fall asleep within the short moments she'd found refuge. How she'd lost the posse was beyond Vivian. She imagined the slave-woman had taken much time in planning her flight so she would know where to hide, which also meant she knew how to hide and not get caught. She would have almost had the upper hand if Vivian wasn't aided by technology.

"She's hiding in the roots of that dead Oak. There's a lot of mud and water under there." That explained how her scent had been lost to the dogs.

"How do you suppose we get her to come out of there without us being seen?" Lourdes asked.

Vivian grumbled. That was a good question. She smacked an ornery mosquito from her neck and thought up the quickest plan she could. "Since the perimeter fence is up we can do a virtual simulation, angry bees,"

"In the dead, muddy roots of a tree? Not bees. Scorpions are more believable."

Vivian considered Lourdes' suggestion before introducing a third option—mud wasps. They were native to the area. "We need to catch her from behind, so I'll take the left flank and you take the right. Once she comes out I'll get her in with the intermezzo. You hold yours at the ready."

It took a little longer than Vivian had expected, but the simulation did work and the slave-woman did come bolting out of her hiding place. Before she could let out a scream, Vivian had her frozen within the time-net. She had only gotten a few paces away from the woman when Lourdes' intermezzo shot off cutting through the active path of Vivian's net, unlocking it. The slave-woman reanimated.

Panicked, Vivian lunged at Lourdes yanking the intermezzo from her hands. She quickly turned toward the slave-woman who obliviously batted at her muddied clothing, aimed the intermezzo at her once again but hesitated in firing when Lourdes called out her name.

"Vivian!"

Vivian flinched. The slave-woman turned to face them, her chocolate brown eyes locking with Vivian's. Both Vivian and the slave-woman's faces contoured in utter horror. Vivian quickly pulled the trigger on the intermezzo.

Once again the woman was frozen in time. The horrified expression hadn't budged, nor had the slave-woman's pointing finger and outstretched arm. She was pointing at Vivian. Vivian wanted to point back. Even through the mud, the sun-bleached hair, tattered slave clothing, and skin sun-darkened a shade or two more than hers, the slave-woman bore an unsettling resemblance to Vivian Leona.

CHAPTER 3

(Present Day)

A glob of mucus and spit landed at Vivian's feet, snatching her out of her assessment of the man.

"You think I can't see your darkie skin through that mask? I see that look in your eyes, negress!" Tucker John shouted. "You just buuurnin' to have a romp with me, ain't you? Y'all like animals in *heat*, aching for the touch of a white man! GO ON! Turn me loose. I'll give you what you want so bad!"

His voice was a fowl hiss, the look in his eyes intent, dangerous. "And when I'se done with you, I'se gon' catch that other negress who done run off and I'se gon' whip the hide right off ya'll's backs!"

Vivian stepped away from him. Her head was spinning again. She was going to collapse, thinking about the slave-woman, her twin through time. She was the reason that Vivian wore the mask. The same way Vivian mistook Tucker John for John Jay was the same way Tucker John would mistake her for the slave-woman that he hunted down like an animal. Their likenesses were so close Vivian had no choice but to keep her face covered.

There would be no mistaking of anyone's identity now. Vivian had already sent the slave-woman—Vivian, she was also called Vivian—back to 1837.

(Ten days earlier)

"She looks exactly like you, Vivian!" Lourdes panted and pointed, her grimace somehow resembling a grotesque smile.

14

At first glance, it was almost like looking into a mirror. The other woman wore Vivian's face even if it were framed in a different fashion; round cheekbones, aquiline nose, naturally arched brows, long lashes and chocolate brown eyes that had always been called demure—John Jay said they reminded him of melted chocolate—full lips that set above a smooth pointed chin and narrow jaw line.

Vivian nearly collapsed staring at the frozen visage of her time-twin. Her legs felt as useless as cotton-candy, her heart beating with an erratic tattoo making it near difficult to breathe. She couldn't even blink.

Lourdes grabbed her shoulders still calling her name. As if burned by her touch Vivian snatched away. If she was tender before, now she was completely raw with anxiety. *Call Raul.* The thought came unbidden to the forefront of her mind. She could call Raul. She *should* call Raul, her Century Cell Group Leader. Raul Manuel would know what to do, she prayed he did. But how could she let him onto her property without letting the posse out?

There were too many variables on the table, most of them unknown. She couldn't afford the gamble. All she needed was a bit more time to fix this, find John Jay, put everything back in order and then—

The tracker recalibrated again, the sound of it punching a startled scream from her belly. Gaining her bearings, she took a step away from the slave-woman and Lourdes, mentally distancing herself from the shock of her time-twin. She quickly took note of the tracker's readings and got a visual of the posse's location. They were just on the other side of the rise and fall of a few hills and pastures not a full two miles away from them.

Sweat tickled her temples and the side of her cheek. She smacked the moisture away with several more mosquitos that dared make a meal of her. "The posse is on their way. They'll be here in less than five minutes. I can already hear the dogs." She narrowed her eyes and looked in their direction.

Lourdes extended her hand, her throat rising and falling as if she struggled to swallow. "They probably heard you scream. I need my intermezzo back."

Vivian glanced back at her, shook her head before pointing her eyes back in the direction of the posse. "Not a chance. You almost got me with that thing last time. You wait here with her," she pointed at the slave-woman without looking at either of them. "I'm going to net the posse and the dogs from the hill. Once I give you word that they're frozen, you are to head back to the house, send me a sled and a Drag Net. There wasn't one with the intermezzos and we'll need one to get them back to the E.P. I'll also forward you their stats, make sure they are all green to go back to 1837 within the next few hours."

She didn't wait for Lourdes' response. She quickly ran toward the hilltop and waited for the posse to come. What a surreal picture it all made, standing on pasture land and Georgia's red clay, looking down on a posse of hateful humans who called themselves men, hunting a defenseless woman just because of the color of her skin.

Vivian never wanted to get this close to that part of history, stare inexplicable hatred in the face. No, she'd left the foul stench of all things antebellum to those within the Ministry of Time who had stronger constitutions than she. She almost agreed with the ideology of the timeline she was surveying in 4037 concerning that behavior. Ethnic hatred and xenophobia were indeed diseases, but in Vivian's mind, they were more forms of mental illness that had uncanny ways of spreading like plagues. Still, she viewed them as curable, unlike the denizens of the New Golden Age.

Without a hitch, she had the posse netted and waiting for transportation back to the E.P. She had just barely finished assessing both the men and their beasts when the same sound that she'd heard when the slave-woman and the posse emerged from the E.P sounded again. Her breath caught in her lungs.

"John Jay," his name had hardly left her lips before she took off in full sprint in the direction of the E.P.

"Lourdes! Someone else has come through the E.P! It's John Jay! It has to be John Jay. Send the sled, *now!*"

She didn't wait for Lourdes' response but kept on running. At the edge of the creek bed, the sled met her. She hopped on, not wasting a single moment to draw up the cover even though that would have given her the ability of greater speed. The lag in velocity did afford her a few moments to consider her direction. It would do her no good to go toward the E.P if John Jay was headed for the manor house.

She looked down at the tracker. It had finally recalibrated and located the individual who had come through, but he wasn't heading toward the manor. Instead, he was following the exact path that everyone else had gone. It was like he knew where they were headed. Vivian's pulse sped again. She was suddenly grateful for her lack of speed. Reasonable conjecture pricked her. What if this wasn't John Jay either, but another posse member looking for the runaway slave? What if she was heading right into the mouth of a lion?

She decreased her speed and waited out of sight of the new arrival. The thickness of the wooded area framing the figure's riding path hid her like a blank.

Within a few short moments and he came into view, easing his way through on horseback, rifle across his lap.

It was almost completely dark then; the gentle glow of fireflies danced in the clearing darkness of the sky, but Vivian could still see his large frame and broad shoulders swaying with the easy gait of the horse he rode upon. She could almost make out the color of his shirt, and the paleness of his long hair beneath the worn leather cowboy hat brushing the tan overcoat he wore. The hat's brim caste a blue-black shadow over much of his face but not the beard that hung down to the bottom of his breastbone.

The sudden rush of blood to her head nearly knocked her unconscious. This was *not* John Jay.

Swallowing down the bile of disappointment, she stilled her breath and raised her intermezzo. She'd do him like the others, identify him in history, verify his future, and send him right back to where he came from. Then she'd call in Raul. She had no other options now. She couldn't leave the E.P open much longer nor the perimeter fence engaged.

With a whip of blinding movements, the man had his rifle raised and aimed directly at her. Tree bark flew outward from the impact of the shot. The shattered evidence of it was only a foot away from Vivian's head. She crouched low against the tree, adrenaline numbing her from the pain the tiny cuts the debris had made on her face and neck.

"Found you," the man's tone was matter-of-fact. There was no humor in it, more an edge of boredom.

Vivian's mouth was cotton. Her body trembled like it had been bitten by frost. She'd never been shot at! She ducked and pulled herself further behind the trees covering her head. Her intermezzo lay several feet away from her. She'd dropped it with the gunshot.

Cold fear pressed her painfully against the rigid bark of the tree. The man had dismounted and was heading right for her.

"You ain't think it was gon' be that easy to get away from me, did you? Now you know I could'a took your fool head clean off your shoulders, but under the circumstances, I'se feeling mighty tender-like right now,"

Vivian's ears perked. That voice . . . it was John Jay's but the accent was all wrong. His words sounded like the heat of the day had melted them together into a thick drawl just as soon as they passed his lips. But it was *his* voice.

"John Jay?" She couldn't help herself but say his name even as her voice cracked.

The man growled. "Hell yes, it's Tucka' John! You mind me, gal! Com'mon now! Get your black @$$ out from behind them trees over there before I let that fool posse set them dogs on you! You know them dogs don't cotton to thick-minded folks,"

It was John Jay! But was it John Jay? It had to be. John Jay was finally home, but he had a rifle aimed at her and had already shot once. And there she sat in the heat of the night, her face now stinging from sweat and tears that coursed through her wounds and she was totally unarmed.

Each step he made in her direction only forced her heart to kick harder against her ribs. She didn't want to hurt him, couldn't, not even if he wasn't John Jay. She needed her intermezzo—but she still had Lourdes'!

With clumsy fingers, she managed to free it from her deep pocket only to drop it near her feet.

"Jesus, please!" She hissed.

"Don't be involvin' Him in yo' mess. Hell, He ain't gon' stop what you got comin'. You done begged for this."

Stifling the need to scream, Vivian steadied her quaking fingers, counted to three, and without a second thought sprung from behind the tree and shot the intermezzo. 'Tucker' John shot his rifle as well. The bullet went still, suspended in the air, caught in the time-net of the intermezzo aimed in the path of her thigh.

The terror-filled scream that burned her insides rent from her belly and drove her to the ground with gulps of tears. She choked before emptying her stomach in the grass, the black shadow of the man cloaking her.

He was a statue and Vivian was bullet free.

She forced herself to breathe easy, taking air through her heated lips and exhaling it through flared nostrils all the while staring at the metal ball that still glowed hot in the time-net. She'd have to trap the bullet somehow, dig the other from the trunk of the tree. All evidence of that day would have to be sent back to 1837 along with the man who called himself Tucker John. But for that moment, all she could do was sit and stare, pulling at the grass as if it were the very heads of her head.

19

What had she done? What was she going to do?

The moon washed a pale blue glow across the forested path causing inky shadows to dance around her like mocking demons. She needed to move and she needed to move him. She forced herself to rise, taking careful steps toward him—her John Jay—and his aimed rifle. She'd been staring at him long enough for the sky to turn black and a true chill to chase through the air. She knew her husband's face. She knew his hands, his eyes. She knew him, but what had happened to him? Time had twisted him in such a way, turned him violent, took his mind…changed his name.

She'd heard of time-breaks. It was a common part of education within the Ministry of Time. There was always that risk in Time Surveillance, losing one's mind and a grip on reality. But John Jay's mind had been tested just like hers. Rigorous tests and training had been applied to ensure they could withstand the regression on the timeline.

Both of them had passed. But nothing was said about anything like this. She'd never heard of a single case where a person had been lost in their nexus gate for a matter of hours only to reappear on the timeline a completely different human being. But somehow, John Jay had.

Her body shook like a dry leaf in the autumn wind with each step she took toward him. Her eyes blurred with fresh tears and her skin itched more from fear than the bug bites that dotted her flesh.

She quickly scanned his structure. She had to be certain it was him and not some freakish look alike like the slave-woman she'd encountered. She prayed it was so. If that were the case, she'd just keep looking for her husband. She would contact Raul and get more hands in action.

Her heart sank and another cry parted her lips. The results were a one-hundred percent match for John Jay. The slave-woman was an eighty-six percent match to her even though at first glance they were identical.

This was John Jay? All she could think was that he had been lost a long time through some tangent, and had lost himself and his mind in time. What was she going to do? What was going to happen to him now? What would she tell their families, or John Jay's best friend, Marcus Taylor? Marcus had warned her to take care of him and she had failed. Vivian's insides went ice cold.

Where was Lourdes?

(Present Day)

Vivian turned without a word and left Tucker John to his cursing threats and spittle, again. She'd feigned her calm control for a week and could do it no longer. Lourdes would have to medicate him today. He'd worn her nerves thin with his threats and bellowing.

Where was Lourdes?

CHAPTER 4

Where was Lourdes? Vivian slid the door in the wall shut, ripped the mask from her face, and pushed the nervous sweat from her forehead. She walked as far away from the laboratory as she could, finally ending up at the front entrance of the house dropping her weight down on a cushioned bench in the foyer.

Sighing, she rolled her eyes up the white walls, across the mahogany barreled ceiling, before allowing them to flutter closed. Somehow she could still hear Tucker John screaming at her. It amazed her that in such a large manor she could still hear the man cry out like a rabid animal trapped within her walls.

The Animal. Slaves had called him that for the way he'd tracked them and maimed them with the little, wicked inventions and traps he'd made and set for them, and how he made sport of them before returning them to their oppressors. They said he moved after them barefoot, wearing nothing but his breaches, covered in Georgia's red clay, hair pulled back in a mess of twigs and debris, his rifle strapped to his back, ropes, and blades secured to his waist and the scent of nature covering his being.

He was like a ghost in the shadows, a lone wolf thirsty with bloodlust. It was a rare thing when he hunted dressed as a man, but even still he was nothing but an animal.

Vivian wondered if this moniker had more to do with his thrashing and howling than his hunting. And what a waste of a man he was. To be a racist, foul-mouthed, violent drunk, he was extremely good with his hands. She'd gone through his belongings and found little contraptions he had. One had sliced through her finger, drawing blood, with the same fiery bite his words did.

Wasted gifts poured out on a wasted man.

She dropped her face into her hands and leaned forward on the very verge of crying again. She had never cried so much in her life and she couldn't have been in a worse place or era to do so. The New Golden Age was no place for fountains of tears.

Amid the restored outward Zen beauty of that society, structured upon a foundation that believed peace was precious and thriving in one's interconnectedness to nature was the key to harmony, was the dark shadow of the fear of uncapped emotions and differences.

According to the ruling ideology, differences as well as emotions left to their own devices produced contagious diseases and viruses through vehicles of fear, emotional violence, and racism or xenophobia, which then produced chaos.

Chaos was the loss of control, and to lose control was to gamble with the quality of life for future generations. It was an affront to the New Golden Age, a threat to perfect peace, and the purification of the human soul.

The past attested to these truths.

A person born into the world during that time was bred into a society that was rightfully questionable in the view of someone like Vivian, a person who understood the need for tears.

Sure she appreciated the simple lifestyles, warmth of smiles, tenderness of conversation, rustic and yet full diets, and the breathable flow of linen clothing for most seasons. It somehow kept the mind at ease and often blinded from the spiked-pit-of-death that lay below. One false step, one laugh deemed too hardy, too many tears at the loss of a loved one could lead to the immediate extermination of life.

*The loss of a loved one…Too many tears…*She began to choke on the offensive things at that very moment, struggling to hold them down.

"You shouldn't look like that so close to the door, people might think you are sick with sadness. *Tristitia Lacrimo Murbus*, or 'Sad Disease'." It's highly contagious, thus dangerous."

Lourdes pushed the ten-foot tall door closed behind her. Vivian hadn't even noticed that she had come in.

"Where have you been? What took you so long?" She straightened up on the bench, sniffing back the moisture that had clogged her nose.

Lourdes robotically showed her the bag in her hand. "I was picking up the items you requested from the Cleric's Office and pharmacy, and I had some other errands to run. I hadn't seen my mother in a few days you know?" She slid off her conical hemp hat and hung it up on the wall with the other two that were already there. "How is," she paused, looking down the hallway. "...the patient?"

She shook the bag by Vivian's ear when she didn't get an answer. Vivian sat up straight once more, she had rested her face back in her hands again. Taking the bag she peered inside, noting the one tucked inside the other, and gave a sigh of relief before she shifted the contents and looked back up at her assistant with a raised brow. "And the parts for the nexus gate?"

It was because of the missing pieces of the nexus gate that John Jay had gone inside of it to do temporary maintenance. It had almost been a year since he had ordered the pieces and for some odd reason, they still had not been shipped back from 6037. John Jay was missing because of that. He was still missing because she hadn't figured out how to find him.

Lourdes shook her head. Vivian answered her question. "He's alive like he was yesterday and the day before that. He's in 'okay' health, considering the condition of life that he lives, and for his age. Contrary to some former historical belief, slave foremen did not have the greatest of living conditions."

Lourdes suppressed a scowl. Vivian noticed.

"This isn't a pity party for him in the least. I'm merely answering your question and making an observation. Anyhow, I need you to medicate him today. Sedate him if you have to. He's been screaming his head off for hours and it's only going to get worse. Right now he is attacking me, later he will be begging me for help." She stood and walked out of the foyer. Lourdes followed behind.

"What are you going to do? Torture him? You can't do such things."

Vivian gave her a look. "Lourdes, the thought never crossed my mind. However, he is going to think I am torturing him. He is a functioning alcoholic, which means he drank regularly and heavily. It's been ten days for him without a drink. The medication for his liver, which was not in the greatest condition, has held back the symptoms of withdrawal. He is to take his last dose for that, and then comes the really fun part."

She entered the large kitchen and pulled out one of the four boxes in the bag that came from the Cleric's Office. "This, we will start giving him within the next forty-eight hours. You have to give him his last liver treatment first and then we will go in with this."

She handed the container to Lourdes who studied it in her hands. "What is this?"

A wan smile shaped her lips. "*XBalance*. That is to help him with the pain of detox, but it won't work until the symptoms are evident in his body which means,"

"Forty-eight hours. Great."

Vivian reached across the cold granite island top and squeezed Lourdes' hand. "I'm sorry."

***

Tucker John growled and pulled his body up against the restraints one last time. He felt the straps digging into his upper arms and wrist, across his chest and abdomen. Almost blacking out, he dropped his head back down into the cushioning at his back.

He didn't have a mind to study the room again. That was all he'd been able to do besides scream.

White. Everywhere he looked, everywhere he was able to see, he saw white. White walls, white linens, white ceiling, large white counter and simple stools to the right of him at the center of the room, white cabinets. There was no other exit or entrance besides the one at his back. The way them wenches sounded when they came his way indicated they were making a descent so he was in some lower-level room, done in white because there were no windows.

He closed his eyes and waited to catch his breath. For three days he had been trying to break free. For three days he had been screaming at the top of his voice during the times that he was awake.

He kept being put to sleep! He didn't know how, but they were putting him clean out. There were two of them though, both females, one white the other a brown-skinned wench wearing a white, porcelain mask. "Two females," he said, his voice was so dry, hoarse.

He tried to remember how he got there, how he had been taken prisoner by two skinny women who couldn't have weighed more than a hundred and twenty pounds apiece, especially not the white one. She couldn't have been more than a hundred and ten if that.

They're probably some vigilante pair of anti-slavery-temperance-busybodies. At least that must have been the white woman's conviction. The black wench must have been going along for the ride. None of that mattered. Tucker John was going to get free and he was going to put both of them in their places.

His hardly calm attitude suddenly flared up again when he heard footsteps coming his way. Like the last times, he didn't hold back. "Wench! You got yourself five good seconds to turn me loose or," his words halted at the tip of his tongue. The white woman stepped into the light of the room. She didn't bother making eye contact with him. She hardly acknowledged his presence.

Tucker John relaxed again. He was angry, and he was tired, but the little woman in the room wasn't bad to look at for a good second, even if he wanted to ring her tiny neck.

He leaned his head back and took in her form. There really wasn't very much to see from the billowy fabric that hung over her body. The floozy wasn't wearing nothing more than a long-sleeved nightshirt and ankle length drawers. "Who are ya'll?" He would try to be civil with the woman, see where that got him. Even loose women liked to be talked to nice. It made them pliable and he intended to work her for all she was worth.

***

Lourdes checked the medical equipment and recorded his vitals. He was in very good health now, one treatment away from excellent, the detox not being considered. She sighed. His broken, backwoods English was grating her nerves. She could hardly understand him, the fact that she had even thought of him as 'backwoods' disturbed her all the more. That, she was going to keep to herself. Derogatory assessments of another person were viewed as toxic by the great minds of the New Golden Age, but treatable if gotten out of hand. Embarrassment over her mistake flushed her cheeks. She was one of the purified. She knew better.

"I *asked* you a question!" Tucker John snapped. Fist clenched he tugged toward her to no avail. "I swear fo' god I'se gon' have your hide once I'se free! You and that *negress* running about here in your *undergarments* like a pair of whores! Her I understand, but a white woman? Ain't you got no sense in your fool head about propriety? Not to mention kidnappin.' That'll earn you a hemp necklace and a few inches to your puny height."

Lourdes could hardly hold back her laugh as she opened the container of his last liver treatment and set it aside. Who was he, a slave foreman, a filthy bounty hunter, to tell her anything about propriety or what was legal? She had read his history, what was there anyway, Vivian had as well. There was nothing nice there, and yet he thought himself in a position to speak about what was proper. She almost snorted. If he was this bad she hated to imagine what he was going to be like once the detox began. That was enough to make her stop laughing altogether.

From what she'd learned, alcoholic detox could be a deadly thing if not monitored and treated properly, not to mention messy. Alcoholism was simply unheard of in her day and age. She and Vivian were going to be flying blind for the most part. The last thing they needed was a dead body on their hands. But then if he simply died on his own, all they would have to do is reopen the nexus gate E.P and shove his hateful corpse right back to where it had come from, add closure to his pitiful life story, give it some redeeming value—he died. The Century Cell Group need never know he was ever there.

She had completely lost herself in thought when she heard him ask the question again. Finally, she responded. "Who do you think we are?" Her eyes flashed when they met his.

Tucker John growled. "If I knew it, would I be asking?"

Lourdes picked up his liver medicine and carried it to him. Tucker John's muscles tensed again, and as had become his way, he jerked against the restraints. Lourdes proceeded with his treatment, loading the medicine into his Osmission, a noninvasive form of injection, no needles required, only a skin connection between medical applicator and patient.

"You shouldn't jerk like that. You're not only hurting yourself, but you could damage our equipment which would not make Vivian very happy." She bit her bottom lip and her eyes slowly edged toward Tucker John.

"Vivian?" He shouted. "Vivian the one behind that mask? That treacherous harpy! I should of blowed her head off when I had the CHANCE!"

"Clam. Down. If you keep fretting I'm going to put you back to sleep."

"It'd be in your best interest to kill me now." He snarled, foamy spit catching in the matted hairs of his beard. "Cause I'se gon' skin you and that ungrateful wench! You yankie b!*#%! You some kinda naked abolitionist?!"

"I'm no yankie, those don't exist. Nor am I an abolitionist, those don't exist either, but then neither does slavery or slave foremen." Lourdes snapped and began the sleep sequence. "You will be out in thirty seconds." Without another word she turned and left the laboratory wishing she could wash off the filth of his presence and the chill that had tingled her flesh the moment she let Vivian's name cross her lips in his presence.

***

Tucker John jerked even harder at his restraints. The heat of anger made him bite his tongue but he couldn't even register the pain for the rage or the fog of drowsiness that was suddenly assaulting him. It was all still so dull what had happened the night he'd found Vivian hiding behind the trees. He remembered very little and even less as his eyelids pressed downward. He did remember firing at her once, twice and then... ...nothing....

CHAPTER 5

Vivian leaned her head back in her leather chair and let the *Paz* or 'peace' medication, an emotional sedative, run its course as old digital files of *Tommy Dorsey* played around her. She was never one for taking pills, especially not ones that inhibited natural emotional functionality, but these were special circumstances. The pressure around her had her on edge.

Lourdes had been right. Expressing any kind of emotion that could be seen as negatively contagious was a health crime in 4037, and she was nothing short of soggy with tears and wrought with anxiety. If a denizen saw her and reported her, the clerics Office would be involved, questions would be asked, a team assessment conducted to ensure that they were still 'capable' of remaining within that thread of time.

Questions could not be asked, nor an assessment done. John Jay was still missing and a viable explanation as to why the Cleric's Office had not been contacted sooner to aid in his recovery was nowhere near her train of thought. Now, in order to deal with the grief of losing her husband, and being stuck with his evil past doppelganger, she was taking medication that leveled out her hormones in a bizarre but effective way.

It was another mark against her, taking the *Paz*. She knew with the history of *Paz* that she was paddling through very troubled waters but she had to take the risk. The *Paz* was allowing her to process what she was feeling without actually 'feeling' it, which meant what was left of her cover in 4037 would not be compromised. She was still able to search for John Jay and hold the fort until he was successfully recovered, and he would be.

Lourdes' being able to simply go to the pharmacy and retrieve the tiny pills for her without there being any issues was a plus. The Cleric's Office would never know that the medication was for Vivian and not Lourdes. There was no reason for them to suspect a thing.

As it stood, the rules of surveillance were different for Lourdes and Vivian. Those borne during the New Golden Age were 'restricted' from actual time travel although they were able to learn of the Ministry as well as aid the work of visiting clerics. In the language of the New Golden Age, they had been 'encouraged' to refrain from the act of time travel as a means of 'minimizing emotional pollution and cross-contamination'. Still, Lourdes, being a native of the day had certain 'privileges' that Vivian did not, even though both worked within the Ministry of Time. *Paz* was one of the privileges.

The medication was no longer utilized in 6037. It actually had been declared an illegal substance since the year 4078 when the Silent Revolution had ended bringing a complete end to the New Golden Age, which was a good thing despite the fact Vivian was indulging in both now.

She stared up at the smooth, hand-hewn cross-beamed ceiling of her private office. How the craftsmen had managed to work the wood in such a way that it looked as if a machine had cut them reminded her of how men had worked the telling of history to make it seem just as smooth and flawless. The truth was, like those beams, the closer one looked the rougher and gnarled things appeared. Still, the deliberate crossing of the wood beams further told the tale of how time was truly calculated. Sadly, Vivian couldn't bring herself to see how any of what was happening to her and John Jay had any brilliant meaning in the fabric of time and the folds of their personal story.

Clasping the obsidian stone upon her chest, closing her eyes, she couldn't help wishing that she and John Jay had been sent to 4078, or anywhere else in time besides where she currently sat, but no. She had wanted a time filled with boiling conflicts. She wanted to aid in the historical documentation that brought understanding to the harder times in history, bear firsthand witness to what people in her time viewed as absurd.

She wanted to know—just like everyone else, really—when and how the Silent Revolution had begun in the first place. No one knew, not yet anyhow. She wanted to be the one to give that revelation to the people of her timeline. The people of the future owed their lifestyle to the Silent Revolution. No, they owed their very existence.

From it was birthed programs like IGE or Isolated Genomic Extraction. An expensive work and project, centered solely around undoing what the New Golden Age had done.

Where the New Golden Age had sought to eradicate the spectrum of melanin and ethnic divides, aiming for the 'perfect golden man', IGE specialized in bringing them back; isolating similar ethnic strands within couples and producing 'designer' children. Two people seen as Asian could bring forth an African child via the program. They could restore the spectrum of the human race.

Vivian, her beautiful brown, the coil of her hair, the slope of her nose and fullness of her lips, was a result of IGE, as were her parents and their parents before them. She owed it to the world to find the key to their restored existence. That is why she had chosen that point in time's crossbeams, so smooth and yet so rough.

The New Golden Age was certainly nothing to be trifled with although its exterior glowed with an alluring luster of peace, balance, and tranquility. Vivian had learned the truth of it the hard way. Hours driving into days, fading into a near two weeks, with no sign of John Jay had left her teetering on the precipice of no return, fighting fiercely to hold onto the original passion that had led her two millennia back in time to the place her feet were now planted...alone, without John Jay. The irony mocked her. The tension was meant to drive them together, not tear them apart.

She hardly knew if she still felt the same passion for things anymore. The inward battle of pleasure versus her current pain was bruising every fiber of her being. But the discoveries, the vastness of knowledge she acquired over the years argued that it was worth so much more than her present moment. She couldn't deny that.

"But none of it is worth John Jay," she sniffled. The realization that she would have never met him in the first place, had it not been for the Ministry of Time, pinched her heart.

There was also the call to legacy she had to consider. Her family was known for making great differences for the future through surveillance. It was her duty to do the same. It was her duty to go beyond what any of them had ever done. She existed because of their sacrifices and in return, she too would sacrifice. She'd meant to, every cell of her being vibrated with the need to. She needed to do her part in restoring the fragmented threads of history, tell the true story.

Humanity had a keen way of writing history from a very shallow viewpoint. surveyors of time helped to broaden the scope, to affirm or disprove what had been penned in centuries past. Vivian wanted to do her part in that great work. She wanted to show the roughness of the beams for what it truly was, expose the splinters even if it meant her hands were the ones pricked, and they'd been more than pricked. Tucker John was evidence of that.

She laughed recalling an incident of another surveyor's failure. It was far less dangerous than hers. It had taken place in the early 1900's. The surveyor had mindlessly used a cellular phone while walking directly in front of a film recorder. It wasn't until the 21st century that a news reporter discovered the blunder, and made mention of the incident. The surveyor responsible was nearly permanently removed from duty but was only suspended from Fieldwork in the end.

At first, Vivian thought the punishment wasn't suitable for the crime. The agent could have shifted the very sands of time and history, and knocked everything off course all because of a single moment of negligence. What Vivian had done was far worse. With one breath she had shattered to dust the two most important rules of surveillance. Worse yet, her mistake, her negligence was living, breathing, and eating at her core in the midst of one of the most precarious and dangerous times in history.

Forty-thirty-seven seemed perfect and within that guise lay all the conflicts and inhumane decisions that were being made on a daily basis in order to maintain that 'perfection', decisions based solely on what was deemed logical without an ounce of real compassion. If a person was denied the right to feel the gambit of their God-given emotions with totality, how could they even understand how compassion or empathy worked?

She had hoped that she, like her parents, grandparents, and great-grandparents, would be influenced in such a positive way in coming to understand the root cause of the negatives within the societies she surveyed, that when she and John Jay returned to their timeline they would be primed to help in current 'causes' of their day.

She had hoped that the 4030's would also push her and John Jay closer together, remove the dullness of their marriage, give them both a common goal and victory that would banish the competitive wedge that had been driven between them.

She squeezed the pendant even harder and felt a tear push from the corner of her closed eyes with the same subtle sweetness that the notes for the horns playing around her pressed from the twisted brass. The very thing that had brought her and John Jay together—The Ministry of Time—had been the very thing driving them apart.

Vivian had become more of a success than John Jay within surveillance even though he'd had more time in the Field.

As a team they were successful, but Vivian, getting all the credit, being the Lead, only chilled things relationally. That was never a good thing for a marriage that had been assigned and was not a love-match, to begin with. Assignments seemed to have a less forgiving foundation even if they had far less emotional expectations in the beginning.

She finally brought the pendant to her lips and kissed it. She loved John Jay now just as he had begun to love her, no matter how strained things had become. John Jay had given the pendant to her on their seventh wedding anniversary, right before they came to the 4030's. He'd acknowledged the rift and wanted to work through it. The pendant was his promise.

It was nothing but a smooth white stone to the naked eye, but when held up to the sunlight and slowly turned in a clockwise motion, a beautiful inscription of love could be read. *"You made us worth it. You made the breaking beautiful."*

The lack of love, at first, the life-changing agreement established via a program that paired mates together based on their career paths and other practical variables had made for a cordial start but a very rocky and seemingly competitive present.

Nevertheless, they muscled through the rubble of broken expectations and even hearts, as it turned out. They wanted to survey. Neither wanted to divorce. Neither wanted to go through the counseling and pre-assigning programs required for a surveyor union. And they would have chosen to be reassigned to other surveyors. No other union would have made sense.

Surveillance could be a lonely life and even inconvenient, not to mention impractical if a surveyor married a civilian. Surveyors stood the risk of being gone from their spouses while on a Field study for up to a decade of linear time, not to mention the centuries or even millennia that would separate them from their civilian family.

This was not the only way to be paired with a marriage match, people still met and simply fell in love, just not Vivian and John Jay. But they did love each other now…they just had to work at it a little harder. She had to give him room to shine. Love did that, helped her realize his need. It also helped her to be more patient with him

She had not been John Jay's first assigned match. She was thirty-one years old, four years younger than him so she had not been put into the lottery for matching when he had first applied. He'd told her about his first match, a woman called Tara Mills. They'd gotten close, far closer than a typical pairing would within the time they were together, but things shifted, he'd said. A month before they were to legally wed and be assigned to a surveying site in the Field, Tara quit the program, and John Jay, which had devastated him. Marcus Taylor, John Jay's best friend had mentioned it several times to Vivian.

John Jay said Tara chose a love marriage instead, that it broke his heart at first—they were in love—nevertheless, he was glad that he now had Vivian. Despite their current issues, he said she made them worth it, the breaking they were both experiencing beautiful. They were growing, together. That was all that mattered in the end.

Vivian would have cried recalling the words at that very moment, but the *Paz* had kicked in, dulling the pain, so instead, she felt nothing. John Jay was gone. She had no idea where he was, if she would ever see him again, dead or alive, how to even really look for him now, and she felt…nothing. She almost felt angry thinking about Tucker John in her laboratory, but the chemical within the tiny pill quickly suppressed those feelings as well.

She leaned forward and brushed the sleepiness from her eyes. She still needed to consider what she was going to do about Tucker John. She realized that she had made a major mistake in keeping him, but the genetic structure read she had done on him when he had come through the E.P said one hundred percent match for John Jay, John Joseph Spruce. There was no reason for her to conclude otherwise, and by the time Lourdes was able to talk some sense into her, it was too late. The window of time that she had to send Tucker John back to 1837 slammed shut, with a reverberating echo that almost made her ears bleed.

Unlike the other four people and the animals that came through the portal, 'Tucker' John *Josephus* Spruce, had no record of life existence past the day that he came through the gate. History recorded that he had never returned to the plantation. His horse was found wandering by a river bed so it was assumed that he had fallen off and drowned since he didn't know how to swim. His body was never recovered, nor were any of his other belongings, so Vivian had kept those too; the rifle, the clothing, the saddle bag, and its contents. She had them locked away from sight, but they certainly were not out of mind.

She couldn't in all good conscience—what she felt she had left of a good conscience—throw a would-be dead man back in time alive, past the date of his death. She only had two options set out before her; she could euthanize him, which wasn't really a reasonable option to her, or she could wait six years to the day and send Tucker John back in time. He had to return on a Sunday evening, in the same month a few moments after he came into 4037. Sending him back at any other time or day could possibly disrupt the timeline.

If she sent him back too soon, he would run into a past version of himself. If she sent him back too late, he could survive his presumed 'river drowning' and the entire course of history could be changed just by that one man surviving.

Vivian wanted to believe that her reasoning for keeping him alive was because, despite his horrendous personality, he hadn't asked to be in 4037, he had nothing to do with John Jay's disappearance, and in the end, it was Vivian's own haste that had pulled him forward through time. It was her desperation that led her to keep him.

Even now she couldn't bring herself to tell her Cell Group leader, Raul Manuel. The thought had clawed at her mind several times since, but too much time had passed. Although Raul was a reasonable person, not even he could reason with what she had done.

Now they were walking what appeared to be nothing more than a burning tight rope. Time was working against them. If Tucker John was going to spend the next six years in that era, he was going to have to undergo a major mental and behavioral conversion.

She cringed and dropped her head to her desk, pain twisting her insides with sharp-edged daggers of angst that not even the *Paz* could dull.

None of what she was presuming to do was going to be easy. Truth was, it was practically illegal and dangerous, but what were her options? Information from the last two-thousand plus years was going to have to be deposited into Tucker John's mind in order to get him up to speed on the history and ways of the world they were in.

Depositing the information was one thing, and it didn't break the code of surveying since he would drown in the river in six years with every glimpse and experience of the future that he would receive—yet another tight loophole. What he would choose to do with the information in the meantime was still totally up to Tucker John's free will. But with the way he talked, Vivian wasn't so sure that Tucker John could change, or even survive in a world that looked like his at first glance, but was completely contrary to the ideology that he was bred to believe was normal and God-ordained.

She was willing to give him the chance to do so nonetheless. She could also perform a 'Clearance' procedure on him, wipe his memory clean, just to be safe. She'd wipe his mind of every gained memory from this point forward and send him back to his timeline completely reverted to his old self. She would have to worry about getting John Jay on board with her plan when she found him *if* she found him.

Vivian finally allowed her mind follow the path of her emotions and grow numb even if only for that moment. She would let Tommy Dorsey soothe her into peace while she thought of nothing but John Jay.

Funny. John Jay didn't care at all for Tommy Dorsey's music and yet it was calming to her, one of her favorite things. She somehow managed to smile at the irony.

***

Lourdes crept into her own bedroom and eased the door shut behind her. She let out a deep breath she felt like she'd been holding from the very moment she walked out of the lab. She couldn't help it. She had done it, she had said Vivian's name!

She covered her mouth with her hands as a rush of nerves fluttered in her belly. She thanked God Vivian was drowning herself in that dreadful music and couldn't hear her.

She suddenly felt a tinge of resentment chill her spine. How could Vivian sit in her office and play that horrible music? She knew Johnny hated it! That somehow took the edge off what she had done. She had told Tucker John Vivian's name. She'd promised Vivian that she wouldn't and she had done so anyway.

Tucker John made her feel hateful. Vivian was the reason why Tucker John was still there in the first place so it was her own fault that Lourdes had let her name slip.

She growled and pushed away from her door. She didn't know how much longer she would be able to handle any of this. Vivian was depressing, Tucker John was revolting, and overall she just missed Johnny. She sighed again and fell backward onto her bed. She wrapped her arms around her midsection and pretended they were Johnny's. She then removed one of the bobbles from her ears and waited until it caught the sunlight, revealing the image of Johnny's face. She smiled as a tear slid out the corner of her eye.

"Please come back soon, Johnny. I love you."

CHAPTER 6

Magnus Sanderson. For a man who was deemed one of the most pleasant of beings to live in the year 4037, he seemed to always have the facial expression of someone who was sucking a lemon. He'd been assigned the Head of the Cleric's Office exactly three years and six months ago to the day. His leadership position was given via a message sent to the Cleric's Office from the year 5041—his proper time position—by way of the Cleric's Office in 6039.

His assignment was unusual for several reasons. Protocol required a team of three Chief Clerics to run any given office per decade. Their assignments were given within five years of each other, with a steady rotation of leadership every five years, each cleric serving as Lead for five years of his or her decade term in the Chief office. That meant as one Chief Cleric exited another entered, as was the cycle, always maintaining a leadership of three.

Magnus Sanderson counted as the fourth and superior Chief Cleric, sent in completely outside of the rotation. It was a temporary position, but one that went without much questioning for obvious reasons—a man called Aiden Schulsler. Schulsler's name had become law no matter what date or time a body resided in. Because of him, Magnus was able to step into the 4030's Cleric's Office and conquer the Chief position with just one look and Schulsler's weighty referral.

The reality, however, was that Magnus had been strong-armed out of a very comfortable retirement, all because of the man. "*A debt to be paid.*" Schulsler had said via a personal message, a debt that had been eating Magnus' stomach lining into nothing for over a decade. Magnus never talked about it; his debt to Aiden Schulsler. Few people knew about it, nor would they ever. Magnus' chilly blue eyes and tight smile made it clear that his connection to Aiden Schulsler was not a topic that was welcomed into the conversation.

Sitting at his desk in the Cleric's Office, his wiry mouth didn't even attempt a smile as he listened to the report brought to him by his 'personal' Front Office Assistant, as was Clarence Mantov's title. Clarence was more Aiden Schulsler's guard dog or insurance policy to make sure that Magnus complied with his assignment. Magnus didn't care one bit for Schulsler, he hadn't before and he certainly didn't now. In the end, he was powerless to protest against him, as were others. The vile man had become a Senator for goodness sake!

He turned his attention to his assigned task from 6039, verifying the actions of Team V. Leona-Spruce 4034-44G.US. Lourdes Berry, Assistant Surveillance Agent to John Jay Spruce and Vivian Leona, had visited the Cleric's Office and collected the two prescriptions that had been ordered by Vivian Leona while making off-handed mention of two others she'd ordered from the local pharmacy.

Getting *Paz* from the pharmacy was something Magnus understood, although it was illegal for a minister of time that was not of the New Golden Age to possess. Vivian and John Jay were not of this era. Still, extreme emotional suppression could prove difficult for even the most seasoned surveyor. *XBalance*, a substance given freely through the Cleric's Office, also could help with chemical balancing among other things. It was a cure all, aiding with neurological imbalances, auto-immune disorders, physiological imbalances; the list went on. It was a health reset button, bringing a person's entire system to equilibrium.

What put things into question were the request for a liver treatment through the pharmacy and *Spadds* (Syntheses of Peripheral Applications and Data Download Supplements) through the Cleric's Office.

Magnus drummed his long boney fingers across the top of his lacquered desk, his lips pushing out into an even deeper pucker. "How many *Spadds* were ordered, exactly?"

Clarence looked down at his clipboard, the holographic screen read 'four.'

"There were four complete sets of *Spadds* ordered. They were placed in a single container." Even though the young man was pretending a role at Schulsler's behest, he tended to do more than an efficient job. That was to be expected. Clarence's real line of work required him to be thorough.

"And they weren't ordered by decade or century?"

Clarence shook his head. "No sir. They were ordered by millennia, each treatment containing two applications."

Magnus stopped drumming. "That would seem like enough to fry one's brain...one would imagine. Apparently it won't." He pinched the flesh between his thumb and pointer finger, activating his recording system. It was a delicate implant, also ordered by Schulsler. He brought his middle and index finger to his lips to log in his report only to hesitate, remembering Clarence's presence.

"That'll be all, Clarence. Thank you." He offered him the wiry smile and as always Clarence exited the room without another word. Magnus put his attention back to his report. "Findings are conclusive with given testimony for the date. Four millennial *Spadds* treatments, open prescription of *Paz* via the pharmacy, and final liver treatment, all retrieved by a Lourdes Berry."

He watched as his verbal information became digital and began to log and balance along with the notes that had already been prerecorded prior to his and Clarence's arrivals. Beneath the skin of his two fingers, a light code flashed for verification. His implants had been pre-loaded with testimonies and documentation from 6039 forward. All the information that was in accordance with what was previously recorded logged in as 'green', meaning valid. Anything that showed up yellow would mean 'unknown information' and would warrant investigation. Nothing had showed up red which meant 'undeniably false' and would warrant immediate action by the Cleric's Office in 6039. No red, no action, no worries for anyone involved, yet.

Magnus prayed it would continue that way. Somehow he knew trouble was waiting to rear its nasty head. Schulsler was involved with this after all. Nevertheless, he couldn't help holding on to the hope that the sooner Vivian Leona's testimony was verified the sooner he could return to his point in time and be rid of Schulsler and his watchdog, Clarence, for good.

***

(48 hours later)
Tucker John dreamed he was back home, not on the Georgian plantation, but in 1817. He was fifteen years old again, living in the Carolinas. His mama had just given birth to her ninth child, and John was helping with family upkeep. He wasn't the oldest. He had four older brothers who had run away from home and from their daddy as soon as they could stand on their own two feet.

Tucker John should have followed their lead. He'd spent many a day and night, and on more than one occasion, weeks, running in the woods as a child, hiding from his hateful daddy. His daddy's torment began the moment John could stand upright and had the sense to run.

His daddy, Ashford or 'Ash' Winston Spruce, was a hateful, violent man who wasn't worth the raggedy, stinking pants he wore. He kept the family in vulgar poverty, swearing up and down he couldn't find a single job that would pay him well enough to take up his time. He blamed John's Irish mama for that; said her blood and heathen Catholic ways spoiled everything. So he decided not to work at all and focused his attention on terrorizing the ones who loved him.

He was a lousy drunk.

Ash spent most of his time away from home which was a good thing. Mama knew where he was, but she never said a word about it. She was too afraid to, too angry, but she knew. The private sickness in her genitals that she'd gotten had come from him, and he had gotten it from someone else.

John had started working on the York plantation a few miles up the road to help his mama and the other little ones survive. He mucked stalls, mended fences, did the other work the plantation owners didn't want their slaves doing lest they die and the plantation owner be out of money. But John did the tasks and he did them well. He earned himself a decent amount of scars in the process, but it kept food on his mama's table and a roof over their heads, even if only barely.

He was dreaming about the last day his daddy had come home. John had just finished up at the plantation and Mama was getting some peas and hot water cornbread ready for supper. They had barely finished prayer when Ash came in. The stench of stagnant creek water, urine, stale liquor, and the brothel he had rolled out of, filled the room and shut the mouths of everyone except the new baby who managed a to give a good cry before finding his own thumb and sucking it. Mama's eyes were stone.

"What you lookin' at, *woman*? Don't ya'll youngin's mind your daddy no more? Nobody greet me at my own door no more?" His arm swept through the air with the same laziness as his slurred words. "Rotten lil' bastards! I bet ain't none of ya'll mine no how, especially *you*!"

He pointed at John, who at the age of fifteen stood a full head taller than Ash, and all of his other sons. John had taken after his mama's kin; fair hair, light eyes, and tall, solid stature. John would be at least six feet three inches in height by the time he stopped growing. His mama said he looked like one of her uncles, but Ash would hear none of it.

He grunted, staggering over to where John sat. John wasn't at the head of the table. He never sat there. Sometimes he sat on the floor in the event his daddy would come home and raise hell like he was doing that day. Usually, he managed to eat and run to the woods before Ash ever knew he'd been there. Some days he was just too bone weary to move, ignoring the warning in his senses that his daddy was near, conceding to take an undo beating and go to bed by the fire rather than hide out in the cold.

Ash stood over him, his sloppy belly pushing against John's shoulder. Drool slid from his mouth and beard and into John's hair.

John didn't budge.

"You in my seat, *boy*."

John's eyes stayed down in his plate. His nostrils flared and his jaw clenched but he still didn't move. It wouldn't have mattered. Everywhere he went was Ash's and Ash made it known. John was not welcome.

"You hear me, boy? I says you in my seat. You had better mind me 'fore I lose my temper. You lazin' round here like a good for nothing, ain't earning your keep!" He was in his ear now. He smacked the back of John's head and laughed.

"Good god all mighty! You even smell like them niggas in the field. Is that where you be spending your time, playing with them black wenches?" He stumbled and laughed. "Nah, you ain't been with no negress. You ain't no man." He nudged John again.

"Leave him be, Ash. I mean it this time." John's mama's voice rang with a warning that John had not heard from her before. Even sick, she seemed fierce. She'd had enough of her husband coming around and disturbing the fragile peace she had managed to maintain in the home. She especially didn't want him around due to the sickness he had given her. Even the new baby had been infected by it just by coming out of her.

Ash wobbled again on his feet but caught his balance. "Or what? What you gon' do, Mary?" Ash snarled and grabbed John by a fist full of hair, pulling him to his feet by the roots. "What the *hell* you gon' do, Irish whore!" The younger children scattered toward the other end of the room. The baby cried out as if his hair had been pulled.

"I said, no MORE!" Mary shouted and rushed toward Ash.

Ash pushed her back with his free hand. She fell backward onto the floor. Her other children—no more than toddlers in age—reached for her. Mary snatched away from them when she saw John still caught in the clutches of his own daddy. John took each fist to his face and body as if he were a full grown man himself. He was the size of one but only in height. He was still just a boy with long limbs waiting for the rest of his body to catch up in growth. Screaming again, Mary scurried from the room.

John broke loose of Ash's grip, shoving him backward one good time before landing him a good punch. He could have hit him harder, knocked what was left of his rotten teeth clean from his skull, but he didn't. Ash was still his daddy, never mind the fact John couldn't shake the fear of him.

Ash fell down with a whirlwind of slurred curses. John's heart was in his throat, fear in his veins. He finally reached down for his scrambling daddy, but caught a knife across the forearm instead. Ash had barely made it up to his feet, and John had hardly had the time to register the shock and the pain when the rifle echoed through the planks of the shack and Ash's head jerked back in a spray of liquid red.

Awake, Tucker John's head pounded as if the gun shot had exploded the back of his skull, as if in the dream his mama had shot him and not his daddy. He had never felt a pain like this before. His body felt wet and cold and his hands wouldn't stop shaking. He also felt the urge to vomit.

He rolled his eyes opened with the pressure of pain and screamed from his gut. What was happening to him? They— simple-minded *Vivian* and the white woman—they were trying to kill him. They had poisoned him! He cried out again, panic and anger squeezing at his lungs, yet all he could think about doing was getting a drink—a nice kick from the sweet burn of aged liquor. He needed to get free and he needed a taste! He leaned his head back and felt his body arcing against the pain and the need. He jerked his arms forward and felt the straps give way a little.

Hope coursed through him, fueled with extreme desperation. He jerked at the restraints again and again. The bruises he had already acquired from his earlier bouts with the bed straps hollered at him, but he kept pushing until his right arm broke free. With trembling fingers and blurred vision, Tucker John frantically worked on the restraints on his chest and waist before releasing his left arm and legs.

He swung his feet off of the bed and lost his balance on the cool, smooth floor. His bare feet made a high pitched squeak as they fought to stay up right. "Shhhh," he whispered. Delirious, he eased himself upward. He was not quite standing and not quite squatting. It was a safe stance. He was too disoriented from the pain and the need to stand upright, and he was still too uncertain about his whereabouts, knowing only that he needed to go up if he were to get free. He needed to be ready to spring into action if and when he had to.

He eased his way to the end of the hallway. It was the only exit that he knew of. He gulped and his eyes went blurry again. He was still shaking uncontrollably. D@^& you, Vivian! He clenched his fists to keep them from shaking. *I'ma whip the black right off your back soon as I get the chance!*

He froze still but only for a second. The door at the other end had been opened. He pressed his body against the cold wall and waited, fists still clenched. He listened to the footsteps. It was the little white woman coming. She had come so many times that he recognized the sound of her stride. As soon as her face moved past the edge of the wall, Tucker John took hold of her. He didn't keep her long in his grasp, but launched her aside before clumsily running through the corridor and out into the house.

He wasted no time searching for the main door. He just needed a way out. Instead, he took the first option that came into view. The window with the path of pale light acting as a beacon was as good an exit as any. He stumbled for it, only to fall against the near invisible mesh that covered its opening. He cursed as the contraption fell away even as he fought to stay upright. Regaining what was left of his balance he stuck his head out first to see how far he would have to jump down. The house was on somewhat of hill. From his wavy vision, he guessed he didn't have more than a six foot drop to the ground.

He was wrong.

Fifteen feet, a badly sprained ankle, and a several yard roll into thorny bushes later, Tucker John was back up, but limping away to safety. He looked back at the whitewashed manor and spit. He would return to it, as sure as his name was 'Tucker' John Josephus Spruce, he would return! As soon as he found himself a doctor, got himself a drink, and his rifle, he was going to pay Vivian and that white woman a visit they were never going to forget.

Nobody messed with Tucker John. Nobody!

***

Lourdes crawled to her hands and knees. She waited until the dizziness shook off before she stood up. Her scalp at the nape of her neck was throbbing. Her hair wasn't long at all but Tucker John had grabbed two fists full of it and tossed her to the other side of the room as if she were a six-pound infant. As she recalled, he had lifted her off the ground by the hair and sent her sailing.

Anger and fear rushed through her at the same time. How dare he put his hands on her? She hadn't agreed to this. This was not supposed to happen! This *animal*, Tucker John, was *not* supposed to happen!

Whimpering with tears, she managed to stand, favoring her right knee. She limped out of the lab and in the direction of the office. She immediately set up the perimeter fence. Tucker John wouldn't get very far mostly because his health was about to take a serious nose dive without the *XBalance*, and because he was trapped again.

Rubbing the throbbing ache of her knee she wished for a rainstorm. The animal was wearing nothing but linen trousers. She hoped he would catch his death and die! Startled, she rebuked herself for the thought. She had never had such hateful thoughts before, never experienced this level of emotion. Tucker John was certainly sick with anger and he was clearly contagious, very contagious!

"*Iragravatus*, disease of rage," Lourdes touched her cheeks with the backside of her hands, wondering if a fever came along side such feelings. She knew that whenever she was with Johnny she felt feverish all over, but in a pleasant way.

None of this was pleasant. None of it.

***

Vivian rushed into the office from the garden, dirt still on her gloved hands. She came back into the house as soon as she saw the perimeter fence go up. She hardly spared Lourdes a glance before she asked what was going on.

"He got loose!" Lourdes cried.

Stunned by the words, she turned on her heels and rushed for the laboratory. She was back in the main office within seconds. "What do you mean he got loose? How?"

"I don't know!" Lourdes shot back. "I was on my way to give him his *XBalance* treatment when he ambushed me—"

"How did he get loose, Lourdes?" Vivian's body was shaking. "He was strapped down!" This was beyond dangerous, not just for Vivian and Lourdes, but for everyone around. Tucker

John was a threat to anyone he came in contact with. Worse, they were a threat to him and the timeline.

"I already told you, I. DON'T. KNOW!" Lourdes' breaths came in heavy gulps. "He must have broken out of the restraints. He's been yanking at them for days!" She sniffled and rubbed her knee again.

Vivian pinched the bridge of her nose and forced herself to calm down. The perimeter fence was up. The house was in the center of it. Tucker John wouldn't get very far on foot while going through alcoholic detox.

"Are you alright, Lourdes? How badly did he hurt you?"

Lourdes didn't look at her. "He pulled my hair and threw me to the floor. My knee is bruised, but I'm okay I think." She wiped away more tears with the back of her hand.

Vivian nodded. "Good, good. And great work putting up the fence." She rushed back to the laboratory and came back to the office again with an intermezzo kit, *XBalance*, and her porcelain mask. "I'm going to go find him. While I'm gone, give yourself a health scan, make sure you're not more seriously injured than you think." She began to pull on the mask. "I'll be back as soon as I find Tucker John. Keep a line of communication open, please." She quickly turned to leave.

"You won't need to wear the mask, Vivian!" Lourdes called after her, her cheeks burning pink.

"What was that?" Vivian had long since grown impatient. She wasn't normally like this.

"The mask is useless. He thinks you are the slave-woman." Lourdes stood, the blush of pink washed away leaving pale, ashen skin in its wake. "The other day I-I accidentally told him your name."

CHAPTER 7

"I accidentally told him your name."

Lourdes' words gnawed at Vivian's eardrums. Another rush of anger and anxiety hit her in the belly. She was going to lose it completely. When was the last time she had taken *Paz*? "You told him my name? *Why* would you do that?" Her voice was a sharp whisper.

"I didn't mean to! It slipped out!"

"Why were you even *talking*, Lourdes? All you had to do was give him the liver treatment. That was all!"

"I wasn't talking to him!"

Vivian scowled. She folded her arms tight around her body, shifting her weight from side to side. She had suddenly lost direction.

"I only told him to stop yanking on the restraints and then I said you, Vivian, would not be pleased if he damaged the equipment."

Vivian's jaw ticked. "Did you say anything else?" She needed to get out of the house, not just to find Tucker John, but to get away from Lourdes. For three years she had put up with her mistakes and her insubordination all because John Jay had told her to give Lourdes a chance, arguing that she was young and of a different culture. Over and over again, he pleaded with her to have patience with their assistant.

At first, even John Jay seemed awkward around Lourdes but he had somehow managed to muster the patience and grace to work with her. Vivian had as well but now she was far from gracious. And, with Tucker John thinking she was the slave-woman he'd been hunting, the situation was only going to grow worse.

Vivian had already decided to reveal herself to the man and explain the confusion with their time-twins, but that was going to happen only after he'd taken his first *Spadds* treatment. By then she would have had the chance to prove the truth and reality of the timeline he was currently on before unmasking herself as slave-Vivian's two-thousand-year-young twin.

Now, there was no grace to be had, no buffer to cushion the blow just enough to ease Tucker John into his new and temporary life in the 4030's. Lourdes' slip of the tongue had probably hardened him even more to reason, leading him to believe that the very slave he was hunting down had been holding him hostage for nearly two weeks. The young woman was always slipping at something, always needing John Jay to come to her rescue. Unfortunately, he was still missing.

Frustrated, Vivian tossed her mask on the side table. It broke on impact. No, Lourdes telling Tucker John her name wasn't Lourdes' fault. It was Vivian's fault for putting this kind of pressure on her. Lourdes wasn't used to any form of real conflict. She was born and bred in a time where reason and logic without any emotion, ruled all things. Emotions—strong emotions—were weaknesses, deficiencies—deadly contagious diseases that Lourdes never failed in calling by twisted, Latin names.

Lourdes' nerves must have been frayed dealing with Tucker John. She was raised to be at ease within all situations, which in Vivian's deduction of the behavior, meant indifference and complete incapability of empathy or true compassion.

Vivian shouldn't have chickened-out with Tucker John. She should have been dealing with him herself, from the very moment she started taking *Paz*. If she needed *Paz* to continue with his ranting, there was no telling what Lourdes would need. Truth was Vivian needed to get a grip and stop taking the pills herself. She knew better, knew what they were capable of.

She asked Lourdes again, "Lourdes, did you tell him *anything* else? Let me know so that I can be prepared to handle this."

Lourdes sniffled, blew out a deep breath, and then met Vivian's eyes. They were perfectly still. "No, Vivian. I didn't tell him anything else."

***

Tucker John limped, mostly crawled, farther away from the manor, staying as hidden in the shadows and the trees as he possibly could. He knew how to hide just as well as he knew how to hunt. Running from Ash since his legs could move had given him the prowess to do it and do it well.

But he'd never been this bad off before. He was always hale when he went on a hunt. With Ash, he was little more than bruised but now he was on the worse side of ill. He felt like he had influenza. It was in the heat of the summer in Atlanta, Georgia, and he was chilled to his marrow. He also couldn't tell which way he was going anymore. He felt like he was moving around in circles. His head was still pounding and the sun was hurting his eyes something fierce, and no matter how much he tried, he couldn't stop the voices from talking in his ears.

Vivian and the White woman had bewitched him!

He moaned and pulled his body deep into the shadows of an Oak. He felt like he had been running for hours and he was beyond exhausted. He looked a fright and felt even worse. He was practically naked and filthy as a field-hand. Briers had caught the hairs of his head, beard, and chest when he jumped from the window. Worse, his left ankle had grown nearly three times in size.

He brought his fist to his forehead and cursed. He'd warned Mr. Jefferson, of Jefferson Plantation, not to send out that backward posse to fetch Vivian. He told him they would only muck things up and get in his way, and for the first time in his life, Tucker John hated that he was right. Vivian had gotten away, caught him instead, and the posse was probably still riding around chasing after their own sorry backsides! And the way things were looking, Tucker John was going to be the one to die because of it.

Sickness suddenly seized him. He clutched his middle and emptied its contents in a patch of dark earth and grass. Nausea came at him almost as quickly as the sudden need to sleep. Sleeping was dangerous, but he was hurting so bad and he was so thirsty. Water wouldn't sate him. He needed something stronger.

He bit down into the flesh of his hand to chase away the rising need. Then he leaned his head back and ceased to fight against the oppressive beast of exhaustion that brought with it horrible dreams—that of his child-self, running with blurry eyes through the whipping limbs of trees as the snarling beast of Ash Spruce chased after him, thirsty for his blood.

***

Vivian glanced down at the tracker. Tucker John had covered a good distance in the thirty minutes he'd been on the lamb. He'd managed to find the densest part of the property to hide in which troubled Vivian. She was going to have to go after him from where she was on foot. And he was still a good distance within the shrubs and trees.

She tightened the strap of the intermezzo around her wrist this time. She had his rifle locked away, but Tucker John was a man of a more primitive nature than she. He didn't need a gun to do her harm. Even going through detox he could still pose a considerable threat to her just because of his size alone. He was six feet, three inches tall, weighed about two-hundred thirty pounds; all solid mass. He'd already hurt Lourdes without a single thought and could have done more if he had the time. He probably wanted to rip Vivian limb from limb.

With a quick prayer, she powered down her sled and prepared to go for him on foot. She flinched. The vehicle gave off a sound akin to a deep hum or a sigh when it was placed in neutral. She hoped Tucker John hadn't heard it. She kept her finger near the trigger of the intermezzo.

CHAPTER 8

Houuuuummph.

Tucker John's heart was already beating like a race horse's. It stopped when he heard the sudden sound coming from beyond the trees. His instincts tried to kick in, but they were slowed and dulled. Had he been healthy he would have sensed them, most likely Vivian and the white woman, coming from at least a half a mile off.

His sensitivity to the presence of others had heightened with each surprise punch or kick he had received at the hand of his own daddy—a sixth sense developed out of the need to survive.

As ugly of a root as it was, Ash Spruce's cruelty had sharpened his senses in a way that he was able to track down and best anyone who came against him. He'd learned to anticipate a person's movements and remain several steps ahead of them, all because he could sense them, smell their scent and intent as if it were smoke on the wind.

Had he been healthy, he would have already tracked down and ambushed whoever was coming for him. But he wasn't healthy, he had been poisoned, and was probably only a few short hours from death. The best he could do was hide. But he refused to go down hiding. He was going to fight to his death, and take down as many of his adversaries as he could.

Grinding his teeth, he pushed up from the ground and hid himself as clean out of sight as he could. Blinking stinging sweat from his eyes, he waited. He wasn't going to be able to stand for too long. The ground beneath him was already pitching again.

He watched the figure of a woman press into his path and suddenly come to a stop. Vivian, it was Vivian! The wench's back went ramrod straight. She hardly got his name past her lips before he lunged at her, throwing his body hard against hers, bringing her to the ground. She landed with a winded thud and gasped for air. Tucker John bared his teeth, fighting to lock his arm around her neck from behind. He was going to snap it right in two!

He cursed his muscles for betraying him, putting up as much force and strength as a seven year old child. Vivian tore his arms away and clawed at the ground. She was trying to grab something she had dropped, its silver finish shone beneath the ground cover of leaves and twigs. Tucker John reached for her arms, impeding her retreat. She'd brought this upon herself. He'd never wanted to kill the wench, but just like a rabid dog she'd turned on him. She'd left him no choice.

He did his best to keep his body on top of hers, using his dead weight and his legs to tangle her up. He grabbed hold of her thick ponytail, looping it around his hand several times and tugging back on it like he would the reins of his horse. Vivian cried out, and swung back at him with a sharp elbow to his jaw.

Tucker John saw stars. His head felt like it had been split with an axe. His grip loosened on Vivian's hair, but his hands quickly found their way around her neck as she flipped onto her back beneath him. His face was only a few inches from hers, his crazed eyes staring into two dark pools of determination. *Not fear*. Why wasn't she afraid? She knew what he could do to her. He'd set her straight before, but this time she wasn't afraid, not in the least.

She should've been. He intended to send her straight to Hell!

"You treacherous, whore!" Foamy spittle slid from his dry lips. "I'se gon' rip your skull clean from your ne—"

Ziop. Cahsssssss.

The threat cost him. A sharp pain pierced him in the side of his neck. His eyes rolled into his head and his body seized with a gut-wrenching spasm, arcing him backward. Vivian pushed him over onto his back and quickly scooted away, kicking him in the shoulder in her retreat.

Tucker John's eyes managed to settle and find Vivian's. The look of determination in her eyes had gone, leaving behind it anger. Even on her knees she looked like a lioness stocking her prey, not an escaped, feeble-minded wench, who had by some form of witchcraft, gotten one over on her Overseer, a man who'd spent so much time with her that he could have been mistaken for her master.

Again his body seized with a pain so intense that it brought tears to his eyes and made him whimper like a child. What had she done to him? His breath caught in his lungs and was only able to escape through the tremors that followed the seizing. Tears fell down the side of his eyes and burned the little cuts he'd gotten while on the run.

"What you do to me, Viv-Vivian? Why?" He had to ask. If he was going to die he wanted to know how. From her, he needed to know why.

His query was staccato, caught between a gasp for air and a pained moan, and he was in pain, a great deal of it. *XBalance* had a different effect on every patient, but the first treatment was notably the worst depending on the circumstances, and the only one that brought with it a level of pain.

Vivian already knew he was hurting from the beginning stages of detox, but the *XBalance* had amplified that with a fiery ache all its own, coupled with extreme spasms as if it were purging the toxins from his body through brute force.

She wished that Tucker John was still in the lab. Had he not run she could have put him under and let him sleep through the agony. With all the hateful things he'd said to her, the short-lived tussle he'd had with her, she still hurt seeing him like that. Again, with the tears in his eyes, and the fear in his voice, she couldn't help but see John Jay writhing in agonizing pain.

She dropped down to her knees and eased toward him. Tucker John snarled at her, his eyes puffy and bloodshot. His skin had flushed bright red and was most likely burning as if being licked by the sun.

She made her voice soft, non-threatening. "I'm not trying to harm you. I'm actually helping you,"

Tucker John moved his head from left to right. "No, you done killed me! Murderer! They gon' lynch you good for this. Hell, I hope they BURN YOU!" His face tensed again and his mouth gaped open. It was another seizure in his muscles. He gasped when it ended, the sound ripping through his dry throat was akin to tumbling boulders.

"You won't die. This is healing you. Your body has not had alcohol in a long time. You are going through what is called 'detox'. What I gave you hurts for now, but it *will* ease the pain."

"LIAR!" He shouted in between seizes. "You d@#%ed liar! You back-stabbing liar!"

"I am not *lying* to you John-*Tucker* John! You need help—"

Panting, he clawed at her, fingers curling like angry hooks ready to rip through her skin. Vivian stayed out of his reach. His eyes were wild, foamy saliva collected at the corners of his mouth.

"I should'a blowed your nigga' head OFF! I should'a let Jefferson hang you that last time you done run off! I should'a set your @$$ on fire my D@^$%^ self! You hear me, nigga?! You worthless heap of tar! You ain't nothing but a feeble-minded, voodoo *witch*! You done cursed me! You done cursed me straight to hell!" Pain took hold of him again and he gagged as if he were being choked.

Vivian shook her head and stood. She couldn't watch him go through the seizing and be cursed each time he caught his breath. It was difficult for her to accept that he wasn't John Jay. Why couldn't she reconcile it? Regardless of her idiocy, no one with a heart could manage to bear witness to that kind of suffering and cursing, no matter how horrid the one suffering was. She couldn't stomach the sight. She couldn't stomach wanting to beat him with her own hands either, only to be haunted by her mind lying to her, telling her that she had abused John Jay.

Her nightmares would replay her beating a suffering John Jay deep in the woods of 4037 Georgia, and with the way, Tucker John was talking, and the frustration she was feeling, Vivian wasn't sure if she could stop herself from beating him to death if she began hitting him at all.

It was settled. She would leave him out there, hidden in the trees. He would suffer greatly alone, but at least he wouldn't die with the treatment at work. She would come back for him later and put him to sleep.

Sensing her retreat, Tucker John reached out for her. Panic contorted his face. "Don't leave me, Vivian! Please! Don't leave me out here! I'se sorry! I-I apologize. I swear fo' *god* I apologize! Please, Vivian! I'se hurting real bad," his breath trembled. "I'se sorry, please help me...please?"

Vivian cupped her ears and quickened her strides. She was feeling way too much, the weight of it all nearly driving her to her knees. She took in a sharp breath. *Paz*, she hadn't taken the *Paz*. She shouldn't have left the house without taking it.

"PLEASSEEE!" Tucker John shouted again before gagging and pulling his knees to his chest. He flipped his body over to his belly and tried to crawl after her, but was drawn back into fetal position only a few desperate feet away from where she stood.

He cried out again, his arms stretching out to her, the muscles in his back flexing like carved marble. She would not listen to him. She could not look at him. Instead, she ran from the path and back to her sled.

She hadn't gotten far before she heard him cry out again with absolute terror, and begging.

"God please help me! Don't leave me out here, Vivian! Please help me,"

Vivian had never heard anyone cry out like that, especially not for her. How could she ignore it? She couldn't.

"ALRIGGGHHHTTT!!!" she hollered. Her fist clenched at her side, tears pricking her eyes. What was she doing? All of this was a mistake, but what was she doing? She turned on her heels and rushed back to where Tucker John lay. He looked small and pathetic, face down in the dirt, tiny scratches with crusted blood on them dotting across his bare flesh, torn soiled trousers, matted filthy hair, his ankle twice the size of a softball, anchoring him down.

Compassion overshadowed her good reason. Guilt for her mistake of keeping him in 4037 compelled her. His begging her with tears almost winded her. Things were so out of whack. Had he not ambushed her, she could have frozen him and taken him back to the lab before giving him the *XBalance*, but now that she had given it to him she couldn't suspend him, at least not until the *XBalance* had fully bloomed inside of him.

She squeezed the pendant at her neck and dropped to her knees by Tucker John's head. The look on his face was nothing less than grateful relief, no matter how short-lived it might be.

Tucker John grabbed her arm with such force he nearly pulled it out of socket. Vivian winced.

"Thank you! Thank you, Vivian! You's an angel of the Lord!" He kissed her hand. The briers in his beard and chest hair scratched at her skin. Her jaw clenched from repulsion and the sharp pain of his tight grip on her arm and hand.

Her nostrils flared and her own body trembled from the forces at work within her. She eased her free hand over his mouth, squeezing his face and lips, careful not to let her hand wander over his nose as well.

It frightened her to think how life could toss a person into the throws of such predicaments in which they could be made to act contrary to their own nature, beliefs, and morals. But it had done it to her. Everything she valued and preached as gospel seemed to have been thrown out the window as rubbish and an animalistic, calloused version of her had sprung forth, even if for only a dangerous moment.

Never once had she ever considered killing a soul! She had problems killing spiders, but right at that moment, alone with Tucker John and the venomous words that he cursed her with, and then the sudden wind of him singing her praises, rage, and wounds to her bleeding heart made her want to kill him with her bare hands.

She prayed again and forced herself to settle for her tears instead of spilling his blood.

Her hand remained pressed against his dry lips, some of the briers pocked through her flesh. She knew they must have broken through his as well. He grunted, struggling against her pressured hold to no avail. She didn't care. She spoke through clenched teeth. "Be *quiet*, Tucker John. Don't say a single word. Not. One. More. *Word*! Understand?"

Anger, hurt, the thought of betrayal beat against her chest. Touching him was like a break in her covenant with John Jay. If she was going to stay with him, she needed not to think of *him* at all. She needed to think of her husband or else she would abandon Tucker John completely, leave him there with not another treatment and let him die. Timelines and history be dashed!

Tucker John nodded quickly but he kept his mouth shut once she removed her hand.

Vivian tried to free her other arm from his grasp but he wouldn't release his hold. "I'm not going to leave you. Please, let go of my arm. Now. Let Go!"

He slowly and reluctantly let her go but tried to grab for her once he was hit with another spasm. Vivian kept her arms out of reach until the spasm ebbed away, moaning within herself to block out the pathetic sounds of his whimpering. Then, when the moment had passed, she forced herself to gingerly lift his head unto her lap.

He groaned from the movement. She felt his body tense and then relax at her touch. He exhaled with relief, his brow suddenly smoothed with an eerie calm. Vivian's chest clenched.

John Jay had been the only other man to lie in her lap. Where was he? Why had God let this happen? She pressed her lips tightly closed and tried to hold back another moan, this time to smother her raging ache.

Heated tears fell from her eyes and onto Tucker John's hair and face. Again he took hold of her arm, but not as tightly as before, only to ease his large, rough, hand into hers. Vivian didn't pull away, instead, she gently brushed his head and face with her free hand, occasionally plucking a twig or brier from his face and chest hair, tearfully shushing him, almost lulling him as she wept.

Quiet washed over them. His eased breathing fell in rhythm with the gentle strokes of her hand against his face, and her fingertips across his scalp. For that moment she imagined he was John Jay and a false serenity washed through her.

Above, the sun peeked through the canopy of the woven fingers of the trees and glided over their bodies like a warm lace blanket of golden, kaleidoscope light; peeking as if the scene in nature's eyes was shameful to witness. Nevertheless, surrendering to the intermission from the chaos around them, both Vivian and Tucker John closed their eyes, yielding to the touch of the other, in silence.

CHAPTER 9

"How are you feeling?" Lourdes asked, slipping into the library where Vivian sat with her head cradled in her hands. She had been sitting that way for nearly three hours, holding her head or staring at the illuminated memo that hovered in the near darkness just above her desk.

It was from Raul Manuel, her Century Cell Group Leader. The perimeter fence had been activated several times and he wanted to make sure everything was okay. Vivian had yet to respond in detail, but she did send him a 'green flag' marker, indicating that there was no emergency.

She hated to lie. It wasn't in her character to do so…at least it hadn't been before.

Now she was thinking about the reason for her lie. She and Tucker John had gotten back to the house well after dark the previous day. She'd moved him in herself after suspending him with the intermezzo and utilizing a transportation net. She and Tucker John had sat in the heat of the Georgia summer for nearly eight full hours before the *XBalance* came to full bloom in his body and Vivian was able to freeze him.

He was resting now—something Vivian was unable to do— washed up, and put back in his restraints, fully under sedation. He would be awake in a few hours again, but the new security measures she'd taken to secure him would hold him in place far better than the precautions she'd previously used.

Before, she had employed the sole use of archaic, padded, straps. Shielding him from modern conveniences had been her initial goal. Now that her cover was blown, and she had to tell the truth about herself, refraining from modern forms of restraint was no longer something she had to do.

64

She yawned when her mouth opened to answer Lourdes' question. She was beyond exhausted. Once she had gotten Tucker John situated, she returned to the nexus gate. She couldn't help but look for John Jay again, a task that seemed nothing short of fruitless, especially since the gate continued to register him as being in 4037. She deduced it was recognizing Tucker John's location which was a problem that went beyond weight or measure.

She covered her mouth and let another yawn pass. "I'm alright." She looked up at Lourdes wondering if she'd discerned her lie. The younger woman's expression was less than convinced and dancing around the edge of anger. Vivian offered an apology.

"I'm sorry. I'm sorry about everything." She rubbed her face with her hands. "I've spoken so harshly to you, Lourdes, since this all began, and you don't deserve that. You've done nothing but try and help me with this." She sighed. "I'm trying to sort everything out. I'm doing my very best."

She dropped her face back into her hands and leaned over her desk, not before closing the memo. Her efforts were nothing more than failures. She couldn't even stay in the room with Tucker John for too long. She'd managed not to smother him while they were in the woods, but that was because he'd stopped speaking, and she forced herself to believe he was John Jay, something that had made her sick to her stomach. Besides the temporary fix that pretending gave, she couldn't pretend forever.

Lourdes took the seat across from her. "How do you suppose to 'sort' this out? This isn't a minor problem. This isn't a discovery of inaccurate historical documentation. This is a broken man, a man from the ancient past, an ugly one, a highly *diseased* one."

Vivian studied Lourdes through the cracks in her fingers. The room was dark but she could still see her. Lourdes seemed suddenly forward. Perhaps Tucker John tossing her to the other side of the lab by her roots had pulled that out of her.

Lourdes continued. "He is loud and violent. He has hurt me, and by the way you looked when you came home, I could tell he tried to hurt you, too. He is a dead end. For you, he is clearly a quandary without solution. But there is always a solution, Vivian. You just have to accept it."

Vivian let Lourdes' words settle before she responded. "So, what do you suggest, Lourdes? What is your solution?" Vivian knew her answer. Lourdes' easy grey eyes gave that away with such indifference that it made Vivian's blood boil.

"Euthanasia."

Vivian said the word with her. Leaning back in her chair, she bit down on her bottom lip. She had to remind herself that she had requested this era for her and John Jay's surveillance. She wanted an era that would affect her, make her a better person so that she could change her future, heal her and John Jay's past. They needed a victory, together, one that would remove the strange thread of jealousy that had caused him to resent her success. Sure, the annals of time recorded their triumphs as first being hers as the Team Lead, but he was also mentioned.

It just wasn't enough anymore, living in her shadow. He'd confessed that to her to her pain. They needed a victory that would bear his name alongside hers not behind it. The 4030's were just the timeline they needed, not only to survey but to see things clearly, grow together, like the team she'd always believed they were.

It was believed that the Silent Revolution sprouted its roots in that decade, right there in Georgia. Vivian wanted to know why. She wanted to discover exactly when it began, and what its catalyst was, or who. She then wanted to use that knowledge for a greater good, write the name of the man or woman in the history annals of her time and beyond, celebrate the hero and heroines who had given her timeline the ability to exist just with the genesis of a single idea and declaration—"*For the martyred we march on, lest the living die.*"

The Silent Revolution had shaped the very century that Vivian lived in. Her very existence, the program that allowed her to be, was birthed from the reawaking that came from it. Differences in ethnicity or race were no longer shunned but celebrated, with passion and grace while emotions like anger and elation were once again understood, welcomed.

Living in the 4030's amid a sea of indifferent people who found death to be the solution to nearly every problem, even the problems that weren't problems, was an entirely different realization altogether. Reading about it was one thing, living it another. In the three years that she and John Jay had spent in that Field, eleven people whom she had come to hold dear had been euthanized for 'issues' ranging from grief or extreme elation, all of them deemed highly contagious, dangerous diseases, dressed up in fancy Latin words.

Feeling too much, allowing one's body to explode with addictive chemicals had become a crime punishable by death if it wasn't contained.

Listening to Lourdes offer euthanasia as a solution to the unwanted presence of an inconvenient, foul-mouthed, hateful man, made the words that had been branded to the Revolution itself sound off in her head once again. The words certainly applied now, even for a person like Tucker John, a man considered nothing more than an animal.

Tucker John had done many wicked things in a time where his actions were not seen as such. No judge or jury in his timeline would find him guilty or sentence him to death for any of them. Though conscious of the truth of his actions, what right did Vivian have to play judge, jury, and executioner to him, two full millennia past his recorded death?

For Vivian, Tucker John was not a quandary without a solution. To her, he was the living who was not meant to die in that day, and he certainly wasn't going to die at her hand.

She took a deep breath before answering Lourdes, selecting her words with the tender care she would use with a child.

"Euthanasia sounds really simple to you. It is simple on the surface, but it's a lot more complicated than you think. Never mind the fact that he, no matter his sins against humanity, did not ask to be here in the first place. He shouldn't be here." She spoke slowly and calmly. "I cannot, in all good conscience, put him to death for my and John Jay's mistake."

"John Jay didn't do this. You did."

Silence.

Vivian bit back the fiery retort that burned her tongue. If her memory served her correctly, which it did, it was Lourdes who insisted that she not involve the Cleric's Office, that she hold off on involving them in their debacle. Why Vivian had chosen that moment in time to heed her advice, she was still trying to figure out.

Lourdes shifted, folding her arms across her chest. "So you're not going to consider euthanasia?"

"No, Lourdes. I'm not. As a Minster of Time, doing so would be ethically wrong. You should know that by now. He is out of his timeline for one thing. He is in the future, his future, and that in itself is a crime, *our* crime," she pointed between the two of them. "I don't need to make things worse by killing him."

"The Cleric's Office *will* find out about him. And then the Government will be involved. They will come for him, and they will put him down, and when they do, we will be in a lot of trouble. They may euthanize me for this, you, they'll just send home."

"So, tell me again then, why you insisted we not tell Raul about this when we had the chance? I know I was inconsistent with my decision regarding involving him, but in the end, when I had felt like yielding and calling him in, you urged me not to do so. Why?"

More Silence. Lourdes' nostrils flared.

Vivian put her head down again, resting it in the crook of her arms. She said nothing, letting the silence fill the atmosphere. She hoped Lourdes would get the message and leave her alone. Her mind was incredibly tired.

Lourdes spoke her name several times before Vivian finally responded. She had not gotten the message. It was to be expected. John Jay was the only one who could get Lourdes to follow directions without a debate.

She said, "This is not a conversation that we are having, Lourdes. Not now. We'll take this one step at a time. We'll consider our options once he is fully detoxed, euthanasia excluded."

"Our options? What options, Vivian?"

"There are options. You just don't want to see them right now." She sighed again.

Lourdes scooted closer to the desk, placing her hand near Vivian's resting head. Her voice was an ominous whisper. "The most foolish thought a woman can have is that she can convert the heart of a wicked man, and he is *wicked*. You know it's true. Don't delude yourself."

Vivian pulled her head from the nest of her arms. "I don't think that I can convert him!"

"Yes, you do, and all at John Jay's expense! You intend to waste precious time on him, time that should be spent locating John Jay. I've read your logs. I understand the math. I understand procedure for time transportation. Because there is no record of Tucker John surviving past the date you brought him forward in 1837, you would have to wait six full years, to the *day*, before you could send him back. Six years is a long time to live with a wild animal, but not if you have schemes of domesticating it."

"Lourdes, you are wrong." Vivian's jaw clenched so tightly that her teeth began to ache. "Furthermore, you have no right to talk to me about my husband!"

"Yes, I do! I know what was in the package you had me get from the Cleric's Office. It wasn't just *Xbalance*—"

Vivian cut her off, anger darkening her face. She smacked the desk with her fist, glad that the large object was acting as a partition between them. "You had no right to snoop, Lourdes! And you don't know what you are talking about!"

"I didn't snoop, Vivian! I had to sign for that package which meant I got to see what was in it. I have done nothing wrong. I'm giving you sound advice—"

"Your advice is not sound! He cannot die in the future. It would be unethic—"

"History says he is dead already! What difference does it ma—"

"Recorded history has gotten it wrong many times! That is why the Ministry of Time exists! Why do you think we surveyors even exi—"

"He is DISEASED! Look what he is doing to me!" Lourdes' voice trembled with the shake of her voice. "I-I'm anxious. I think horrid things about him. I fear I have caught his filthy sickness of hate and anger and—"

Vivian shot to her feet. She'd heard enough. "Then leave, Lourdes!"

Lourdes flinched as if she had been slapped.

Vivian stared hard at her. "You're in complete conflict with what I am doing, and I don't blame you for that. My actions, my reasoning, are foreign to you. But you need to be reassigned. You've never honored me as your superior, you have always questioned any decision I have made. You are doing so now—"

"With good reason! You're not being rational!" Her eyes were large, the whites in them shown in the dark of the room.

"What do you know about being rational? You've just blamed your poor behavior on an ignorant man lost in time, a man you've spent less than a full hour with while he's been awake. Anger is not a disease! Assessment of a person's character—be it negative or positive—is not a contagion that needs to be sterilized! All these things are part of the human experience.

"Our behaviors are ours to choose. They are the product of our God-given free will. This is how we learn to respect one another, by dealing with a person's character flaws, even the vile ones. How we do so is our choice."

"That is why I said to euthanize him, Vivian. That would be the most humane and respectful thing. The right choice,"

Vivian took a deep breath and sighed from her belly. "I will no longer be in need of your assistance, Lourdes, but you are still under the confidentiality clause, so I suggest you move along, quietly."

Lourdes stood up with a shudder. "No, that won't work. It's too late! I'm in too deep. If this ship sinks, I'll drown right along with it, even if I am reassigned tomorrow. Don't you get it? You have not only jeopardized your own future, but mine, and John Jay's too. And all for what? For that relic in the lab!" She pointed a stiff arm in Tucker Johns direction.

Vivian scowled. "I've heard enough. Watch your tone, Lourdes." She finally rounded the desk and closed the gap between them. "You're from this century so, like I am doing with Tucker John, I am going to give you the benefit of the doubt—"

"Benefit of the doubt? For what, Vivian?" Lourdes was smug, her pert chin rising in challenge.

Vivian met her head on. She didn't want to be cruel, but she needed to be frank. Time was working against them and if the Cleric's Office did catch wind of Tucker John, if the Government got involved, there was no telling what they would do to him, to them, now that so much time had passed without a report of any of it. Either Lourdes was going to work with her or she needed to leave. Either way, Vivian was going to give her a taste of reality.

"I'm giving you the benefit of the doubt for your emotional inadequacies, your delusions about the worth of life or the lack thereof, and your ignorance, all of which are your shared character flaws with the 'relic' in the lab. The only thing is they were present in you long before he got here."

Offense flashed in Lourdes' eyes. She choked on her own breathe, but she remained quiet.

Vivian continued, her tone firm but seasoned with pleading. "But since I am not from this timeline and have you in physical age and maturity by almost seven years, I am going to give you a bit of helpful advice. Life is precious. It is a gift from God. Yes, it is unpredictable, it can be difficult, but it is precious. Its value cannot even be measured.

"I don't know about you, but I believe in God, Lourdes. I believe what He said when He stated that 'to whom much is given, much is required.' I believe because I have more knowledge, more education, and more power than Tucker John, that I am obligated, *obligated*, to treat him with mercy even though I don't believe he would do the same to me.

"In the face of my requirement, at the call of mercy, as a Minister of Time, I am choosing to honor the gift of life, by giving *him* time. Here is my advice to you. If you have the opportunity to honor God, to preserve and change a life for the better, you should take it, Lourdes, whether the change is guaranteed or not. Because it could be that that one life that you took the time to change, shifts the currents in the sea of human existence for the whole world, and the future generations to come. If that sounds like conversion to you, then yes, I am hoping, *praying*, to convert Tucker John, or at least preserve him, until I can place him back in his timeline."

Lourdes shook her head, her arms folded around her waist. "There is nothing that you can do that will change him. He will cost us everything. And after learning about some of the things he has done to people, to women…to the slave-woman…I don't believe there is any value left in him at all. As far as I can see, he is in the red. Euthanasia is mercy for a person like him."

She turned to walk out of the room. "But, I'll stay on, not just because I don't see a way out of this, but because I owe it to John Jay to do so. That's what he would want me to do."

Vivian's voice came out as a whisper. Lourdes' last statement, the implication, though small, nearly knocked the wind out of her. "John Jay isn't dead, Lourdes."

Lourdes offered a wan smile before leaving Vivian's office. "I never said he was. Anyhow, I think it's best I stay at my mother's for a day, see how she's doing, cleanse my emotional output. There are at least three vaccines at her house. I'll be back, and ready to work once I get my head as far around this as I can. I just hope you know what you're doing."

CHAPTER 10

Sweat tickled the crevice of his nose and cheek causing him to shift uncomfortably in his bed. Magnus was never one to appreciate the heat, especially the kind that made his clothing cling to his body. It put him in a foul mood which is why he had mostly stayed indoors during the last three and a half years. The heat and humidity were why he had retired ten years ago to milder climates at all. The sooner this assignment was over, the better.

He pulled the sheets from his body and stepped into his home office. The 'Instrument' that had been sent to him from the Cleric's Office in 6039, was calibrating.

The Instrument had never been used before. It didn't even have a name besides 'the Instrument'. All that Magnus was told was that when 'Static waves'—whatever those were—were being made, the Instrument would calibrate. Three and half years and nothing had happened. He should have known that on one of the hottest days of that year, the darned thing would calibrate!

Part of him was almost convinced that Aiden Schulsler had planned it, counted on stifling days like this just to grate at his mood. The man hated Magnus almost as much as Magnus hated him. It was a bizarre thing to know that grudges could transcend the threads of millennia, and still buck and stab with exacting and painful execution.

Magnus, however, did not have it nearly as bad as some of the others on Aiden's I-owe-you list. All he had to do was dredge through heat and humidity thick enough to scoop with a spoon for a little while longer, verify a few facts on the timeline, and then he would be free of Aiden Schulsler for good...he hoped.

Others on the Schulsler's list had not been as fortunate. Magnus had wronged him, and thus fallen in his debt, but his wrong doing was simply the result of a bad draw, while the others had come at him with bloodlust.

He rolled his head on his shoulders, working out a kink that had been growing at the base of his neck. He leaned over the small object in the darkness of his office before finally sitting as the strange bright grey glow began to ebb from its sensors. Like wisps of cigarette smoke they danced, giving off enough illumination to dimly light the entire surface of his desk by the tiny currents of what appeared to be electricity coursing through them.

Magnus covered his mouth and offered a delighted laugh. Science and surveillance were such amazing things, full of delightful surprises. This was a grand surprise. He quickly reined in his excitement. He didn't have a single concern about the Governing authorities catching wind of his 'overt expression,' as they may have called it. Instead, he wanted to verify what he had seen rather than get excited over a hoax. For all he knew, the very creator of this device could have scheduled for it to go off like it had.

Again his mind drifted to Schulsler. Although Schulsler had not created the Instrument, he wasn't above to having the thing rigged. The man loved to play cat-and-mouse. Those who knew Schulsler on the wrong side of his manners, quickly learned to play along and hope he got bored of them sooner rather than later.

Magnus played along.

He quickly dressed and grabbed his best walking shoes. He checked for the strongest readings on the Instrument and followed the coordinates to the source location. From what he could tell, he would be walking for at least two hours before reaching his destination, somewhere near Balm Hill. That was maybe seven miles away, not too terribly far from his private home or the Cleric's Office, but far enough considering he had to go on foot.

The Instrument was too sensitive and fickle to use on a sled. The Static trail would be lost, or so he'd been told. He was just glad that it was still in the early morning. The sky was still black and dotted with stars. The sun hadn't shown its face. If the heavens smiled upon him, he would be able to verify more information concerning his bizarre assignment and make it back home before his skin began to tan.

***

Tucker John felt cool air blowing steadily upon his face. He nestled deeper into the comfort of the bed linens before startling himself awake. He was in a bed! No longer was he in the woods with his head nestled in the warmth of Vivian's lap.

That was twice that she'd brought him to this place without his knowing it. He cursed inwardly. He tried to sit up but found that he'd been strapped down again. Each movement he made gave off the scent of soap. She or the white woman had bathed him; more like violated him which only made him angrier.

He couldn't remember the last time he'd taken a bath. He wasn't much on keeping up with his weekly bathing. He would splash water here and there; take a dive in the river when the heat was too much, but the hip-bath on Saturday he missed quite a bit. He didn't attend Church much apart from the holidays, and even then he missed service sometimes, so keeping up with a weekly bath in preparation for entering the Lord's house was not much of a priority.

But now he'd been bathed, and laid up in the bed like an invalid woman! This, whatever it was that was happening to him, must have been his punishment for being such a heathen. His mama had always warned him not to be like his daddy, told him not to stray from beneath the protective hand of the Lord, but Tucker John hadn't listen. God hadn't done him much good from his view of things. God had taken his mama from him not soon after she had blown his daddy's brains out. The baby didn't last a good week without her, and before Tucker John could blink through the tears of their loss, his lily-livered, eldest brother had beaten down the door, and taken everything that he had left.

He still remembered Ashford Junior's words and the stink of them. Ashford, as he was having the other 'dandies' he had connected with call him, barged his way into the shack like he was too good to be there, as if he had never seen such poverty, even though it had bred him. He was a hypocrite, just like their daddy he was named for.

The law wasn't far from Ashford's back, either. He said he had brought them with him because he didn't want any trouble or a fuss out of 'the animal'. He threw the hateful name at Tucker John as if he was Ashford Senior himself. The verbal blow all but winded him. His brothers knew the wound the name had caused him. His eldest brother no longer seemed to care. All Ashford wanted was the three little ones, and since he was the eldest he had the right to have them.

To the law, Ashford Junior had made it sound like he was doing his duty before God by taking the little ones with him, but the look in his dark eyes said otherwise. His actions had nothing to do with the Lord. It was nothing more than a move of desperation that drove him back to the shack, vomiting scripture and robbing Tucker John of the little ones. Ashford was no more a Godly man than Tucker John. No, Ashford's sins were worse. He lied on the Lord and pretended religion where Tucker John just kept out of God's way.

Ashford had somehow managed to marry a homely gal with a healthy inheritance, but, with all the wealth she owned, she had proven to be barren and inconsolable over the matter. She wanted children, children that looked like her "lovely" Ashford. When Ashford had gotten word that their mama had murdered their daddy and then died herself, leaving three children under the age of three, with no one to fend for them besides Tucker

John, Ashford saw his opportunity to provide for his wife something she would otherwise not have.

He would give her children, children that looked like him, and they would be his blood even if they weren't his seed; the twins, Harry and Carl, were three years old, and Willa' May had only just turned two.

The only thing was, Ashford wanted nothing to do with Tucker John. Tucker John's presence would be a 'blight' upon the Blake family name, so he said. That was the new surname that Ashford had taken, Blake. He shunned the name Spruce like he shunned his past. His wife, Ingrid was the only child, and the one with the powerful name, so Ashford took hers upon their wedding day, and so would the only three people in the world that cared a lick for Tucker John.

Tucker John was going to be alone and utterly forgotten, a lone Spruce in a dead forest. His other three brothers, who had run off after Ashford Junior those many years ago, were already dead and gone as well. Mark and Louis caught influenza their first year out on their own, and William met his death at the end of a sheriff's rifle. It was a robbery gone bad.

Ashford wanted nothing to do with any man called Spruce. The only reason he'd seen fit to leave Tucker John with the few dollars he did was that the lawman said it was wrong to take the boy's family and leave him with nothing. And that is what he essentially had done, left Tucker John with nothing, but a hard heart, bitter wounds, and a few dollars from his fancy billfold to balance the scale.

Tucker John cried so hard those following days that he couldn't speak for a week. His heart ached so much he wept until it never ached again. He took up drinking just in case it tried to. Alcohol had a way of numbing the pain. That was one thing he did inherit from his daddy, which was the other break in his mama's advice. The only difference was that, although it kept Tucker John from feeling and crying, it had not kept him from earning a living and being right good at it.

Alcohol and cold discipline had become his steady companions.

But yesterday, yesterday Vivian had done something foul to him, and it hurt him with a pain that he not only felt clear up and through his hair follicles, but she had also made him cry like a baby. He sounded like a pig being slaughtered!

"Downright *pathetic!*" He spat. She had humiliated him in a way a man should never be humiliated by a woman, least of all a cotton-picking wench. She had him begging at her feet as if she was the Queen of England! It made his blood boil thinking about it. She had disrespected him something fierce, him, a white man! And after all the kindness and favors he'd given her.

"That treacherous negress got some nerve,"

He didn't know where she'd acquired her recent grit. Maybe it was from the little white woman. Back on the plantation all he had to do was give Vivian one look and she dared not step out of line. She knew what would happen if she did.

She was beyond thick in the brain—body of a full grown woman with the mind of a child no older than five years old on a good day, he reckoned. He'd figured she'd been born that way, the result of a weak buck mating with one of the females. It was her mental capacity that made her so easy to control, wrangle in. But when she did step out of place it didn't take much to set her back to rights.

Yesterday, however, she fought against him, bullied him into submission, and then she'd squeezed his face so tight she'd made his inner cheeks bleed. His eyes narrowed and his nostrils flared. He rolled his tongue around his inner mouth, assessing the damage.

She had *never* touched him like that! He would have pitched a fit right then if he had not begun to recall the way she stroked his face and scratched his scalp while he was hurting afterward, she even held his hand. Never mind the fact she was the reason why he was in pain in the first place.

He closed his eyes and leaned his head back thinking about it. Her hands felt so nice against his skin, like warm silk. He wondered what she had done to get her rough, calloused palms so smooth. She even smelled pretty. He clicked his teeth recalling her fragrance. She never smelled like that before, but it was good to him. As fighting mad as he was, as pierced as he was by her ungrateful betrayal, he wanted to smell her all over again.

The carnal thoughts of her somehow managed to abate his desire to read her her last rights. She was simple-minded after all. He was still going to teach her a lesson for what she'd done to him though, but for the time being, he was going to meditate on the softness of her hands and the pretty scent on her skin. When he got her back to the plantation, and once her backside heeled up from that whipping she had coming, he was going to take his time smelling that sweet fragrance she had acquired. He was even going to have her scratch his scalp again.

He never much cared that she wasn't worth a lick talking to, being as weak-minded as she was, in addition to her already inferior black, female, mind. He never had much to say to her in the first place. But, dang it all, if she didn't want to please him when she thought he was mad at her. If that attribute didn't come in handy in a full grown female when a man needed a bit of attention, Tucker John didn't know what did.

His only problem was he needed to figure out how in Sam Hill he was going to get himself free again and get Vivian back in place.

His eyes looked around the dreadfully sterile white room. Things had certainly changed since he run from it. He'd had that book, *Frankenstein*, read to him once or twice. The book gave him nightmares. He imagined the room looked exactly like Frankenstein's laboratory did, just stark white.

Maybe Vivian and that little white woman had schemes of changing him into some kind of Frankenstein monster. Maybe they were part of some half-naked-temperance-abolitionist-cult.

It seemed farfetched, but so did a full grown man, armed to the teeth, being rendered defenseless, and kidnapped by two tiny women who traipsed about in their undergarments.

And the attitude that Vivian was wearing…It almost made him believe she had been play-acting her former condition all these years long.

Tucker John was keen on character. He was a people-watcher. He had a natural talent for calculating a person's next move based on their behaviors and subtle nuances. If he paid enough attention, he could tell how they got to the places in life they were in to begin with. He'd had so much taken from him by the ones he had trusted, that he had to learn to keep a watchful eye on everyone, just in case they had plans of robbing him blind too.

That's how he'd become one of the highest paid and sought-after bounty hunters and overseers his side of Georgia; his sensitivity to movement and his discernment for behaviors.

Something had clearly happened to Vivian, something had changed her bad, and by the looks of things, her wanting to 'help' him was her trying to change him too, make him part of their naked-devil-worship-Frankenstein-cult. He just couldn't figure out how he hadn't seen this coming. He had foreseen her running off again, though, and he'd let her, with the intention of teaching her a good lesson, but he had not anticipated any of this.

He suddenly found himself praying, a practice he had never found value in. "Now, Lord," he cleared his throat. "I ain't much on praying. I'se tried to stay out of Your way, and I believe You done the same for me, but I knows when it's time to be humbling one's self and I'se at Your feet…humbling myself."

He waited a minute before saying anything else. He felt foolish for even praying at all, but the sudden image of his mama's face flashed into his mind, and out of respect for her, out of respect for his predicament, he kept praying to her God.

"I ain't got a clue as to what that negress and that nasty lil' white woman has up they sleeves, but I'se begging for Your help, Lord. You knows I'se always been a man who take care of my own needs. I ain't never asked nobody for nothing I couldn't get my own self. But Lord," he shifted his jaw as if he were trying to work down a chunk of tree bark. "I need help in this. You know I'se a man of my word. And I promise on my *mama*, if You help me in this, I'll," his jaw clenched. He tugged at the restraints, just testing his own resolve, wanting to see if he could free himself before he made a promise to his mama's God that he didn't want to keep.

A blue light came on with his jerking, and slowly rolled up his feet, and eased up the length of his body. He panicked, sucking in a sharp breath that made his throat burn. He could feel his body relaxing, going back to sleep again!

He panted, fear filling his belly. He quickly uttered the rest of the prayer as the light neared his chest. "I promise, sweet *Jesus*, if you get me out of this I'll turn my life to You! I'll do right. I'll be Yours forever! I'll—"

The blue light rolled over his head and turned off again.

Tucker John was fast asleep.

CHAPTER 11

Lourdes turned the key at her mother's house. Balm Hill was a good five and a half miles away from Vivian's. She was glad that she'd made it there before the heat of the day. She would have baked for sure in the sunlight even with her conical hemp hat and breezy linen pants and blouse. Her movements were also slower than usual since the community market was being set up and traffic clogged the walkways.

She grumbled under her breath. That was one more extra chore she had to help Vivian do among other things. Their first offering for the farming co-op was due in few weeks.

The sounds of calibrations were but a low hum coming from the basement, but they were enough to shift the sourness of her attitude, sending her stomach into delighted flips and turns. She rushed for the basement door, nearly falling as she took to the stairs. Her feet pounded hard as she jumped down the last three, and dashed toward the homemade nexus gate she had hidden away.

It had taken nearly a half a year to get it working and retrofitted once the new parts had come in from 6036. But it had worked.

She sat in front of the make-shift nexus station, fixing her hair and straightening her clothing as if someone would see her. No one could. All that was before her was a wooden desk threaded with gold bands that had been welded to a golden basin. Tentacles of wires sprouted out from the basin and poured unto the stone floor and into the framing of a glass box that stretched seven feet across the back wall and jutted nearly three feet out. The design was simple and only a step above crude, but it was a functioning nexus gate.

Blowing out a calming breath, she wrapped her hands around the basin. Its contents shifted and swayed before settling into circular ripples set off with the rhythm of a pulse. It moved as if it were alive, with the flow of oil, despite its appearance of coarse gold dust. She and Johnny had discovered it. He called it 'Static'.

Closing her eyes, she let her face hover over the static, speaking into it. "Johnny? Are you there?" She brushed an anxious tear from her eye. "Johnny?"

"I'm here," The static rippled with his words. From somewhere in space and time, somewhere hidden and unknown, John Joseph Spruce answered her. His voice was recognizable but distorted as if he were speaking through water, but even with that, he didn't sound like his usual self. Something was very wrong.

"Johnny? What's wrong?" Lourdes choked on panic. She couldn't handle anything else going wrong. The Animal was more trouble than she could manage as it was.

"I…I-I did it…Open the gate, Lourdes. I need you. I need to be with you right now,"

Lourdes' grip tightened around the basin. "I can't open the gate. Listen to me, Vivian—"

John Jay cut her off. "Is dead, *Baby*," the static trembled with his weeping. "I caught her. I didn't wait. I-I," he kept stuttering. Lourdes tried to speak but he wouldn't let her. "I hanged Vivian, Lourdes! I killed my *wife*! I did it for us, but…" The static was an even vibration with his steady cry.

Lourdes' jaw clenched. Hearing Johnny cry and call Vivian 'his wife' made heat rise within her core with a dangerous ire. *Jealousy. Invidia Contagio.* She bit down on her tongue until she felt the sharpness of her teeth pierce through. The pain would draw her attention away from the infection seeking to pollute her. She couldn't afford to be infected with anything else.

"Please, open the gate. I need you,"

Lourdes shifted her jaw. "I can't do that, Johnny."

There was a dead silence before he spoke again. "Wha-What? I don't understand,"

"Vivian isn't dead." Her tone was flat, deflated. She could taste its bitterness like the irony tang of blood that coated her tongue.

The static leaped, but then leveled again before John Jay flew into a hysterical rant. "Yes! Yes, she is! I hanged her myself, I watched her die! Don't do this to me," he panted. "Don't bandon me now, Lourdes! Open the d@M# gate! Please!"

"I can't! Vivian, your *wife*," Lourdes hollered back. The angst rolled off her tongue like rain down a windowpane. "…is here, in 4037, very much alive! It didn't work. Everything went wrong—"

John Jay shifted from weepy to irate. "No, she isn't, Lourdes!"

"Yes, she is! I'm sorry, Johnny. I've been waiting for days to tell you this!" She cried. "But you were hiding in the static. You were supposed to have made contact with me five days ago. I've been going out of my mind, Johnny! I didn't know what to do. I don't know what to do."

"Why is she still there? What did you do? What did you make me do?" He shouted again.

Lourdes flinched, giving into sobs. "I didn't do anything! Vivian took the intermezzo. I tried to get her, but I couldn't, and before I could fix things he came through, and she thought he was you and—"

John Jay cut her off again. The chocking claw of tears tearing up her throat allowed him to.

"Who came through?" He already knew the answer. Just thinking about the beast who called himself Tucker John, made his skin crawl. The man was vile, made him feel like he was looking at a diseased version of himself.

"The Animal," Lourdes mumbled the name the slaves and his own daddy had given him, the one she and John Jay had adopted for him the very moment they had discovered him. He was a foul creature, vicious and without regard for life. The way he'd hunted and tortured those he'd seen as his prey was barbaric, if not extremely calculated, which only made him even worse.

He'd viciously maimed slaves meant to be returned to their masters. Those sentenced to die met slower deaths. All of them were gruesome in nature, born of the blackest, most hateful heart.

It hadn't taken long for John Jay and Lourdes to determine that 'Tucker' John Josephus Spruce was beyond redemption. He wasn't even worthy of a name.

Silence flooded around them. Things were supposed to have been simple. The plan was air tight, static tight. They'd timed it out perfectly. Vivian would open an E.P, and the slave-woman called Vivian would come through the gate, right were Lourdes had placed it. Lourdes would freeze Vivian Leona, and send her to 1837 in the slave's place, before sending the slave back in time to die herself.

John Jay would be there to catch her before any harm came to her, or before she found a Cleric's Office. He would do away with her, return to 4037, and claim it was all a bad accident. Then they would say as a result, he had found the static. The world of surveillance would praise him for his discovery and pity him for his loss.

The plan was harsh, but it was the only way for him and Lourdes to be together. This was meant to be. They were meant to be. He knew from the very moment he'd laid eyes on her. What he'd been denied in Tara, what had been eating him alive for years, what Vivian reminded him she would never be nor could ever give him, had been handed to him in the 4030's in the person of Lourdes Berry.

It was divine.

Time had given him back what he had lost all those years ago. This was to be his chance to be completely happy. It was a gift too sweet not to take. It had most importantly given him the static; the way to make it all happen, the way to prove he was just as good at surveying and discovering, as Vivian Leona, if not better. He wasn't just her Tech, who happened to be her husband, a man whose surname she wouldn't even take as her own unless things went her way with their current Field Study. He should have never married her. But if he hadn't, he would not have found Lourdes.

He'd been given a golden opportunity and so he was taking it. If there was another solution, he would have taken that as well. But there wasn't. Vivian wouldn't understand just walking away. She only understood winning. She only understood being at the center.

Letting go of their failed marriage would have pushed her from her limelight, it would have made her a failure. She would never willingly take that title. John Jay had to dispose of her if he were to ever be free of her. He loved her but the bitter resentment that she had born inside of him was too much to let live on.

Still, he couldn't let the Animal get a hold of her. He knew what Tucker John had done to the slave-woman, and he couldn't stomach anything like that happening to his Vivian.

Unlike his horrid doppelganger, John Jay wasn't a murderer, not really. Time simply had better plans for him. It meant for him and Lourdes to be together. But he had to fight for it. And he would.

He'd proven the depths of his devotion when the time had come. The moment Vivian stepped through the portal into 1837, John Jay froze her with the intermezzo, put a burlap sack over her head, a rope around her neck, and set her swinging from the nearest tree.

He had proven himself.

He nearly hung himself right next to her once the deed was done. He'd been so torn apart by second-guessing his actions. He hadn't even noticed the strange fashion of her clothes, or the slight differences in the woman's physical appearance that were suddenly coming back to memory. The trauma had blinded him so.

Now, hearing that she, his Vivian, was still alive and that he hadn't murdered her as he had mournfully believed, somehow changed things. The guilt for his ghastly crime washed away. Its sway over him turned off along with the fountain of tears he'd been crying as if they were on a timed switch.

The slave-woman, according to history, was said to have been lynched that day anyhow. By his sudden reckoning of accounts, he hadn't done any harm. He hadn't murdered anyone. He'd actually done the poor woman a service. He had kept her from groping, drunk hands, biting dogs, and a gang of rapists that would have made her final hours beyond hellish.

The way he was beginning to see it, he had been used to mercifully euthanize the poor woman, something the culture of 4037 would applaud.

"What are we going to do?" Lourdes finally asked, her voice soggy with tears.

John Jay calmed himself within the 'nothing' of time. This was not the plan that he wanted to use, but Vivian's tenacity and greed for glory left them no choice. The very reason they were in the 4030's in the first place was because their joke of a marriage was dying. In truth, it was dead before it had even begun, no matter how hard he tried to convince himself otherwise. Vivian wasn't Tara. He didn't love her like that, and he never would.

His agreeing to a ten year Field assignment at her side was his last ditch effort to salvage something he never truly wanted. He was meant to be a surveillance specialist, a Team Lead, an adored husband. He was none of those things with Vivian. With her, he was little more than an accessory, one she loved in a certain way, but not one she needed. As far as he was convinced she only wanted to try and salvage their marriage in an attempt to save face, let the world and time know she was successful in everything.

Now he wished she had been the type of woman who knew when to give up, knew when to throw in the towel. If she had, during their first turbulent year in the 4030's, none of them would be in the position they were in now. She would have accepted that she didn't have to be the name on everything, that their marriage was passionless, and lacked romantic love on his end. She would have allowed him to tell her the truth about him and Lourdes, and she would have left the marriage. The slave-woman would not have been hanging dead from a tree at his hands either, nor would he be in the static preparing another plan of action.

He would not be a murderer!

This was all Vivian's fault! Her ambition would be the death of him if he didn't stop it. He was going to stop it.

"Johnny?" Lourdes finally cut through the silence. She could bare it no longer.

"Plan B," he said with an urgency that made Lourdes jerk back again.

She nearly swallowed her tongue. Plan B was not a plan. It was something they'd imagined in a fit of passion, a dark solution to their problem. But it wasn't a viable option. They'd both agreed upon that.

"What? Wha-*No*! We can't do plan B!"

"We don't have a choice! Vivian is still alive. And that thing is in my house! You know what he's like. You know what he'll do to her if he gets the chance—"

"Is she all you care about?" Jealousy was not a feeling Lourdes had really experienced. She didn't know how to hide it. She needed a vaccine, fast. She would gnaw her tongue off if she didn't.

"Lourdes, don't do that to me," he whispered. "I'm where I am because I chose you. I choose us. This is our dream. But that doesn't mean I want him to hurt her. I don't love her, but I do care about her."

Silence.

"Please, Lourdes. We're going to have to do plan B. It's going to require tweaking since the *Animal* wasn't part of that one either but, I think I've learned enough about the static to make this work. Besides, Vivian won't be the first agent to break down in the Field like this. Actually, she is a prime candidate. This is going to work.

"We're going to be together. No one will be able to tell us 'no.' No one will interfere. If we do this right, and don't make any mistakes this time, they'll even give us their blessing."

***

Magnus pinched the flesh between his thumb and pointer-finger, turning off his voicepod. The documentation for that moment had been verified, all of it. Although he was less than pleased—more repulsed—there was nothing that he could do. What was done had been done, and it could not be altered. He wasn't there to change time, only survey it, and confirm or disprove its accuracy. Lives depended on it.

He did, however, cheer his spirits with the prospect of further study on what was being called 'static.' Since there was no record of it in his original timeline, he had high hopes that perhaps he was the one to have figured out how to get rid of it all together.

It seemed a nasty business, the static. But conquering it was just the thing a retired surveillance specialist could do, a mark of honor he wouldn't mind receiving. It would be a silver-lining to the dark cloud of working for Aiden Schulsler.

CHAPTER 12

Vivian felt the numbness of the *Paz* settling in. Taking it had become a necessary evil, one she needed to abandon soon. Unfortunately, the need for it was a result of her unintended houseguest.

Steadying herself, she opened the wall to the lab and took her time getting down the corridor to Tucker John. He should have been awake. The sooner she got the ball rolling on his 'conversion,' as Lourdes had put it, the better for all of them, including John Jay.

Plans had changed so quickly. She initially wanted to ease Tucker John into the state of his new reality, gently pull the sticky bandage back from his hairs, but that was no longer an option. Vivian needed to rip the bandage off and be done with it. Tell him the truth. Tucker John already thought she was the runaway slave, which further complicated things. She needed to set him straight fast if she could, and begin the *Spadds* treatments as soon as possible.

In less than a week, she was due to give a progress report to her Cell Group on her, and John Jay's surveillance and research. The last thing she needed was paranoia over Tucker John. She needed to have the assurance that he was headed in the right direction.

She also needed to ask him a few questions about the rifle he had in his possession when he came through the emergency portal. It was the rifle—a *Winchester Model 94 .30-30 Lever Action Rifle*—that had aided in her confusion over who he was to begin with. Ruminating over the issue—after verifying that Tucker John was not her husband, but somehow owned a relic that wasn't even invented until nearly sixty years after his death—had made her sick from fearful confusion for days.

Nothing was making sense and it frightened her to her core.

She could hardly keep anything down from the anxiety that boiled inside of her. All she could imagine in those prior moments was that John Jay had somehow damaged several timelines while being lost, and in the process had lost his mind.

It wasn't unheard of, for a person in the Field to have a break with reality, develop a deadly form of PTSD. The Cleric's Offices did a thorough job in ensuring everyone that went into the Field was mentally stable and sound, that they could withstand shifting variables, stay grounded. But some still managed to break, even though the occurrences were few and far between.

No matter how firmly rooted, the human psyche was still as malleable as wet clay and could be changed under the right pressures and circumstances.

Where the rifle was involved, Vivian was shrewd enough to hold off on tackling that issue until Tucker John proved he was within a reasonable mindset to give her answers concerning it.

Drawing to his bedside she immediately checked his vitals, grateful that he was still sleeping from the second sedation. She had taken extra measures with him this time. At a certain point of tension on his restraints, the computer would be notified to sedate him. She couldn't chance another escape. Things might not work in her favor a second time, especially since the community co-op was setting up shop nearby for the exchange of goods in preparation for the winter months. She needed to get her goods ready as well. Just one more log to add to the mounting fire.

She stood near Tucker John, marveling at the strength of *Paz*, how it enabled her to look at his face and feel nothing at all or at least process what she was feeling as if it were nothing. The strain and burn of lost hope that the man could have been her husband but wasn't, held no emotional sway over her in that instant.

Now, she only stared at him with an edge of indifference.

She still couldn't understand how the nexus gate had gotten things so terribly wrong and was still getting it wrong. Tucker John didn't have the same fingerprints as John Jay. He was even missing a couple back molars and John Jay had all of his teeth. From Vivian's own assessment of the man's physical appearance, alcoholism and liver damage aside, she would have said that John Jay and Tucker John were a ninety percent match at best. That was still quite close to one hundred, but close was not identical. That truth hadn't kept them from slipping into the tangled mess they were in.

Reaching above his head she punched in a command code. His eyes peeled open. His nostrils flared as he took in a deep breath and startled when he saw her standing over him. Instantly, his color began to rise, his expression pinching in an angry scowl.

"How are you feeling?" Vivian asked, her head slightly tilted to the side.

Her voice was irritatingly calm. Tucker John growled. "How'n the hell you think I'se feeling, *Vivian*? You kidnapped me, d@%4 it! Done some voodoo hoodoo magic on me. Had my body all tied up in knots! You got my a$$ shackled to this bed!" He jerked his arms upward. The blue light came on again. His eyes flashed.

Vivian leaned over him, did something with the wall above his head. The light, as well as the calming sensation in his lower body, ceased.

She said, "Because of your recent escape, I've had to take some precautionary measures in your treatment. Any time you lose your temper and become physically explosive, that light will come on, and you will be put to sleep. This is for your own protection. Do you understand?"

He jerked his arms once more. Vivian touched the wall again.

"What in Sam *Hill* are you doing, Vivian?" He was about to tug again but the raise of Vivian's brow made him think better of it. Blowing out several deep breaths through his nostrils, he tried to calm himself. He needed to get free and the only way he could do that was by playing along. He also needed to see what had gotten into her head, out think her.

She, being a woman and a mentally inferior negress, should have made his task easier than blinking. It was the little white woman who might show a bit of a problem, but not as much as a man would. Tucker John could handle this. Before, he had been too irate to work Vivian's mind. Now he was steady.

His tone came out easy, gentle, but mildly corrective. "Vivian, you're not acting like yourself. You ain't never been prone to disobedience, least not of your own thinking. Your fool mind is too weak for all that. First, it was that nasty buck, Mo, who done got you in all that trouble before. Filling that lil' head a' yours with foolishness. Must'a given you a headache, all that talk 'bout running off. And now," he shook his head. "Now some wicked lil white woman has got you doing *awful* things,"

Vivian folded her arms across her chest.

Tucker John took note of the gesture. "Now, I'se a mite bit upset with you over all this here, and rightly so, but, if you mind me, and turn me loose, I won't be too hard on you. You just tell Tucka' what that wicked woman have you doing, turn me loose," he emphasized. "...and I'll take care of it all, put in a good word with your master, tell him to let me discipline you my way this time."

He offered her a gentle smile. That, along with his promise of a recommendation, should have been enough to procure his freedom. Vivian however didn't budge. She didn't even break a sweat. She usually cried, got nervous when he used that tone. She'd second guess herself, beg for mercy, offer him favors in exchange for it.

She wasn't now.

"First, that 'little white woman' as you refer to her, has a name. She is to be called by that name only. She is called Lourdes. That is the first thing. Secondly, my name—"

Tucker John cut her off. "Vivian, I know you d@m# name, fool!" His sudden frustration caused him to jerk too hard. The blue light came back on.

He roared in frustration.

Vivian punched in the override code once again and spoke on as if the incident with the light and his growling hadn't happened. "Yes, Tucker John, you know my name. The problem is you take liberties in using other names that are in a word, disrespectful. My name is Vivian, not 'fool', not 'wench' and certainly not 'negress' or any other adjective that you can think of. You are to call me nothing but Vivian from this moment forward. Understood?"

She didn't give him the chance to respond, instead, she went straight to the point trying her best to explain their near impossible situation. "There's been a great deal of confusion, not only on your part but on mine as well. Because of that confusion, you're here."

"Cause you confused I get strapped in a bed like an invalid, and you run about in your knickers?"

"Tucker John," she took a deep breath. The *Paz* should have kept her from feeling frustrated. She clearly needed to up her dosage, albeit, carefully. She was already toeing a dangerous line with taking it. She took a few breathes and chose cold hard facts as the best option to douse the fire of the situation even though it would only fan the flames of others. "You're no longer in the year 1837. You are in the year 4037,"

Tucker John raised an annoyed eyebrow. He went to speak, but she raised her hand to quiet him. That set him off. "Don't *shush* me! I ain't no child! Respect your betters, neg—"

She blocked his lips with her hand. He jerked, tried to bite her, and once again she had to override the sedation process. "Tucker John, listen. You were looking for a runaway slave—"

"You, Vivian!"

She shook her head. "No, not me. I'm not the woman you were after. I've never been a slave. Slavery no longer exists. It hasn't in the Americas for over 2,000 years."

"Vivian, wench or no, ain't nothing fouler than a drunk female talking nonsense. You been on the bottle? Lord have mercy! Get me out of these here straps. Now!" He managed to not jerk.

Vivian stepped away pushing back more frustration. He was making her heart race, he was so stubborn! What did she expect? Would she believe him if the tables were turned? Not likely.

Talking alone wasn't going to convince him. She should have known that. She decided to employ the use of visual aids, show him some undeniable truths. The worst that could happen is he would faint, but she could always wake him up. She went to her tech desk. The smooth, white, surface began to glow. She ignored Tucker John's intake of breath and quickly compiled images and projected them on the open air of the room with the flick of her fingers, one of them was that of his slave-woman.

Like dust motes dancing upon the rays of the sun, tiny, green, electric spots appeared a few feet from the tech desk and began to swarm and churn before spreading outward. Having brightened to near white in color, they suddenly stopped as if suspended in time. Tucker John's chin fell to his chest. Vivian noted his accelerated heart rate and gave him a small dosage of *XBalance* to level him off. He calmed, awakened, but was still afraid.

At least she had his attention.

Standing next to the mass of dotted light she said, "As I said, I am not the woman you were pursuing." She gave a verbal command to the computer. "File V2541151837."

Again the mass churned, connecting and multiplying like human cells at their first dawn of prenatal gestation, rapidly shifting as artificial cells and tissue formed, mimicking the genetic data of the woman they were recreating. In a matter of seconds, a full-color nude, four-dimensional image of the slave-woman floated in the center of the mass of light, some of the extra electric particles dancing around her like bubbles in water.

As expected, Tucker John's face, drained of color and went slack, his eyes rolled back in his head, giving way to faint. Vivian woke him up.

"I know this is a lot, but I need you to focus." She said. "I can't imagine how difficult this is for you—"

"Good Lord Almighty!" He shrieked, eyes pale and wide. "This some witchcraft-Marry Shelley-Frankenstein, blasphemy! Vivian, you gon' bust the gates of hell wide open! Fooling with that ole' sloop foot devil! I don't want no parts of it. No sir! You can ride that ole' goat alone! Turn me loose, d@^$ it!"

He was panting now. She couldn't give him any Paz. He wasn't even finished with his *XBalance* treatment. Paz would throw everything off. She settled for allowing him to be sedated instead.

Tucker John saw the light come on and began to buck with full-on rage. He cursed, kicked, and jerked like an angry, suffocating, fish out of water. "You turn that thing off! Mind me!" Spittle flew from his seething lips.

Vivian didn't suspend the sedation program which she knew was going to infuriate him. She woke him up again but allowed him to be put back to sleep several times over.

Tucker John had to realize that he was not in control. She was.

The final time she waited a good ten minutes before waking him. When she finally did she could tell she had his attention, even if the only reason why he was looking at her was to do her harm. She positioned herself next to the projection of the slave-woman. Even with her life-like form slowly rotating within the water-like mass of energy, Tucker John's hard glare stayed on Vivian, his mouth tight.

Vivian ignored it. "This is your Vivian." She pointed to the image of the woman's body. Tucker John's gaze didn't mover from hers. "Look at her, please."

Still, his gaze didn't budge. He didn't even blink.

"Tucker John, look at her."

He finally chuckled, mocking the frustration that had tightened her jaw. "Vivian, I done seen many ah' drowned negress before. What I need to look at that one for?"

How quickly he had deduced what was before him as nothing more than a water-aided pallor trick, all at the expense of her time-twin. Anger broke loose inside her. She felt her feet carrying her toward him. How could he be so smug?

She grabbed his crown and beneath his chin, keeping her hands out of the reach of his teeth, and turned his head. She was firm, but she didn't hurt him. Tucker John's body tensed. Vivian hollered. "Look at her, Tucker John. Look at her! That is not me! That," she pointed behind her. "That is your Vivian! Not me. Not. Me."

She withdrew her hands and stomped toward the rotating image. "Look at her body. You've seen it before. The stripes on her back, you put them there. And then you used tar to fill them up," she turned her back to him and lifted up her tunic. "There are no stripes on my back. Do you see?"

She let down her shirt only to kick off her shoes. They were nothing more than slippers, but she needed to make her point. "I stand, flat foot, five feet, seven and a half inches tall. She was just barely five four." She held up three fingers. "I'm sure you can count. That is three inches in height difference, nearly four.

"Look at her hair. You cut it yourself the last time she ran from you. It's just below her shoulders when not covered or pulled in a bun. Mine is to my waist. File V2541151837F."

The mass of energy churned again, this time projecting an enlarged image of the slave-woman's head. Tucker John startled again, but he stayed conscious, his complexion washing in a sickly shade of gray.

"Note her nose. It is slightly pushed to the left, mine is centered." She leaned close enough for him to see the smooth, symmetrical curve of her aquiline nose.

She continued, "Note the scaring behind her left ear, the tear in the lob, and the burn near her right temple," she walked toward him. His eyes followed her. She pointed to each area on her face that she had pointed out on the slave-woman's. "None of those marks are on me. I have my own scars, but none of them match hers. File V2541151837DC." The image opened its mouth. "Do you see that? She is missing half of her front top tooth, two of her lower left molars. I have all of my teeth, every last one of them, and none of them are chipped."

She stepped back and called up another file. Her hands trembled. "File…File JJS632234034." She didn't look at the image but kept her eyes on Tucker John. Astonishment washed over his face. He had to see that the man in the mass of energy was him or a similar reflection of him. He had far shorter hair, a clean-cut face, was fairly thinner even though he had a much softer and less defined midsection, less toned arms and legs, and paler skin, but the image was exacting enough to drive home her point.

"Like I'm not your Vivian, you aren't my John." Her voice caught in her throat. The Paz had worn off far quicker than expected.

Terrified, Tucker John's eyes pulled away from the image of the man and locked again with Vivian's.

Vivian took a second to check his vitals. The last thing she needed was for him to die from a fear-induced heart attack. His pulse was accelerated, but he was still in the safety zone.

"This is an image of John Jay, my husband." Tucker John flinched at her declaration. She continued. "His name is John *Joseph* Spruce. He was born on March thirteenth of 6002."

Tucker John slowly shook his head, one eye narrowing. "Nah. You just told me this is 4037." His expression changed from fearful to something akin to haughtiness. He shifted in his restraints, a stern composure resting over him. "Vivian cut the parlor tricks. Ain't none of this gon' save yo' a$$! You in a heap of trouble, not just with your master, but with me now." His temperament began to sway. He was a terribly hardheaded man.

Vivian closed the gap between them. She placed a stiff hand on his chest. His heart was still racing despite what his expression said. He flinched when she touched him. She entered the command and suspended sedation once again.

"I don't expect any of this to be easy for you. I'm struggling to explain it. But you need to recognize, Tucker John, that you are no longer in a position of control or power. This is not the Georgia you know as home. You are not my overseer, and I certainly am not your enemy, your bed-warmer, or slave."

She moved her hands to the restraints. "These are not on you to solely protect Lourdes and me from your violence. These are on you to protect you from the dangers that await you if you leave this property unprepared. There is no one out there that you know. No one. Everyone is gone. Everyone you loved, everyone you knew, they are all dead. The only help you have is me—"

Vivian flinched. Her breath caught in her chest. She slowly stepped away from his bedside and wiped the thick mass of spittle and mucus from her face. Her back turned away from him.

Tucker John hoped she was shamed, hoped his spittle knocked her off the pedestal she had put herself on. How dare she say a single word to him about the ones he loved? How dare she make a comparison of herself to them? Vivian had hit him hard with that one, viciously reminding him who he was, what he was—the lone Spruce in a dead forest. He had no power and he had no control back then. Ashford Junior had taken all of that away from him, and what he had fought so hard to earn, Vivian was trying to snatch away as well. His head began to pound from the stress of the thought. He would die before he let that happen to him again!

Slowly, Vivian turned around to face him. Their eyes met again in that instant, Tucker John noted the pain he saw in hers. Yet he noticed that she shared a similar resentment for him that he had for her, and rebellious curiosity—a frightening tug of war. He would not let her win.

He dared not believe that what she said was true, would not allow it. But something in his gut made him feel the threat all the same, that both of their worlds had been turned on their heads and they were grappling to stay out of the abyss. Somehow he knew that Vivian was just as strapped down and boxed in as he was, hanging on a wing and a prayer. It was her own fault and he intended to make her pay.

She said, her voice tame, nearly a whisper, "Because I'm aware of your ideology, and the culture in which you were bred, I'm going to do my best to be gracious and merciful to you as you go through this program," she slipped on a glove and pulled out a silver pill. It looked like a metallic teardrop the size of an apple seed. "But if you spit on me or at me again, I will put you to sleep for a very long time, so long that you won't even remember me when you wake up."

Tucker John clenched his teeth. He could tell by the look in her hazel brown eyes that she was being square with him. He swallowed down what he had waiting for her, but he couldn't swallow down the hatred that was burning inside of him for her. He was indifferent toward her before, even if only a tiny bit tender. He kept her company because she was convenient. She had always been an easy fix to a need; bed company when he wanted it. Now, he wanted nothing more than to snap her neck. He'd never been so indecisive.

"This pill in my hand is called a *Spadd*. This will help you understand. Unlike the other medication I gave you, this will not cause you any pain."

Tucker John's voice was low and rough as gravel when he responded. His eyes narrowed. "I ain't taken no pill."

Vivian sighed, exhaustion spilling off her like the sweat that dampened his sheets. "Tucker John—"

"I ain't taken no pill. I'd rather go to my grave than take anything from you."

Vivian wiped her face with the back of her ungloved hand. "That is exactly where you will end up, sooner rather than later if you don't. But I won't fight you. And like it or not I'm the only help you have."

She touched the wall above his bed one last time. The blue light came on at his feet and he screamed.

Wishing that things had been as easy as she'd hoped but conceding that she'd known better, Vivian waited until Tucker John was fully asleep before placing the *Spadds* treatment beneath his tongue, praying he'd be a different man when he awoke.

CHAPTER 13

Traveling through time through a nexus gate was like blinking. One minute John Jay was in his era, and within a millisecond he was somewhere else, centuries or millennia away.

Static didn't work that way. It wasn't so straightforward.

While the nexus dealt with the purity of time, static dealt with the possible remnants of time; the elements that were still waiting to be used. It was filled with 'possible' moments, perfectly measured sequences that could replace anything that already existed with something new and different.

Or it could leave a hole, an elusive and fleeting memory of something, something vaguely remembered. It was like a filler of sorts.

At least that is how John Jay had come to see it. That is how he and Lourdes had planned to describe it when they finally reported its existence to the Cleric's Office, earning him a name. There were no blink-of-time landings with static. Each step, in whatever direction in time, was less fixed, like walking on quicksand without completely sinking, although one could, he supposed.

He had no choice but to continue his navigation through the static. Before, he had only used it to conceal his whereabouts. He had stepped through it—bypassing the exit of a nexus gate—to do away with the slave-woman when he believed she was his wife. But stepping through it caused tears in the fabric of time. It distorted his visibility, made him ghost-like. He appeared hollow like thin smudges on glass, only seen through periphery, and even then, by just a vague glimpse, one that left the seer wondering if they had seen anything at all.

Lourdes had told him that.

Although he was complete and whole to the touch when tethered within the static, the visual density of his substance was still anchored within the static itself. He could only get that substance back by breaking away from it all together. To do so, he had to go properly through a nexus gate.

That would have to wait.

Setting his aim toward the future, he urgently began to track specific segments of time. He was going to use the static to do the unthinkable. He didn't believe that he could rewrite time, but if he could black it out, remove tiny bits of it and shift others to give a presumable reality, then he and Lourdes would have what they wanted. No one would be able to prove that anything besides what he and Lourdes told them was the truth.

The day would definitely come when they would ask. When they did, and when the two of them gave their answer, no one would have any reason to doubt them. All possible doubts would be erased.

John Jay would work the static on his end. Lourdes had to keep the Animal from being reformed, and then everything would fall perfectly into place, just as it was meant to.

They would deal with Vivian later.

***

As usual, Tucker John was irate, the only difference was, now he had a larger vocabulary and a greater reference of knowledge—two millennia worth—even though he still spoke with a deep southern drawl, and kept his words loose and broken. The only silver lining was that he was at least dialoguing about his new reality, even though he still didn't fully concede to its validity, and was struggling greatly with his documented past.

"Ain't I living in my future?" he shouted at Vivian.

Vivian rolled her eyes. She had explained it more times than she could count, and Tucker John still wouldn't let it go. She hadn't even managed to bring up the issue of his rifle. "That's precisely the problem. You are here, and you shouldn't be. It's damaging to timelines and history."

"Then you're thinking all wrong. You don't know what you're talking 'bout!" His voice raised another octave.

"Tucker John, be calm. You already know the consequences of these kinds of outbursts in this century!"

"Nah, I ain't gon' calm down! You sitting hear tuggin' my strings, trynna play me like a piano! You said traveling to your future can't be done, ain't been done, but here I am. That fool posse was here, and the other Vivian, according to your own testament." He raised his brow and arrogantly folded his arms across his chest.

Vivian had given him back the usage of his arms only the day before. It had been three days since his first Spadds treatment. It seemed that the first one had tempered him, even if only a little. She still didn't fully trust him, so she kept his lower body sedated so that he couldn't run away and get them all into trouble or himself killed.

But she was growing more and more irritated, not just with Tucker John, but with everything. She had yet again, been unsuccessful in her search for John Jay. Her research, and the very reason she was in the Field of 4037 had been disgustingly neglected—as if it truly mattered anymore—and she hadn't even had the time to think about the Review and evaluation she was supposed to have with her Century Cell Group and the Cleric's Office.

Raul Manuel, her Cell leader, had messaged her several times. She'd responded to his questions as vaguely as she could without being suspicious. But even he seemed to be losing patience with her. He'd even gone as far as to question her team's necessity within that timeline. He further argued that they had been there for years and still had come up with nothing, not even a hint to the cause of the Silent Revolution. Teams usually had unearthed some clues to their query within the first two years.

That had grated on her. She knew his argument was only meant to light a hotter fire beneath her, and it did, but the wrong kind. Very little work had been done in her efforts to discover the source of the Revolution since John Jay had vanished, and very little probably would be done if she couldn't get Tucker John to comply.

It didn't help at all that she and Tucker John had been going in circles on the same topic for nearly three hours. "Yes! Yes, you are here, and look at the damage!"

"What damage, the damage you done caused to my manhood? You treat me like I'se a child, like you'se my mammy, or something. Now, if that ain't damage I don't know what is."

She ignored his mocking. "As I said before, there are many reasons why this is no good. We can't or rather, 'shouldn't' travel to our futures for one simple reason. People would stop living, they wouldn't enjoy life. They would be focused on death. Or worse, people who knew the day of their death would skip right passed it.

"That kind of occurrence would cause massive ripples in time, knots even. Look at what's happened since you came forward, and think about what would happen if I listened to you, or listened to Lourdes, and sent you back to 1837, today."

Tucker John snorted. "I ain't skipped out on my own death. I didn't ask to be here."

"Maybe not, but the deed has been done," Tucker John went to speak but Vivian continued her thought. "...regardless of whose fault it is that you are here." The hateful man seemed to remind her of her fault in bringing him forward every chance he got. He was openly resentful over the matter. Kidnapped, he said she'd kidnapped him, arguing that nowhere in time was that legal. He was right and he was angry.

Vivian couldn't blame him. She pressed her fingers into the tension knots at the base of her neck. "I've told you, Tucker

John, the day that you came through the E.P, was the day that history records you as having died."

He shook his head and looked away from her, grumbling under his breath.

"There's no further documentation of you. Believe me. I looked. Your body was never found. Your horse returned to the plantation without you."

"And how in the hell did I supposedly die, Vivian? Did your twin put me six feet deep?"

Vivian bit her tongue. She hadn't told him how he died. She didn't see the point in doing so, but she did see the danger in it. He could go back to 1837, avoid his death, and live on, armed with the knowledge of the future. If she was going to tell him how he died then she would have to 'clear' his mind in order to send him back without incident, wipe his mental slate clean, all the way back to the very day when he first came through to 4037.

Yes, he would be older, but it wouldn't matter. It was hardly likely that he would pass any mirrors. He would just go back in time and die as history had written it.

She wouldn't have told him about his death in the first place, but that was the only acceptable explanation for why she had kept him and would keep him in the 4030's. It was the truth and her defense against his insistence that she had intentionally kidnapped him.

Tucker John turned toward her again, sizing her up with a flippant look. "Cat got your tongue? I have the God-given right to know how I'se supposed to meet my Maker. You holding me here against my will. You owe me that much."

She sighed heavily. He did have the right to know. If she didn't tell him he would probably kick up more sand until she did. She would have to sedate him and give him his next treatments that way, which would only make him angrier.

Everything was beginning to seem so hopeless. But she wouldn't give up. Giving up on him would mean she'd have to give up on everything. She couldn't do that to John Jay.

But what if she couldn't help Tucker John to conform to the current times? What if she grew so stressed that the clerics became truly suspicious and decided to investigate? None of that would be any good. Her head throbbed at the thought. Nausea tickled the back of her throat. "According to history, you were presumed dead by drowning in a river. You couldn't swim, and you drowned." There, she'd said it. She would just have to 'clear' him later. By then, she would have John Jay to help her. Life would somehow go on as if none of this had ever happened. She would even clear herself if the need arose.

Tucker John was silent far longer than usual. His gunmetal-grey eyes burning into hers before his face contorted, and he slapped is numb thighs with agitated hands. "Bull$#!*! I ain't drown in no d@#$ river!"

"Tucker John! Mind your tone!"

"No, sir! That's the dumbest thing yet I done heard come out your crooked, black lips!"

"Epithets! Avoid using them. And what's dumb about it, John? People drown every day!" She stood.

He glared up at her, his mono-lid eyes wide. "John? Who gave you permission to call me just John, Viv? And where exactly does history 'presume' I drowned? Far as I saw, this land we on, look the same as it did in 1837, could still be 1837 by my reckoning."

"So what, it looks the same? It's not the same. And you still drowned in the river. Consistent landscaping doesn't change anything."

"There is nothing but creeks here, Viv!" His arms stretched wide. "Never mind the fact I can swim!"

"Then you slipped! You fell and bumped your head, fell unconscious and drowned. I don't know. I wasn't there. The point is, this is the timeline. You don't exist past that day." She paused to catch her breath. She was tired again. "So, I can't send you back, not now. Not for a while, unfortunately."

His glare deepened. "Can't or won't?"

"Both." She matched his glare.

"What? You'se a'feared about what I might do to your twin? You think by tying me up for six years, I'se just gon' forget?" He leaned forward. "You can't protect that wench from me. I always get my way. As far as my reckoning, she's as guilty as you are for my current predicament. She gon' get what she got coming to her even if it takes six years for her to pay the piper. Hell, I'se a patient man." His mouth curled in a devious smile.

Vivian didn't know if he was trying to bait her or was telling the truth. It made her stomach protest even more. She clenched her teeth. "She's already dead. Lynched. They put a burlap sack over her head and slung her up from a tree like she was nothing. So there is no one left to protect from you, but you, from yourself." She swallowed down the bile that had risen up her throat.

Tucker John's tanned face turned florid, his chest rumbling with an angry growl, and his eyes enlarged with heated anger. "Som'a b!#%^!" He punched the bed. His voice echoed throughout the lab.

Vivian startled. "Tucker John!"

He pointed an accusing finger at her. "Don't Tucka' John me! Your stupid a$$ done got that wench killed! Ya'll playing god, pulling unsuspecting folks through time!"

"What difference does it make to you? You would've done the same thing to her. You've done worse!"

"What lie you preach?" His chest puffed from the offense.

"Come on! You treated her like a plaything. What is it that you all called women you kept around for bedtime, 'Fancy slaves'? Bed-warmers? You tortured her. You beat the flesh from her back. You beat her with your words. You cut off her hair to humiliate her. You raped her—"

"Like hell I did!" His eyes were blood red. Veins protruded from his neck and forehead. "I ain't rape nobody! Negress or no!"

"Oh, so every time you made her lay with you it was consensual?" Vivian was now the one doing the mocking.

Cold silence met her mocking for several moments before he answered her. "I didn't pin her down." His eyes glinted in a rakish way, darkening as he stared at her. There was almost a spark of blasé humor in them. The look was vile. "And she never said no." He finally grinned.

"As if she had a choice. I'm sure Vivian, like everybody else who knew you, knew better than to tell you no. You didn't earn the nickname 'Tucker' by being congenial."

"Shut your fool mouth."

"Why? Does it bother you that you didn't get to murder her? Is that it? She was a notch in your belt of manhood, but not a knot in your noose?"

Her Paz had clearly worn off. She was taking his remarks personally. She was taking what had happened to the slave-woman personally, and goading him because of it. She wanted to hurt him like he had hurt the slave-woman.

Tucker John hocked spit on the floor.

Vivian bristled. "I told you not to spit at me, Tucker John,"

"D@#$ you, and your rules! And d@#^ your presumptions of me. Vivian is dead cause of you. Not me!" He tried to rise up from the bed but couldn't having forgotten his sedated legs. "I woulda' beat the black off her high-yella' hide, but I sure as hell would'na slung her up from no tree,"

"You don't know that!"

"I ain't like you, Viv!" He tapped his temple with his finger. "I think before I make my moves. I wouldn'a needed to lynch her. But you snatched me forward. You let that posse get at her," he clenched his jaw and let out a gust of air from his nostrils that would have rivaled the angriest of bulls. "I promise you one thing. I bet she would've preferred my whipping, or my bed, over a rope 'round her neck. But I'se 'spose you proved your point. Moving forward in time is mighty dangerous business, ain't it? Sure 'nough was for Vivian."

Vivian fell silent. She wanted to hit him. He was such a cruel man. And yet his accusations somehow put her mind to thinking. What if he was right? What if the slave-woman had been murdered because she had selfishly kept him in 4037, even though something deep inside of her kept screaming that he was not John Jay?

She blinked back angry tears. She wouldn't let him see her cry. He would take to her tears like a hungry wolf to bloody meat.

Her voice cracked when she spoke. "What's done is done,"

"Sure 'nough is."

Her jaw ticked. "The only thing I can do now—besides what the Government of this era says is a help to you and your 'glowing' condition—is to help you to become acclimated to this time period, help you survive here until the time that something else can be done for you."

She walked away from him, slipped on a glove and grabbed the next dosage of his Spadds treatment.

He shook his head. "I ain't taking no more pills. They ain't worth a lick outside of given me nightmares, pumping my mind full of stuff I can't sort out." His voice was low.

"That's not true, they—"

"I said I ain't taken no more pills. Mind me."

Vivian ground her teeth. Mind me! Mind me! She hated it! "And I told you, that you're not in control, that you need these, whether you believe me or not. But I'm not going to argue with you about this every time you need a treatment." She went to reach over his head. She was going to sedate him.

Tucker John lunged at her like a bullet from a pistol. His lips drawn back in a snarl, his large fist raised to hit her.

Vivian startled at first, stumbling back a step and nearly losing her balance as fear slapped across her face. She managed to right herself, quickly squaring her shoulders and firmly planting her feet. Her chin raised and her eyes narrowed in defiance. This time the tears fell.

She swiped them away with quick, rough strokes. "What are you going to do?" Her voice cracked again. "Hit me?"

Tucker John didn't say a word he just seethed, his large knuckles bone white, and his red face easing into an angrier purple. There was more than a battle of wills at play between them. It was a full-on war, a deadly thing.

She said, "I don't know about that other Vivian, but I promise you, 'Tucker' John Josephus Spruce, if you lay one hand on me in violence it will be the last thing you do on this side of heaven...or hell! I don't care where you end up, but I will kill you. Timeline and ethics be d@^#$!" She stepped toward him, her jaw set and her fist clenched at her sides, her hazel eyes brewed dark as they bored into his. "Try me."

Tucker John's eyes twitched. Something about the set in Vivian's jaw and the ire in her eyes made him falter in his intentions. Only his mama had shown such starch in the face of a fist big enough to lay her flat with one hit. The similarity stalled him.

She said, "You have tested my patience for the last time today. I've grown weary. You can either do as you're told, for your own sake, or you can call my bluff, and see what happens." She drew even closer.

He could tell she wasn't bluffing. Too many thoughts ran through his mind, too many foreign modes of rationalizing presumed consequences and repercussions that he could face at her hands if he did strike her. But at that moment, he knew her choosing not to kill him as a consequence wasn't likely.

All those thoughts, along with her searing accusations about his character put him in a place of shame that made him feel weak even though he wouldn't own it. He would have never felt that way if not for those cursed Spadds treatments!

Nevertheless, he could own the fact he wanted to live, and he wanted his freedom. He wanted to taste the revenge he had coming for Vivian Leona from 6037. But if he called her bluff with one silencing hit and she did as she had said and killed him….

He wouldn't risk it. He lowered his fist, and opened his mouth, his eyes sharp as a razor's edge, his nostrils flaring. It took everything in him not to put his hands on her.

Vivian snarled. She grabbed him by the wrist and dropped the pill in his palm. "Give it to yourself!" Her voice cracked as she stormed out of the lab.

Tucker John flinched. The pill had started to dissolve in the moisture of his hand! Fear caused him to quickly lick up what he could with his tongue. As much as he was still struggling to believe it, he couldn't deny he was no longer in his Georgia, 1837 Georgia. That was a very dangerous thing. He had been alone and ignorant before in his life, and had he not taken the bull by the horns as soon as he did when he was a young man, he would have died off just like the rest of his family. He would have been eaten alive by those with power, those with knowledge.

Because of this woman, this Vivian, and her mistake, as she so lightly put it, he was back in that place again, angry, ignorant, vulnerable and alone with his life hanging in the balance. He might as well have been a little child again, hiding naked in the cold dark of the woods like an animal being stalked by his own daddy.

That was the problem with those who dubbed themselves powerful because of what they knew. They saw lesser men's lives as things to be toyed with, as if they were collateral damage for 'mistakes'. Tucker John had learned to make those kinds of people pay for their careless ways. He would do the same to Vivian as soon as he got the chance.

CHAPTER 14

Vivian cried so hard that she vomited. Her face was puffy, and her body shook. She could hardly catch her breath or even speak when Lourdes knocked on her bedroom door. She was careful not to open it or even speak outright before she had gotten a bit of control. She was grateful that in all the chaos she had at least remembered to record all of Lourdes' tasks for the day, placing the list in the main office of the house. She was reluctant to send it via clipboard. That could be traced by the Cleric's Office, and they couldn't take the risk. She was even gladder that the main office was on the other side of the house on the first floor, nowhere near her bedroom, in the event she had another crying fit.

She had gotten so worked up over Tucker John that she worried it might have been a side effect of *Paz*. She needed to pace herself with the tiny pills, but she couldn't help it. Tucker John's character had the same effect on her as someone driving rusty nails beneath her fingernails.

Spitefully, she almost omitted telling Lourdes to feed him. She was going to do it herself, but after the hostile brawl they'd had, there was no way that she was going back into the lab for anything, least of all to feed him.

She simply couldn't understand how a person could be so hateful. No one was perfect, not even her, but to be that odious.... To make matters worse she had allowed his nastiness to draw her in, to the point she threatened to take his life.

Worst of all, she meant it.

She started crying again. She wanted John Jay so badly. She needed him there just to hold her. John Jay made her a better woman. She believed that even if sometimes she struggled at being the best, most attentive wife, even though he'd admitted he didn't truly feel the same connection with her. The very fact they had taken such a long Field assignment to spark the romance in their marriage was proof that he at least agreed that both of them needed work. He made her want to try.

But Tucker John, he only brought out a darkness in her that she didn't even know she had. She'd begun to wonder if Lourdes was right, if she should just go ahead and euthanize him. His body was never found after all. Maybe euthanizing him wasn't the wrong answer.

He had gone through two *Spadds* treatments already, had been able to successfully pass an informational examination, and even though he, for a brief moment, seemed less volatile, he had quickly reverted back to his nature. It was as if he was mocking her, pocking fun at the facts because he still saw them as nothing but lies. Or he just wanted to see her sweat.

His lack of commitment, justified or not, was causing her to break her commitment to everything. She seemed farther away than ever before. She hadn't been able to spend enough time looking for John Jay. Her work, her research had grown cold. What about her mission of discovery? What about solving the mystery of the Silent Revolution? She was hardly keeping up with the farm chores which meant she would fall behind with the community co-op, another demand of the New Golden Age; unity through codependency.

If Tucker John could just go away, she could at least do something, something worthwhile, even if she failed to find her husband. She shuddered at the thought. The time she was losing was probably making the feat even harder. There must have been a reason why John Jay hadn't contacted a Cleric's Office wherever he was. She prayed he wasn't hurt or worse.

The strangling thought of John Jay dying, lost and alone somewhere in space and time, only made her think about euthanasia again. She quickly rebuked herself when her own words sounded off in her head, *Life is precious.* What right did she have to take Tucker John's? Where had the benefit of the doubt gone? Where had her heart of mercy gone? The truth was that some things were just too heavy to carry, and Tucker John's two-hundred and thirty plus pounds of muscle was becoming far too much for her, especially with threatening fists connected to it.

"No, I won't do it." She finally told herself, thinking again of the mantra of the Revolution, *"For the martyred we march on, lest the living die."* In that moment she was not thinking about Tucker John, she was thinking of herself. She was not from 4037. She knew better than to even consider killing the man.

If she put him to death, she, the Vivian Leona that had been raised in righteousness, forbearance, honor, and truth, would die right along with him, leaving nothing but a poor shell of who she once was. She could hardly imagine how she was going to survive with the shadow of this season always reminding her of her mistake, even once she and John Jay made it safely home.

If Tucker John was in her era, in the 6030's, he wouldn't have been considered for anything close to euthanasia, at least not because of the words he hurled at her. He would have had to have harmed someone for that, and apart from throwing Lourdes aside in his poor escape attempt, he hadn't hurt anyone, at least not like he had the slave-woman. What he had done to Lourdes did deserve some kind of justice, but not death. It was the things he'd done and planned to do to the slave-woman once he got back to 1837 that made Vivian's heart grow hard toward him.

Her stomach turned again, thinking about the poor slave-woman's life. She hadn't even made it to twenty-four years of age, she was mentally handicapped, had birthed nine children of her own, the first at the age of eleven, all of which were stolen from her and sold. She had been abused by several different men in every way possible—Tucker John included—and had found her bitter end on a hangman's noose.

"I could've helped her," Vivian moaned. "I shouldn't have sent her back." If Tucker John died and the slave-woman died she could have at least given her time-twin six years of peace before sending her back to her death. Instead, she gave her a day and a half of running in fear before it all came to a dreadful end. Yet another mistake for Vivian to add to the mountain growing at her feet.

She pulled open the drawer to her nightstand. The bottle of Paz rolled forward. She popped three of them in her mouth, and lay back on her bed as they dissolved. She sighed as her body relaxed. With her eyes closed, floating on a sea of numbness, she thought of John Jay. The evaluation with the Cleric's Office was in two days. She needed to be relaxed.

She shouldn't have talked to Tucker John.

CHAPTER 15

Tucker John was woozy. He could hardly focus on the broken *Spadds* treatment, present reality, and his own hallucinations. His mind was battling with accepting what was past, present, and future, what was real and unreal. For the first time, he wished he was tied down, and that the blue light at his feet would turn on, and put him to sleep.

He felt like he was running without moving. Centuries, broken and distorted, moved past him like streaks of splattered paint. He would never be able to make any real sense of any of it. He had struggled with the other treatments, and they were whole and in order. He could feel the order.

This one, however, had been corrupted when Vivian dropped it in his hand. It had begun to break down. Some of the information literally fell through the cracks of his fingers, leaving fractured fragments, and threads of what was considered bygone eras, to stretch across his mind.

Amidst the rolling tides and breaks of time and history that were being thrust at him like a violent storm, were the images of two wicked, black sirens; Vivian Leona and his Vivian, the slave and the free. Both of them baited him, taunted him, tempted him, eluded, and seduced him. They brought him such pain. They ruined him with soft gentle hands.

Hours, it seemed he had been like this for hours when suddenly, the running of time ceased, and the 'Vivians' faded into the back of his mind like hot breath evaporating from cold glass. Sweat stung his eyes as he pressed them closed. The smell of parsnip soup and hot bread made him open them again. He was suddenly very hungry.

Lourdes stood before him holding a tray of food. He wondered how long she had been there. It must've been long enough for her to see him struggling in his mind. The look in her eyes, that she quickly altered, told him so. The way she revised her expression, the quick switch from disgust to sheer indifference, mingled with a touch of willing servitude, put a hook in Tucker John, drawing up even more suspicious thoughts of her than he already had.

Had she maintained her disgust, he would not have thought twice about her—he knew she didn't care a lick for him. Most people didn't. Had she slowly changed her expression, touched it with a bit of embarrassment for having been caught, he would have overlooked it completely. But she had quickly schooled it and hid it away. That spelled out deceit in Tucker John's reckoning.

Lourdes was a pretender.

He'd seen that quick change before amongst many of slaves, and even foremen in his day. Some of the slaves that the masters thought most loyal with their innocent ways were the very same ones who were grinding glass into their master's supper and feeding it to them with eagerness and prayer. '*Oh Lord Jesus, Massa' I prays you gets better. I'se worried near sick with death myself over you. Wass' we gon' do if the good Lord take you?*'

Most people missed these nuances, not Tucker John. Those overlooked messages meant life or death.

He looked at the tray in Lourdes' hands. "Where's Viv?"

"Viv?" She raised a questioning eyebrow.

He made sure to keep his tone in check. Lourdes was not like Vivian. Although he distrusted her, Vivian seemed forthright for the most part. Lourdes had a sneakiness about her. "Why are you here? You ain't been here for the last couple days." His voice was gravelly.

Lourdes set down the tray. "I've been here. I've just been busy with other things. I have to admit after you hurt me, I was afraid to come back in here." She rubbed her neck as if it still pained her.

Tucker John studied her. There was some truth to what she was saying. Good. She should be afraid of him. "So why you here now? And why is it ya'll keep feeding me soup in these funny shaped bowls? And ain't no eating utensils. I swear ya'll some silly acting females." He pushed himself up, still unable to move his legs.

Again Lourdes schooled her expression. "Because Vivian told me to feed you. She has me feed you soup because it is lighter for you to digest. She says *Spadds* can be nauseating, and cleaning up soup is an easier task should you not keep it down. You don't get utensils because you don't need them. You have figured out how to drink from the sip-lip and clean the bowl with the bread?" The bowl was shaped like a teardrop with a little lip at the top point which allowed the soup to be blown, and quickly cooled sip by sip.

She said, "It's convenient really. Besides, Vivian doesn't trust you with sharp or blunt objects, understandably so."

He sneered. "What kinda' business ya'll two running where a negress is calling all the shots, telling a white woman when to jump and how high? She got you playing house slave, gal. 'Take him soup. Clean up his mess. See after his business.'" His voice cracked dreadfully as he tried to sound like a woman. It almost made him laugh.

Lourdes didn't hide her frown this time. She hated Tucker John's racism. She hated him. She slowly allowed herself to smile. His own words showed that the treatments weren't working at all, not by her estimation of things. No wonder Vivian had locked herself in her room.

This would be an easy go, keeping the Animal an animal, keeping him at Vivian's throat until she would have no choice but to put him down. Tucker John had not changed a bit. Lourdes was just going to throw some more kindling on the already blazing fire.

"Vivian is the lead in this surveillance. I'm fresh out of the Academy. Even though her husband, John Jay, has more years in surveillance, Vivian has handled more cases successfully, so she is the Lead. Whatever she says goes. I'm only their assistant."

Tucker John's eye twitched. Lourdes had to turn away from him to keep him from seeing her elation. Not only was he a racist animal, he was a diseased chauvinist and probably a misogynist by default. Nothing was more absurd to a person like him than a black woman in charge of white people, especially a white man.

Tucker John wanted to spit! Vivian had subtly explained to him about John Jay, the man floating in the glass tube, how he was supposedly her husband. She didn't give him details even though he'd demanded them. She certainly hadn't mentioned that she was in charge of him. That was beyond emasculating!

He waited as Lourdes picked up the tray again and set it near him. He wanted to reject it, but his stomach protested the thought. Besides that, if Vivian wanted to kill him, she wouldn't use ground up glass in parsnip soup. She was using pills to torture him already. She would go for something far fancier to put him down. Even Lourdes could do better than poisoned soup.

He slurped the soup up from the sip-lip. Some of it fell onto his beard. He said, "What I can't come to understand is why two white folk is letting that black b!%@# tell them what to do. She done turned ya'll into criminals." His brow rose, and he pointed a finger at Lourdes. "Kidnapping a law-abiding white man is a deadly crime."

Lourdes folded her hands in front of her, her brow raised in challenge. "She tells you what to do."

He snorted again before soaking up some of the thick broth with a torn hunk of bread and tossing it in his mouth. He really didn't like Lourdes. "She don't tell me what to do. She holds a knife to my man-parts, and threatens to make a lady out of me if I don't comply. I don't have much choice in the matter. She ain't done that to you, seeing as you ain't got such valuable anatomy. Figuratively speaking a'course.

"You just weak and don't know your place is all. Apparently, neither does that idiot boy she call her husband, the one ya'll say done got his fool-self lost."

"Johnny isn't an idiot! And he isn't a *boy* or a fool! He's a man." Lourdes scowled, her voice strained with a growl.

Tucker John froze still, soggy bread just an inch away from his open mouth. Lourdes' sudden anger was a surprise to him. Vivian hadn't even responded like that over the man. He tossed the bread in his mouth. "What? This 'Johnny' your brother or," he narrowed his eyes, and appraised her from head to toe. No, he wasn't her brother, not even a cousin. *A female don't get mad about her brother being called a boy. An idiot, sure, but a boy...And she certainly didn't growl about it. Besides, Johnny-boy was from some other period in time.*

His beard hid most of his grin, but Lourdes could still see it in his eyes. Her checks flushed. "You're the idiot, Tucker John. You're the one sitting here in a bed against your will, not me, and not Johnny!" She felt a surge of shame calling him an idiot, but she couldn't help herself. Johnny needed to come back soon. Tucker John was infecting her so!

She kept going. She pointed at the bowl in his hands. He had devoured it in less than three minutes, slopped it up like the animal he was. "You're the idiot that takes food from strangers who hold you captive. How do you know Vivian didn't poison it? How do you know I didn't?" Her heart was racing. She was going to need Paz or another vaccination.

Tucker John released a ruckus laugh. Chewed-up bread shot from the back of his throat and landed on the bed linens making her gag.

He said, "Don't get your knickers all knotted, darlin'."

"I'm not your darling!" Her fingernails dug deep into her palms. She startled at the thought of wishing it was his face.

Tucker John took his time settling down from his laughter, but the smile didn't leave his eyes. "No, you're not." He wanted to call her out about John Jay, had already done so subtly, but knew better than to come straight out with it. He wasn't in a position to do so, besides that, it wasn't his business. If he had, he could imagine what she would do. The food may not have been poisoned this time, but he didn't want to give her cause to poison it the next time she came bringing bread.

"And ain't no need to threaten nobody, especially a man who supposed to drown. So simmer down, get your feathers in order." He licked his lips.

Lourdes had stomped toward the exit, but turned on her heels when she heard him. There was a hint of delight in her eyes. "Oh, so Vivian has told you that you drown?" She slowly, darkly, walked back his direction. "So you know what she plans to do then?"

He met her gaze. He'd ruffled her feathers good and had done so unintentionally. From his own experience he found flustered women did one of two things; storm off in a huff and try to beat a man with silence, which never worked, or they would say far more than they should—a mix of hard truths and far out lies.

Lourdes was going to talk. It was up to him to sift out the facts from the fiction.

He kept his eyes locked on hers, and his mouth shut. He didn't need to say anything more. He wasn't even trying to bait her, to begin with, and he had caught her like a fat, catfish. All he had to do was give her his undivided attention and wait.

Lourdes made a sorrowful face, laden with sarcasm. "If she's told you that you drown, then she's told you that she's going to have to 'clear' your mind before sending you back to 1837." She drew even closer and shook her head. "Clearance, as it is officially called, is like cutting out a big chunk of your brain, removing information, memories. It's a practice generally reserved for people with PTSD or post-traumatic—"

"I know what PTSD is." He cut her off. He did know what it was. The solid *Spadds* treatments had given him that information. He didn't need her to waste time explaining it to him.

She was smiling now. "Right, the *Spadds* treatments told you. Well, Clearance will take all of the 'painful' information and memories away that have been deposited by the *Spadds*. You won't remember a single second that has taken place since you've been here, not what has happened, or will happen within the next six years if you manage to survive that long. You'll just be plain old, ignorant you, back in 1837, set and ready to take a bath that you will never dry off from.

"By then, Vivian's little project of 'Tucker John Conversion', will have reached its end, and served its purpose for her. Which means you'll meet your end shortly thereafter. That's Vivian Leona. She's very thorough. She doesn't care for loose ends." She offered another smile. Dead air lingered. Lourdes was done talking.

Tucker John's face was stone. Eyes still on hers, he handed her his empty bowl, his tone easy as if she hadn't said a single word to him. "Make sure you clear these here dishes when you go, gal. You gotta' keep your mistress happy, now. Wouldn't want Viv putting no hooks in your hide for mis-stepping in front of the company." He winked.

Lourdes snatched the bowl from his hand, and left in a huff, leaving him alone with his thoughts.

So Vivian was going to patch him up only to send him to his death, fix him to her standards before knocking him back down to the dust he had crawled from. And it was dust! All of it. The *Spadds* had shown him that much. If what he'd learned was true, people like him didn't matter, they weren't even remembered. Hell, no one even bothered to look for his body once he supposedly drowned!

Vivian thought the same about him. He was nothing. He could tell by the way she spoke to him like he was ignorant that she thought he was worthless. That's how her kind, the know-it-alls, and blue-stockings, treated folks. She never called him ignorant like Lourdes had, but she was thinking it. To her, with all that learning she'd had, she must have believed he was nothing but filthy, stinking trash, or as the snake, Lourdes had put it, a project.

He had indeed become Vivian's mistake and she was going to paint him up and hide him away as long as she could before burying him where no one would ever have to know about him. "Like hell, she will! I ain't nobodies Frankenstein-monster!"

His blood boiled. Vivian was nothing but a blue-stocking, a female dandy! He despised dandies!

Lourdes, he didn't give much thought to. As much as she attempted to hide it, the woman was as clear as crystal when it came to her feelings toward him. She hated him to the core, but she was a being of very little power. Tucker John could tell that by her deceitful ways. She was the slave grinding glass into Vivian's supper, bedding down with Vivian's husband in secret, while pretending to be some kind of loyal assistant to her cause.

As dreadful as it all sounded to his ears, he had gained some very useful information, not only about Lourdes but Vivian and her hellish schemes for him. He had hated taking the *Spadds*, hated the way they made him think, and second guess his natural view of things. He hated the nightmares most of all, but he was going to keep taking them no matter how much they twisted his mind.

If Tucker John didn't learn anything else in life, it was how to beat a person at their own game. He would eat up Vivian's knowledge, every last drop of it, and then when he was finished he would eat her alive with the very tool she thought to tame him with.

CHAPTER 16

"Theoretically, I think what she's planning to do is kind of amazing. Don't you?" Raul Manuel's brow rose nearly as high as the black curls of his hairline. An apprehensive twinkle danced in his dark eyes. "It just makes me nervous, is all."

Vivian pried her lips open and searched for an appropriate response. She'd come all that way for this impromptu meeting with Raul and had only answered a few questions concerning the Cleric's Assessment and Review. Mostly, Raul had apologized for his criticism of her lack of so-called progress, while the rest of the meeting had been high-jacked by the work of Surveillance Specialist, Yasmina Flytch.

Under different circumstances, Vivian would have reproved the man for his lack of professionalism. However, with her own sketchy circumstances just waiting to boil over her poorly controlled cook-pot in the flavor of Tucker John Josephus Spruce, she kept quiet and thanked God for His amazing grace. Besides that, she liked Raul.

She said, "I'm not sure what you're referring to. What about Yasmina Flytch?" She'd heard of her, didn't think too much of her or her antics in surveillance. In Vivian's estimation, Yasmina pushed too hard, like she was trying to prove something to the world at any and all cost.

Raul's brow rose higher. Choking with a shocked laugh he projected the news reporting from his clipboard unto the nanoids that hovered in the air above his work desk. A large, smiling face of a woman with massive dark curls and pale green eyes appeared before Vivian with a screaming headline. Yasmina was gearing up to pull three back to back doubles in the Field all in different millennia!

For the briefest moment, Vivian's own mistakes and fears fell into the shadows of her mind. Two 'doubles' was toeing the line with a time-break. Nobody's resolve was that strong. Jumping to one timeline was hard enough, but to leap from three different millennia in a six-year timeframe was insane. It gave the words 'foolish' and 'reckless' new meanings. Vivian startled when she heard the words slip from her mouth.

"I agree," Raul countered. "…but we have you to thank for it." Vivian froze this time. Raul swiped through the article until he stopped at a section that made Vivian's blood run cold.

"She's doing this because of me," In Yasmina's own words, she had stated that, *'The ambitious drive of Vivian Leona has been the catalyst for my career. She has been like a beacon to me, and the greatest mark of thanks I can give her is to outshine her. And I intend to.'*

If words had fist each one had landed unrelenting blows to Vivian's pride. She'd thought Yasmina Flytch foolish and reckless, and yet, as of a few weeks ago, there had been very little difference between their careers and exceedingly great poor choices. Since John Jay's disappearance, Vivian had been the poster-child for foolishness and recklessness.

Raul dropped the article back unto his clipboard. "Oh don't look so unnerved. Everyone wants to outshine their hero. They may not put it in such tasteless words but," he shrugged his shoulders before leaning back in his chair, "I'm glad to know that I'm not the only one who sees doing a triple-double as unwise. But what can we expect when you cast such a big shadow?" He winked at her and smiled.

Vivian forced a smile of her own and reminded herself to breathe. John Jay had used those words as he skirted around asking her for a divorce back in their timeline. If only Raul knew what was lurking in the darkness of her shadow now….

The remainder of the meeting passed in a blink. Raul never got back on topic, never really gleaned what was necessary for him to know for the Assessment as her Cell Leader. Clearly, Yasmina's wave of ambition had knocked him off his axis

Moments later Vivian left the Cleric's Office in haste and only slowed her retreat when she was a good two miles away. The heat of the day and the rising sickness in her belly made her head pound. She should have ridden the sled but decided on going on foot. She thought it would help her clear her mind, that, and give her some much-needed distance from her houseguest.

She wove her way through Tall Acres, the township sitting between her large spread and the Cleric's Office. This time, on her way back home, she tried to take the time and soak in the tranquil beauty of it all, but the reality of what lay beneath the breezy façades and the placid smiles only seemed to scream at her with the same harsh growl of Tucker John's curses.

The same way he looked like her husband but was nothing but a hateful racist, murdering, drunk, was the same way that Tall Acres looked like the perfect society but that perfection came at the cost of the lives of any who behaved like normal human beings.

Perfection was simply not humanly possible.

Her temples throbbed, even more, the lie of it all clawing at her chest as the scent of spiced air from the Co-op Super Market clogged her nostrils with the threat of nausea. She quickened her pace toward home. She needed to escape. She could feel herself falling apart. She was nearly in full sprint when she was called to a halt by a Peace Officer. He approached her with a wary smile, his gloved hand slowly lifting as if he needed to use caution to reason with her.

"Is everything alright, miss? You look," he appraised her. "…unwell."

Vivian chuckled and lightened her posture. "Oh no, Officer. I'm fine. It's just I left home without my sled and thought I had more time to run my errands by foot, and get home in time for my chores than I actually do. I didn't mean to startle anyone. I just wanted to get home as quickly as possible." She smiled again.

The Peace Officer gave her another appraisal before dropping his hand and returning her smile. "Would you like for me to carry you home on my sled? I wouldn't mind at all."

Vivian's heart bucked in her chest. She didn't want anyone from the Government anywhere near her property. "Don't trouble yourself, Officer. The lesson of later chores and a later dinner will be a welcome reminder for me to pay closer attention to the choices I'm making."

The Officer dipped his head in acquiescence before moving from Vivian's path. The few people who'd witnessed the exchanged eased back into their tasks as if nothing had happened. In Vivian's timeline, nothing would have been counted as happening. In this timeline, the threat of a hysterical contagion breaking out had just been put to rest.

"For the martyred we march on lest the living die," she whispered under her breath as she resumed her pace. She couldn't afford to lose it. Too much was at stake. It was bigger than just her and John Jay. It was bigger than Tucker John.

CHAPTER 17

Magnus took a few days off from going to the Cleric's Office. With the permission of Aiden Schulsler, he was able to leave Clarence there just to keep a watchful eye on things.

Watching the Cleric's Office was indeed an unusual assignment. Never before had a Cleric's Office been under future surveillance, not until 4037. Whatever was supposed to happen during that year was supposed to affect even the Cleric's Office in 6037 and beyond, which was why Magnus had been brought in by Schulsler.

Aiden Schulsler; always the ambitious one, always striving to build his platform off the accolades of accomplishing the impossible. That 'bug' must have been in the air. Magnus had read about Yasmina Flytch and her planning to pull a triple-double in the Field. *Stupid woman*. But Schulsler...he knew something about this timeline, more than what he was letting on. He was so determined to make sure that things played into his hands that he'd forced Magnus out of retirement and back into the Field, setting Clarence Mantov at his heels.

Magnus could hardly stand either of them.

Clarence Mantov was a strange and peculiar young man, quiet and seemingly harmless. Other than the obvious threat that he worked for Schulsler, there was something ominous— predatory—about him. At the least he was helpful, Magnus conceded.

He pulled out the tools that had been given him for the usage of studying the static. The unnamed instrument, the one that had picked up the waves of the static had collected a strange, golden-copper, grainy residue at the base of its prongs. Magnus had been told that this was what solid static looked like. It all seemed so farfetched at first, but now looking at it...even such a small sample of it fascinated him.

With a pair of lightweight tweezers, he drew clumps of static away from the prongs and deposited them into a safe container. On the prongs the static looked like a type of rust but in the container and to the touch, it was malleable, like a thick gel or liquid. Magnus likened it to coarse gold dust.

He curiously blew his breath against its surface. It rippled like water in the container. The feeling, however, that bounced around in his mouth was bizarre and unexpected. It was as if his breath had been scooped away, like the space within had been filled with solid, invisible nothing. Frightened, he stood up and away from it, brushing his tongue with his hands, drawing back in the feeling of saliva and moisture.

Clumsily, he activated his voicepod. "Static, is-is as described. It appears rough to the touch but is *fluid*. Even in small trace amounts, the substance acts as a vacuum; it takes, but refills the area it has taken from with," he paused. What had his mouth been filled with? He nervously checked it again with his tongue, ensuring that all of his teeth and other bits were still there. "It fills whatever has been made void with what I can best describe as solid nothing. It is tangible and yet, unseen, and indefinable, leaving one with greater curiosity, but without an inkling of what they are curious over. It's almost like weighted air."

He waited until all the information in the voicepod was affirmed for that session before deactivating it again. He would have to come back to the static later. It had frightened him. All he could do was stare at it from a distance before he built up enough courage to explore it further, most likely on another day. More so than anything, he was curious to know what Schulsler knew about it.

***

John Jay wasn't exactly sure where he was going to begin his static processing. Lourdes had suggested that he just go to the future and erase Vivian altogether from the memories of those closest to them. He quickly shot down that suggestion. There were a number of very good reasons why he would not do what Lourdes was suggesting. One of them was because he knew she had offered it up out of jealousy. He couldn't understand how she had become so infected with it. There was no reason for her to be jealous of Vivian. He had chosen Lourdes and had hoped he had proven his need for her by having euthanized the slave-woman by mistake.

He simply told Lourdes that erasing Vivian would not suit their cause, never mind the fact he didn't know if erasing her was even possible. Like it or not, they needed her. Vivian eventually being done away with, in the manner she would be done away with, was their only leverage for sympathy.

They would tell the authorities that, through the tragedy, the wretched senseless loss of her, he and Lourdes had come to find comfort in each other. He would tearfully, woefully, ask permission to stay in 4037 with Lourdes, even if that meant his sterilization—a consolation prize to his having never wanted children to begin with—arguing that he couldn't face a future without Vivian. The clerics would offer him Clearance to forget the pain, and he would decline. He wouldn't want to not remember his wife.

Eventually, they would give into good reason and allow him permission to stay in 4037 with Lourdes. After all, it would be the Cleric's Office in 6037 that had made the mistake and gotten Vivian killed in the first place, her pending time-break aside. Malfunctions in their system would cause the loss of all records of their team and thus contact with them.

It was a sketchy plan, but a good one. It would work. He would make it work. Surveillance Specialists had lost their grip on reality while in the Field before. Vivian would prove no different.

Nothing was going to keep John Jay from having Lourdes. He'd lost Tara and he wouldn't lose her again. He all but shuddered thinking how the two women were like equal drops of water; the same in form. He'd lost Tara in the 6030's and found a better version of her two millennia back in time. The burning ache that had all but consumed him, even if it had been blunted by the presence of Vivian, had raged with a new fire the very moment he laid eyes on Lourdes.

But not only was he getting the woman he deserved, he would also get the glory that was due him. He was better than a simple Tech. Everyone should have known that. They would very soon.

He only had to figure out which moments in time he would have to blackout from view via the static in order for the snowball effect to occur, sending their plans forward at full-speed. He decided to start with every second after Vivian and Lourdes opened the Emergency Portal, after the slave-woman and the posse came through. He needed that moment visible because that is when he and Lourdes would testify Vivian had begun to have a time-break and a loss of mind, leading to her subsequent death by hanging. It would be either a suicide or murder by the Animal. He hadn't decided which yet. John Jay's discovery of the static is what they'd say had set Vivian on edge to begin with.

He also needed to blot out every scheduled Clerical Assessment from that point on. He needed to make it look like there had been a mistake that took place in 6037 that made them lose contact with him and Vivian in 4037. With their faulty nexus gate, broken contact with the Clerics Office in 6037, and no conclusive time records of their team in 4037, he and Lourdes would have to put up their perimeter fence to keep the Animal— the man Vivian had brought forth in order to take John Jay's place—in so that they could capture and euthanize him. The fence, like the nexus gate, would malfunction for a time, and not go down for a long while afterward.

He and Lourdes would appear as victims of a string of dreadful circumstances. Records, aptly edited by his hands, would become visible again after about a year or two, with him and Lourdes being stuck together to cope with the tragedy. That is when they would say they grew to love one another. Pity, as a result, would earn him and Lourdes what they most wanted.

It made his stomach ache with mourning, and sour with the pain of being a widower just thinking about it. Blowing out a breath, he readied his resolve. It was going to take him some time to shift moments from both 4037 and 6037.

He decided to shift the static in 4037 first. It seemed more easily accessible. He would run forward again as soon as he was finished. Then, when he had completed his work in 6037, he would return home and deal with the Animal himself.

No one that vile deserved to live. Vivian should have known better. He and Tucker John were nothing alike, nothing at all.

***

Vivian stretched her neck. She had slept wrong while locked in her room. She'd been there since her impromptu meeting with Raul Manuel and later the run-in with the Peace Officer.

The latter encounter had rocked her. She didn't bother eating anything since then. Her appetite was missing in action since her near violent encounter with Tucker John when she'd attempted to give him his *Spadds* treatment. She felt like a complete idiot because of it—fighting with him.

Tucker John. Why was she having such a hard time not taking his words to heart? Why couldn't she get her heart to understand those poisoned words were not coming from her husband's mouth but Tucker John's?

He was not her husband! He was nothing like him.

That was still almost as hard to swallow as the fact that she was so much like Yasmina Flytch. It terrified her, actually.

Reason should have schooled Vivian to get help when John Jay had vanished the same way it should be schooling Yasmina not to do a triple-double in the Field. Yasmina was truly setting herself up for failure, toeing the line with a mental time-break.

Fueled by the numb emotions and her ever-active thoughts, Vivian forced herself to return to her research, building a believable progress log for the Assessment, before resuming her seemingly futile task of figuring out how John Jay had gotten lost through the nexus gate, and where in time he could possibly be. She had been at it for hours, working clear into the late afternoon of the following day, back tracking in the logs, trying to find some anomaly.

It had to be an anomaly that caused John Jay's disappearance. If she could find that, she would be able to locate him and bring him home. Instead, all she found was a string of holes. The more she looked at the logs the more they appeared as Swiss cheese, like the nexus gate was eating away at its own memory.

Why hadn't the Cleric's Office in 6037 sent the pieces they needed to repair the gate when they had asked? This was their fault, all of it; John Jay missing and Tucker John's presence!

She massaged her forehead, realizing it was just as much her fault. Had she reported what had happened, instead of allowing herself to foolishly listen to Lourdes, Cleric's Offices all throughout time would have been looking for John Jay, and could have already safely returned him to her.

Frustration was beginning to suffocate her. Anxiety was the noose. She had never been this inept. It was her knowhow and her quick thinking skills that had won her the headship of her and John Jay's surveillance team.

Now, she felt like a newbie at the Cleric's Office, completely wet behind the ears and unequipped to handle a yearlong log of purchase receipts let alone a nexus gate! Everything was getting away from her. She hadn't even gone to give Tucker John his next treatment.

She kept putting off having to see him again. She only wanted to see John Jay, and if she had found him in those burnt up hours she had spent running in circles, she would have asked him to deal with the monster she had locked in the lab. But she hadn't found him and Tucker John was still there, her brain was frazzled, and her research was suffering. Everything was.

She pressed her hands against her belly and tried to steady her nerves. She was better than this. She believed God wouldn't put more on her than she could bear, but she truly felt like she was being crushed under the pressure. She needed to calm down, get her mind at ease to be prepared for the Cleric's Assessment and Review, get her offering ready for the Co-op market and give Tucker John his treatment.

Lourdes couldn't give it to him. She had gone to see about her mother again. In all the chaos that had taken place, Vivian had not even asked how Alba Berry, Lourdes' mother, was doing. Lourdes wouldn't be back to work before tomorrow afternoon, which left Vivian with the full plate.

With everything before her, she was beginning to worry about Alba too. Alba had been battling several different symptoms over the last year and a half. Lourdes said things were under control, but Vivian knew better. She knew if Alba didn't get it together and fall in line with the rest of the emotionless society, she would be considered incurable—a health liability— and euthanized without another thought.

Lourdes, and anyone else near Alba would be quarantined for three days before being given seven days to mourn her loss in an appropriate fashion. All of this before they were demanded to move forward with emotional balance and ease, completely free of such toxic expressions that loss could bring.

At least Vivian had remembered to have Lourdes feed Tucker John before she had gone. She'd told her she would take care of the *Spadds* treatment herself since Tucker John was so aggressive when it came to taking them. But now she was completely undone and would be like a lamb being led to the slaughter if she went to force another treatment on him, especially since he hadn't eaten in the last few hours either.

He was screaming so loudly that it seemed he was in the room right next to her. His cutting curses and ugly threats were beginning to make her nauseous again as she battled between concentration and anger of her own.

She dug into her pocket and pulled out her pill bottle. "Be careful, Vivian." She told herself as she looked at the bottle. She'd taken three *Paz* as soon as she'd returned home and they had quickly worn off, they were such tiny pills, not to mention addictive. No, she would be okay. She could handle this more than she could handle the effects Tucker John was having on her.

Frowning, she decided to up the dosage. She needed a calm mind to treat him, and an even calmer mind to get through the Cleric's Assessment tomorrow morning. Despite Raul's distracted and yet positive attitude, and clearing up of the misunderstanding concerning her surveillance, Vivian still felt wretched.

She was becoming a proficient liar, a quality she wished she wasn't so apt at mastering, especially when it demanded she practiced on beautiful souls like Raul. In contrast to what she'd told him earlier that day, as far as she was concerned, her research had completely stopped. She had some information, some things to report, but not much. Her nicely prepared log was a lie.

She also had to give a report of Lourdes' work ethic and ability as a cleric. She thought she might have to blur some of the lines of reality when it came to Lourdes as well. More lies. Even if she was an okay surveyor, she had a very hard time with honoring the chain of command.

That was only the tip of the iceberg. But she refused to waste any time meditating on the shortcomings of Lourdes Berry. She would eventually have to come clean about her lack of ability, but for now, she just needed to get past the assessment and figure out how to solve the weightier problem of having two Mr. Spruces.

With a few flicks of her wrist, she peppered six pills into her hand and dropped them beneath her tongue before making her way to the nexus room.

She would spend a few minutes there as she waited for the Paz to kick in. Then she would go and see about Tucker John when her dulled emotions allowed it. She would do more searching for John Jay as well. She could do this. She had to.

CHAPTER 18

Lourdes had been rebuking herself since her argument with Tucker John the other day. She'd even cried after talking with Johnny about their disrupted plans. She could tell that he was disappointed in her for losing her temper, even though he encouraged her not to be too hard on herself about whether or not the Animal knew of their relationship. It would be only a matter of time before he was dealt with, Vivian was gone, and they would be together.

But she hadn't anticipated things to be even worse once she returned to Vivian's home the following morning. Tucker John's cursing reached her ears the moment she opened the front door. His voice was so hoarse it was obvious he had been screaming for a long time. Frowning, she covered her ears.

"Vivian?" She called out but got no response. Tucker John hadn't killed her that much was certain. He wouldn't have been cursing her name and demanding she come to him if he had. She noted the time on the grandfather clock. It was well past noon, nearing one. Vivian had the Cleric's Assessment at eight thirty that morning. Assessments were lengthy, but no longer than two hours, three at the most. She had to be somewhere in the house.

Quickening her pace she searched for Vivian throughout the house, finally stopping at the nexus room beyond the kitchen. She pushed at the slightly ajar only to have it stop mid-swing with a soft thud. Something was blocking it. She shoved it again.

"Aghhh…" The door slammed into Vivian's head again. Lourdes slid into the room, her neck and ears burning red. This wasn't good!

"What are you *doing*, Vivian? How long have you been in here?" She grabbed Vivian's arm and tried to help her to her feet. Disoriented, Vivian pulled out her of her grasp.

Her hair was matted, the grooves in the wooden floorboards had made divots and creases in her face, and a pool of saliva glistened where she had been lying. She moaned and touched her head where the door had beaten into it.

Vivian was groggy. Someone reached for her and again she pulled away out of their grasp before scooting out of their reach. Her head was spinning and her vision blurred. The last thing she remembered was standing up to go feed Tucker John and then…nothing. She rubbed her eyes. The light from the noonday sun was giving her a migraine.

She gasped. It was noon! "Oh no…Oh no…" She should have been panicking, but she was dragging instead. A strange, dizzying euphoria was rolling through her. "Wha-wah," she grabbed her head again to stop the ringing in her ears. "What time, Lourdes? The time?"

Lourdes scowled. "It's almost one in the afternoon! Have you been sleeping on the ground this entire," she didn't complete her question. The look on Vivian's face, her overall appearance had answered her loud and clear. "You slept passed the Cleric's Assessment?" Her voice rose and strained.

Vivian's adrenaline shot her to her feet. Her swimming equilibrium knocked her back down. She landed hard on her backside. But at least she was coherent. "What time is it? Did you say it was after one?" She moaned. She had missed the Assessment! She had never missed an Assessment.

Lourdes' stomach took a nose dive. The last thing she and Johnny needed was for the clerics to pay them an in-home visit because of negligence. If the clerics came to the house they would know Johnny was missing, they would see the Animal, and start an investigation. They'd lose everything. She'd be euthanized!

Ice ripped through Lourdes' veins. Johnny had told her to keep things in order. This was beyond that. She began to panic. "I told you, Vivian! I told you this was a bad idea. I told you he was nothing but trouble. Now the clerics will come!"

Vivian shook her head. "No, no…I've never missed an Assessment. I'll reschedule. We'll be fine. We'll," she clearly hoped they would be fine. The look on her face was evidence that she hadn't even convinced herself of that.

Lourdes suppressed a growl. "How are we going to be fine? Do you hear him?" She opened the door wider for Vivian to hear the ongoing, livid, chorus of Tucker John. She hoped it made Vivian's ears bleed.

Vivian leaned over and pushed the door closed. She didn't want to hear Tucker John's name, let alone his voice. It was his barking that had stressed her out last night to the point she couldn't focus. Because of him, she had taken too many *Paz* and had passed out, sleeping through the Assessment.

He was proving to be a lot more trouble than she had anticipated.

She told Lourdes what had taken place the night before; how she had lost track of time looking for John Jay, but only found holes in the nexus logs. She told her how stressed she'd become due to Tucker John's screaming and had taken a few too many *Paz*.

Lourdes plopped down on a cushioned bench near the door, a distant look in her eyes. Vivian had managed to stay upright in her seated position without wobbling. She held her balance by keeping in close proximity to the wall. "Lourdes, I need you to get him something to eat, please, and give him his treatment. I'm in no condition to do that." Her voice rasped. "He needs the treatment."

She went quiet not knowing what else to say; staring blankly outward like Lourdes before she finally broke out in tears and sobbing.

Lourdes' head jerked back in her direction. She felt Lourdes staring at her in amazement. It was likely because she had never seen her cry. She had never really seen her break a sweat, not until recently, not until Tucker John.

More tears fell. She felt Lourdes awkwardly kneeling beside her, patting her back with an equally awkward, stiff hand.

"Don't, don't cry, Vivian. Sorrow can be contagious. We don't want the Government involved because of prolonged sorrow." She didn't bother mentioning the condition's Latin name. For that, Vivian was grateful.

Still her shoulders slouched. Why had she picked the 4030's again? Yes, it was because she wanted to be in the boiling point of historic moments. She wanted to discover the root of the Silent Revolution. She wanted to be isolated enough from the familiar to give herself and John Jay the time to fall in love, truly in love. She certainly had gotten what she asked for as far as boiling points were concerned. "I'm doing my best, Lourdes. I know," she hiccupped. "I know you don't get it about Tucker John, right now I am questioning it myself. I know you want me to euthanize him because it makes sense to you. But it's not the right thing to do."

She sucked in her bottom lip and tried to stop crying. It didn't work. She was angry and she was wounded, and now her reputation, along with everything else, was going further down the drain all because of the very man whose life she was trying to preserve.

She hiccupped, "He, *Tucker John*, is costing me so much!" She swiped tears away from her face and neck. "My name, my reputation. My husband. I can't even find John Jay because he is here! I don't want to hurt anyone, you know?"

She looked into Lourdes' eyes. Lourdes was still, practically unblinking. "But everything I do to help him is met with resistance and cursing. I just don't know right now if any of this was worth it."

She shuddered. She couldn't bring herself to say if she thought Tucker John was worth it. Instead, she pushed herself upward and eased her way to the door. Lourdes stood up with her. "Just please get him fed and treated. I'll make an attempt at damage control with the Cleric's Office."

Lourdes didn't move.

"Please! Go now." Vivian finally snapped. She said nothing else, just dragged her feet down the hallway and out of Lourdes' sight.

Lourdes felt her own cauldron of anger boiling within her. *Caput Furorem, Head rage.* It was ironic really. She found herself completely furious with Tucker John, not just because she hated him, but because he had made Vivian sob like a helpless child. She counted Vivian as her enemy, the mountain in the way of what should have been hers, but who was Tucker John to stab at her? He owed Vivian the very breath he was breathing.

But it was Vivian's own stupid fault. She should have listened to her and gotten rid of him before things got as messy as they had.

Tight mouthed, Lourdes stormed to the kitchen. She poured what was left of the cold, parsnip soup into a bowl and carried it down to the lab. Tucker John looked just as worn as Vivian did from all the screaming. He fell silent when Lourdes walked in only to start up again.

"Well, it's about *time*! What ya'll tryna' do? Starve me to dea—" Before he could finish Lourdes shoved the cold bowl of soup into his chest and began to walk away. Some of the liquid spilled onto his stomach. Tucker John flinched from the chill of it and tried to catch the bowl before the rest poured over the bed, but it fumbled in his hands. More than half of it splattered on the floor. "Soma' b!%$#! This soup is ice cold!"

"Don't eat it then!" Lourdes hollered back before storming out of the lab.

CHAPTER 19

If Tucker John had been angry before, he was enraged now. This was the game Vivian was playing at? She thought she was going to starve him into submission? Feed him cold slop until he conformed?

He'd never conform! But he would fix her and Lourdes for their schemes. He'd fixed others like them, and he had no problem doing it again.

He ground his teeth, his mind drifting back to a distant memory. It was only a year or two after his family had been busted apart. It was then that he earned the nickname 'Tucker'.

He'd been working at a little watering hole that had a few 'good time' rooms in the back when a man wanted to relax in the company of a lady who wasn't his wife. The work was hard enough as it was, it smelled horrible and brought in the kind of men who reminded Tucker John of his daddy. The owner of the place, Big Bobbie MacArthur, wasn't much better. Everyone knew better than to mess with Big Bobbie, even Tucker John knew better. It didn't matter one lick that he almost matched the man in height.

When Big Bobbie wasn't drinking from his own barrels he was taking free samples of the women he'd hired on, saying it was their payment for room and board in addition to the coin they had to dish out to him.

The only reason Tucker John was there was because he was hungry. No one would hire him, even for the old jobs he used to do on the nearby plantations, due to the shame that surrounded his family name. Out of money, he couldn't feed himself. Neither could he afford to make the lien payments on his family property. It wasn't long before he lost it to the bank along with the few fragile threads of dignity he had left.

He had no other option but to crawl into the bullying shadow of Big Bobbie and stay there for nearly a full two years.

He did his best to stay out of the man's way and even the patrons. His determined efforts didn't always pan out. He'd worn a great deal of spit, been baptized with several slop jars when he tried to get the non-paying whore-mongers out of the rooms without killing any of the girls. He had earned enough black eyes, split lips, and bruises to last him a lifetime within his first month.

Having an almost sated belly kept his mouth shut. Getting a drink to numb his mind every few hours, helped him tolerate the constant abuse that had come from Big Bobbie, and some of the other regulars.

But all of that changed with the same sharp turn that the weather took one November afternoon. Too much drinking, in a sorry attempt to warm his bones, had gone on even for Big Bobbie's large frame and mind to reckon with. Doused up to his eyeballs with his homemade drink, he began to walk with a foolish courage, giving his fingers over to play with things that were not his to toy with—Tucker John's pay—which in Tucker John's estimation was his very own life.

"I don't owe you nothing, boy. I ain't giving you one half of a red cent! Dogs don't need coin. All they needs is scrap from they masta's table." He spat out the words when Tucker John had come for his pay for the work he'd done that week, and even tossed a hambone at his feet to heighten the insult.

Seeing the hunger nearly drive Tucker John after the bone, Big Bobbie grinned, eyes bloodshot from spirits, and wild with a hateful fire. He mockingly, tauntingly, pulled out the exact number of coins that he owed him, slid them from the top of the table into his meaty paw, before dropping them, one by one, into his dirty shirt pocket.

Patting the bulge, still holding Tucker John's gaze, he offered drinks to the house and gave doubles to the men who'd caused Tucker John the most grief. *"Drinks, for all, courtesy of the Animal."*

Tucker John held his tongue but felt a spark light in his middle the moment Big Bobbie called him an animal. White-knuckled, and so full of rage that he had no room for meat, he walked out into the cold November storm, determined to cool his mind and even wait another day to try Big Bobbie for what was his when the man had sobered down.

But Big Bobbie wouldn't budge, and neither would Tucker John. He wasn't going to let anybody else take what was his by right, not even the feared Big Bobbie MacArthur, especially not after he had called him an animal! He'd let it slide the first time because the man was in his cups, but the second time, and right on the heels of cursing Tucker John's mama, had taken the shackles off him and set him loose like a hurricane beating against the shoreline.

Most of what happened after that was nothing but a rage-induced blur of hard, bloody actions dealt in full by the butt of a rifle. When it was all over with, Bobbie MacArthur had lost his left eye, all of his front teeth, and slept for two days after Tucker John got into him. Tucker John walked away with several knots, cuts, and a bruised rib or two. He also earned the nickname 'Tucker'.

He was only seventeen, wiry compared to Big Bobbie, but taller than most, and could move a lot quicker and rebound from a good hit much faster. He'd also learned his way around a rifle. He had beaten Big Bobbie with it, not seeing any sense in wasting good shots on his rotten flesh. He beat Big Bobbie like he wanted to beat Ashford Junior or his no-good daddy. He beat him until Big Bobbie's brain was shaken and the man slurred his words, and walked with a limp for the rest of his miserable life, all the while messing himself since he had lost sense enough to hold his bowels.

When folks around town started telling the tale, they liked to say, *'That John Spruce sho' put that Bobbie MacArthur to sleep that night. He tucked him in right like he was his mama!'*

Riding on the wind of people's strange admiration of his ruthless violence, Tucker John made quick business of the other patrons that had grieved him in the past couple years, and even some of the whores, making a nasty public display of them if they couldn't pay him the tax that he had placed on their heads for his pain.

He got away with all of it. The sheriff hadn't been too keen on most of the men Tucker John had business with, and so he turned a blind eye, quite like he did when he allowed Ashford Junior to rob him of his family.

What Tucker John had earned wasn't the kind of reputation that would have made his mama proud, but it was one that he could live up to, one that made people think twice before messing with him or what was his. If any man—or woman—mis-stepped, he only gave them one chance to do right by him before he sprung into the act of 'tucking them in.'

His reputation and ways of quick movements and clean shooting had won him many jobs with bounty hunters who gave him skills to match what God, and the back of his daddy's hand, had naturally given him in the way of understanding people and their character ways. And when a wealthy plantation owner, with the right amount of silver, came calling, Tucker John was converted to an overseer, keeping sharp his new skills with any slave who dared buck authority or try to run.

He was one of the few overseers who had just as much say with the Master of the Plantation as their closest house-slave.

The days of his humiliation had gone. Hell, even the patent office had contacted him about the fancy slave-hunting inventions he'd concocted. He was an outright success! No one dared slop him or even think to disrespect him, but Vivian Leona had. Vivian had strung him up in that bed. Let him starve for a day, and then sent that *sneaky* Lourdes in to throw cold soup at him!

He slowly set the bowl down and pulled the soiled nightshirt from his body, not giving a single care to the fact he was now completely naked underneath the bedsheet. He hadn't worn slacks or undergarments since the day after Vivian had scratched his scalp in the thicket. Since then he had a set of tubes invading his private parts that cleaned and pumped out his body waste—more humiliation to make her pay for.

Lourdes eventually returned, still moving with haste and spite. He trailed her with his eyes. "Where is that black b!T#% you call you better? I want her in here. Now." He didn't raise his voice. He'd done it enough damage. Vivian had done it damage. And there was no need in questioning Lourdes about throwing the bowl of soup on him. He knew her kind.

Lourdes slid on a protective glove. She still hadn't looked at him. "She doesn't want to see you. Or hear you for that matter."

"Oh, she gon' hear me, Lourdes. I don't know what game ya'll call ya'll selves playing at but—"

With an angry growl, she cut him off.

Lourdes clenched her jaw to keep from shouting. She was still livid with Tucker John for making Vivian miss the Assessment and cry, but she was even angrier with him for how his behavior had further complicated her and Johnny's situation.

Vivian had already talked to the Cleric's Office. She tried to reschedule the Assessment with Quinn Ellington, the Chief Cleric in Rotation beneath Magnus Sanderson and was denied. They were going to come to the house instead, at an undisclosed time. If it had not been for the ordering of the *Spadds* treatments they might have rescheduled, but with that order placed and received, the perimeter fence being activated several times, coupled with Vivian's absence at the Assessment, red flags had been raised. The Cleric's Office wanted to talk to everyone on the team now, Johnny included.

"This isn't a game! You ape!" Her hands fisted. "You've ruined everything! All you had to do was shut your mouth. But you couldn't do that. You had to scream, and curse, and stress Vivian out. Now she has missed the Assessment—"

Tucker John sneered. "Ain't like you care one stitch for her. You stink with hate for her! Ain't no need to pretend with me, Lourdes. And I don't give a hot d@^% 'bout no 'sessment, neither!"

Lourdes laughed. Had she been that obvious with Tucker John in regard to the way she felt about Vivian? Apparently so, if he was calling her out on it. "This is not about her alone. You don't get it. She's missed the Assessment. Now the Cleric's Office is coming here to do interviews with not just Vivian, but with Vivian's entire team. Only one problem with that, Johnny is gone! We're ruined because of you!"

"What the hell I care about her being ruined. She ruined my good name by stealing me here! I ain't never lost no slave 'til now, causa' Viv! Everything I worked for is gone. According to her reckoning of history, I die a failure!"

"You are a failure! No one remembers slave foremen, especially not ones who ran around in nothing but filthy trousers and bare feet. No one cares to. That wasn't a profession, it's an embarrassment! You, Tucker John, are a savage animal, the blight of history, the worst of the worst."

He inwardly reared back as if struck. Ashford Junior had called him 'blight' when he'd left him with nothing. It amazed him how it cut him open hearing it from the insignificant wench who stood before him. The worst was her calling him an animal.

Lourdes continued. "There's nothing redeemable about you, and yet the only person who is willing to give you a chance, you spend tearing to pieces! You systematically sabotage yourself, and you're taking her down with you." Her eyes darkened. "And because she goes down, I go down. Only thing is, I'm willing to do what it takes to not let that happen. If a problem has a clear solution, I will take it."

She moved closer to him, but she was still well out of his reach. Walking the length of his bed, she took visual stock of him. Her expression shifted in several different directions, and her cheeks blossomed pink as her eyes finally covered the length of him. Her widening gaze lingered upon him before moving upward toward his bare torso and chest and finally reaching his face again. She obviously had not realized until that very moment that he was naked beneath that thin sheet.

Tucker John's jaw ticked watching her. He didn't care for her imprudent gawking, but he was too proud to cover his silhouette with the heavier cover. He wouldn't give her the satisfaction of having known she'd embarrassed him.

Lourdes smirked. "I can almost see why Vivian keeps you around. But the reality is you're like a lame horse, pretty to look at for the most part," she bit her lip and let her eyes appraise him again, more color darkening her cheeks. "But useless and bound to die. Vivian ought to just put you down. But she won't, even though at this very moment she is considering the option. I know her though, and I know she won't do it. She needs a bit more convincing."

She wagged her gloved finger. "That's where my assistance comes in." She pulled out his next *Spadds* treatment and held it between her gloved fingers, just close enough for his blazing eyes to see. She could hardly keep from smiling. "The funny thing is there are only so many of these little pills that we have on hand. Vivian insists that you still take them. It doesn't matter. Every time you call her a 'black b!$#%' or 'negress' proves that they're wasted on you.

"And that's why, as her assistant, I'm here to help her. The sooner Vivian realizes you can't change, the sooner she'll listen to reason and euthanize you like she should have done the day you came through the E.P. And when she finally does, you and your diseased mind will cease to exist, and so will all of our problems." She dropped the *Spadds* to the ground and stomped it with the heel of her foot.

Tucker John felt his body lunge forward, but he was stopped by sleeping legs and the restraints that kept them in place. Lourdes laughed outwardly seeing him struggle for balance. He could only sear her with his glare.

"Really? Now you want to take them?" She laughed again and even clapped her hands. "It's too late. You've done enough damage. The only thing left to do is to contain it, and that starts with getting rid of you."

Tucker John pushed himself back upright, his breathing deep, controlled. "You shoulda' never done that."

"You shouldn't have made Vivian miss the Assessment!"

"So what, you her protector now?"

"Call it what you want. If keeping my personal interest in a safe place means protecting Vivian, then yes, that's what I am, her protector, for now."

Tucker John slowly exhaled. "Let me tell you something, Lourdes, the worst place to be is in between me and my enemy, and that's where you done placed your fool self."

Lourdes huffed and shook her head. "You still think she's your enemy, after all she's done for you?"

"Ya'll both are." Fury burned in his chest, but he held its flames at bay.

"News flash, Tucker John, this isn't 1837, and I'm not afraid of you."

He closed his eyes and calmed himself. Readjusting his sheets, he licked his fevered lips. They were hot with ire. "You should be Lourdes, you should be very afraid. You have no idea the kinda' hell I can rain down."

Lourdes hummed. "If only you were going to live long enough for me to find out. I mean, when Vivian hears that you threw your food like a child, stripped down naked, and cursed her as your worst enemy, she is going to be three steps closer to doing exactly what she needs to do." She held up three taunting fingers.

Tucker John took a look at the lab. There was a trail of parsnip soup on the floor and he was naked as a newborn baby, never mind his prior whooping and hollering.

Lourdes finally removed the glove from her hand, scooped up the wasted *Spadds* treatment, and tossed them both in disposal as she made her way toward the exit hall. "Well, my work here is done. Thank you for playing along. And one more thing," she lingered at the exit. "I dare you to tell Vivian that I did this."

She placed her hand on her chest and with her free arm pointed to the mess that had been made. She even pointed to the place her heel had destroyed his *Spadds* treatment. "I wouldn't even make mention of it if I were you. With all the fuss you've put up, and the mountain of trouble you've caused with the Cleric's Office, she won't believe you. She might even be moved to kill you herself. One can only hope. Thank you for making this so easy."

CHAPTER 20

Vivian Leona had missed her Assessment at the Cleric's Office. Clarence Mantov made a quick note of it in his clipboard. The message instantly went to Magnus' voicepod. It was another incident that had been verified as correct within the timeline.

There were so many holes, so many black spots that covered that decade that it was virtually impossible to make heads or tails of most of what took place. It was as if the 4030's had been vulgarly assaulted and left without a voice, and no one even knew it was happening.

The same could be said for other leagues in the future, but no one was privy to that, not yet at least. Some details, results of John Jay's tampering, would remain unmentioned in the reports, even though Clarence would deal with them personally, and soon since the holes in the timeline were proof that he was about to get his hands extremely dirty.

As far as Aiden Schulsler was concerned, the holes were none of Clarence's business. He was there for one reason and one reason only; to keep a close eye on Magnus Sanderson, make sure the man kept his nose clean and did everything Mr. Schulsler had instructed him to do.

Clarence just had to make sure that he, himself, fit in, and didn't give anyone any reason to suspect something was 'off' with him while he watched Magnus, thus the ruse of him being Magnus' dutiful assistant.

Clarence was an excellent study in the art of pretending. He had just over two decades of work under his belt within his given profession, was a master of slipping through timelines undetected, and had kept each of his clients happy, and their names unknown. That was until he made Aiden Schulsler's acquaintance. It was tricky business, that, delicate really.

The gentlemen who'd hired Clarence to 'handle' Mr. Schulsler clearly had no idea of Mr. Schulsler's true character and capabilities. They couldn't just leave well enough alone. As a result of their arrogant ignorance, and Clarence's failure to allow his gut to guide him, he became a victim of a forced conversion into Mr. Schulsler's permanent 'hand' for hire.

They had damaged Aiden Schulsler's physical hand and now he was taking theirs.

The difference for Clarence, within this new arrangement, was that he was no longer receiving any monetary rewards worth mentioning for his efforts. What he got in return for his obedience to Mr. Schulsler was the gift of his life in exchange for him handling those who had hired Clarence against him in the first place. The only other time he had found himself on the losing end of things was as the result of a fixed hand of cards, costing him a fancy *Winchester Model 94 .30-30 Lever Action Rifle.*

Being that he had been the one to fix the game to his opponent's favor, as he had been instructed to do, Clarence did not count that occurrence against his overall abilities and success scores.

The odds with Schulsler, however, had not been rigged in the least. It was all a token of destiny. The man was just slippery and far more cunning than anyone truly knew or understood, all without ever being deceitful. This, Clarence respected. Those traits ran heavy in Mr. Schulsler's blood.

The deal between him and Mr. Schulsler seemed fair enough in the end. Mr. Schulsler was still alive, which meant Clarence had failed his clients, Clarence should have been dead himself, was seemingly helpless against his former prey—which was a position he had never been in before—but since Mr. Schulsler was all about the bigger picture, a gambler known to play his cards close to his chest, Clarence became, not so much his victim, but his employee.

At least for the time being. As it was, Mr. Schulsler being alive proved a great reward for Clarence.

Still, there were more powerful people than Aiden Schulsler after all, people to whom Clarence had given his full allegiance, and since his presence in Mr. Schulsler's life proved in their favor, they left him on his leash. Eventually, they would break his hold, but until then, Clarence was at the man's beck and call. Thusly, whenever he needed one of his critics encouraged to comply with a given demand or have their cords ripped, Clarence was the one to do it, discretely of course.

The unfortunate thing—for Mr. Schulsler's critics, as they were called—out of seven people on his list, three had not survived Clarence's visit. Things were looking promising for Magnus, although his survival didn't at all mean that he was free from Mr. Schulsler's chokehold.

Once in Aiden Schulsler's debt, you were in his debt for the rest of your life.

***

Quinn Ellington, the Chief Cleric in Rotation, was none too pleased with Vivian's absences and had made that fact known to her without hesitation. Being that Quinn was not from 4037, and was aware that neither was Vivian, she'd wasted no time in trying to suppress her irritation. Absence was just not acceptable, not even for a decorated surveyor like Vivian Leona. Even Raul had agreed, although he had not been keen on Quinn's disciplinary approach.

Quinn wondered if her harsh response toward Vivian was a direct result of her own pregnancy, that, and being overheated the last few days. She didn't know. What was done was done. An unannounced Team Review would be conducted.

She comforted herself with the knowledge that because Vivian had such a clean track record, the Team Review would not be too much of a hassle for either party involved. It would be quick, easy, and painless. Vivian Leona was known for running a tight ship, and yes, that should have been enough cause to cut her some slack and simply reschedule the Cleric Assessment, but Quinn did find it odd that she had placed an order for multiple millennial *Spadds* treatments.

That kind of thing was not against protocol, but it was curious. And why had her team activated their perimeter fence so many times within a three week period? Vivian's absence that morning didn't help, neither did Quinn's unborn babies, taking turns in tap dancing on her bladder. Her nerves were beyond worse for the wear.

Nevertheless, she realized that she had most likely jumped the gun. She would have to send Vivian a 'comfort basket' as they called them in 4037, really it was nothing more than a glorified fruit basket, extend an olive branch for the inconvenience, and interruption the clerics would cause Vivian's team.

They would all laugh right through it in the end. Vivian and her team would get a stellar review, and everything would continue forward as if there had never been a single interruption. No harm, no foul, and no problem.

Vivian was a very rational person after all. She would get past this. She probably already had.

***

Vivian could see no other option. She'd spent the entire afternoon mulling over what she could possibly do to avoid the coming storm of the Cleric's Office. Raul had called, and after talking to him, she was beyond convinced that she should stop her charade and tell everyone the truth, the truth about John Jay going missing while doing maintenance on their faulty nexus gate, and Tucker John coming through the E.P in his place.

She sat in her room and told the account out loud to her reflection in the mirror. The more she listened to herself, the more incriminated she felt. She had already raised several red flags of her own against her conduct, and mishandling of the situation.

That wasn't good at all.

If listening to her own testimony made her frown with disbelief and disapproval, how would it cause a woman like Quinn Ellington or a calm-hearted man like Raul Manuel to react?

"They're going to think you're insane, that you've had a mind-relapse in the Field. Fantastic." Growling, she cupped her face in her hands.

There would definitely be disciplinary actions. She feared to think what they would be. Worse, how would it all affect the efforts in finding John Jay? For that matter, what would he have to say about her choices? No one had done what she had done, especially no one with her ranking. The clerics would hit at her for her misconduct, and they would hit hard. She would be made the example—the sacrifice for everyone to watch burn.

She cringed at the thought.

In the end, she found herself facing the same question she had been battling with since it all began. If she told the Cleric's Office the truth, what would they do to Tucker John? Part of her argued that she shouldn't care. It was Tucker John's fault that they were now being investigated. Another side of her reasoned that it wasn't his fault at all. That wasn't the first time he had raised a grating ruckus. No, he had been screaming since he had been awake.

His usual antics shouldn't have led her to overdose on Paz. There was really no one to blame but herself for that. She was understandably stressed out about John Jay missing. She hadn't felt like herself since then, but she couldn't blame Tucker John for that either. Blaming brought no solutions in the end, it only made her mind crank and reel in a thousand useless directions, and Lord knew she was already battling the symptoms of being completely scatterbrained.

"I'm stressed and it's throwing my hormones out of whack. You're a hormonal wreck. You need to get it together." She rebuked her reflection. "People are depending on you, whether they realize it or not." Tucker John's scowling face painted itself on the canvas of her imagination.

Having exhausted her own ears and mind of solo reasoning, she reluctantly invited Lourdes into her session, voicing again her reasons for considering coming clean with the Cleric's Office. If, for no other reason, gaining access to the full gambit of resources available to the Cleric's Office was one that was too grand to ignore. The Cleric's Office would surely have greater success in locating John Jay, even if that meant the most severe consequences for Vivian.

Who knew, maybe the Cleric's Office would side with her and not allow Tucker John to be euthanized since he was only a victim in what had happened, as ironic as it all was. Sure, there were seemingly fragile agreements set up between the clerics and the Government of that time, but the Government only had jurisdiction over people of their timeline and no one from the future. The problem was that the agreement did not include people from the past. Tucker John was somewhat a free agent.

Lourdes quickly shot down her reasoning. The clerics would not understand, she argued. They would send Vivian back to 6037—without John Jay—to face whatever consequences they deemed worthy of her poor judgment. Lourdes would be removed from all surveillance and clerical work, and would most likely be euthanized for depression. As for Tucker John, he would definitely be put down as well. He had no rights, and as far as history was concerned, he was already dead, so the Government would be doing the world and all timelines a service, something she clearly agreed with.

After a few rounds with Lourdes, the mirror again, and another bout with crying, Vivian had come to a decision. It was the most frightening, but it was the only one that she could see that benefited all parties involved. It would provide them all with what they needed most—it would buy them more time.

CHAPTER 21

Lourdes stayed on Vivian's heels. Vivian couldn't seriously be considering doing what she was headed to do? This was *not* the best plan. It was the absolute worse decision that Vivian had ever made, besides keeping Tucker John alive!

"Don't do this, Vivian," Lourdes whispered, pleaded. She'd felt the once healthy glow of her face slip into a ghastly white the moment Vivian headed for the lab. Her fingertips had even grown cold from the sudden shift in Vivian's attitude. She would have rather her be locked up in her room, sobbing pathetically, than this. This was insane.

Lourdes stopped right in view of Tucker John. It was as if a glass wall had been placed between them. The greater the distance she kept the better. She glanced at him and then at the back of Vivian's head. "Vivian," Vivian ignored her.

Tucker John didn't need a single word to be said to decipher what was going on. He had no details, but what he could gather from the anxious ticking in Lourdes' muscles, he knew whatever it was, was going to be in his favor.

He offered Lourdes a curious nod, and then made himself comfortable, turning his attention to Vivian.

She took her time in meeting his gaze. It was as if she was still undecided in whatever it was that Lourdes was trying to convince her not to do.

She finally took a seat and rolled it close to him. She was also smart enough to stay out of his reach. He noticed the muscles around her eyes contracting as she took in the room; the soup on the floor, his soiled nightshirt in a heap, and him naked as a jaybird.

He glanced at Lourdes and found her scowling. She had obviously told Vivian about his 'tantrum,' and things had not gone as she'd predicted. Vivian hadn't taken those three steps forward that Lourdes had hoped she would.

All the better for me. He almost smiled.

More silence lingered, only broken by Lourdes' pleas. Finally, Tucker John spoke up. "You got something you wanna say to me, gal?" He tilted his head trying to angle his face so that he could see more of Vivian's.

"Vivian. Don't do this!" Lourdes hissed.

"Viiiiiv," He practically sang her name. He could tell it made her skin crawl. That made him smile.

Vivian's body shuddered as the air escaped her lungs. Her face turned toward Tucker John's. Clenching her fist she forced herself to look at him, staring into his gunmetal grey eyes.

There was strangeness to the moment. It was as if she could feel his soul, though quiet to her ears, screaming out at her in cold indignation, almost a threat. But the way he stared back at her meant he could hear her soul screaming with the same force and gale. Somewhere between them was an invisible line that they both could sense. They were each waiting on either side of it, waiting to make their move—rabid dogs hungry to attack.

"Vivian, please think this thro—"

"Lourdes, please, leave the lab, and wait for me in the library. I'll be up in a moment." Her decision had been made. Nothing would change it.

"This is a mistake." Lourdes retorted. Vivian pressed her eyes closed.

Tucker John cleared his throat. His voice was still very hoarse. "I thought you ain't wanna talk to me no more, Viv. Why such a quick change a' heart?"

Vivian stood and filled up a vile with water. She handed it to him. The glare in his eyes meant he'd noticed her care in not allowing her fingers to touch his when she did so. He managed to brush his fingers against hers just before she pulled away just to spite her. Throwing her a rakish grin, he drank down the water.

Turning, she headed to a nearby cabinet and began to rifle through it. Pulling out a fresh tunic, she handed it to him. "This isn't a change of heart," she said. "It's an unexpected change in circumstances."

Tucker John pulled the new tunic over his head. "Is that right?"

She took another breath, stilling her irritation. She hated how his words melted together when he spoke. "Yes, Tucker John. By the looks of the room, I'm sure that you've already heard." She sighed, using her foot, and his old tunic to mop up the parsnip soup. It was as if a wild toddler had been there. She didn't have time for children. She was grateful that John Jay agreed with her on that, no matter how much his mother, Emlen Spruce, had nagged them for grandchildren.

"What is it? I can tell you want something, just a'feared to ask for it?" He seemed elated with his assumption of her fear. He liked people being afraid of him. She, however, was not. She only feared what would happen if things went wrong.

"No, Tucker John, I'm not afraid to ask you," she kept mopping up the soup.

He narrowed an eye. He didn't believe her. She didn't care. "Contrary to your previous assumption of me, and my 'inability' to think things through before I make my move, that is exactly what I am doing, thinking this through." She scooped up the soggy tunic and dropped it in a disposal.

Tucker John followed her with his eyes. Her taking her time in asking him whatever it was that she wanted to ask him was beyond irritating. *Just like a female! All filled up with foolishness and indecision.* He hated being strung along.

"Well, you done thinkin? I'd hate for you to get a headache over whatever it is you got rolling about in that head a' yours." He made a circular motion with his hand.

Vivian wiped her hands and took her seat again. Her tone was surprisingly calm. "Yes, Tucker John, I'm done thinking."

"Well, what the hell you want?!" She opened her mouth to speak, but he cut her off with a raised hand, pointing his long finger at her as a warning. "Before you go into you 'dissertation' about whatever it is you call yourself asking of me, you need to understand one thing. Whatever you ask of me is gon' come at a cost to you."

Vivian didn't flinch at his words. It appeared she already anticipated he would make her pay for whatever she requested of him. And he would take his time in doing it. According to her, he'd have six full years to do so, more if things played into his hand. He had no plans of going back to 1837 to die. He wouldn't.

He felt an energy rise up within him. The tides of the power struggle between them were churning in his favor. He thought about his previous prayer to God for help, and nearly choked. This was going to cost him, too. He would worry about that later.

She said, "I figured it would. Nevertheless, here I am."

He opened his arms wide. "And here I sit, a captive audience."

Vivian made her proposition brief and clear. She explained the situation with the Cleric's Office, sparing him the blame, he'd noticed. She told him that they would make a surprise visit for a Team Review and Assessment. She stated the obvious, that John Jay was nowhere to be found, but Tucker John was present.

"I'll save the telling of the consequences and repercussions that could take place should the Review fall through, and if the Cleric's Office were to discover who you really are for another time." She said.

Tucker John's ardor declined a few notches anticipating what the future could hold for him if anything Lourdes had already said was true. He had to give it to Vivian. She'd known he was gearing up to jab her hard in the ribs with his demands before that very moment. By the look on her face, she'd known before she had even come to him with her request, that he would indeed gain some very valuable ground. What chaffed him most was she also knew he wouldn't get it all, not like he had hoped. Good thing he was a patient man.

He should have known better, that Vivian had already mapped things out in her head. She knew what he wanted, and she knew what he would do. She took her measures to safeguard against him as best she could and she'd done a fine job of it. In an instant, she'd nearly managed to douse his fire with a murky reality, almost forcing him to put away his smoking ace as the reality of the situation settled in. The invisible line, the power struggle was evident once again. Smart. This woman was so unlike his Vivian, and certainly unlike Lourdes who wore her emotions out in the open, and spilled her intentions like the parsnip soup that had sprayed the floor. Vivian, unfortunately, did not. She could be riled, had been riled, but even then she kept her mind to herself, telling only what was necessary to be told. He wondered what she might be hiding in that very moment.

"So lemme' put this in simple terms," he said, "You want me to dress up like your idiot husband, and put on a show, like a circus monkey for some folks who might find a reason to kill me if I don't?"

"Correct." She was extremely calm.

"What's in it for you?" He pointed at her. He was no fool. He knew her concern for his life only went so far, by his estimation of things. "This about that boy ain't it? If you lie to me, won't be no deal." His gaze was cold as ice.

She leaned back. "I don't need to lie. I just need time. Truth is, I'm not, nor have I ever been, interested in killing you or having anyone else do so for that matter. Even in the face of your crimes against others in the past, I refuse to play judge, jury, and executioner. I simply want to put things right, and I need time to do that."

"You want me to conform in order to buy you some time so you can send me back to 1837 to drown." It wasn't a question.

He couldn't resist the threatening growl that surrounded his words.

Vivian ran her fingertips at the edge of her hairline and stopped at her temples, giving them the gentlest of rub. "Tucker John, I don't know how else to make myself clear to you about where I stand in regards to your death. I just want my husband back. Your death is not my doing. I simply have no intention of preventing it since it has already taken place. It would be unethical."

"To hell with your ethics!" He shooed her with his hands. "I ain't gon' be that easy to buy, Viv."

"I didn't think you were for sale." Her tone and posture, her decided stance on his pending date with the Grim Reaper, made him want to knock her down several notches.

All in time. He thought.

She continued. "I'm only giving you the option to help yourself."

"Help *you*." He countered.

"Helping me is helping you. What's it going to be?" She stood, looking down at him, her hands akimbo.

He considered her for a moment. He wasn't keen on lying, but he wasn't keen on dying prematurely either. The fact that Vivian was offering him the weak olive branch in her hands was a sign that she was in a corner and had no other options left. This would be his stepping stone. He would take what he could get until he was in a position to take everything. He would eventually put the wench in her place. For now, he would do like her and buy himself some time.

"Fine. I'll dance your Johnny-jig for a spell," he scratched the hairs on his chin, a grin stretching across his lips. "But here's what you gon' gimme' in return…."

CHAPTER 22

"There ain't no *meat*? Ya'll living in the big house. Where's the *meat*?" Tucker John looked at his plate with disgust, shoving the vegetables around with his fork. "Vegetables ain't nothing more than *orphan food* all by they-selves! They needs meat to parent em' up right!"

He sat at the head of Vivian's dining table. Vivian was in the seat to his right, Lourdes to his left, his solid chest jutted out. He was the Alpha male, the ruler of the roost. *Just as God intended.*

In return for his compliance with Vivian's request, one of the things she would have to give him was the right to eat at the head of her table. He would eat from the same dishes that she and Lourdes ate from. Now that war had indeed been openly declared between him and Lourdes, he couldn't take any chances. Lourdes was desperate. She would poison him as soon as she got the chance.

"There's meat," Vivian answered without looking at him. She slowly chewed a roasted sweet potato.

"Well, can I *have* some?" Tucker John huffed, not hiding his attitude. Why should he?

Vivian sighed. "Lourdes, can you pass Tucker John the meat, please?"

Lourdes pursed her lips without giving any further complaint about the new 'arrangement' within the home. Instead, she silently followed directions, clearly still stunned by Viv's decision. She knew that she'd converted Tucker John into more than an enemy for herself. The harpy was now corned thanks to Vivian. Things were playing right into his hand of divide-and-conquer. Lourdes was afraid, just as he warned her to be.

He stared down at her from the slope of his nose, making her keep a firm, white-knuckled grip on her fork even as she passed him the covered plater of beef.

Scowling, he yanked it from her hands, dropping its lid on the table with a bang, before shoveling several pieces of beef tenderloin onto his plate. "I don't know what woman call herself serving a man supper and don't give him no meat if she got it! A man needs meat! He ain't worth a hill a' beans, and can't even move a hill a' beans living off a lady-diet. Ya'll been feeding me soup like I'se an infant, and soon as I get out the bed ya'll gimme' salad and no meat!"

Vivian continued to eat, but Lourdes broke her silence, making a comparison between him and John Jay. She loaded her fork with sautéed asparagus. "John Jay is a man, one of the finest I have ever known—"

"Yeah, I bet he is." Tucker John interjected. He'd heard Lourdes ask Vivian how she thought he could possibly pass for John Jay? She'd emphasized how they were nothing alike. *Nothing at all.*

Lourdes ignored the intent of the statement. "He is. And he is a vegetarian."

"What's that now?" Sucking gravy off his thumb, his brow rose.

"John Jay only eats fruits and vegetables. He never eats anything that has a soul, and he is a man."

Tucker John's jaw bulged from the amount of beef he had shoved into it. He pointed his fork at Lourdes. "Well, that explains whole a hell of a lot! Especially why that boy couldn't keep no order in his house. Sitting up here, call himself married to a negress, got a lil' white woman acting the part of slave. He's only eating greens like a dang gum deer, and prolly skittish as a rabbit, no doubt. Boy needed some meat! He all out of order. Good lawd almighty, just wrong! Way out of the natural order of thangs."

He soaked up some gravy with his bread and hummed as the flavors burst in his mouth. "By the way, Viv, this is some mighty fine gravy you done throw'd together, best I ever done had. Better than my own mama's! And that's sho' nough saying something."

Tucker John's open smile caused his mono-lid eyes to form sparkling grey half-moons. Vivian looked away from him, forcing down the flash of emotion that had sprouted in that one neutral look alone.

"Tucker John, you agreed to mind your tongue and the epithets." She took a drink from her glass and stared at him. *Mind the line*, her gaze told him. *You're loose, but not free. The balance is still tilted in my favor.*

Tucker John hummed tauntingly challenging her with a look almost as if he'd heard her very thoughts. His brow flickered upward before settling. Smacking his lips he rubbed his hands together. "Now listen here, soon as I'se done, I wanna see my room. Meal like this demands a good nap."

Vivian pushed around the vegetables on her plate. She'd long since lost her appetite even though she'd forced some food down. She'd be ravenous later if she didn't. But how, after everything she'd told Tucker John, he could smile and think about naps was beyond her. He had to understand the gravity of the threats that were weighing over their heads.

He didn't resist the urge to stretch. *Yes, lawd. That's exactly what I needed, a good, long nap.* Tucker John refused to live within the walls of the lab any longer. If he was going to be John Jay, he was going to get to sleep like he did. He was not going to be Vivian's experiment or Lourdes whipping boy. Tactical repositioning was a must. Being bound to a bed with dead legs left him vulnerable. There would be no more blue light putting him or any other part of his body to sleep. He was totally in control of his own person now.

Vivian would also be giving him time and access to other educational resources, knowledge of the nexus gate, as well as the ability to administer his own *Spadds* treatments.

Like it or not, he needed every shred of information that he could get his hands on. Knowledge was power. When he was a bounty hunter he had learned to gather as much information about his bounty as he could. Not knowing his target left him open to being the target. Vivian and Lourdes were like two loaded pistols aimed at his head. The year of 4037 was the rifle right at his back. One false move and he was a dead man.

"Your room?" Lourdes' eyes grew large as she parroted his last words. She hadn't known that he was getting a room beyond the lab. He'd made mention of it just to rub her hide raw. *Divide and conquer.*

She turned toward Vivian, her face washing a sickly shade of grey. "He's not staying in the lab? You didn't mention this to me," she dropped her fork only to snatch it up again as soon as her eyes met Tucker John's. She swallowed so loudly it could be heard.

Vivian took a sip of her water. "I mentioned what was necessary for the time we had to talk."

Lourdes pressed her lips, her eyes skirted from Viv's to the smirk Tucker John had for her, and then back to her plate of orphaned greens. Staring down she said, "Obviously you failed to mention much of the arrangement the two of you have made."

"I told you what you needed to know." Vivian glared.

This, keeping Lourdes in the dark, was also according to his will. None of his rights were Lourdes' concern. Vivian was to tell her only what she needed to know, which wasn't much of anything. To tear down whatever alliance the wenches had, he needed to keep them in confusion. Keeping the two from communicating, and subtly loading them with negative speculations about each other would do that quite well.

He still needed to take his time and play each card he had carefully. Trigger-happy hunters always missed their kill. He needed to deal with them while assuming his freedom and the new identity he was taking on. He'd handle John Jay soon enough. Taking the man's life, as he planned to do once the fool was found, was no sweat off his back. One of them had to die, after all, might as well be Johnny-boy. Had he been a man in the first place, Tucker John would have never been pressed under Vivian Leona's heel, he would have never been tempted to stay beyond his timeline, and current circumstances notwithstanding, he was sorely tempted.

He took another bite of beef and stretched again. He liked the way Lourdes' discomfort was making him feel. "And, I think I'd like a bath, too. One ah ya'll need to fetch me some hot water," he stopped himself, suddenly seeing the image of modern plumbing in his mind. He smiled with expectation. "Now wait a dog on minute! My room had better have one of them built-in showers and a tub."

Daily bathing was Vivian's demand. Remembering the nice smell of the soap she had rubbed him down with, he conceded without much argument. He looked her way. "We gotta' room with both of them in it, shower and tub? Why the hell am I asking? Sure we got one of them. This the big house!" His laughter was so ruckus that it made both women flinch from the volume of it as meat particles shot out from the back of his throat.

"We?" Lourdes nearly choked. "This isn't your house." She glared, rubbing her ear that was closest to him. Obviously, his laughter was too much for her. Hell if he cared.

He tore off another piece of beef and chewed it with an open mouth. "Ain't yours neither," he countered.

Vivian pushed her plate away and wiped her mouth. She looked absolutely ill. "The room on the third floor, I'll show you to it after you've finished with your meal."

She was going to have to show him more than that. Tucker John wanted to see the entire house and the end of the property. This place was now his battlefield. He needed to know what he was working with. He still would have his limits, 'precautionary measures' as Vivian had called them, but he would figure out how to overcome those in time. He always did.

He raised one finger, scrapped the rest of his food into his mouth, dumped his water down the back of his throat as if it were a glass of liquor, following it with a wet and obnoxious belch before he too shoved his plate forward. Wiping his wet beard with his hand he stood up. "Done." He hit the table with two gavel-like fists. "Let's get going, Viv." He offered Lourdes a wicked smirk. He didn't mind letting her know her days were numbered.

She turned away from him, reserving the disgusted frown for Vivian, mouthing out the words *'This is a mistake.'* Tucker John didn't miss the exchange.

Viv sighed and walked away from the table without a word.

***

Magnus had built up his nerve again. Of course, it was a new day, but he hadn't slept well at all since his first encounter with the static. His mouth still felt cottony no matter how much water he drank. The feeling unsettled him, but it made him respect the glittery-gold substance.

He watched it closely. He didn't touch it, nor did he breathe on it, but it seemed to be moving, vibrating. Before, when he had followed the Instrument to Balm Hill, he heard a chilling conversation, voices like breathy whispers coming through the smoky glow that drew from the Instrument's prongs. He wondered what he could hear from the static itself.

He placed a sensor to the side of the static's container and listened carefully to the ripples. He turned his head, trying to gain a better frequency. Grinding metal; that is what he was hearing; a sharp cutting sound that irritated his inner ear. The sound was reported to be the result of one thing; information being ripped out of time, space, and memory.

Palms sweating, he reactivated his internal clipboard and reread the notes that he was given about the static. The lines moved across the palm of his hand. What he had heard was consistent with what had been reported. Next, he recorded a new log entry. This time the data entry logged in as yellow.

He cursed. What had he expected, for everything to be smooth sailing, no inconstancies or unreported information? That hardly ever happened. Besides, he was sixty-five-years old, too old to be that naïve.

He quickly forwarded Clarence a note about what he had heard and the color of the data entry. In light of the grinding metal sound, it was best that the information was doubly recorded, just-in-case.

CHAPTER 23

Vivian sat in the window seat of her bedroom staring out into the dark of the night. The thick moist air blew in and settled within the linen threads of her nightdress. With clumsy fingers, she pulled several long, black tendrils of hair from her face. Hardly paying any conscious attention to what she was doing, she nervously worked out the fairy knots that had formed in the humid breeze of the night. She snapped several strands of hair in her mindless efforts before tucking the misplaced lochs back away from her face and binding them in a braid.

She could hear Tucker John's footsteps move across the floor and stop right above her. He couldn't sleep either. The excitement of his presumed victory must have kept him awake, that, and simple curiosity.

He'd turned on his bedroom light several times already, flicking it on and off again like a child would until finally leaving it on. Its glow interrupted the darkness that Vivian's eyes had adjusted to. Glaring at the ceiling, she moved away from the window. She should have suspected he was nothing more than fascinated even though he'd managed to keep his enthusiasm well-hidden during their tour of the home and grounds.

He'd taken his time scrutinizing everything that she showed him that day. He touched things, stared at them in silence which was usually accompanied by narrow eyes, a frown, or simple indifference. When something really fascinated him in a less important way than the others, he whistled, loudly. Whistling had been his initial reaction to the house itself. Vivian nearly got a migraine from its sharp resonance when he first stepped foot into his bedroom and ensuite.

The suite made up the entire third floor, sparing only a few square feet for a modest-sized storage room.

Just like with his bedroom lights, he'd run water and repeatedly flushed the toilet. It was nothing short of a miracle to him, indoor plumbing, causing his eyes to spark. Vivian had the unpleasant chance to encounter those same sparkling eyes he'd flashed her at the dining table when he'd done a poor job of complimenting her gravy.

But, just like his open smile had amazed her, so did the notion that a man who didn't care for bathing by the way he smelled when she first made his acquaintance, was suddenly eager to take a bath just because hot water ran out of the pipes. 'Tucker' John Josephus Spruce was a far more complex and curious creature than she had given him credit for. There was a great deal more to him than the rough, bristly, exterior and coat of terror he wore like a second skin. That was what he allowed people to see, what he wanted them to see. But there was something more beneath. Vivian just didn't know what and wasn't sure she cared to find out.

What she did know for certain was that truly vile human beings had no spark to their eyes. Twice in one day, Tucker John had uncovered that he was simply hiding his light in the darkness.

Lourdes was wrong. He was redeemable.

That didn't mean Vivian would be underestimating the level of threat he held. He was still a very dangerous man, even with the spark and the curiosity.

What struck her most was what he didn't find intriguing. She had wrongly assumed that he would have been more taken with the nexus gate, shown the same awe for it as he had the simple lamp in his bedroom. The first time Vivian laid eyes on a gate all she could do was stare—wide-eyed, and wide-mouthed. It was ingenious. If it had a simple switch, she would have clicked it on and off just to see it work.

Tucker John, in his less than imaginative practicality, did not share the same enthusiasm.

(Earlier that evening)
"What'nah hell is this?" Tucker John pointed a long finger at the large wooden door frame. It jutted out on all sides by three inches and had a single thread of gold that ran along its inner seam, and even across its threshold, forming a perfect rectangle.

"It's the nexus gate."

He gave Vivian a warning stare, a sharp brow arching upward. Their agreement would go very sour if she tried to pull the wool over his eyes. He'd said as much. Vivian assumed the look was meant to be her first, and only, warning.

She casually shrugged. His warnings meant nothing to her.

"This ain't nothing but a doorframe, a mighty large doorframe, but a doorframe." Easing his head carefully through it, he peeked at what was beyond. The 'doorframe' was on the back end of a room that was seven feet deep and twelve feet long. It was like a Butler's pantry, empty besides the single desk and chair that were pushed against the wall and a narrow bench that ran perpendicular to those, pointing into the greenhouse.

"That there is a glass hallway to a greenhouse." He turned around, folding his arms across his solid chest and looked down at her, his mouth a tight line. "You think I'se a fool."

Vivian looked him in the eyes and slowly shook her head. "No, I don't actually." She moved past him and touched the framework of the nexus gate. Gold thread aside, it matched the rest of the massive, dark, rough honed wood framing throughout the manor.

To a person who knew nothing about surveillance, time travel, and nexus gates, the gate appeared to be nothing more than a massive doorframe, just as Tucker John had deduced. Few noticed the matching wood trim with a thin gold inlay that mimicked a chair rail, running through the nexus room, through the metal framing of the glass room beyond it, and even across the edge of the work desk.

Hidden in plain sight. That was an excellent mark to its engineering. Nexus gates were intended to blend seamlessly within any time period, after all.

She said, "This is the nexus gate. As surveyors, we need to blend with our surroundings as does our equipment."

Tucker John rapped his knuckles against it. "This thing don't lead to no past or future, gal—"

"Don't call me 'gal'." Vivian's brow was the one to arch this time.

Tucker John sighed and rolled his eyes. "Viv, that goes into a greenhouse." He pointed toward the greenhouse.

"It does. All nexus gates are connected to greenhouses or sunrooms. None of them are made from usual glass. The glass that is specially constructed for the gates helps with light refractions, etcetera. It's a utilitarian type of camouflage for time travel that provides either food or leisure. It's absolutely brilliant when you think about it. We hide the gates in plain sight." Her brow gathered when she looked at him. "You took the *Spadds*. You should know this already."

Facing the gate again her gaze longingly followed the rough lines of the dark wood. "Something's wrong with this one. That's why John Jay is missing...and you're here. It thinks you're him." Tucker John gave a fowl snort. Vivian stifled a bristle but couldn't keep her eyes from stinging. She touched the bottle of *Paz* in her pocket but thought better than to take one. Her head was still fuzzy from earlier. She could keep it together for a little while longer.

She moved past Tucker John. "Let's finish up the tour. It's getting late."

(The Present hour)

Frowning, Vivian rubbed the back of her neck. The tour with Tucker John had gone relatively smoothly even though she masked her fear of his presence like the greatest of actresses, often resisting the urge to freeze him with her intermezzo even though he had made no sudden move to harm her. But what was it going to be like with him moving about the house freely all the time, as well as in the fields, having access to the farming equipment? They desperately needed his help to get things ready for the Co-op delivery.

The thought didn't settle well with her, but she had made the decision. She had chosen to set the lion free rather than leave it safely within its cage. Tucker John's less contained presence did help her think with a clearer mind. The threat he now posed was the push she needed to search harder for John Jay. As if she could give any more to her diligent efforts than she had already given.

Forcing herself to bask in the looming shadow of danger was not her initial plan. She had, however, taken extra measures to ensure that she and Lourdes were safe with him loose. She also wanted to make sure he wasn't a flight risk. That's why she'd put him on the third floor. It was a long way down should he decide to jump. She could also anticipate his arrival before he made his appearance.

He none too pleased with the safety measures she was putting in place against him. And, true to his character, he let it be known.

(Earlier that evening)
"I ain't no d@$^ dog! You want me to wear a collar!"

Vivian held the necklace out to him. It was a simple circular medallion strung up by a leather string. But for all its simplistic appeal it was like the nexus gate. Woven within its internal construction were sensors remotely connected to an intermezzo program.

Tucker John had to wear the medallion whenever he was outside of his bedroom or else he would be frozen still via internal intermezzo.

Vivian answered him. "It's not a collar. It's an insurance policy. Let's just be frank. You don't trust me, and the feeling is mutual. Although I have done nothing to harm you, *you* have tried to harm me. So, Lourdes and I do have reasons to be wary of you, even though we need each other's cooperation right now."

He snatched the necklace from her hands. "It's a dang collar. You wanna' put something inside me and make me wear this here dog leash." He glowered. "If you was me, would you put this thang on? Would you let me put some bug under your skin?"

Vivian sat down and rubbed her face. He had every right to be angry and offended. It was a type of collar that she was giving him. When he had first told her that she would have to turn him loose from the confines of the bed and the lab, Vivian rejected his demand flat out. She made it plain that she didn't trust him to not do her or Lourdes bodily harm in any way. He knew what she was alluding to. Being a man with no real moral scruples in her estimation, how could she trust him to not take advantage of either or both of them? Who would keep him from it?

Lourdes was barely five feet two inches tall and weighed no more than a hundred and ten pounds. Though narrow, Vivian was taller and heavier than Lourdes, but even the extra weight she carried wouldn't count for very much against Tucker John's size and demeanor. Sure, Vivian, like all other Ministers of Time, had been physically trained to defend herself. She could handle her own, within reason. More than anything, she was trained in the art of *fleeing* harm.

But there would be very little hope of flight from Tucker John. His livelihood was made on giving chase. What was more frightening was that he was a healthy, solid man, who stood a head taller than she, outweighed her by hundred or more pounds. That weight difference was made up of nothing but dense muscle. He was twice her girth from shoulder to shoulder, and could probably outrun her without even losing his breath.

He had spent the better part of his life physically brutalizing anyone who didn't give him his way. Vivian wouldn't chance it no matter how riled it made him.

She understood that, through his ignorance and indoctrination of archaic social codes, he thought and behaved differently than she. His beliefs and views on women—black women especially, having been labeled as sexually insatiable and free for the picking—were indeed in line with the ways of the world in 1837. Those ideologies left no room for misinterpretation, *Spadds* treatments aside. Vivian couldn't take the risk without a safety net. She couldn't risk Lourdes' safety either. She needed him to comply, and this was the only way to procure that compliance.

Tucker John met her concerns by giving her his word laced in a vulgar spray of curses and a rant about him not being an animal, before trying to calm himself and simply saying that he would never violate her or Lourdes in *that* way.

"Now look here," he said, raising his large hand in the air as if being sworn in under oath. "I understand your concerns, no matter how foolish they is. But I done told you I ain't no *rapist*, no matter what you think I done to your time-twin." His jaw ticked. Vivian leaning toward the notion of him being a rapist had made him so angry he could have ground his own teeth to powder by the way he was working his jaw.

Vivian held her ground. "I hear you, but you, just telling me that, isn't good enough."

His face was florid, the icy glare in his eyes made her spine turn cold in a way it never had before. Before, Tucker John was no longer strapped down to a bed, paralyzed from the waist down. Now he stood on two solid legs glaring down at her with fiery indignation. All he had to do was grab her and—

"I ain't that fool you call your husband," he spat at her. "I'se a man of my word. If I says I'se gon' do something I make good on my promise, positive or no."

Vivian swallowed down the dryness in her throat, careful not to avert her gaze. She couldn't show him weakness. "That's exactly why I insist that you take the implant and the medallion."

His scowl deepened. Vivian's fingers grazed the intermezzo in her pocket. She prayed she wouldn't have to use it. But just like Tucker John had demands, so did she and he wearing the medallion, and accepting the implant was one of them.

She said, "Not too long ago, you swore before God that you would kill me, remember? You being a man of your word is all the more reason for me to put you under restriction."

Snarling, he plopped down in place, thrusting the medallion's cord over his head and neck, and with an irritated sweep of his hand showed his yielding.

Vivian released the breath she had been holding, taking the seat across from him. "I'm going to place the sensor just beneath your skin," she said. "The medallion works in tandem with it and allows intermezzo pausing without an actual intermezzo being present. If you are anywhere inside the house, besides your bedroom, without the medallion on, the sensor beneath your skin will activate."

Tucker John's fist clenched and a deeper red began to grow up his neck and saturate his face. Feigning calm, but adding a hint of force to her voice she said, "If you're in the house or on the property and seem as a threat, at any time, I will use a small remote to freeze you as well. I can and will override the sensors program for my and Lourdes' safety. Understood?"

His gunmetal eyes burned unblinkingly into hers, but he said nothing.

Vivian shifted her weight and gave him a scowl of her own. "At the end of the day, Tucker John, I'm not you and you're not John Jay. You want freedom. This is the only option. It's the medallion or you forfeit the use of your legs, one of your arms, and will have to use a house-sled to travel on. So what's it going to be?"

Tucker John gave a derisive snort and folded his arms across the breadth of his chest. The strain of his solid arms pushed beneath his linen sleeves until the fabric was taut as a drum. The evidence that he wanted to take hold of her and snap her in two, but he was doing his best to keep his hands to himself, was seen in his posture.

"What do you think, Viv? I got this stupid thang around my neck, ain't I?"

Her mouth wavered. "Good. As I said, as long as you're in your room you don't need to wear the medallion."

A sharp smile contorted his face, sarcasm lacing his response. "Thank you kindly for your beaming generosity. How shall I ever repay you?"

Vivian sensed the threat within the question. Tucker John was scheming alright, but there was no need to address that at the moment. She would just keep her eye on him until the Cleric's Team Review was behind them, and the Co-op harvested and delivered. What choice did she have?

(The Present hour)

Vivian heard Tucker John's footsteps move away from the window. After that evening, and the minor surgery she had done on him, she wondered if the implant underneath the skin of his inner left ankle was causing him pain and keeping him awake. She laughed at the ridiculous thought. Tucker John had endured far worse than what she had given him that evening and kept going.

Apart from the implant being the size of a flattened mustard seed, it would go unnoticed by the clerics, and Tucker John would not run the risk of agitating it since he had such a wide gait.

She pulled back the bed sheets and slid underneath them. They were cold against her skin. She wasn't used to that. John Jay always went to bed before she did and had warmed the bed for her.

Her chest constricted. What was she going to do if she couldn't find him? How could she return home alone? Apart from having to live with her own gaping wound from having lost him, how was she going to be able to look his mother in the eye and tell her that she had lost her only son, no, her only child, and only living relative?

She rolled over on her side in a fetal position as the ache gripped her. Try as she might, she knew she was not going to get very much sleep that night.

CHAPTER 24

Prisoner or not, Tucker John had never had it so nice. He reckoned if he was going to be caged it might as well be a gilded cage. He had grown used to suffocating heat, water that was as warm and murky as urine, clothes stiff from dirt and sweat, lying on straw, bug-infested, ticks or even out in the elements.

Truth was he didn't have to grow used to any of it, the good or the bad, least of all the straw ticks. Tucker John had not known any better for most of his life. He had even believed the straw ticks were a grand step forward from laying on the floorboards and patch-worked fabric that he had slept on as a child—when he wasn't hiding in God's nature from his daddy—and clear up until the day he had earned his name 'Tucker'.

Now he had a bed, a real four post bed fit with fine linens. Nothing was threadbare. He couldn't even raise a complaint about the bed he had slept on in the lab. Even that was like sleeping on a dream. He had been given fresh clothes to wear each day, too, even if they reminded him of undergarments.

Vivian's house was surprisingly cool compared to the humidity that clung in the air outside, and the water he drank was as good as wine! Even the food he had been given was rich. Soup wasn't anything but dressed up liquid, but it had been tasty and filling. He had never eaten so well, even with all the money he had earned as a bounty hunter and top-notch overseer.

For him to be her prisoner, Vivian Leona had treated him extremely well.

He frowned not knowing what to make of it. It mostly chaffed his hide. He wanted to believe it was only because she needed him to pretend to be John Jay, be slave labor, but she had treated him well before the Team Review or Co-op was even mentioned.

He lay back letting his head rest against the soft, cool pillows, crossing his feet as he smiled briefly before the screaming red knot on his ankle jeered at him. He sat up and ran his thumb across it. The heat from the bath he had taken had soothed it so that he could hardly feel the pain of it anymore, no matter how dull of a pain it was. The implant Vivian had given him reminded him of a mosquito bite, slightly puffy and red. The blasted thing even had the gall to itch!

He touched it again and the roughness of his hands brought to mind the softness of hers. She ended up having to touch him quite a bit before the day was through and although every touch of her hands meant a loss to him he couldn't say he hadn't enjoyed her hands being on him. He was a warm-blooded man after all.

Had the tables been turned, had he been the one putting an implant in her, he would have done everything possible to cause her pain. That was his way when it came to his enemies. He made sure to make them suffer. That's how he got folks to respect him. If his name and face were associated with a pain they would never forget, they would never cross him again.

Vivian had not treated him so. She did put his arms in restraints before she got started with things, and he had let her. She touched him so delicately, numbing the area of his ankle before inserting the implant. He had flinched from the dull pinch and pressure, a swear word, and several grumbles passed his drawn lips.

Vivian gingerly steadied his foot. Looking up at him she had apologized for hurting him. He met her sincere gaze with a scowl.

When she was done with that she went to work on his hair. He had known that he was going to have to be shorn like a lamb, but he had not expected her to be the one to do so.

(Earlier that evening)

His hands were fisted, clenched hard against the restraints. His jaw was just as taut. It wasn't the shaving and cutting that bothered him, it was Vivian coming at him with the razor that made him tense.

She was right, he didn't trust her.

"I'll cut your hair first, before I shave you." She said.

"Why can't I shave my own self? I done it since I'se a man? I know my way 'round a razor."

Vivian considered him for a moment before setting the razor down and reaching for a brush instead. "If the tables were turned, would you give me a razor?" She waited for his response. He kept his mouth closed. "Exactly. I realize I'm going to have to earn some level of your trust, just like you have to earn mine."

She stood behind him, just out of sight and began pulling her fingers through his long hair. It was well past his shoulders. Tucker John hadn't properly combed or cut in ages. He flinched when her fingers caught in a knotted patch of it. Again she apologized. Still, he said nothing. Slowly she brush through the long strands, sectioning them off then working through them until they shinned.

He felt himself relax even though he had wanted to stay angry, resist her. But her hands on his scalp did something to him. Curse it all if he weren't the dog he had argued against being, and she hadn't found that sweet spot behind his ear that might as well have made his leg go to kicking, the way he succumbed to her touch.

She worked silently, wetting his hair and cutting it. When she was finished she reached for the razor again. By then, he'd all but fallen asleep with the brushing, and cutting, that he didn't resist her, even as the sharp blade slid from the bass of his throat, and over his jawline. When she was finished, she wiped his face down with a warm, damp towel. Even that was gentle.

Sitting down in front of him she studied her work, but only for a few quick moments before taking her hands and readjusting the hair that she had left on his head. One eye narrowed and her bottom lip drawn in, she brought some of the hair at the top of his scalp up and over a bit before smoothing back the shorter hairs that edged his face.

Tucker John's eyes stayed closed as her warm, soft hands, gently moved across his temples and passed over his ears as she brought the direction of the hairs together at the back of his head. She did so several times before she finally stopped. By then, he was done for.

The stillness caused his eyes to draw open to half-mast. Oh, Vivian Leona had worked some magic on him at that moment, worked him until anger was the farthest thing from his mind. He forced himself to swallow.

Vivian's arms were still behind his head when their gazes locked. Her hazel-brown eyes sparked and seemed to melt like chocolate, making his stomach flip, and his mouth run dry. She was still a female after all. There was that pressure too, the shout in her gaze he was growing accustomed to, except this time it wasn't a shout that met him, there wasn't even a line. He didn't know what it was. Whatever he was looking into made him feel alive, exhilarated like he was free falling, and hell would be iced over before he lied and said he didn't like it or want it.

He sucked in a breath to speak, but her fingers stilled his lips. He wasn't in pain nor was he delirious. He could've shaken her off but he didn't dare.

Vivian's expression shifted, turning from the open curiosity to pain and guilt. She shook her head. "Don't...say anything," she whispered, her voice strained. She drew her fingers away and stood up, turning her back to him, moving out of his reach. At that moment he cursed himself for having let her tie him down. Had his arms not been restrained he would have certainly taken hold of her that very instant, and worked her with a bit of magic of his own.

No, he wouldn't have forced her to lay with him, but he would have definitely stolen a kiss, sampled a taste of her pretty mouth and full lips with his own dancing slowly and gently with hers, until he left her dizzy and breathless, like putty sliding through his fingertips.

He smiled at her back, knowing had he done so she would have slapped him clean across the face, maybe even given him a nice shiner over it. Vivian was definitely the kind to do so and he would have let her. He would have even taken being completely restrained again because of it.

A kiss like that would have been worth it.

His gaze drew up the back of her frame from her feet to her crown. No, she most certainly was not the Vivian he knew, her smarts aside. A man remembered the silhouette of a woman, the nuisances, slopes, and curves of her even shrouded in darkness when he had been with her enough times. Vivian Leona didn't have his Vivian's hips or thighs, her solid waistline or the slope of fuller breasts.

This woman may have had a better diet than his, but she didn't have the same roundness to her. Her shape was much quieter, understated like a sweet whisper. It was less provoking to his senses and baser desires, and yet, somehow all of her was provoking his senses and desires at that very moment. What she lacked in shape she made up for in the way she carried herself. She had a confident, steady fire that could burn or simply warm the bones. Enemy or not, Tucker John was not blind, and he was far from immune to it. He knew that now.

Vivian's temperament stirred him on the inside something fierce. It was like a quiet storm, not hot, not cold, almost a mixture of both. It was like humidity that had a chill to it. He didn't know how to describe it exactly, it mostly made him fighting mad, but in the spaces between her touch, and gaze, and touch again….

He settled for the momentary confusion and the sudden delight it had brought to him. One thing he knew for certain was he wouldn't be calling her Vivian anymore. He was just going to keep calling her 'Viv'. She was indeed her own woman.

She incited him, even more, when she turned back toward him until he noticed the spark in her had completely gone, leaving behind a dull, glazed-over expression and lightless eyes.

(The present hour)

Tucker John stared at the wall recalling what had taken place. Viv had pulled a small container from her pocket and dropped something into her mouth that extinguished the light in her eyes.

He shook his head. What difference did it make? The woman was still his enemy, her and that cockroach Lourdes! He needed to stop thinking about the silky heat of her skin, wondering about the taste of it, and concern himself with saving his own!

He gingerly touched the roundness of the sensor on his ankle. It wasn't deep. All he needed was a clean knife and a steady hand, and then he would be rid of it. He had carved out enough metal balls to be able to withstand such a pain. His only problem was getting his hand on a knife sharp enough to do the task.

He didn't fret. He could use a sharpened stone if the need arose.

Standing again, he went to one of the several windows of his room. There were sixteen all total; six on the left side of the room, six on the right and two right at his back when he came up the stairs into the room. There was also one in his bathroom, and one he reckoned was in the storage space next to it.

Windows. He had already looked out of most of them. There were no trees close enough for him to latch on to and shimmy down to the ground, and he was very high up. Jumping straight down was out of the question.

He had no immediate plans for escape. Something like that was going to take time, but he needed to know that he could get out of the room if the need arose. He finally looked at the linens on his bed. There were enough of them to rope together and they were certainly strong enough for such a need.

A tiny seed of guilt tried to wiggle its way to life in him. He plucked it out with a growl. He wasn't plotting to break his word, no sir! He promised to let Viv put the bug in him. He never promised to leave it there, and he certainly hadn't given her his word that he would not try to leave. On the contrary, he had warned her that he was going to get the upper hand, and he would.

He gave a good hearty yawn and felt sleep suddenly hit him between the eyes. It had been a very long day. He made his way to his bathroom, relieved himself and then took an appraising look at his reflection in the mirror. He was looking at a stranger. He hadn't seen that much of his face in years and neither had the sun. Viv had given him a cream to put on his skin to help even out the coloring. Just to be contrary he wanted to not use it, but he did look like a raccoon by the eyes.

Begrudgingly, he slathered it on his face and finally made his way back to his bed, turning out the light with a simple wave of his hand. The linens were cool and welcoming to him. He felt his heavy eyelids closing and a smile bloom on his bare face. He had much to do in the days to come. It was best he got some rest in the meantime.

Those two wenches down below had no idea what he had in store for them.

CHAPTER 25

Vivian waited for Tucker John in her office. The integrated display of her clipboard illuminated from her desktop, but she paid it no mind. Instead, she continued to stare intensely out the window, chewing on the tip of her thumb. She hadn't even noticed that he'd entered the room until he rapped his knuckle against the doorframe. She jumped at the sound.

Shifting her gaze to the clock on the wall, she addressed him. "Good morning, Tucker John. You're right on time, excellent."

"You wasn't at breakfast." He lingered at the threshold of the room.

Vivian stared at him, unable to read his expression. She ceased to try. "I wasn't hungry." More than anything she felt sick to the stomach. The last thing she had in mind was breakfast. She hadn't slept a wink either. Queasiness aside, at least she didn't feel irritable.

The *Paz*, she knew had side effects. "Take a seat, if you would please, and then we can get started. I have a lot of things I need to see about today apart from grooming you for the clerics." She pointed toward the chair across from her. "They're going to want a thorough progress report, and I honestly don't have that yet."

Tucker John folded his arms across his chest but didn't move.

Vivian felt his eyes on her. It made her skin tingle. "Is there something wrong? Did," she raised a brow and touched the skin beneath her eyes. "Did the salve irritate your skin? It looks more even-toned from here."

Tucker John shrugged and finally entered the office. He sat down and jabbed a finger in her direction. "We have an agreement. You 'spose to eat every meal with me, you and your cream-colored wench—"

She sighed. *So much for not being irritated.* "You're angry about breakfast?"

"This ain't about no breakfast! I don't shine to being cheated is all. If you say you gon' do something, *do* it, 'specially if you think I'se 'spose to do what you ask of me."

"Tucker John, I didn't cheat you or default on my end of the agreement. You said I was to eat every meal with you—"

"Right. And you didn't."

"I didn't eat anything this morning. I got up, did my chores in prep for the Co-op delivery and then came straight here." She rubbed her forehead, her eyes fluttering shut. Nausea tickled the back of her throat. "I have no intentions of cheating you, not even with the trivial request you've made,"

She quickly raised her hands realizing her poor word choice. Tucker John was very sensitive to those sorts of things. One wrong word and the day would be spent arguing. "Trivial was the wrong word. What I mean to say is that that request is not as weighty as the others you've made. It pales in importance to things like you wanting to learn legal languages of the age, mechanics of computer systems, improving your literacy. That's what I meant." She offered a smile but met a stone expression.

"Every request I made is important. It's in your best interest to honor each of 'em."

Tempering her own ire, she pressed her lips. "Tucker John, don't threaten me."

"Not a threat, Viv. This 'bout respect. I don't care if your appetite is gone for the rest of your days, you had better be at that dining table for my next meal, and dare not miss another." He peered over at the clock. "Time is ticking. Clerics could be here any minute now. You gon' want me on my best behavior.

That's purchased at the price of your obedience to my every request." This time he did smile.

She leaned back in her chair. She had no illusions that their 'arrangement' was going to be anything but difficult. She was just hoping the difficulty would wait a day or two before rearing its ugly, little, head. "This isn't about respect for you, is it? This is about you trying to put a 'black female' in her place." She made quotation marks with her fingers.

He raised his chin, his gaze darkening. "Don't pretend to know me, Viv. I ain't no book for you to read. We have an agreement is all."

"From your end, it seems like more of a manipulative power play."

Tucker John raised his bare foot onto her desk. Dirt, evidence of his own work outdoors, caked his soles. Vivian grimaced as he pointed to the sensor underneath the skin of his ankle. "We both have our leveraging tools, don't we, Viv?" He put his leg down and rested his forearms on her desk. "Just don't miss another meal." He stared into her eyes.

"Fine. Now may we get started with your education?"

The two hours spent tutoring Tucker John on everything John Jay, was far more work than Vivian had anticipated. More than anything, she needed him to, not only look like her husband but carry himself like him. Reshaping Tucker John's gait was the easiest part of the entire process.

Tucker John told her that playing the part of a 'dandy' didn't take much practice. All he had to do was walk like he had a rod rammed up his nether parts and no one would be the wiser. To her chagrin, his mocking portrayal of what he thought John Jay might have walked like was spot on.

The speech therapy was not so easy. She had compiled several sound bites of John Jay speaking for him to copy. Sadly, she felt as if she would have made better headway cutting down a large tree with a steak knife than she was with getting Tucker

John to sound like John Jay. There was too much timber to his tone, never mind the near-impossible task of hardening his pronunciations.

He was just as frustrated as she was with the entire lesson. Vivian had heard more growling out of him in that short time period than she had during all the weeks he had been present.

She rubbed the back of her neck, before pressing her hands together in prayer position. "Please try not to use the contraction, 'ain't.' Remember to pronounce the 'R' in 'your', curve the 'U' in 'you', because the word is not pronounced 'ya,' and for the thousandth time, the only time you use any word that sounds like 'eyes' is when you are referring to the ones you see out of!" She smacked the desk and huffed, biting back a growl of her own. "And let's not forget your disappearing 'g's!"

Tucker John smacked the desk in turn. "Hell, Viv! Calm yo' self! I'se trying! You ain't got no patience, woman! We only been at this for an hour or so. I feel like I'se learning a new language o' somethin'!"

You are. It's called American Standard English! Biting her tongue, she rolled her eyes, more frustrated with herself than with him. He had been trying. She could tell by the way the bulge grew between his eyebrows that he was indeed putting forth a sincere effort. It was new and frustrating to him. What he had done for a living required very few words. He was a natural and skilled hunter, not a linguist.

Sighing, she stopped the next recording before it began. She couldn't bear to watch the holographic markers that Tucker John would produce with his spoken attempts at being John Jay contradict the originals one more time. The discrepancy was a glaring reminder that this man was not, and would never be, John Jay no matter how much work he put towards trying.

"Let's just leave this, for now, Tucker John." She calibrated his clipboard with hers, making sure the sound bites were ready for him to practice later on, preferably alone. It would also give him time to figure out how clipboards worked. Really, she was killing several birds with one stone. She slid the device toward him. Brow still furrowed, he lifted it from the desk, swallowing its size in his large hand.

She said, "That is your clipboard. You'll be able to gain access to any information that you'll need from within it, or for specific purposes, any computer station in the house. As it projected the sound bites, it can project anything else that you decide to access. It also acts as a writing station should you care to keep notes. Of course, it does several other things, but we'll try and keep things simple for now."

"You say I can connect it elsewhere, even the nexus gate?" He looked up at her, his brow still tied up in a blond knot.

Vivian took a few moments to answer. She already had a headache. She really didn't want another argument. "No, I have not calibrated that clipboard to access the nexus gate. That wasn't part of our agreement. You asked to know about the nexus gate. I've shown it to you, and I have no problem talking to you more about it, but as far as you accessing files from it, trying to operate it, absolutely not." She shook her head.

His expression darkened. "And why can't I learn how to use it?"

"Think of the nexus gate as another razor that I'm not entrusting to your hands. Besides, you have enough things to learn. You shouldn't even be worried about the nexus gate, let alone, one that is malfunctioned and unpredictable."

Tucker John's eyes followed her as she rounded the desk and stretched. Vivian couldn't help but think of him as a calculated beast stalking its prey. She casually slid her hands into the pockets of her linen pants. Her fingers quickly found the remote to the sensor in his ankle. The shot of adrenaline his stalking eyes gave her was all she needed to take a firmer hold of the urgency to find John Jay.

Tucker John sucked his teeth. "And where are you going?"

She stole another look at the clock. "I have work to do. I still have a reputation to uphold, and tasks to be completed. We did come to the 4030's for a purpose. I intend to accomplish it no matter what." *For the martyred we march on lest the living die.* She would keep marching on for John Jay. She would find him and the root cause of the Revolution. That was their dream. She wouldn't lose that, too.

"You can spend some time in the library studying whatever it is you like. I, however, suggest you practice more of John Jay's vernacular. Who knows, the clerics could come today. It's best that you're as ready as you possibly can be. We'll be clear after three this afternoon. Protocol prohibits visits after three. I'm going to be in and around the lab for the rest of the afternoon."

"Except for lunch time." His gaze bored into hers.

Vivian was tempted to ask him why he was so obsessed with her eating with him. She quickly reminded herself that it was his power play, but something within her told her it was far more than that. "I'll be there for lunch, appetite or not. If you have any other questions, Lourdes can help you with those."

Tucker John shook his head. Throwing his arm over the back of his chair he said, "Lourdes is gone. She left right after breakfast, said something 'bout tending to her mama."

Vivian folded her arms across her chest. "Again? She was just there the other day." She frowned. Something was going on with Alba Berry, she prayed it wasn't serious.

Tucker John continued. "She said she would be back before supper, but lunch was up to you to tend to."

If Lourdes was going this much to see her mother, she must have been worse off than Vivian thought, especially if she hadn't taken the time to tell Vivian that she was leaving. It was that or she was still angry over Tucker John being allowed to move freely about the house and grounds, and she needed an excuse to leave. If it wasn't for him, Vivian would have gone to check on Lourdes' mother as well. She really liked the woman.

But who is checking on John Jay while you're looking for the start of revolutions and paying visits to people who are safe and sound in their own beds? Who's going to find your husband, Vivian? That's your job.

She chewed her lip as if it were her very thoughts she was gnawing on. She still needed to check on things with Lourdes. "Okay, well I'll be around the lab if you need anything. If it can wait, please, let it wait. If the doorbell rings, don't answer it. I'll see to that, and lunch apparently. Also, if you decide to study out on the property be cognizant about the perimeters I've set for you."

He stood. "I thought you said I had access to the whole of the grounds. How am I supposed to get them chores done on a short leash?"

"I did, and I didn't put you on a short leash. I just don't want anyone growing suspicious, asking you questions that you don't have the answers to. We don't get company all that often, but neighbors are neighbors and they know us well enough to recognize that you're being peculiar as John Jay. As you well know, chores are done in the morning,"

"Chores is done when you get 'em done. Could take all day."

"Just be careful, alright." She began to gather up a few items from the desk to take with her to the lab. A framed picture tumbled to the floor at Tucker John's feet. He reached down and grabbed it before she could. The image became animated. Tucker John startled and nearly dropped it but quickly gained his composure staring at it with a keen eye.

The animated image was one of John Jay. When the image was still, he was smiling brightly—the perfect candid shot captured in the midst of laughter. He had his arm slung around his best friend, Marcus Taylor's neck. Now, he was laughing. The sound made her dizzy with guilt.

"Who's that buck next to your John? Is that your brother?" Tucker John stared at the picture a few seconds more before handing it to her.

She scowled at the word 'buck,' and carefully pulled the frame from his hand, pausing the image once more. Her brow met. "No, that *man* is not my brother. I don't have any siblings." She ran her fingers down the glass of the frame as if smoothing it out from the fall. "That is Marcus Taylor."

"Who's he?"

Vivian closed her eyes as her stomach clenched. She didn't want to think about Marcus. "He's John Jay's best friend. They're like brothers. They've known and loved each other since infancy. He is a Minister of Time as well, in a different division of the Clergy." Her voice grew quiet.

"Hm." Tucker John shrugged. He didn't have any other response than that. Turning on his heels, he left for the library without another word.

CHAPTER 26

Vivian set the picture frame back in its place and felt a role of anxiety set off a storm in her belly. Marcus wouldn't take it well knowing that his best friend was missing. It would do absolutely nothing for her and Marcus' non-existing relationship to find out that she had lost John Jay. No, it would only cause a war between them. Worse, he would do everything possible to destroy what little reputation she had left within the Ministry of Time.

Marcus had never supported her and John Jay's union. He said that settling was the worst thing that John Jay could do. He had even gone so far as to tell Vivian the same thing. Sure, he said it was nothing personal, argued instead that he knew his friend loved another woman, loved his first assignee. John Jay still loved the other woman even though it had been a few years since she had rejected him.

Tara, her name was Tara.

Vivian argued that there had been enough time to silence the wound in John Jay's heart, that compatibility, and mutual respect, could and would, win out. Marcus only insisted that sometimes time was not enough and that compatibility was irrelevant.

Looking back over the strained years and the feigned perfection she and John Jay had displayed as husband and wife, she hated that Marcus had been right, no matter how diligently she was working to prove him wrong yet again.

She could still remember the day Marcus confronted her. She even recalled the scent in the air as his words thrust through her like a blunt knife breaking through bone….

(Several years prior)
Vivian had been hungry, but she wasn't anymore. The smell of Peking Duck had gone from tantalizing to nauseating all in the matter of seconds laden with ill-spoken words. Marcus Taylor looked squarely down at her. He wasn't a man of minced words or one who got muddled up in distracting emotions. He wasn't like John Jay who wore his heart on his sleeve.

Vivian kept her expression cool even though she flinched as if he had stung her. He had stung her.

Marcus took her coolness as his cue to continue. "It's not you, Vivian. I would be remiss not to state the fact that you are extremely intelligent, you have excellent pedigree in your career field, and you are tenacious. Everyone can see that you have a brilliant future ahead of you. John Jay does well on his own, but at your side, the sky will be the limit for him within surveillance. He knows that. And let's not forget you're extremely beautiful. I get why he accepted this assignment of marriage to you."

Vivian blinked far deeper than she had intended. Marcus pityingly touched her arm. She gently pushed his hand away. "Are you insinuating that the only reason he would unite with me is that I have a pretty face and can advance his career? You do know there are more variables applied to career marriage assignments apart from career field."

Marcus' dark brown eyes didn't waver. They were as emotionless as his dark, brown face. "Vivian, this is nothing personal against you. And I'm certainly not trying to belittle you. But let's be clear, career aside, your qualities aside, I know John—"

"I know him too!" She interjected.

"You know what a computer analysis, simulated Field scenarios, and a few short meetings have told you. I, however, have known him all of my life, all of his life. He doesn't love you. I don't think he ever will. And I don't believe you will be satisfied with that in the long run, just like I know he won't."

Vivian took a step back. "Who are you to make that kind of judgment call?" She looked away from him. She was never one to shy away from any challenge, but there was something so formidable about Marcus Taylor that she felt like she needed to escape, like she was being bullied. "This conversation is over, Marcus," she took a few more steps away before he grabbed her arm.

"*Listen*, Vivian," his voice lowered, he practically whispered. The severity in his tone stilled her. "John Jay is still stuck on his first match. Tara hurt him. No! He ripped his own heart out and gave it to her. It's gone. Had you been first, had Tara never happened, you would have my blessing—"

"That was a long time ago," she could hear the tears in her own voice. She tried to pull her arm free.

Marcus loosened his grip. "It wasn't long enough, not for him. I've never seen him that low," his face grew into an unreadable expression as he reminisced. Closest Vivian could think to describe it was 'troubled.' Marcus looked troubled.

He continued, "...and I promise you, he's still climbing out of the darkness. He's closer to normal than he has ever been, but he's not there yet. Not quite."

"How do you know I'm not the one he needs to help him recover?" She forced her jaw to still and her eyes to look into his. Why had she agreed to meet him for lunch?

Marcus only shook his head. "Vivian, you're a smart woman. Don't put yourself in that emotional trap. You may win yourself some gratitude for helping him heal in the end, but you won't win his heart, and at what cost? Do yourself a favor, and walk away. Ask for a new assignment. Neither of you has confirmed your match agreement, so just walk away." He released her arm.

Vivian's nostrils flared. "Aren't you asking me to do to your friend the same thing that, what's her name, Tara, did?"

Marcus lowered his head, his eyes closed as he bit his lip. "No, Vivian, this is different."

"How is this different?" She all but shouted. Several heads turned and looked their direction, abandoning their conversations and Chinese street food out of curiosity.

Marcus ignored them. "He loved, Tara. He still does. I'd go as far to say that he is obsessed. But he doesn't love you."

"He will. In time, John Jay will love me, as I will love him. All it takes is time. We will be a success in surveillance. We are both dedicated to the Ministry. I'll make him happy."

"And what about you? Who's going to make you happy? I promise you it won't be John Jay, not with him constantly daydreaming about an elusive woman."

The two stared at each other for several tense moments before Marcus finally broke the silence. "I've said all that I can to you. And believe it or not, it's for your own good as much as it is for John Jay's. This marriage is a disaster waiting to happen. This is his last shot at trying to heal himself of Tara, and it won't work. He's using you as a rebound and you're playing right into it. And when the smoke clears you will only end up just as wounded as he is if you don't listen. I'm asking you to listen." He dipped his head in a slight salute before turning to walk away.

"I won't," Vivian said to his back. "I won't listen, because you don't know everything. You can't see into the future."

Marcus' back went rigid. Closing the gap that had grown between them, he faced her again. "You're a big girl, Vivian Leona, so you can do as you please. But I'm warning you that if my best friend ends up more lost because of you, you will have me to deal with. I can promise you that."

Vivian went to respond but was quickly cut off.

"Just. Walk. Away." With that Marcus disappeared into the crowd, his warning fire branding itself on Vivian's mind and eating up her conscience like his long strides ate up the road before him.

(Present Day)

Leaning against her desk, Vivian recalled the warning in Marcus' words. Her head was suddenly pounding more than it already had been. She couldn't seem to figure out what would be worse if she failed to find her husband; John Jay's mother's tears, Vivian's own heart turning to dust, or Marcus Taylor putting her head on a silver platter, right before Tucker John sucked the meat from her bones.

Drawing in a trembling breath, she clutched the white obsidian at her neck and blessed it with a kiss. She prayed she wouldn't have to find out. She just needed to find John Jay and everything would be alright.

CHAPTER 27

(Year 6037)

Marcus Taylor rubbed his eyes with the heels of his hands. He had pulled an all-nighter at the Cleric's Office, again. It was all part of his duty as Surveillance Monitor. Whenever a team of surveyors was sent into the Field, he would go with them, get them situated, and make certain they followed the instructed protocol for timeline insertion. When they were extracted from the Field, he was the one to meet them and ensure they'd exited their host timeline in an orderly manner before escorting them back to their present time, also a matter of protocol.

It was an honorable job within the Ministry of Time, but it wasn't the type of position that earned him many friends. Grading and rating each team and often penalizing them with sanctions if things were not done by the books, generally earned its fair share of frowns. His last Field recovery had been a complete disaster which left him with miles of data and reports to be filed. If he had his way, that team would never be allowed in the Field again.

Collins, his wife of nearly a decade, was going to be furious with him again for staying the night at the office. Even after so many years of marriage, Collins still didn't like it when he was gone from home longer than the two weeks per month that he was expected to be away. She would cut her eyes at him and give him the silent treatment, serve him cold dinner when he got home. If she said anything to him at all, while she stewed, it would be 'family first, Marcus.'

Collins was a stay-at-home mother and artist. One of them had to be a constant in the lives of their children. Though Collins was rising in recognition in the art world, bills still had to be paid, and Marcus, spending one extra day away, wouldn't hurt anything.

In the end, he would have to woo her with pouting eyes and kisses behind her ear, just like she liked it. It was a glorious sacrifice he was willing to make. Eventually, Collins would yield to his advances and tell him again how much she loved his dark brown skin. She couldn't stay mad at him when she could smell his skin, she would say. She always said it was like art to her. There were archives filled with painted studies of him to prove it.

Marcus bit his full bottom lip with the anticipation of finally getting home to her. He hoped the kids would be in bed. Sometimes Collins let them stay awake just to get at him when he stayed at work so long—three mountains of love that he would have to climb in order to get to his queen. He adored his children but he wanted some alone time with his wife.

He looked at the motion photo of his children. The three of them ran in circles through their yard, bubbles streaming around them with laughter echoing from their smiling faces. They were getting so big. The thought made him frown. John Jay and Vivian were the children's godparents. They weren't even halfway through their ten-year surveillance yet. The kids would be almost as big as they were by the time they got back to their millennium. All that time would be lost; time they could never get back, even if it was for a good cause.

He laughed at his own hypocrisy. "I get it, Lord. I need to spend more time with my own family, even if what I'm doing here is for a good cause. I hear You loud and clear."

An exhausted yawn escaped his lips as he finished up the last of his reporting. He stopped and glanced around his office, an eerie tingle crawling with a chill across the back of his neck. He could have sworn he'd seen someone there, felt their presence in the room, but there was no one.

Shifting his shoulders and shaking off the feeling, he gathered his things. He turned out the lights in his office he headed for the front door, rapping his knuckles on the cleric's counter as he passed. "Hey Sinclair, they got you staying the night here, too? Don't fall asleep. I know how you kids are." He chuckled.

Sinclair, the interim desk cleric, waved her hand and smiled without taking her eyes from her clipboard. The holographic comic hovered in the air just above her lap. "Good night, Mr. Taylor. See you in the morning, assuming Mrs. Taylor doesn't kill you this time for being late."

Marcus clucked his teeth. "Ahhh she won't ever follow through with her threats. She couldn't live without me." He stopped at the door and turned around. John Jay and Vivian were on his heart again. "Hey, Sinclair?" He shifted the bag that hung over his shoulder.

Sinclair looked up at him from her clipboard. "Yes, Mr. Taylor?"

"Can you do me a quick favor, check and see if there are any status reports on surveillance team V.Leona-Spruce4034-44G.US?"

Sinclair nodded, hopped down from her seat and began her search. "Getting a head start on your next expedition? Pulling someone home early?"

Marcus shook his head. "Nope. Just checking up on my best friend is all."

Sinclair smiled, then frowned, her head leaning to the side like a puppy that had heard a high pitched noise. "Hmmm," she pushed her dark mop of hair back from her face and looked closer at the information. "That's bizarre."

Marcus stood on his tip toes and leaned over the high counter. He was six feet three inches tall. "What is it?"

Sinclair shook her head and then climbed back in her chair, clipboard in hand. "Your friend is fine."

Marcus raised a brow. It was moments like these that made him wonder why the Cleric's Office interned teenagers. "What do you mean, he's fine? You just said something was bizarre."

She waved her hand. "It must have been a glitch, it's probably nothing."

Marcus sat down his bag and made his way to Sinclair's side of the counter. "Our systems don't have glitches, Sinclair. What did you see?"

Sinclair moved her hair again and pointed at the viewing bay of the computer counter. "When I looked up the team there was a yellow marker for a Cleric's Team Review—"

Marcus' face contorted. "Team Review? Vivian Leona has never had a T.R."

"Well, that's what the system said at first, and then it was gone and everything was green. That's why I said it must have been a glitch. Or somebody in 4037 is negligent at the Cleric's Office and input the wrong information right before fixing it. People aren't perfect even if you think our systems are." She scrunched her nose and made a face.

"Don't be sassy, Sinclair." Marcus tugged the end of her hair and then looked at the viewing bay again. "Are you sure that's what you saw?"

She gave him another look. "Mr. Taylor, you're the one who's been up all day and all night. I've only been up for a few hours. I have these young eyes, too. I'm fit and ready to go. So, yes, I'm sure. If I see anything else come through that is about that team I'll let you know. No worries. You can trust me."

Marcus gave her an uncertain glance before curbing it with a smile. "Alright then. I'm off. You be good. I'll see you in the morning. And trash the sass or else when you become a surveyor I'll make each of your trips hardcore with all my regulations!" He winked at her before leaving through the door.

Sinclair playfully stuck out her tongue.

***

John Jay moved from the darkness of Marcus' office into the light of the Cleric's Office. Sinclair's head turned up in his direction. He went still. She, just like Marcus, had seen him in her periphery but had not seen him at the same time. He watched her head turn carefully about the office. Eventually, she shifted in her seat and turned her attention back to her clipboard.

Lourdes had gotten the message about the T.R just in time. Had she waited any longer he would have missed her warning and his moving the static he had previously moved would have been in vain. The damage would have already been done. He quickly filled the spaces in 4037 with tiny holes. The Cleric's Office would no longer remember a Team Assessment and Review needed to be conducted in 4037 for Vivian's team. Quinn Ellington was needed to sanction the surprise visit and she was out of the office for personal reasons. The message she'd left for whoever had taken her place had been intercepted by John Jay as well. In the end, there would be no record of a T.R in 6037 or 4037.

He breathed into his palms. The residue of the static felt like grit and glass against them, burning them with tiny little cuts each time he shifted moments and manipulated time. He clenched his jaw. He felt like he had rope burn. His first act of manipulating static had burned him so deeply, he'd fallen unconscious. Moving recent events in time was like slicing through them with hot iron, older moments was like massaging coarse sandpaper. He stole a glance at his hands. Even with his hollow shell, he could see what looked like blood on them. No matter, he could survive it. It would all be worth it in the end.

Vivian Leona has never had a T.R. Marcus' words only fueled his determination. Vivian. He still couldn't shake having loved her in a way, but the unending shadow she cast had made him resent her. He'd told her as much before they'd been assigned to 4037 before she requested the New Golden Age, and the right to discover the cause for the *Silent Revolution.*

We'll do this together. She'd said. *We'll call it the discovery of Vivian and John Jay Spruce. We'll work on us. All we need is time.*

How nice of her. He scowled at the memory. All of her bright ideas and yet she hadn't even realized that she still put her name before his even if she was willing to one day take his surname as her own.

It was always about her and her need to shine. But not anymore. He would have his double-win. He'd be the hero, named and decorated an expert surveillance specialist—as he should have been in the first place—and not just a Tech, once he revealed his findings regarding static. And Vivian would get none of the glory.

He'd had time to tighten up his plan of action against her. He'd say his discovery drove her mad. Vivian was the ambitious one, after all. She was the Lead. She wanted the glory, but he was the one to make the discovery and thus the one in line to get it, and she just couldn't deal with it.

Her bringing in the Animal from 1837, trying to domesticate him, was all in an attempt to get rid of John Jay and have the Animal be her puppet in his place. Madness in the Field happened every so often. Vivian would be painted as one to lapse. John Jay, however, would have to destroy the Animal once it turned on Vivian and killed her as vile beasts from his timeline often did women of color. Then he and Lourdes, the woman he was always meant to be with, would be together.

But had that yellow marker remained in place, Marcus would have volunteered to see what was going on with him and Vivian. Marcus would have argued that something had to be wrong with them and would have requested a special expedition to see about them. Because Marcus was in such great standing and had so much pull within the Cleric's Office, his request would have been granted.

That couldn't happen. He couldn't let Marcus see any of this. Not yet. If Marcus knew what he was doing, it would kill him. He would hurt over Vivian's death. He had come to like her, John Jay knew that. Her being gone would be hard on him and Collins, it would even hurt John Jay's mother.

He had gone to see her too, planted a kiss on Emlen's cheek while she slept. Even in his hollow form, he felt the warmth of his mother's skin on his lips. He was going to miss her terribly.

He had even gone to see Tara. She hadn't known he was there either. She would have blushed to know he watched her bathe, ached for her with a hunger as he watched her long, blonde tresses, slick with water, hug her curves. He'd watched her before. He'd watched her for nearly a year after their breakup, and for the longest time, she hadn't known. When she'd found out, when she caught him, she responded with such fear that it all but blackened his heart. How could she not have known how much he loved her?

Tonight though, he'd gone as far as to touch her. He'd smelled her skin while she slept, and toyed with the blonde curls that wound lazily around his fingertips. Had her husband not been there he would have laid next to her.

His lust for her gnawed at him. He wondered if his watching Tara, his want for her, was a betrayal to Lourdes. He'd told himself it wasn't. Looking at Tara was like looking at Lourdes. They were two equal drops of water. Tara's hair was long like Vivian's but she was the exacting likeness of Lourdes. The only difference was that Lourdes loved him. She loved him unto death. She craved his closeness and welcomed the way he watched her, protected her. Lourdes would never leave him or break his heart, never, not like Tara had. She'd never look at him with fear.

He flexed his hands and his palms protested. He would let them rest a bit before he took to moving any more static. He needed to create white noise in 6037 and even in some parts of the prior years involving his and Vivian's team. The Cleric's Office needed to forget about them until 4039, and then when they realized they had fallen off the grid with no cleric reports, a red marker would rise and a Monitor would be sent to the 4030's from 6039 to see about them.

He and Lourdes would stick to their story about the static, Vivian, and the Animal. They would tell how the Cleric's Office of the 4030's had cut them off because there was no record of them there either. They would be made like Adam and Eve in a garden in the American South, left to support each other and ultimately love each other.

It was a devastatingly beautiful plan.

***

(Year 4037)
Magnus shifted the conical hat on his head. Even in the coverage and shade of Balm Hill's healthy foliage, it was a very difficult task to keep out of the licking heat and fire of the mid-day Georgian sun. He exhaled and tasted his sweat as it rolled back onto his lips and tongue.

He was several steps beyond miserable in that heat.

The Instrument's prongs were coated thick with more static dust. Lourdes Berry was back in her mother's home again. Ironically, He had not seen or heard anything from Alba Berry, Lourdes' mother. That was a yellow marker that would have to be sorted. He already assumed the worse in her regard.

He sat listening and recording all that he heard. Lourdes and John Jay had had a very short-lived conversation the other night, something about an animal being let loose in the house and a Team Assessment and Review being scheduled. Magnus had checked the clerical schedules the following morning and all evidence of a scheduled T.R. had been erased. However, there was still a note from Quinn for a comfort basket to be sent to Vivian because of the inconvenience. Those were several more marks that were verified in green in his voicepod. Lourdes had also been instructed by John Jay to continue on with her side of the plan.

Magnus had a vague understanding of what Lourdes was supposed to do, minus a few hardcore details. He would verify what he could when the evidence presented itself.

He repositioned himself and took a gulp of cool water before pouring some of it over his face and down the back of his neck. He had been gathering evidence for the last few hours and it seemed like it was never-ending. He would melt before it was all said and done.

He should have packed a lunch.

CHAPTER 28

Thunder rolled overhead with such a force that it shook the house. Lightning struck in the distance and flashed enough light to make Tucker John's pupils constrict. It was the light or the fact that for the seventh time in three weeks he watched Lourdes creep out of the house in the middle of the night when she thought no one was the wiser.

He realized that Lourdes had probably gone off far more times than he had known but when he had taken notice he noted that she always left on the days that she had stirred up trouble between him and Viv. And now the lava-hot tension between them was nearly unbearable.

It baffled him how Viv in one moment could go from being agreeable and tender with him, like when she put the sensor in his ankle and shaved him, to being an absolute harpy out for his blood.

It had been twenty-three days exactly since she had let him roam free and within that span of time Lourdes had managed to keep him and Viv at odds for a complete week when he put the days together. That was a lot of undermining and clever scheming Lourdes had done. And in all of it, she had mostly managed to keep her nose clean and make him look completely at fault. Little did she know it was only because he was allowing her to.

It was a risky war tactic on his part to play along, put on the show of belligerence even though the truth was he did want to ring Lourdes' scrawny neck. But the end would surely justify the means. So, he allowed himself the freedom of a good rant just to gauge how either wench would respond. He only gave them what they needed to see, baited them enough to learn their ways.

Every situation he walked into was no different than the day Lourdes had tossed cold soup at him and convinced Viv that he had thrown it about the room in a fit of rage. The only problem he was facing with his tactics wasn't that he gave Lourdes the exact reaction she was fishing for but rather he couldn't quite gauge Viv's.

Viv was completely unsteady and growing worse with each day. It was something he had begun to attribute to the tiny pills she kept hidden in her pocket, the ones she slipped beneath her tongue more often as of late. Because of their effect, he couldn't tell whether the woman was coming or going, even though he had a pretty solid read on Lourdes and had for a very long time.

Viv occasionally leaned to Tucker John's side of things but more often than not, she sided with Lourdes. After all, she didn't trust him, and she knew Lourdes, or at least she believed she did. *If the woman only knew the truth...* Viv's ignorance only played in his favor. If she was blind to Lourdes then she wasn't going to see what he had coming for her no matter how closely she kept her eye on him.

He'd managed to glean enough about the duo to be able to construct his plan of assault and Viv had given him everything he needed to know about dear old Johnny-boy. But what he needed most was to get both Viv and Lourdes securely under his thumb while ensuring that John Jay never came back, or at least if he did, he would be just as trapped as his wenches that he, too, would be securely under Tucker John's boot.

He hadn't yet decided if he wanted to blackmail the trio into stepping aside while he disappeared in another timeline, or if he would take Johnny-boy's life altogether. Truth was, he was leaning more towards the former option, having already firmly decided he was not going back to 1837, ever.

He had no plans of dying before a ripe old age, especially not because of drowning in a mud puddle contrary to what Viv had told him was destined to happen. He had resolved, a long time ago, that he would be the one to write his destiny and no one else. Granted, he had sworn to Jesus that he would turn his life over to Him if He got him out of the prison he was in with Viv.

The good Lord had honored him and he was mostly out, mostly, so he had to consider that the Great Almighty had a say so about what his future would hold. Nevertheless, going anywhere without electricity, indoor plumbing, modern medicine, and conveniences was totally out of the question. He'd been spoiled while in his binds and would except nothing less than better than what he'd recently experienced.

What he'd learned from his solid *Spadds* treatments gave him a lot of excellent options. The early 5000's held a lot of promise, should he determine he was not going to just take over John Jay's cushy life. Taking his life would mean being stuck for good with the likes of Vivian Leona. That he couldn't cotton to. No sir! The simple-minded Vivian was hard enough to keep in line at times and she knew Tucker John was her better. Viv would only conform for a hot minute before she rebelled and pulled the rug clean out from under him. He could tell that by the glint in her brown eyes. She was a formidable foe, sure enough.

Fact was, the woman thought too much and had far more of an opinion than any female should have, especially a black one. That was evident by her latest show of reprimand.

This last collision with her and Lourdes had left him locked in his room for the greater part of the day and all of that evening. Truth be told, his temper had gotten a hold of him and his mouth went off. He was still angry over it. Viv came right back at him with a fierceness. She laid into him with a tongue lashing that made the hairs on his neck stand on end. Thinking about it made him bristle. That woman's mouth was fierce when she was out of patience. To prove her power over him, she froze him, locked him in his room like he was a child, and sent Lourdes up with one 'orphaned' meal that was overdone, and had clearly fallen on the floor. That was Lourdes' special gift to him. The plate of dirt-kissed vegetables sat untouched by the door.

It only made him angrier than a hornet when Viv dropped that word 'grooming' on him again. He didn't like it one bit! It only fueled his suspicions of her, that she thought of him as trash in need of cleaning, or worse yet, a tramp dog at her mercy—an animal. He gripped the leather strap around his neck with white knuckles. The intermezzo medallion she'd put on him only fortified what she thought of him.

"I'ma fix both them wenches!" He grumbled along with his stomach. He couldn't figure out who he wanted to strike more, Lourdes for causing him so much trouble or Viv for burning, and shaming him with her words.

He laughed at the irony. There he was, plotting to keep Lourdes and Viv at odds, and he had for the most part, but Lourdes had managed to out weasel him and keep him and Viv at odds all the more. That was twice now that she had managed to get Viv so riled up at him that she had suspended him with the intermezzo in his ankle. Lourdes was proving to be far more trouble than he had anticipated.

He suspected she would be. She had declared war with him the day she destroyed his *Spadds* treatment. But he had to admit, looking back over the events of the day, that he had sorely underestimated her.

It wasn't the first time he'd misjudged an opponent. He nearly lost his life the first time that he had done it with a bounty, and still had the scars to prove it. He wouldn't make the same mistake with Lourdes. At least now he knew her way of doing things.

Cleary, she was up to something far more underhanded than anything she had already done, and contrary to the song and dance she had been performing for Viv, he knew her leaving had nothing to do with a 'sick mama'. Lourdes wanted him dead and gone, and she was scheming to get Viv over to her way of thinking. Whatever she was up to while she was away was clearly not in his favor. He needed to find out exactly what she was sneaking off and planning. That meant he had to follow her.

He tore one more line of linen bedding and tied it together at the base of his homemade rope. He had no plans of escaping. From what he had learned, Viv had put herself in a very bad place with the Cleric's Office by keeping him in the future, losing her husband, and not reporting any of it. Lourdes was an accomplice to the crimes. That gave him a great deal of leverage. All he needed to do was tip the balances even more. He could hold them hostage for as long as it took for him to polish his end plan.

He was going to hog tie the two of them with the truth of their mistake, and not let them go until it suited him to do so. He would control the reins of his life and theirs. As long as Viv didn't find John Jay in the meantime, Tucker John would be able to rule the big house like it was his own. Hell, he'd even do it even if that fool boy showed his face.

It seemed like a sweet enough exchange for his being abducted for the next six years.

He got to his knees and placed his ear to the floorboards. Viv was snoring lightly. She must have taken some more of them tiny pills. That was a good thing. The last thing he needed was for her to watch him slinking out his window by a rope he had made from linens she had stored in his room.

Pulling up his pant leg he did one final check of his inner ankle. The spot where the sensor had been was still bleeding but only a little bit. He'd had enough of Viv freezing him up. Twice was two times too many. So, in a fit of angry desperation, he'd used a garden spade to carve the sensor from his skin.

Being responsible for all of John Jay's farming chores, chores he was able to make quick work of since he had done that manner of work during his youth, gave him easy access to what he needed. Usually, Viv would check all of the tools when Tucker John was done with his work, making certain that all of the semi-sharp objects where in their proper place before she locked them away. But, because Lourdes had set one of her traps, Viv and he had ended up arguing, the tools didn't get checked, which gave him the chance to pocket the spade before she turned on him and froze him.

The spade had already come in handy with getting the sensor out of his body. He could use it as a weapon while tracking Lourdes if the need arose. He would put it away as soon as he got back to the house. Viv would lock him back in the lab if she found out he still had it. That meant he needed to find the other intermezzos, and stash those away as well.

He was going to have to move fast tonight.

He stuck his head out the window and his eyes watered from the gust of strong, warm, wind that beat against him. It was going to be a precarious slide down his makeshift rope to the ground below, but at least it wasn't raining yet. He would have to find Lourdes' trail quickly. If it did rain he would have a hard time trying to find her, and an even worse time trying to get back up the wall and into his window.

He tucked his clipboard in the linen bag he had made, and threw that over his shoulder. Then he checked the tension of his rope one last time before slinging his legs out the window and lowering himself to the grass, nearly fifty feet below.

CHAPTER 29

Magnus tucked the Instrument within the inner lining of his overcoat. After two hours, Lourdes had wrapped up her business at Balm Hill and had already headed back to Vivian's property. He would have headed back to his home as well if it wasn't for the dark figure he spied entering the house shortly after she'd gone. At first, he'd thought it was Clarence. He'd assured Magnus on more than one occasion that he'd been watching him, that he was always watching him as par Schusler's instructions. The thought made Magnus' skin crawl.

He eyed the figure as closely as he could, well enough to divine that it was not Clarence, although its silhouette was completely masculine which raised a yellow marker on Magnus' voicepod. Curious, he moved closer to the house to get a better view. The static had gone silent, so he wouldn't be able to hear anything.

Part of him said to turn around and head back home, let Clarence deal with whomever it was lurking around, but he knew that he couldn't do that. His assignment was to fill in all the gaps and holes that were evident in the timeline, record all flags raised by Vivian Leona and her team. This was a yellow marker. This was clearly a hole. He'd do his part and let Clarence handle the rest if the need arose.

He did one complete turn about the outer perimeter of the house before stopping at the basement window. Whoever had entered into Alba Berry's home was down there now. He carefully lowered himself to the ground and peeked into the window just behind the bushes, the glow from the quiet static helped him see everything.

***

(A few moments earlier)
Tucker John waited outside, watching Lourdes through one of the cellar windows. He took in what he saw, noting the desk with a trim of gold, a large gold-trimmed door casing propped up beside it with a man-sized glass box, also fitted with gold lining, nearby. The items appeared to be nothing but cast-off furnishings stored away in the cellar, harmless pieces waiting for a home above the stairs.

But the niggle in his belly, the way they were positioned, wouldn't allow him to believe that, especially not by the way Lourdes was sitting in front of them. It put him in the mind of Viv when she sat in her nexus room, and like the thunder that rolled across the indigo sky, the realization rolled across the forefront of his mind; Lourdes had somehow constructed nothing short of a homemade nexus gate!

She sat in front of the gate with her head down in a large golden bowl. He couldn't really make out what she was doing but it looked like she was talking into it, that, or lapping up water like the dog she was. No one was there with her, that much he could tell. Wisps of smoke framed her head and wrapped their pale tendrils around the nexus gate. For a second, he thought she was doing some sort of strange ritual with incense. He didn't put it past Lourdes to be the type, hoping to cast some curse on him and Viv, but what was she doing with a nexus gate?

Twenty minutes passed before she pulled her head out of the bowl and powered down the gate. The beam of white light beating through the gold trimmings like blood through veins, in tune to a heartbeat, faded into nothing.

Tucker John heightened his focus, memorizing where Lourdes moved her hands across the nexus table and how she disconnected the strange bowl attached to it. He intended to get a closer look at what she was fiddling with. If nothing else, he could link his clipboard with her nexus gate and gain a better understanding of them without Viv ever knowing. And he needed to know them in order to make his escape elsewhere in time. He sure as hell wasn't going to leave his steps to chance and get himself lost like Johnny-boy had.

He waited until Lourdes had turned out the lights and headed up the cellar stairs before he crawled out from beneath the shrubs. Keeping his body close to the walls of the house, he watched her leave in the darkness. He waited until she was over the hill before he moved out of the shadows.

He crept toward the front door and reached for the handle before thinking better of it, opting instead to check the side windows. If Lourdes did have an ill mama inside, going in through the front door would only scare her, not to mention, cause trouble for him. Old doors were noisier than yapping dogs. Nevertheless, he was going inside the house.

It was the third window to the right of the door that slid upward without any resistance. He pulled his linen bag over his head and gently laid it on to the serving butler right beneath the window opening before pulling himself inside. The inner darkness of the room met him head-on. He crouched down for several moments allowing his eyes to adjust to the darkness inside before he took any steps forward, his ears perked for any sound of movement in the house. He could have sworn he was being followed on his way to Lourdes' house, thought he'd seen movement not thirty yards away from him, but the sensation of another presence left just as quickly as it had come.

Now in Lourdes' mama's house, he heard nothing, nor did he feel the presence of anyone else.

Standing outside he had deduced that Lourdes was the only person there. If this was her mama's home, the woman certainly was nowhere to be found. Still, it didn't hurt to show a little extra caution.

The wind howled like a hound but the thunder had ceased to crash, the moon was even giving off a little bit of light. Tucker John was happy for that. The clouds had moved on so there would be no rain which would make for an easier trek back to Viv's manor, as well as a climb up the wall back to his bedroom. He all but laughed. His mama's God sure was smiling on him with good fortune.

He pressed through what he assumed was a small parlor and made his way into the front entry hall. There was another room on the other side of it and a set of stairs just in front of him. He took to the other room first, slowly poking his head into the darkness therein, giving the space a quick once-over. Besides the furniture, vacancy met him, just as he'd expected. Then he headed up the stairs.

Within less than five minutes, he'd toured the whole of Balm Hill's first and second floor, and even gave a quick go around of the attic space. Unlike Viv's manor, the home was modest in size and only had two stories, an attic, and a cellar. All of the bedrooms on the second floor were empty. All the beds were perfectly made but the linens were stale except for in the room that smelled like Lourdes, those linens were fresh, recently used, but absent of a body. No one had slept in the other beds for quite some time, at least several months. He made mental note of that detail and moved on.

Working his way back to the main floor and into the front hall, he headed toward where he assumed the cellar stairs would be. He stopped, only for a short moment, taking a glance at the large image of Lourdes. She stood with an older man who must have been her daddy, and a woman he assumed was her mama. Besides the picture, there was very little evidence of either of the two being present or having been present for a long while.

Narrowing his eyes he took silent steps toward the cellar door, frowning as soon as he stepped down unto the first step. The strange cloud that hung in the air made his clipboard buzz with activity. He steadied it with his hand, and carefully descended the stairs, garden spade in hand. His ears perked, and his eyes drew to the source of the billowy grey cloud that gave a dim glow to the basement floor even in the absence of light. The closer he moved toward the cause of the glowing cloud the more his clipboard buzzed.

Apprehension gripped him, but it wasn't enough to keep him from advancing closer. The fact that he was a good two-thousand years in the future was enough to dust off his hesitation.

He stood in front of the small nexus gate. Its form was simple; crude, and far smaller than the one at Viv's, but it was definitely a gate. His eyes trailed the line of connection between the glass, coffin-like box, the gold-trimmed frame, the table with the bowl that had also been attached to it. He couldn't understand the need for the bowl. Viv's gate had no bowl, and certainly not one that gave off a cloud of glowing smoke.

Two prongs stuck upward from the bowl's rim like antennae. At first glance, rust seemed to heavily coat each prong and spill over the sides of the bowl. But rust didn't shimmer nor did it move.

Tucker John eased forward with the same care he took near a hornet's nest, peering over into the basin where the glow of the cloud was strongest. Like the prongs, it too was filled with the shimmering, grainy material. Like moss, it grew and poured over the bowl's edge traveling along the gold trimming of the nexus gate and embedding itself within the joints.

"Oh, Lourdes, what are you up to?" Shaking his head, he clutched his linen bag. He'd figure out her scheme soon enough, but for now, he needed to take further advantage of the situation before him. He was standing in front of an unlocked nexus gate after all. He needed to get his clipboard calibrated to it, something he had been blocked from doing with Viv's, but Lourdes hadn't taken those precautions. Providence was definitely on his side!

He made certain to touch as little of the grainy substance as he could while he worked to link his clipboard with the gate. He had to allow his clipboard to touch the actual nexus table in order to begin the calibration. Grainy mess or not, he had to advance himself, and if Lourdes felt safe enough to stick her head into its midst, he could definitely take the risk of connecting his clipboard with it.

It took him several minutes to figure out what he was doing, even though he had read up on calibration. Manipulating digital matter that somehow appeared and hovered in thin air, was not something he was used to doing. He was clumsy at first and set off enough curses to light the whole house on fire in frustration but he finally managed to successfully align his clipboard.

Pressing his lips together, stilling the tremble of excitement that shook his fingertips, he pushed the active and launch command that sent his clipboard into full calibration.

He stumbled backward, startled from the strange gravitational pull that yanked his clipboard from his hands, encapsulating it in a circle of golden light.

He cautiously took several more steps away from it, swallowing down his heart and guts that had leaped into his throat. The thing looked like a golden nucleolus hovering in the air.

Nucleolus? Why did he know what that was? "*Spadds* treatments," he whispered before making quick work of retrieving every ounce of information he could gather from the gate. Task complete, he carefully disconnected his clipboard and slid it back into his bag.

Crrshp.

His head snapped back toward the window behind him. He turned just in time to see fabric stretching from a branch before tugging completely free.

His jaw clenched. He'd gotten reckless, not trusting his primary instincts. Someone *had* been following him! He quickly made certain everything looked like it had before he connected with the nexus gate, leaving no evidence that he'd been in Balm Hill, and then, like a bolt of lightning, he headed for the stairs taking them three at a time.

CHAPTER 30

Magnus ran until his heart pounded in his ears and his throat constricted from the wheezing in his lungs. He wasn't in the worst shape, but he had not seriously run anywhere in almost a complete decade, and now he was running in the dark away from someone he wasn't even sure had seen him.

He turned his head back, like he had done several times before, only to find that no one was behind him. He was being paranoid. From the static to this secret assignment, Magnus was simply on edge. He slowed his pace and blew air from his thin lips. He even took a few seconds to bend over and catch his breath. It was when he stood straight again that he felt an iron-hard forearm tighten around his throat, and a sharp point press against his kidney.

His hard-earned breath caught in his throat. He *had* been seen! Where was Clarence?!

"Why'n the hell you spying on me?" The man's voice was threatening.

Tucker John, the other part of the puzzle. Magnus cringed. He'd encountered the one called 'The Animal.' The messy flow of his English was evidence of that. Magnus tried to swallow but gagged instead. Tucker John shook him around before he loosened his grip, but not very much, only enough for him to speak, but not enough for the blood to stop pounding at his temples.

"I wasn't spying on you," he yelped as the point of the spade dug deeper into his back.

"Don't play with me, boy! Prying eyes is always connected to wagging tongues, and I'm fixing to cut yours clean out!"

"With what? That garden spade you have at my back?"

"You seem eager to find out."

"Don't be ridiculous! I—"

Tucker John growled. He moved the spade's point from Magnus' back and pricked the point of it right at his jugular.

Magnus got the message, spade or not, it was still sharp enough to end his life. "Point taken, literally, sir. But I assure you I mean you no harm! It's quite the contrary," he chose his words wisely. He was physically defenseless but he wasn't a fool. He knew how to negotiate. All he had to do was give a little in order to gain a lot, namely his life back.

He couldn't influence the past but he could do just enough to save his own neck so that he could get back to the future in one piece. Clearly, he was going to have to. Clarence was either a liar, or he simply had no intention of intervening. Either way, Magnus was on his own.

He said, "Killing me will be an utter waste for you, especially when you consider that I'm more useful to you alive than dead, Tucker John." He held his breath. He had taken a risk in saying his name. He hoped it had drawn curiosity and bought him some time.

Tucker John froze still behind him. "How you know my name?"

Magnus' nostrils flared as saliva splattered in his inner ear. "I know more than you think! Your name is only one detail. But be assured, my knowledge is for your benefit. As I've said, I mean you no harm," he gagged again. Tucker John's grip had tightened. Magnus pulled at his arm but quickly stopped. The spade was breaking through his skin! "My presence is only for verification purposes and surveillance! It's my job to know and to watch,"

"And report, *wagging* tongue!"

"Not how you think. Not how you *think*! I don't make reports to this Office in 4037. I'm not under their jurisdiction!"

Tucker John seemed to consider Magnus' words. He kept the spade pressed firmly beneath Magnus' Adam's apple, but remained quiet himself.

Magnus took advantage of his silence. "I see that fact raises some questions for you, questions I'm more than willing to answer out of your grasp." He slowly pried Tucker John's forearm from around his neck and moved out of the danger of the garden spade. The feeling of safety was superficial. They both knew he couldn't outrun or out arm Tucker John. He had no intention of trying. Clarence could have been of use, but he was Schusler's dog, to begin with. He wouldn't bark for Magnus.

Magnus would simply offer Tucker John reason and pray that it would be received. He adjusted his clothing and managed to catch his breath again. The look in Tucker John's eyes was threatening, especially in the moonlit night. "I, like you, am not from this millennia. I'm from beyond. Therefore, I have knowledge of this time and certain people who live herein, you being one of them."

Tucker John's eyes narrowed. "You from 6037?"

Magnus shook his head. "Before that time." He folded his hands in front of him. "I will offer you this token, should you choose to take it as the truth that it is. I was not here for you. Actually, I didn't even know that you would be here—"

"Then how did you know who I am? Some wench tell you?" He was obviously referring to Lourdes Berry.

Magnus frowned at his name calling. "No person of this century has told me anything. They are future details. Don't bother yourself with them."

"Oh, I'm bothered," Tucker John's jaw ticked. Moonlight flashed from the garden spade he shifted in his grip. He took a step forward.

Magnus raised an open hand. "Be that as it may, I was here surveying, verifying certain fact points when you arrived. That is all. You've learned enough of the rules of surveillance to know that, even if you were up to no good, I could do nothing to hinder, nor prevent your actions. This may be your present or future, but it is the past for me. I am not authorized to alter it in any way. The only thing I am authorized to do is observe and verify. Don't add unnecessary quarrels to the heap that you already have, Mr. Spruce. The less confusion the better, I would imagine."

"What are you saying?" Tucker John's chin rose.

"I'm saying go home before your hostess awakes and finds her shredded bed linens dangling in the wind outside your window!"

Tucker John's eyes widened with fury. "How do I know you ain't here to sabotage me, that you ain't one of them clerics?"

Magnus smiled. "I survey. That makes me a cleric, a Minister of Time. Magnus Sanderson," he gave a slight bow.

"Then its best I kill you, lessen my confusion, Magnus."

Magnus sighed. "How can I convince you that I am not out to get you? Tell me!" Sweat tickled his temple and it wasn't because of the heat that still lingered long after the sun had dropped below the horizon. Tucker John seemed as unpredictable as the animals he was named for. For all Magnus knew, his death at Tucker John's hand were one of the holes that was left unfilled in the timeline, some sick trick of Aiden Schulsler, hence the lack of aid from Clarence. He prayed it wasn't.

Tucker John shook his head. "You can't convince me."

"Then let me put this on the table because, clearly, you have not considered it. If you murder me, the Governing forces will be involved. They will trace that spade to your hostess. They will come for her. She will be held accountable. Where do you think that will leave you?"

"I've skinned many a' pig and kept my hands clean. They won't find the spade."

"You know better than that, Tucker John. This is not 1837! Here, they work with methods beyond even your scope of expertise. Your doubts at my words are not worth the risk. I'll tell you what I will do. I'll send you a certified message from the Cleric's Office, the kind that will require you to take it in hand from the deliverer, it will need your DNA to do so, proof that I am who I say I am. Your hostess will be powerless to keep you from it. And, to prove I'm legit, I will let you dictate the message yourself. What would you like for me to put in it?"

Tucker John's silent stare made Magnus' blood run cold. It also made him hate Clarence all the more.

Tucker John couldn't see how a letter would make him not want to kill the man and hide his body away. Killing him actually wasn't the best option either, but he wasn't certain that he could take the risk and leave him alive. What if Lourdes was working with him? What if he had been in that house and Tucker John had missed him somehow? For all he knew, she could have told him who he was. If she had, then the stranger before him was certainly a dead man walking.

But he had brought up a good point about Viv. If she was exposed, then so was he, and that meant he was good as dead. He considered strangling the man but that would mean a mess of his DNA being shed. No man in his right mind would let himself be strangled without a fight, even if it was a losing fight. It was all looking hopeless. He had to take his chances and let the weasel go. His gut told him it was the best choice, even though he didn't like it one bit. The wiry snake could slither somewhere and have him put down within the hour, or he might not. Sensing the presence of another nearby only forced his hand.

Sensing the hidden threat only made the silly letter seem like an even less worthy risk, and the thought of killing one enemy before facing another, the better option. "Not good enough," he hissed. "…especially since you ain't alone."

Magnus stumbled backward, fear pulling his ashen face taught with creases and sweat. He raised his palms as if that would fend Tucker John off. "I am alone. I," his brow rose and his face flushed. "Well, my assistant is somewhere out there but,"

Tucker John growled and lunged forward. Magnus all but squealed like a stuck pig.

"I-I have something more! Something about your enemy!" He covered his head with his arms.

Tucker John considered the man, his face grew paler with his announcement. He was desperate, too desperate to lie, and clearly not confident in his unseen assistant. That was promising, especially since Tucker John needed any information he could get and he needed to shed as little blood in the process.

"You got something on Viv? Spill it!"

Magnus stumbled to right himself. "Not Vivian Leona, h-her husband."

"That fool's lost!"

"Is he?" Magnus's pale eyes grew wide as he straightened. "Is he lost, or is that what he wants everyone to believe, what he wants Vivian to believe?" He swallowed hard but took a few more steps backward, his eyes unblinking, his breaths ragged. "John Jay Spruce is not as big of a fool as you think, but he is far more dangerous than you can imagine. Watch out for him. That, that is all I can tell you, but there is so much more you don't know and killing me won't help you. But it will help *him*, and Lourdes Berry."

Tucker John let the tiny cryptic message sink like a lead weight in a pond. John Jay wasn't lost? So said the man from the future, the man who was spying on him, the man who knew his name, and about the rope dangling from his window.

It was just enough to bring Tucker John to heel, and too much to ignore with a quick gamble.

"You're considering the truth of what I'm saying. Good. That's very good. I will still send you the letter tomorrow to ease any lingering concerns you may have. I assure you that I have no intention whatsoever of getting in your way. Just tell me what you'd like me to say and—"

Tucker John snarled and pointed the garden spade in Magnus' face. He hated leaving loose ends flapping in the wind. He hated more that his situation had gotten far more complicated than it already was. "You put whatever the hell you want in that letter, you just make sure it gets to me tomorrow 'cause if it don't I will find you, and I will cut out your lying tongue, yours and your assistant's."

Widening the space between them, Magnus nodded in agreement. "Then we a have deal. You let me go on my way?"

Tucker John hocked spit on the ground. Magnus frowned. "I better have that letter tomorrow." He said nothing else but backed away into the darkness of the trees. The man did the same heading in the opposite direction at a much quicker pace leaving behind the parting words about keeping his sights on John Jay. He reckoned he had no choice but to do so.

Cursing several times under his breath he took off at a sprint back toward Viv's house. He was at least forty-five minutes behind Lourdes but that wasn't a concern of his. She never walked beneath Viv's window when she left or came home. His rope would be well out of her view. His only concern was the wiry man that he'd caught spying on him and his unseen assistant lingering somewhere in the shadows.

He would have to wait until tomorrow to see what would happen with Magnus. He just hoped he hadn't sealed his own death by not taking the man's life when he had the chance, and all over false bait concerning Johnny-boy.

***

Magnus pushed open his front door and slid inside the safety of his home. He locked the large door behind him and was finally able to relax, but only for a short moment. He felt his heart skip a beat recalling his failure. He'd never betrayed future knowledge during surveillance, but if he'd died tonight what use would that knowledge be?

"So that is who was reported as the 'Animal'?" He said. At first, he had thought the name was ridiculous but having had to pry his life out of the calloused hands of the man he knew as Tucker John he wasn't so sure anymore. Only an animal would think murdering a stranger was an acceptable solution to an inconvenience. He was no better than Clarence! At least he knew the animal's intentions. Clarence had just hidden somewhere and watched him being accosted and never once lifted a finger to offer him aid. Some guard dog he was!

He touched his neck and felt the crusted blood that Tucker John had drawn with the garden spade. He wanted to vomit! This was the day that it was recorded that the Animal had used a garden spade to remove the sensor from his ankle, and Magnus was certain he had not bothered to clean the thing off!

He rushed to his bathroom, doused his face and neck with cold water and soap, before applying a topical antiseptic to his wound. He also administered a shot for just-in-case. He didn't know what kind of ancient bacteria Tucker John was carrying and he certainly didn't want to wait to find out.

Magnus had once loved his job as a Minister of Time, but not so much that he was willing to die for it, and that is exactly what he had almost done, died because he had gotten too close. He was going to have to be more careful with his surveillance, or at least let Tucker John know he had to watch Balm Hill as part of his assignment.

He left the washroom and checked his pockets to make sure he hadn't dropped the Instrument while he was running for his life. To his relief, it was well in place. He was still very upset by the happenings and would need to take an *XBalance* if he was going to be able to level out his nerves and sleep.

He grumbled angrily under his breath. He would let the leveling out wait until after he had written his message to Tucker John. Now that a great enough distance was between them, with sufficient security, Magnus was willing to give the brutish man a piece of his mind. He might even throw in a few choice warnings of his own.

***

It was the first of many wraiths to come. Manipulating the static, the cutting through fixed points in time in order to create holes had created them. The cutting had actually acted as a pruner's tool, cutting away branches so many more could grow in their place. The only problem was these branches were born of time. They were perversions of the mother-timeline, filled with copies of people and events that already existed.

It would have been one thing had those duplicates of time stayed in their fixed places, but like John Jay had torn through the fabrics of existence, so too had his wraiths, his copies.

Clarence had watched the shadowy figure from the static. It stepped in and out of the folds of 4037 without even knowing it was doing so. Clarence had to wait for a fixed moment in time, a specific break in the folds of static and reality to align before he could rid all of creation of its presence. Then, just as he would do with the others, he threw it back into the static where it returned to the nothing it was born from. From the static it came, to the static, it and its perverted timeline would return. The original thread of creation would pull back into order, one branch at a time all because of Clarence's diligence and extermination of the wraiths.

His employers would be pleased.

CHAPTER 31

Vivian's eyes were strained. She'd been up since before the sun, looking for John Jay, and no matter what she tried, no matter how many statistics she changed, the nexus gate continued to tell her that he was right there, in 4037, with her. At least there had not been a T.R even though she had somewhat caught up with her research in preparation for it.

She sighed and wiped her hands on her pant legs. The fact that no one had shown up in the twenty plus days that she had been informed that a T.R would take place, bothered her greatly. It made her anxious. All reviews had to be done within a fifteen day period. It was well past that time, and she had not received a single word from the Cleric's Office as to whether or not the T.R had been canceled, which meant it had not.

She had contacted the office several times already and was met with sheer incompetence each time she asked for information about her scheduled T.R. That didn't bode well with her either. It seemed like everything was crumbling around her, the once well-oiled machine of surveillance was on the verge of a major breakdown alongside her personal life. Truth was, it had already broken down, she just hadn't been able to be clear of the smoke.

Lourdes and Tucker John were not helping her feel any better about things. She felt like a clock's pendulum swinging between the two of them in their endless battle against each other, which only pitted both of them against her, once she demanded order. She still had a headache from her fight with Tucker John the day before, and had awakened that morning with a severe case of nausea. He never showed for breakfast, which was a great thing, but odd considering his demands that she be present at every meal. Apart from her not having much of an appetite she had even less of a desire to lay eyes on him, even though at times she would look at him and see only John Jay. Sometimes, to get through the day, she would tell herself he was John Jay, and that everything else was a horrible dream, which only made her feel disgustingly guilty afterward.

She thought herself a hypocrite. She was furious with Tucker John, almost completely despised him, and yet she used his image as a stand-in for her missing husband. She didn't feel that way at present, him being John Jay's stand in. That morning she watched him in the early moments of the dawn in the garden, tending his chores in preparation for the Co-op delivery. He was efficient at what he did, far better than John Jay had ever been, if she were honest, but she couldn't help wishing that he would drop something on his foot or hammer his thumb. She wanted him to hurt the way he had hurt her with his nasty tongue.

She rolled her eyes thinking about their fight the previous afternoon. It seemed like things were only getting worse by the day. They were all in too deep now to wallow in regret, but Vivian couldn't help but toss around the 'what if's'. What if she hadn't panicked when John Jay disappeared and had contacted the Cleric's Office the very second Tucker John had come through? What if she had put Lourdes in her place the very first time she had undermined her authority instead of letting John Jay get her in check? What if she had just punched Tucker John in the jaw the first time he twisted his lips and called her something other than her name?

She startled, her eyes blazing the moment she realized Tucker John had been standing in the room watching her lost in her thoughts. She hadn't even noticed he'd come in. She had belatedly realized the man had an eerie way of either letting his presence be known, or not. He was indeed a predator.

She glared at him long and hard hoping that by some twist in the nature of reality he would suddenly combust. He didn't.

"Good morning to you, too, Viv." His tone was laden with sarcasm. His vernacular was smooth and articulate even though it was still steeped in southern drawl.

Just like that. Just like that he turns it on and off. The voice and tone of the man before her was certainly a contrast to the beast she had encountered yesterday. At least he'd been practicing. Still she held her tongue.

He huffed. "What? You still vexed over yesterday?" He pulled out the chair across from her and sat down.

Vivian's eyes narrowed and her chin rose. "You think that after the vile display you showed, and the nastiness you shot at me, that you can just walk in here like everything is okay, that I should just receive you?" She pressed her lips and shook her head. "When are you going to understand that I am not your enemy? I don't deserve how you have spoken to me. I don't care what you were brought up to believe."

Tucker John kept her gaze as he flicked soil that had been embedded beneath his fingernails onto her floor. "You want an apology or something?"

"Did you come to apologize?"

"Absolutely not."

His face was placid, and yet she could tell he was ready for another war with her. She wouldn't play his game. "Then we have nothing to talk about."

He leaned forward. "Sure we do. I have questions that need answering. Now, you can sit over there and give me the cold shoulder all you want but it'll be your hide tossed in the fire soon as them Clerics come a knocking."

She hated that he was right. It made her blood boil. He was making her blood boil! She touched her pocket. Either the *Paz* wasn't working as well or she was extremely sensitive. "What is it?" She all but shouted.

Tucker John ignored her frustration and looked down at his clipboard. "I just had a few questions in regard to your broken nexus gate."

"Everything you need to know about the gate I have already told you! Now, if you will excuse me." She pretended to turn her attention back to the work in front of her.

Tucker John didn't budge. He glanced at Viv and stifled a smile. Her brown cheeks had burned a lovely shade of red at his resistance. It made his stomach flop. Sometimes she was just outright pretty to him even when she was fighting mad and making his life pure hell, which was most of the time. Had she been a man, he would have hated her a hundred percent. Had she not been his enemy, or according to Magnus Sanderson, not his enemy, he may not have hated her at all.

He'd been considering what Magnus had said, raising the question that John Jay wasn't missing, was dangerous, and that Viv was none the wiser. If that was true, that surely changed things, turned them right foul, if he were honest with himself.

He said, "Before you go off and call yourself dismissing me, hear me out. All roads are going to lead back to you if I answer your cleric friends incorrectly. I'm just trying to be prepared. We have an agreement after all."

Viv pushed away from the desk and leaned back in her chair. "What's your question?"

"How long that thing been broken?"

Viv's brow pulled together. "It's been broken for a while…at least eight months, maybe a year. Why?"

Tucker John raised a finger. He still had more questions. "Why ain't it been fixed yet?"

"Why *hasn't* it been fixed?" She clearly couldn't keep herself from grooming him. "It hasn't been fixed because there are certain pieces, nanoids that we need. Nanoids are—"

He raised his finger again but kept his eyes on his clipboard. "I know what nanoids are."

She grunted. "Right, the *Spadds*. Anyhow, we had to order the nanoids in from the 6030's, but they still haven't arrived yet. Anything else?"

Tucker John looked up at her noting the annoyance that rang in her every answer. "Yes. Is your team the only team in this area that has a nexus gate?"

Wariness clouded her face. Tucker John could almost read her mind. Too bad for her he had already found a nexus gate to link up with. He just wanted to know if it was supposed to be at Balm Hill or not. Instinct told him he already knew the answer. Still, he dreaded her pending confirmation, realizing that if the gate was illegal, especially in light of what Magnus Sanderson had divulged on the evening past, then a great many things would have to change in his war against her.

Part of him wanted her not to confirm what he was beginning to see. Because if she didn't know about the other gate, then she wasn't truly at fault for what was happening to him, she wasn't his enemy, not really. She was just a pawn. But why, and what the hell did it have to do with him?

He said, "Let me ease your suspicions by rephrasing my question. Are there any other surveillance teams nearby that I should know about?"

The wariness lingered. "Not for several miles, at least ten. We're always alerted when another team is stationed in our area even though we are never told who they are or where they're from. We may run into them at the Cleric's Office but we make it a point not to get too familiar with them on that level. That is how we keep our surveying experiences authentic."

"By pretending you don't know your neighbors are not really your neighbors?" It was more of a statement than a question. Viv didn't respond. "So what happens then if say Lourdes' mama, for instance, was a surveyor," he paused. "Is she a surveyor?"

She shook her head. "No, why?"

"People like to follow in the footsteps of they kin. Figured that's why you and Lourdes chose this profession."

"It's why I did. My great-grandparents were part of a program that really influenced the structure of our family.

Surveillance was what prompted them to that call. I joined the Ministry of Time for that reason. Their passion inspired me to come to the New Golden Age." She waved her hand finally aware of her digression. "But, Lourdes, she's first-generation."

"So when you're done with your work here in the 4030's, are you going to leave your gate here for the next team?"

The doorbell rang and both their attention shifted to the front of the house. Viv stood up from her desk and headed for the door when the bell rang again.

"No. We dismantle everything and it returns to our perspective time along with us. Where's Lourdes?"

His jaw clenched as he watched her head to the front of the house. She'd given him the exact answer he needed, but certainly not what he wanted. *D@#$ it all!* Viv had just confirmed what the wiry stranger had spoken the previous night. She had no idea what kind of storm they were standing in. She had no idea what kind of man her husband was. Worse, neither did he.

Things had gotten far more complicated.

***

Vivian quickened her pace when the bell chimed a third time. She hadn't even noticed that Tucker John was right behind her when the door opened. Immediately her heart sank down to her toes. It was someone from the Cleric's Office.

Suddenly cotton-mouthed, she tried to swallow. "Hello. Are you here to conduct the Team Review?" She peered beyond the man. "I thought there would be three of you."

The young man at the door smiled politely and shook his head. "No, ma'am I'm not here to do a review."

"You're not?" Now she was surprised. "We're scheduled for a T.R. If you're not here for that then,"

Still smiling, the young cleric pulled out a capsule scroll, a personal message. It was unusual practice for penned messages to be sent for clerical business but this one had. There was an electronic sensor that had been used to seal it where a wax seal would have been. "I'm here simply to deliver a personal message."

Vivian frowned and reached for the letter but the cleric pulled it away. "No ma'am, this message is to be received by John Joseph Spruce, exclusively. Are you him, sir?" He looked past her to Tucker John. Vivian felt the color leach from her face. She hoped the cleric hadn't noticed.

Tucker John coolly stepped forward. "I am."

"Fantastic! If you would place your thumb here on the seal that will verify your identity, the message will be yours to read, and I will be on my way!" The young man was extremely chipper.

Vivian sucked in a choppy breath. She wanted to protest but she couldn't find her voice. She felt more like she was going to faint instead. If Tucker John touched that sensor, the Cleric's Office would know he was not John Jay! The only thing she could do was clamp her mouth shut the moment Tucker John slid his thumb in place.

Within a matter of excruciating seconds, the electronic seal clicked, the capsule rolled open, and the cleric slid the handwritten message to Tucker John. "Excellent, sir. Ma'am. You two have a great afternoon!" He raised his hand and turned toward his sled.

Vivian gave Tucker a petrified look before pushing past him. The sensor should not have come off! What had just happened? "Is-is everything alright wi-with that?" She pointed toward the cleric's inner pocket.

He touched it through the fabric of his linen vest and nodded. "Yes, ma'am. Everything's fine." He scanned Vivian with his eyes. His brow rose. "Is everything alright with you?"

Her mouth opened again, but still no words came out. She glanced back to where Tucker John was supposed to have been standing. Instead, she saw nothing but an empty doorway and the burn of fearful confusion clawing at her chest.

CHAPTER 32

Vivian swung her attention back to the cleric who cautiously stared at her, her panic rising. Tucker John had left with the message, a message he shouldn't have been able to open, unless….

What was happening?

"Ma'am, are you alright?" The cleric asked her again, stepping off his sled.

"Yes, yes I'm fine." She waved her hands and faked a smile.

The cleric didn't look convinced. "Are you sure ma'am? You look a little ill." Worry lines grew upon his forehead.

Vivian swallowed hard but managed to shrug her shoulders still smiling. "I haven't eaten yet today. There were a lot of chores that took precedence. We're a bit behind with our co-op offering. You understand. It doesn't happen often, but when it does," she used the same lie she had with the Peace Officer.

The cleric's smile returned, exposing his teeth. "Oh, yes! I understand. Just last week I woke up a tad too late and our cow was none too pleased. She was full of milk! I missed breakfast myself and was a bit out of my wits because of it."

He steadied himself once he stepped back up on his sled powering it up. "You might want to try half an *XBalance* if you have any. They work wonders for days like these. Have a great day ma'am."

Vivian back peddled toward her door. As soon as the cleric was out of sight she ran inside and slammed it shut. "Tucker John!" She shouted. No answer came. Where had he gone? She made a sweep of the first floor, and then the lab before it registered to her that he had gone to his room with the note in hand. Retrieving the skeleton key from her desk she raced up the stairs, terror at her heels. How had he opened the letter? Sealed letters like that took a small blood sample, not just a thumbprint.

Her mind tumbled back to the original thoughts she'd had when Tucker John had come through the emergency portal; that he was John Jay and that something had happened to him to make him forget, to break him. She didn't know what to think anymore. "Tucker John!"

Lourdes suddenly appeared on the stairs behind her. "What's going on, Vivian? Why are you screaming? What did he do, now?"

She didn't bother to turn Lourdes direction. "Fine time for you to show up, Lourdes. Don't worry, I'll figure this out on my own. Tucker John, open the door!" She shook the doorknob before beating on the door with her fist. Tucker John still didn't answer. She pounded again.

Lourdes grabbed her shoulder. "What's going on? I have the right to know,"

Vivian turned on her with a fierceness that the other woman had never seen. Lourdes backed away. "Do not put your hands on me again, Lourdes. Go away! Go back to wherever you were before when I called you and you couldn't answer. I'll deal with this. Alone."

"Vivian—"

"Go!" Vivian stared her down until she began to descend the stairs. She took to the door again, this time using the key. It swung open with her weight. She stumbled to catch herself from falling up the final flight of stairs only to clip her shins in the process. Wincing, she called Tucker John's name again.

Peering down at her from the railing with a mixture of confusion and anger Tucker John's shadow fell over her. He glanced at the open door and then frowned, clearly seeing her entry as a form of trespassing. Still, she ascended the stairs.

"Viv, what are you doing in my room?" He eyed her suspiciously with each step she took.

Winded from the trepidation that gripped her stomach, she stared up at him. He only stared back, the note refolded and secure in his hand. Vivian's eyes looked down at it and then back at him. "John Jay?" Her voice shook with uncertainty.

Tucker John's frown deepened. "What are you doing barging in my room, Viv?"

She drew closer to him. Her eyes stung with hot tears, her heart beat with an erratic tattoo. The blood test for the letter had confirmed that he was John Joseph Spruce. It said nothing about a John *Josephus* Spruce. But hadn't she done a blood test of her own? Yes, she had. Nothing was making sense, not now, and certainly not then.

"Are you John Jay?"

"What?" His voice raised an octave.

"Are you," she took a breath and steadied herself, ignoring the pressure in her chest. "Are you my John?"

"Are you serious right now?" He folded his arms across his chest. Vivian stared at him, her chin trembling. Tucker John's eyes widened before he burst into laughter. "Good Lord, Viv! You're serious!" He kept laughing.

Vivian clenched her fist hollering at the top of her voice. "Are you my John?"

Tucker John stopped laughing, instantly silencing having been startled by her outburst. Viv was rigid but trembling, her eyes closed, and her shoulders rising and falling with each labored breath she took.

He growled back at her. "Hell no! I ain't that lily-livered, *rat-bastard* call himself married to you, too much of an imbecile to find his way back through a nexus gate, and can't tell a real woman from a cockroach!" His gaze met Lourdes' and followed her all the way back down the stairs that she had snuck up while Viv wasn't paying attention. The look in the little devil-woman's eyes was too much to ignore, too much to cast aside, in light of the letter in his hands, and the warning written by the man he'd held at the point of his garden spade just the night before.

He didn't speak again until after he heard the door shut behind Lourdes and the sound of her swift moving feet bounding down the second flight of stairs. "No! I am not your John! I ain't nothing like him," his tone lowered. "And you already knew that." He pointed a stiff finger at her, the paper message crumpling in his hand.

At his words Vivian's lungs constricted as if each one was a hand squeezing the air from within them. She would have collapsed to the floor had she not managed to clear the three paces to the small vanity pushed against the wall facing her. She leaned against it and strained to breathe.

Her eyes burned all the more when she looked up at him. Confusion was an understatement. She was feeling like a crazy person. She watched Tucker John's feet as he paced the floor, fully committed to the rant that spilled from his tight drawn lips.

"Viv, you done lost your marbles. You sitting around here, pretending like you got everything under control. You ain't got nothing under control, don't even know what you're dealing with! Lourdes don't mind nothing you say. You got my neck in a noose!" He pointed at her again, fuming, veins protruding from his neck and forehead. "You popping them little pills like they's candy and they're making you crazy!"

She lifted her eyes to meet his, violently swiping tears from her cheeks. "Where's the letter, Tucker John?" Her voice was hard.

Tucker John looked at her over his shoulder a disgusted expression on his face. "What?"

She straightened her back, raised her chin, and stuck out her hand. "Where is the letter? I want it."

The sound of crumpling vellum scrapped against her ears as he tightened his grip on the message. He squared his shoulders, staring down the slope of his nose at her. "This letter don't concern you."

Vivian's jaw clenched. "That letter is addressed to John Joseph Spruce. You are not him. I want the letter. Now!"

"Leave my room, Viv."

"This is my house! Give me the letter, Tucker John," she lunged toward him and grabbed at his hand, her nails tearing into his skin.

Tucker John cursed, prying her hands away from him by the wrists, shoving her away from him. Stumbling backward, she bumped up against the vanity again. He glanced at the growing welts and then her, his lips pressed so firmly together they'd gone white. Nostrils flaring, she glared at him, angry tears running from her eyes.

As if he could read her mind, he lifted his chin. "You contemplating violence with me, Viv? Hmm?"

"I want the letter," she spat through clenched teeth.

Tucker John squared himself again. Viv was about to learn her place, and the sooner the better. He would not strike her. He didn't need to. He would pin her down though, laugh at her, and hold her there until her pride turned into shame, and she ran from his room with her tail between her legs.

If Johnny-boy and that wench Lourdes had something nefarious planned that involved him, he needed things under control, under his control, and that included Vivian Leona. "Come and get it."

Viv hollered and threw the vanity to the floor. The mirror shattered. Glass poured across the dark wood floorboards like broken ice on water. Tucker John skipped out of harm's way.

Viv fumbled with the remote she'd torn from her pocket. "If you won't give it to me," she panted, her eyes wild. "I'll take it from you. Then I'll lock you back in the lab where I should have left you!" She clicked the button several times, then several times more.

Nothing happened.

Unable to resist, Tucker John casually leaned against the wall and crossed his bare feet at the ankles. He watched her with contentment. He had been waiting for this moment. He had not known it would feel so good to him, but it did.

Viv mumbled about the remote not working until finally, her gaze met his again. It was then that she realized what he had done. She took in a sharp breath before slamming the remote to the ground, causing its fractured bits to scatter amongst the glass.

Fully enraged, she rushed him, giving no heed to the shards of mirror that crunched beneath her slippers. She reached for his ankle, her words shrill, "What did you do? You broke it didn't you?!"

Tucker John took hold of her wrist again. "Mind your hands, Viv,"

Wrenching her arm away, she stared at him with crazed eyes, her chest rising and falling with each quick breath she took before she darted for the stairs.

He leapt behind her, goading her with his words. His triumphant smile couldn't help but gleam. "Don't bother looking for an intermezzo. I put 'em away in a safe place this morning. They are like razors in your hands. Can't trust you with 'em."

Viv stopped midstride and turned back around. She slowly took each step back up the stairs, her brow twisted, and her mouth agape. Tucker John backed away as if welcoming her to the dance floor, only now he was the one in the lead and she knew it.

His smile was devious as he watched the whirl of emotions converge on her face. "That's right. You don't like this place do you, being powerless? Not knowing what the other person will do to you just 'cause they can,"

They circled each other until he broke the movement and stalked closer to her, crowding her in with his size. "Them dangling your life in your face by a string, and telling you to dance or else." The words tasted good on his tongue. It felt good to watch her squirm.

Vivian stopped moving. She wouldn't take another step. She wouldn't submit to being Tucker John's victim, even though she was afraid. Truth was, she was terrified. But he expected her to fall back in fear, give in to the fear of him that made her marrow quake.

She waited until he was only a foot away before she shoved him back from her. That got his attention, even if he only moved back one half-step to her three. "I never did that to you! I wanted to help you. And look what I have received in return," her breath caught in her throat. She prayed he misread her trembling as nothing short of rage and not fear. It was a mixture of both.

Tucker John caught his balance and glowered at her. "You sure as hell did! And you haven't helped me. You can't even help yourself! You and that assistant of yours was holding me hostage and trying to lord over me, humiliate me. No sir! Not no more! The tides have turned in my favor. I'm the one holding the power now!" He thumped his chest with his fist, the veins in his neck protruded all the more.

Vivian placed her hands on her head. She felt beyond sick. She couldn't even register the fear anymore. "That is what this is about to you…That is what this has always been about to you. Power. Control,"

"That's what it is for you—"

"No!" She brought her hands down and stomped her foot. "No, Tucker John! No, it isn't! This has been about finding my husband, and keeping *you* alive!" She couldn't keep herself from crying, bawling as if he had beaten her with his fist and left her to lick her wounds. "This was about me trying to do what was right when I could have left you at the mercy of the Cleric's Office or the Governors, who would have put you to death the very *second* they realized you were recorded as dead!"

Viv, eyes red and flowing with tears, shook her head with sheer disillusionment. Tucker John felt the weight of it in his belly. He didn't expect that, no more than he expected that John Jay was as villainous as he was realizing, and he didn't like it at all. The memory of John Jay's laughing image, the one Viv kept on her desk, flashed across his mind.

Viv slowly appraised him with her eyes. "You are the worst kind of person," her voice crocked in the most pathetic of ways. It made his blood boil.

"Why!" Defensively he mocked her. Somehow he felt cornered again. "Because I don't *think* like you? Because I didn't have a proper education? Or maybe because I come from 1837, and had an 'unmentionable' profession! Or-or, because I'm an *animal* in need of grooming," the words burned from his throat.

Viv slowly shook her head, her voice startlingly calm. "No...it's because you're a liar."

Tucker John flinched. "I didn't lie to you,"

Viv laughed. "You have browbeaten me with the stipulations of our agreement and yet you have not only broken your end, but you have shattered the little bit of trust I had for you. This entire time I was thinking you were growing despite your conflicts with Lourdes, but no, you were sneaking behind my back, scheming. And you didn't do it because I had harmed you or treated you like you were sub-human or 'uneducated,' or an 'animal'. You did it because of some," she looked up as she grasped for the words. "Some need for control."

"You don't know what you are talking about,"

"Sure I do! I'm going off of what you've shown me. You're out of control so you try to steal it from everyone else. You only care about yourself. You lie because you can. Because you are 'Tucker John' and the world had better *mind* you or else—"

Closing the space between them, he jerked her toward him by her biceps, lifting her up to her toes, leaning down into her face until they were standing nose to nose. He hated her words. Each dart she threw at him penetrated his armor like nothing else had.

"You shut your mouth! You don't know anything about me," spittle shot from his clenched teeth.

Vivian pressed her eyes closed and braced herself. She thought for certain he was going to strike her, or worse. Lourdes had been right about him. He couldn't be trusted.

He said, jerking at her arms again. "You think this is about control? I don't know you, just like you don't know me. And as far as I see it, you don't have a clue what you're doing. This is about me taking care of me, and making sure I don't end up someone else's means-t- an-end, yours and your team's to be exact. You think I don't know about you wanting to clear my mind, steal everything from me, and then drop me back into 1837 to drown?"

Vivian's eyes peeled open.

Tucker John nodded his head. "Yeah, I know all about that." She struggled in his grasp but he only tightened his grip.

His hold on her did not render her speechless. "So you think me refusing to alter the past makes me your enemy?" Her voice shook. More tears blurred her vision but she didn't mask her angry resentment. "I could have killed you the moment I found out who you were, the very second I realized you had no future. But I didn't. I gave you a chance. I put my own safety and reputation at risk to give you an opportunity," she struggled against his grip. "…and you've lied to me. I could have turned you in, got John Jay back, and never thought twice about you, but I didn't!"

Tucker John's nostrils flared with every word she spoke. His grip began to loosen and he stepped back from her.

"Do you know how many times I have had to fight with Lourdes about not euthanizing you?" Cold silence and even harder stares lingered between them. "No, I imagine you have no idea. You were too busy making certain you weren't my 'means to an end'. What is my end, Tucker John? How have I come out ahead in this?"

He didn't answer her. Instead, he released her, and put more space between them. Vivian knew there was no answer, not one that he could use to condemn her. The look in his eyes, the one he couldn't mask with indifference, spoke of the degree with which he was beginning to second-guess himself. All that remained was a display of anger.

Vivian continued, "My own future is at risk now because I chose to believe there was value in your life. You have taken everything from me, or maybe I was the foolish one for leaving it unattended. Maybe I should have done like you and secured myself. Then I wouldn't be where I am now. What do you have to say to all of this? Hmmm?"

"You was going to clear my mind, send me back," he quietly growled.

Vivian laughed. "I never kept that from you! You knew I was sending you back. You knew it! And why wouldn't I? That is your timeline!"

"Did you ever consider that maybe I didn't want to go back?" He sat down on the edge of his dresser and looked at her. He was still visibly angry but had far less fire, and by his tone had completely lost the enjoyment in the moment.

Holding her stomach Vivian moaned. This was far more than she had anticipated. "You have to go back. You can't stay here."

He shook his head. "You can't make me leave, Viv. And I sure as hell ain't going to sit down and let you wipe my mind clean to do so."

Her world was spinning on an unruly axis. She began to pace. "Is this what you do? You play along just long enough to gain an inch so you can take a mile? You gain enough trust so that you can pull the rug right out from beneath people who have gone out on a limb for you?" She let out a full-on groan of tear-soaked grief. "You have no integrity, and shame on me for thinking you could develop some for your own good—"

"Enough!" He shouted so loudly Vivian thought she heard the windows shake. "This ain't got nothing to do with integrity! This has to do with me wanting a say so over my life!" He worked his jaw. With quick strides, he stood over her again. "If you ain't born to nothing, then you ain't *got* nothing! You take whatever you can get your hands on, and you fight to the death to keep it!"

He stared hard into her eyes but didn't take hold of her again. "I ain't going back, not as no brainwashed fool, and certainly not to die. I'm not giving you or anyone else the power to make that decision for me. And I sure as hell don't need nobody telling me that my life has value." His spread his arms at full wingspan. "I know I have value. I know!"

Vivian blew out a breath and turned toward the stairs. She needed to be away from him. The tension in the room was suffocating her. The pending threat was about to break her. She quickly took each step before she stopped halfway down and looked back at him. "And now I know. I know what you are." He flinched with her declaration, all the red of his face washed into stricken white. "We'll let the chips fall where they may, but you, you stay away from me."

CHAPTER 33

Animal, Viv was going to call him an animal. The realization carved at his insides like a blunt steak knife, bruising before breaking open his flesh. Tucker John stumbled after her but was silenced by the door slamming shut. He backed away from the stairs. His thoughts muddied with confusion, and his throat aching from having to swallow down the nasty words he had intended to fire at Viv's back.

His daddy had a similar effect on him, striking him silent with a searing look, treating him like a filthy animal before calling him one. His daddy hated him, and the truth of it had turned his heart to coal. Every time a body called him animal they might as well have been saying, 'I hate you,' 'You're worthless.'

Vivian Leona had stared him in the eye, and without words, had managed to say what wounded him the most. Worse, he didn't understand why he cared what, she of all people, had to say. It was her fault his life was in upheaval anyhow. She was to blame! She had no right to think ill of him. She had no right to hold him against his will, no matter her reasons!

He had done the right thing, breaking free of her hold, hadn't he? Despite what Magnus had alluded to about her not being his enemy, no female had the right to rule over a man. Nobody had the right to make him feel like a fool, least of all Viv. But for some reason, left in the silence and the aftermath of his own plans, he felt like he had gnawed off his own feet right at the ankles.

He closed his eyes and punched the wall, a curse shot from his drawn lips. How did that woman make him question his every move and his own nature? How did she make him feel shame for being who he was? He had been certain and settled in his plans against her. She was his enemy, a lady-dandy, just like his brother, Ashford Junior, and an outright tyrant like Big Bobbie. She needed to be cut down to size! *He* had cut her down, but now that he had, his stomach seemed to sour and a bad taste spread over his tongue like soft butter on warm bread. All this, and he hadn't even addressed the threat of her fool husband yet.

He dragged his hand down his face and ran it over his wet hair. The dampness of his scalp surprised him. He had been so riled up with Viv that he had broken out in a sweat. His eyes managed to move across the mess that was now the entrance of his room. The lovely dark wood vanity lay crippled on the floor. One of the legs had snapped off when Viv had thrown it down, and the mirror shards glistened in the cracks of the floorboards like the tears that had fallen out of her eyes.

He silently stared at them. He could hear Viv's muffled cries coming through the floor. He growled. "Who cares about your crying! I ain't done nothing wrong! You shouldn't have crossed me! You shouldn't have tried to cage me like some d@#% animal! I'm a man! You hear me? You should'a known better!" He hollered at the ground.

He stomped into his ensuite and snatched the waste bin from the ground. He carried it back into the other room with him and began to pick up the pieces of broken mirror. He cursed cutting his finger. Glancing at the shard in his wounded hand sent cold shame running down his spine and over his entire body. He could only see one of his eyes reflected in the tiny mirror. Blood from his finger slowly streamed across it like a crimson tear from his reflected eye. That one eye moved with anger and red from ranting, looked like that of a lunatic. It reminded him of his daddy.

The image shook him to the core. He dropped the shard in the waste bin, quickly bandaged his finger, and pulled out the letter he had received, the letter that had ignited the fire between him and Viv. Unfolding it, he read it again. The first time he had gone over it, he had laughed from deep within his belly, impervious to the words. He didn't laugh this time. This time, he felt the trueness of the rebuke, and he owned the appraisal that had been written of him.

He read:

> *"Greetings, Mr. Spruce from 1837. I promised you a letter of good faith. I am a man of my word. I would have liked to have called our meeting last night a pleasure, but I must assure you it was far from it. Your tasteless behavior and candor left much to be desired. Your blatant disregard for life and your careless disrespect for a fellow human being are insufferable! You, young man, should I be so bold to call you such, toy with things that should not be toyed with—life, to be exact. You fail to see the value in it and it sickens me.*
>
> *You had known me for not even a second and you had deduced that I was nothing more than a fly to be swatted. Because I was doing the honorable thing, and taking care of the assignment that I was sent to do—one that benefits you—I found myself in your clutches where you humiliated me, and turned me into your victim. I had to bargain for my own life, break a code of surveillance, simply because you found me inconvenient in a passing moment.*
>
> *How dare you? Who gave you the right?*
>
> *I will not waste any more ink on you, as I fear you are too ignorant to take my words seriously, but I will give you some tokens of advice since I owe it to the denizens of 4037 to do so. Life is not a child's playground. It is more a game of chess. You should be careful how you*

manipulate the pieces because one false move can cost you everything.

You may be thinking that I am nothing short of a coward for hiding behind a pen to express my opinions of you, but it is my belief that when one has encountered an insatiable beast it is best to keep one's distance even if you call to it to stay away from you. This, Mr. Spruce, is what I am doing.

Do take this letter as your first and last warning. Should you seek to find me, or harm me in any way, you will regret it. Drowned men have no rights.

~Magnus Sanderson

P.S. One more pearl of advice from one man to another, do something redeemable with the borrowed time you are on, and ditch the spade.

Tucker John closed the letter. Everything Magnus had called him out on in the message, Viv had attested to. He had called him an insatiable beast, an animal. Viv hadn't said the words but when she looked at him before she left his room when she had said she now knew what he was he knew what she'd meant. Magnus had said it, Lourdes, and just about any other person he'd known.

Few had ever thought him redeemable; his mama had though, and so had his three little siblings. There was also a little slave child called Luckette who he'd known but briefly before she died. Luckette, for some reason that only God knew, thought he was sunrise and sunset. Now it seemed that Viv had held the same estimations of him as they had. She'd thought him redeemable. But he'd accused her of thinking of him as nothing more than garbage.

It vexed him to think he'd been wrong. It was easier to do what he needed to do knowing she was just like Ashford Junior or Big Bobbie. But the devastated and disillusioned look in her eyes, when she'd realized how he had betrayed her fragile trust, proved what she had thought of him all along. No, she didn't like him one bit, but she had actually believed that he was worth the risk, that he was redeemable, that his life meant something. And what had he done in thanks besides tearing her world apart like a dry rotted cloth?

The more he thought about it, the more he realized he was no different from Lourdes or Viv's lying, cheating, husband. Tucker John had played a great hand of deceit and taken from Viv just to feed his own need, same as Lourdes and John Jay. And since he was forcing himself to be honest, he had to own the fact that she had not hurt him, and when she had, it was not because she wanted to. He'd raged against her for keeping him in 4037 when he actually had no intention of ever returning to his timeline. His behavior made no sense at all. And yet he was irrevocably in her debt.

He'd become a nasty drunk just like his daddy and Viv had weaned him off that devil's bottle. She had taken valuable time that she could have been using to find her wicked, slippery, husband, and had spent it making him healthy. She fed him, clothed him, and kept him clean, and all she asked in return was for respect. She knew his past and how he had treated people that looked like her, and still, she had been as kind as anyone could be considering her circumstances.

She was right. Anyone else would have killed him on the spot, but not her. He wasn't worth his salt but she had given him a chance to prove otherwise. He hated to admit that he owed her for that or anything. It took a stranger putting those truths into writing for him to come to see them as they were, let alone accept them.

He laughed at himself. The very fact that he was able to actually read was because Viv had given him the access to properly learn how to do so. Before he was just puttering along and guessing most of the time.

He sighed. He could feel the vibration of her moaning cries through his feet. He had worked overtime to squeeze those out of her. She sounded like his mama all the times she had cried over his daddy. The similarity made his bones tremble. He had grown to hate the man who had wounded his mama so, and somehow he had become just like him. "Tucker John, you *are* a blight."

He had never felt more shamed over who he was until that moment, and it was because of the most unlikely of people. He read the last line of the letter again. He was on borrowed time, twenty-two hundred years' worth. Opportunity was right at his fingertips. He didn't have to snatch it. All he had to do was receive it. He needed to do something redeemable with his time, just like Magnus had said. If he couldn't do anything else, he could at least help Viv find John Jay, make her stop crying for a moment, even though he knew the tears would be worse when she learned the truth about the man. Instinct told him that he wouldn't like what he found either, but it was better to have the man in his sights than lingering in the wind.

A warning about him coming from lips born in the future was enough to settle that. He needed to see this situation for what it was and not what he wanted it to be. He was caught in crosshairs of a deadly hunt, one that involved a man, his mistress, and a wife he had clearly betrayed.

***

Clarence broke connection with his 'other' employers. Their instructions were to leave things as they were concerning Tucker John, assuring him that everything would right itself in due time. Magnus had swapped out John Jay's DNA in exchange for Tucker John's in order to send the man a certified letter. In his haste, he'd neglected to put things back to right.

Mr. Schulsler had no idea about the swipe, just like he had no idea about the static-wraiths, or that Tucker John had nearly killed Magnus. But then he didn't need to know. If he ever found out about the DNA swipe he would only feel inclined to tighten the noose around Magnus' neck, and thusly Clarence's, and no one had any time or room for that. Clarence already had a full plate; playing as Mr. Schulsler's hand-for-hire, making sure Magnus did as he was told, securing specific moments within that timeline as per his other employer's orders, all while remaining truly unidentified by all parties.

He had very little patience for any more games.

It was a lot to handle, so many tugging ropes anchored to one man. But things would eventually come to a head, and like his employers had assured him, they would right themselves. So he would keep his ground, hold on against the pressure, and trust the process. What choice did he have?

CHAPTER 34

Seventy-two hours, Vivian had hidden away. She felt soggy and swollen from the tears she'd cried. In it all, she had lost her voice, but that was of little consequence. She wasn't speaking to anyone.

Lourdes had knocked on her door a few times and offered her food. Vivian knew that it wasn't out of generosity or concern. Lourdes was a creature of habit. She wanted to know what had taken place between her and Tucker John, and her only way to get to those answers was to invade Vivian's space by hiding behind a tray of food. Her attempt at ambush and inquiry by way of trickery reminded Vivian of the Trojans and the Trojan horse.

Vivian had eaten, however. She'd waited until the house was perfectly quiet before she would steal away, feed herself, and then rush to the nexus room. She barricaded herself in there for a few hours each night, searching. If there was ever a time she needed John Jay with her it was then.

Tucker John had blindsided her with such force and velocity that she felt like she had whiplash. All the while she had believed that he was making progress. His language had become more tempered, his attitude, though still volatile at times, was noticeably less volatile than before. He had even kept the farm running far better than she or John Jay had. Tucker John knew things about farming that she didn't know but then he also knew things about deceit, and he managed to do both with an air of expertise.

She had taken the chance to look for the intermezzos while she roamed the house, and true to his word, Tucker John had indeed stolen them and hidden them away. If it wasn't for the simple fact that his shotgun lay loaded underneath her floorboards, she would have truly felt powerless against him, against them. It became painfully obvious just the night before that Lourdes and Tucker John had been working together against her.

She hadn't slept that night and had slipped down into the kitchen for something to eat. It was well past two in the morning when she saw Lourdes sneaking away from the house, occasionally looking back behind her before moving on. Suspicion had made Vivian's chest tighten. At first, she thought that Lourdes was going off to report her to the Cleric's Office. She had left Lourdes alone with Tucker John for nearly three days. There was no telling what he had done or threatened to do to her. Perhaps she was fed up.

Her suspicions quickly shifted to disgust when she saw Tucker John slinking down the same path as Lourdes, only a few moments later, both of them heading in the direction of Balm Hill. It didn't take a genius to know what was happening. Tucker John and Lourdes were having a secret affair.

Now that Tucker John was free, he could meet with Lourdes whenever and wherever they wanted. Vivian would no longer be in their way. The newfound knowledge made her despise the both of them. Why couldn't they have just been honest with her instead of stabbing her in the back and the chest? Worse, none of it made any sense. They hated each other or maybe it was just the tension of baser attractions causing them to act as if they did. Again she wondered why they had chosen not to just tell the truth.

"That's just the kind of people they are." She answered herself again like she had the other night when she ruminated over their affair. For some reason, she just didn't see Tucker John being the type to sneak around with a woman. But who was she to deny what her eyes had shown her? At least they kept their activities under the cover of darkness. If the community suspected an affair, believed John Jay was involved with

Lourdes in any way other than professional, their surveillance would be brought to an end, and everything they had hidden would be exposed.

It was already late in the morning and Vivian hadn't heard either of them. She assumed Tucker John was tending to his chores even if she had no clue where Lourdes was off too. She couldn't be at Balm Hill. Alma Berry wouldn't abide her taking a 'married' man under her roof. She wouldn't know about it at night.

Nevertheless, Vivian was grateful for the emptiness in the house. She needed to move freely. There were things she needed to do in the lab especially now since she had discovered something growing on her nexus gate.

She'd been working that prior evening when the strange, grainy matter dropped from the gate. If she hadn't lost her voice she would have screamed from the fright. She wasn't easily spooked, but since her gate had been on the fritz she was overly cautious and anxious about anything coming out of it.

The material she discovered moved like a liquid but it wasn't liquid. It was silent but it felt like it was a vacuum for sound. She didn't know what it was. Had things not been as they were, she would have contacted the Cleric's Office and reported it. Being caught in the continuing snowball effect of her first act of silence, she couldn't. Instead, she carefully scraped what she could of the golden substance into a container and locked it away in the lab. She was on her way to run some tests on it when the doorbell rang.

"Please Lord, not now!" She chewed her lip, coughed to clear her throat, and tried to make herself as presentable as possible. Her hair was pulled back in a massive, frizzy bun, her clothing hadn't been changed in two days, and there was very little she could do about the bags underneath her eyes besides sleep, and she wasn't getting very much of that unless she was full of *Paz.*

She blew out a breath, ran her fingers across her matted hair, patting the strays down, and painting on the best smile she could before pulling the door open. The same cleric from the other day greeted her.

His smile quickly faded at the sight of her. He shifted the basket he was carrying to one hand and pointed at Vivian. "Someone has not taken the *XBalance* that I suggested."

Vivian didn't know what to say.

The cleric waved his hand and smiled again. "You must be on something really incredible in the timeline if you are going at your work like this!" He bounced on his heels and leaned forward. "I shamelessly admit that I am very jealous! Don't tell anyone."

Vivian returned the smile. This one was sincere. There would be no Team Review that day, at least not at that moment.

The cleric offered her the oversized basket. "This is for you, ma'am. There's no signature needed this time," he held up his thumb. "Just make sure to find comfort in it." He smiled again.

Unable to hide her confusion, she frowned. "What's this for? Who's it from?" Her voice was scratchy.

The cleric pointed at the card on the top. "I believe it is from our Chief Cleric in rotation, Quinn Ellington. See?"

"Yes, yes it is," she studied the large basket, confused as to why it had been sent. When she looked up to ask the young cleric, he had already boarded his sled and was well down the path leading off of her property.

Closing the door behind her she pulled the card out from the basket and read over it. Her eyes darted over the printed ink once again, and her brow arched with irritation. "What in the world is going on?"

Frustrated, she grabbed her conical hat and went for her sled. She couldn't deny the relief she was feeling at having not had a T.R, but she couldn't chance leaving the door open for one to suddenly fall upon her. This situation needed sorted, and as quickly as possible.

It usually took her twenty minutes to get to the Cleric's Office on the sled, but with how she gunned the power, she would be there in ten.

***

Tucker John came up the back hills of Viv's property just in time to see her speeding off on a sled. He'd been off on the farm since before sunrise. One of Viv's cows had gone into labor and needed a bit of help since the calf was turned. He'd never liked that kind of farm work. He'd only helped with a calf birthing a few times in his youth and was far from an expert on matters, but he had done enough to ensure that both the calf and its mama survived the ordeal.

The situation, the dislike, the filth, the uncertainty even while all parties involved grappled for life, reminded him of his situation with Viv. The mess with John Jay and Lourdes, him being two-thousand years out of his time, Viv not knowing heads from tails, it was no different from the cow and the calf. It was a mess, an involved mess that could leave all involved, injured or dead if the wrong move was made. The thing of it was he was beginning to see Viv as more the calf than anyone, even himself. She was more helpless and unwittingly at the mercy of others than she knew, which was all the more reason for him to have a sit-down with her.

He'd hoped to be back at the house before lunchtime to catch her by herself. He needed to mend broken fences, secure his standing with her while he prepared for whatever danger might be lurking.

He hated not knowing. Part of him wanted to hunt down Magnus Sanderson and force him to tell him what he was up against. It had to be something nasty if a man was sent from the future to verify what he, of all people, was up to. It put him on edge, made him leery in the same ways he was when Ash was out of sights but lurking somewhere nearby, just waiting for the worst time to come home and raise hell.

Tucker John had at least managed to intercept a written message from Lourdes to Viv saying she was going off to the Cleric's Office to check on any messages that Viv's team might have received before heading over to check on her non-existant mama. She would be gone for a few of hours.

That was all the time he'd needed to search through her things.

He shoved his filthy hand in his pocket to make sure that the earring he'd found in Lourdes' bedroom was still there. It was. He'd offered another prayer to God for direction in how to help Viv and himself in regard to their hidden enemy. He'd literally gone from the pot into the fire, from being Viv's hostage to his time-twins prey. He hated the feeling. Always had.

The thought that came to mind, shortly after his prayer, was to keep an eye on the mistress. Mistresses always seemed to know a bit more than the wives did regarding a man's 'extra' activities, at least that always held true in Tucker John's accounting of things. Sometimes the mistress knew very little, but with John Jay not being as lost as things seemed, Magnus marking him as an enemy, and Lourdes being so desperately out for Tucker John's blood, it only stood to reason that she knew exactly what was happening.

Tucker John spent a few careful moments the day before going through Lourdes' bedroom and closets. From what he had discovered, she and John Jay had been bedding down together for the better part of two years. That began to shine a little bit of light as to why Lourdes had an unauthorized nexus gate in her mama's house. If she and John Jay had a longtime affair going on, then it was possible she was looking for him too. But that reason didn't hold any weight when Tucker John considered his and Lourdes' earlier conversations.

Thinking about her posture from the very beginning only heightened his suspicions that she knew that her beloved Johnny had planned his sudden disappearance. There she was, his mistress, not shedding a single tear, not showing an iota of distress. What she did show was annoyance at Tucker John's being present, as if he somehow was a great inconvenience. That, and the fact she had urged Viv not to contact the Cleric's Office about him being present or John Jay missing.

Then there was the way she tended to further play Viv. She continued to give her best attempts to manipulate Viv into disposing of him. It was as if the little harpy was simply biding her time for something while attempting damage control, all while lying about tending to her mama when there wasn't a single soul living at Balm Hill.

Alba Berry was good and dead, and had been for several months. He'd found the record of her euthanasia last night. The record said that she was infected with an extreme case of sadness, rage, and anxiety—all spelled out in fancy words. Her symptoms were especially heightened whenever she laid eyes on Lourdes. Tucker John thought that was understandable. Lourdes had the same effects on him.

Because Alba Berry had stroked as a result of her emotional condition, she was unable to communicate, and would not cooperate with the medical staff at the hospital. The government had determined that her emotional illnesses were too far gone and deemed it a waste of time to heal her of her paralysis as a result. So they put her to death instead.

That chafed his hide something fierce! The ideology of 4037 made him angrier than a wet tomcat. He was no saint by any stretch of the word, but to put a person to death because they were sad was just madness! They would have killed his mama had she lived during the 4030's. Law or not, Tucker John would have never done his mama wrong, never condemned her for her tears. How in the world was he being accused of not valuing human life? Hell, Lourdes had had her own mama put down. She was as vile as they came.

That still didn't explain why she was speaking into a bowl full of shining sand whenever she sat down in front of her nexus gate. Either she had gone completely out of her mind or she had discovered something new, and was trying to use it to communicate with John Jay somehow. He didn't know for certain but he couldn't dismiss the possibility of communication. He had, in one stride of his horse's hooves, stepped twenty-two hundred years into the future, after all. Why couldn't a bowl full of gold dust connected to a makeshift nexus gate be some kind of mode of communication?

What he did know for sure was that the strange substance had begun to grow on his clipboard ever since he had connected it with Lourdes' nexus gate, and it was starting to appear on Viv's since he had interloped into hers not long after.

He'd always been a quick study with mechanical things. He never would have imagined that the same would hold true for electronics. Hell, he didn't even know electronics existed. But now that he did—and had discovered his gifting—he certainly couldn't waste it in 1837. When this was all over, he needed to start over in a place where his talents could be cultivated. He just had to survive 4037 in order to do so.

He made certain that he recorded the information about Alba Berry on his clipboard so that he could use it later to his advantage. Him knowing the truth and being able to prove it were two different things. He needed to clearly keep things documented. All of it was another log to add to the fire he was building to burn Lourdes and John Jay down. Lourdes knew more about John Jay's disappearing than she was letting on. The pair was undoubtedly up to something nefarious. History had said as much.

At least Tucker John had been able to spot Lourdes' ilk from the beginning. Using the earring with John Jay's face, and the words *'you were worth the time and wait'* inside of it, and the record that proved she was lying about her mama, might be the right kind of leverage that he would need to bring Viv over to his side of things. There was also the possibility that it could make Lourdes tell what she knew about John Jay's whereabouts.

He snorted. He knew no matter how easy it was in theory, he would have a better time selling Viv snake oil than he would with getting her to believe him, even if he showed her his evidence. Women didn't cotton to hearing negative things about the men they loved. Lourdes could have slit his throat when he'd called John Jay a boy. There was no telling how Viv would respond when she found out the truth concerning the man. It wouldn't be in kind, of that much he was sure.

Wiping the sweat from his brow, he pulled the barn door open and led the cow and its calf safely inside. After getting them settled, he tended to a few other chores before heading back into the house. He smelled horrible. The thought made him laugh from his belly.

He had shamelessly become very spoiled with his new way of life. Hot bath water soaking into his muscles after hard chores had become a guilty pleasure. Besides that, his own body odor had begun to offend his nostrils, whereas in 1837 he hadn't really noticed it at all. He needed a bath, and quick, especially if he thought to have a word with Viv once she got back. If she hated him for the way he had betrayed her trust, she really wouldn't receive him if he smelled as bad as his behavior had been especially with the tidings he intended to bring along with him.

CHAPTER 35

Vivian gripped the rim of her conical hat and forced down her brewing temper. She counted inside her head before she parted her lips again. "Clarence? That's what you said your name is, correct?"

The plain-faced man looked squarely at her. If not for the strangeness of his blue eyes that were dark and yet pale, and freckled with bits of green and brown, Vivian would have easily forgotten him. He had the same attractive appeal as a blank sheet of paper, yet his coloring helped him fit perfectly within the New Golden age. Except, Clarence wasn't golden, he was more the color of almond paste, just like his hair. Even his lips were washed out. He was simply blank.

"Yes, Clarence Mantov." He blinked slowly, appearing far from moved by Vivian's annoyance.

She forced a smile. "Clarence, you're the *fifth* cleric that I've spoken to in the last forty-five minutes. And it seems I have no other options since all of the chiefs are in a meeting." She slid the card to him. The other clerics pretended not to pay any attention to her poor attempts at not making a scene. "Please, if you would, read this card out loud."

Clarence raised a brow but read the note. "Dear, Vivian Leona, Please accept this comfort basket as a token of grace and my sincerest apology for causing you any inconvenience with the Team Review. Signed, Chief Cleric in Rotation, Quinn Ellington." He closed the card and slid it back to Vivian. "Is there a problem with this card—"

"Yes!" Vivian settled herself again. "Forgive me, yes, there is a problem. I haven't had a Team Review." She touched her throat. It was beginning to ache.

Clarence held her gaze. "Then you are displeased with the basket?"

"No, Clarence, I'm displeased with the fact that for over three weeks," she held up three fingers. "My team and I have been waiting for a Team Review even though they have to be conducted within fifteen days."

"I explained that to her already," another cleric added. Vivian gave the man a warning glare. The cleric quickly shut his mouth.

"I'm well aware of the protocol, as I already explained to you." She turned her attention back to Clarence. "I have called the office for the last few weeks and have gotten nothing but incompetence in regard to my situation. No one has been able to give me any explanation as to what is going on. All I've been told is that I must've made a mistake. Who makes a mistake like this? Team Reviews are a serious matter. Then today I receive this comfort basket with a printed apology for the inconvenience."

Clarence smiled politely. "Perhaps the comfort basket was sent because you had made a mistake about there being a review, and Chief Quinn only wanted to put you at ease."

Vivian's jaw set, her face stone. Her fisted hand gravitated to her hip.

Clarence gave her another curious look. He said, "Vivian, I sympathize with your situation. Unfortunately, I don't believe that I'm able to assist you with it."

Vivian coughed. What was left of her voice was on its last leg. "Where is Chief Quinn?"

"She isn't here. She's on maternity leave."

"Of course she is," she extended her right hand. "I'm requesting access to my team files from the last thirty days."

"That isn't necessary."

"Yes, Clarence. I want to prove that a review was scheduled and never conducted."

A strange stillness and a cold glint flashed in Clarence's eyes. His smile fled. Vivian shifted uncomfortably as he offered her a thumbprint DNA analysis. "Do you want a Team Review?" He asked, a hint of warning in his tone.

"No! That would be a negative mark on my record." What she wanted was time and assurance that she wouldn't have to keep looking over her shoulders, fearful of the clerics showing up. She already had enough to worry about. "What I want is assurance that I will be able to continue my research without the constant concern that a team of clerics will be at my door interrupting me. It hasn't been easy with this at the back of my mind, especially with your staff talking to me as if I were thick-skulled each time I raised a question about it."

Clarence leaned forward, the look in his eyes pushed her back a step, their color swirling like a darkening storm. He had the most peculiar gaze. It was cold, cold in a way that she could not explain. "Then maybe you should consider not calling. Clearly, there was a mistake. Sometimes, it's best to leave dead bones where they lay buried."

Vivian pressed her conical hat on and tightened it under her chin. She was through talking. "I'll be able to access my records from my station at home, correct?"

Clarence nodded.

She gave him a curt tilt nod and headed for the door before turning back around. "One more thing, Clarence, could you please have the interim Chief in rotation, forward me confirmation that there will be no Team Review in the future? You said they are in a meeting, but I can't wait to see them. Can you have them do that for me please?"

"Yes. It's already been handled." He stared unblinkingly.

"Thank you, Clarence."

With that she was gone, back on her sled, rushing home. She moved just as quickly to her house as she did to the Cleric's Office. She was glad that she had. Something about Clarence Mantov made her uneasy. She couldn't tell if he was threatening her or warning her, or both. Either way, she was glad to be home, especially now having the assurance there would be no trespassing from the Cleric's Office in the near future.

As soon as her foot hit the threshold of the front door she heard movement above her head. Someone was finally home. She tiptoed to her office and then to the nexus room. She quickly connected her clipboard to the nexus station and downloaded all of the files that the Cleric's Office had forwarded to her before rushing off to her bedroom. Just as the door was closing she caught a glimpse of Tucker John only a millisecond after she had inhaled the full scent of his bath soap.

"Viv!" Tucker John called out to her.

She didn't answer. She placed her clipboard down on her desk and took a deep breath trying to still her racing heart. Tucker John pounding on the door only sped it up all the more. She didn't want to see him and she couldn't fathom why he was trying to see her. Wasn't he the same person who had called her a cockroach?

"Viv! Open up. I need to talk with you." Tucker John waited several seconds before he called out to her again. Three days had been enough, hadn't it? She had stopped crying two days ago. She should have been okay to talk. He had no intention of fully divulging his suspicions but he did want to clear as much stink out of the air between them, the sooner the better. "Viv!" He called out again.

Still, there was no response. He left her door and sat on the stairs outside her room for nearly thirty minutes before knocking again. He couldn't keep himself from knocking harder than he had before. "*Viv*, open the door. We need to talk…What I need to say is important." He jiggled the door handle. He didn't know why he was getting so frustrated but he was. Her ignoring him was making his skin itch. "Viv, you can't hide in there forever!"

"Want to bet?" She responded.

He glared at the door tempted to knock it down. "Viv it's been three days. Now that's several meals you've missed having with me," he pressed, drawing at straws. "You promised me that you wouldn't miss another meal according to the agreement that you made...Come out of that room! Let's have a little chat." He waited again and then tossed in a 'please' for good measure. It came through clenched teeth, but it was delivered nonetheless. That was more pleases' he'd used in over a decade.

"Viv?" He said her name again and put his palm against the wood. He hated remembering things that had pained him and waiting in the silence for Viv was making him do just that. His mama had locked herself away once she had blown his daddy's brains out. She didn't eat and she wouldn't get out of the bed. She died not long afterward. The longer Viv ignored him, the more he thought about it, the more anxious he became. No wonder he was feeling the way he was.

Viv finally responded. "Tucker John," her voice was raspy but he could hear her. He watched the dance of shadow and light play beneath the crack in the door as she moved forward.

His brow perked and he softened his tone. "We need to talk Viv. Please."

Vivian's stomach clenched. She could only see deceit in his desire to talk to her. She had no idea what he could have possibly wanted. One thing was for sure, she wasn't inclined to give it to him.

His sudden gentleness was his sick attempt to get her to open the door. It was another Trojan horse. She said, "You tell me one thing first, Tucker John,"

"I'm listening,"

"Is there an intermezzo sensor underneath the skin of your inner ankle?" Silence met her question. She scowled. "That's what I thought. You have nothing to say to me. Get away from my door. Liar!" She smacked her side of the door with her hand and walked back to her bed.

Tucker John recoiled before his fists clenched. He sensed Lourdes in the house and only turned when he heard her on the stairs. She didn't say anything to him. She only gave him a wicked smile as she walked past him. She was so contented. Tucker John's eyes followed her until she was out of sight. He turned back to the closed door before finally walking away.

CHAPTER 36

Lourdes stood in the window of her bedroom and let the heat of the afternoon sun dry her freshly washed skin. It had been a long night and an equally long afternoon, but she had completed just about everything that Johnny had told her to do. Letters to Emlen Spruce, Johnny's widowed mother, had been left at the Cleric's Office first thing that morning. They would arrive in her care in 6037 at separate moments. All of the letters were misdated, of course, a detail that Johnny would take care of, but they were enough to keep Emlen from worrying about him for the next couple of years as she usually did. She would, however, be fed just the right dosage of doubt against Vivian's sanity, converting her into a witness for her and Johnny's cause.

Lourdes had also spent a great many hours working on the perimeter fence. She was far from done with that phase of her tasks, but what she had accomplished was a step toward her finally being able to be with Johnny. She had to reroute the fence so that its failsafe was no longer powered by the Cleric's Offices in either 4037 or 6037. It would be powered solely from within.

She'd gotten most of the fence's sensors to trace back to the nexus gate at Balm Hill. The last leg of the task was to connect the failsafe from within Vivian's house. Once she and Johnny were together, they would activate it and the fence would be impenetrable from the outside for nearly two years. They would, of course, blame it on a technical malfunction, say that, in the fall out with the Animal, they were trapped inside, but in the event that the Governors didn't buy that story, they would still be safe from their clutches for a time.

There was very little that she needed to do in regards to Vivian and the Animal. Tucker John had hanged himself in Vivian's eyes and Vivian had done a fine job of making herself look suspiciously unstable in the eyes of more than half the Cleric's Office. Lourdes had thrown a few extra logs on that fire by pretending to be completely unaware of Vivian ever mentioning to her a Team Review. She even added in a couple of 'mindless' remarks about Vivian locking herself away and frantically working all hours of the night, and then having to take Paz to calm herself down.

That had garnered some wary looks from the clerics within earshot, and even a distasteful sneer from the wiry, pale-skinned man with the ice blue eyes. She had no idea who he was but he turned his gaze away from her when someone had called out the name 'Magnus.' He was one of the chiefs who was rarely seen she'd realized.

She smiled at fate. If it weren't for fate things would not have been working so well in her and Johnny's favor.

She rubbed on some skin cream and then splashed on a bit of perfume. Then she slipped on her peach colored, floor length dress with the wide flowing sleeves. She smoothed it out on her frame and then combed back some of her hair behind her ears just the way Johnny liked it. She'd even been growing it out longer to please him. He said long hair would make her look more like the goddess she was.

She did a turn, admiring herself in the mirror. This is what she would wear on their first night together. She looked perfect, almost perfect. She knew just what she needed to complete her look.

She pulled open her vanity drawer and lifted the false bottom away. She slid her hand into the darkness of the cavity and felt the smoothness of one of the red bobble earrings that Johnny had gotten made for her kiss her fingertips as it rolled by. Pulling it out, she went for the other, her hand searching aimlessly in the dark with no reward.

"Where is it?" She huffed before pulling the entire drawer from the vanity and tossing aside the false bottom. Her heart sank and her face grew hot. Where was her other earring? She quickly rummaged through all her other drawers and checked with frantic eyes around her floor and under the bed for the earring. There was nothing there.

Lourdes' stomach began to sink, the corners of her mouth dipping as she fought off crying. How could she have lost it? She was certain that she hadn't worn it outside of her room in a while, two weeks ago to be exact, and she had put the earrings away shortly after. She had to have. Frustrated, she chewed her bottom lip until it was nearly as red as the single bobble in her hand.

She stared at herself in the mirror again. She wouldn't lose her peace or her focus. She would find the earring later on. Vivian was too caught up in her downward spiral to notice something as insignificant as an earring, and Tucker John was too caught up in himself to cast a second glance at it if he were to come upon it. She let out a breath and shook off the sudden tension that had engulfed her. Things were going to be fine. She and Johnny were on the right track, earring or no earring, there was nothing that could possibly go wrong.

***

(Some place in the Static of time)
John Jay felt his blood curdling as the flesh of his hands and arms seemed to peel back in thin, painful layers. But it was worth it, the pain, the blood, the sacrifice. He was doing this for his name's sake, doing it for himself and Lourdes. He had to keep pushing if he ever hoped to get back to her, ever hoped to establish himself. This would make his mother proud. It would make Marcus proud, knowing that, despite a tragedy, his best friend had made an incredible discovery in surveillance. Marcus and everyone else would know he was far more than a Tech or

the husband of Vivian Leona. But there were so many barriers, bigger than Vivian had ever been, standing in his way now.

John Jay had managed to work out the time with the letters Lourdes had sent for him to his mother. He'd shifted what was necessary in order to do so—making sure each message showed up at a certain date and time—but he hadn't taken into account the subsequent domino effect that would happen in the timeline once he began his work of shifting and blocking out moments.

The static was still very new to him. Events that he hadn't even touched seemed to slide forward, hovering over the dark places he'd purposefully caused, kinking the thread of time, blocking his exit route. The very road that led directly to 4037 was as knots, leading anywhere and everywhere at once. His only option was to shift more static, move the unnecessary events out of his path. He had no choice.

He braced himself and forced his burning hands against the dark golden glow and with a guttural growl watched as more moments faded into the black with each step backward in time that he made, giving little care to the hovering consequence.

CHAPTER 37

Tucker John whistled a catchy tune, mimicking the lovely music that Viv had turned on. He didn't know what it was, but he liked its upbeat tempo and the sound of the horns. It made him want to dance. It also toned down his simmering temper when he considered his continuous, and deathly inconvenient, handmade circumstances. Viv still wasn't talking to him and probably never would again by the way things looked. If worse came to worse he would just have to make her. Women were some of the silliest creatures God ever done made!

He'd never quite cared about anybody not talking to him, especially not a female, and he couldn't wrap his mind around why he cared that Viv wasn't doing so, other than the fact that her husband and Lourdes were up to no good and more than likely trying to kill the both of them.

In situations like these, his usual mindset was every man for himself, but there remained the scathing itch that kept reminding him that he owed her. He also needed her. There were still too many technical variables that he hadn't quite gained his footing upon in regards to the 4030's. Had Lourdes not destroyed his *Spadds* treatment, had the one prior to that not been compromised, he would have been set to go without Viv. As it stood, she was now his missing piece in the time-puzzle, immediate access to pertinent information without having to sift through useless garbage, so he couldn't afford to lose her...not yet anyway.

He wasn't interested in polite conversation with her. To hell with that! The only talk he'd ever really mastered was the art of putting a few hateful choice words together when the need arose. He also wasn't the type to apologize since he didn't make it a habit to misstep. Since he had made a grave mistake with Viv, was walking blindly while she continued to shun him, he was growing more and more restless by the minute, music aside. She clearly couldn't sense real danger. Her silence was more infuriating than any of the words she had hurled at him in the past weeks. The fool woman didn't have a grasp on the severity of their situation! But why would she? She was too caught up in her slimy husband and didn't have the privilege of having a man from the future warn her of his lack of character.

He'd tried for the last few hours to busy himself since his failed attempt to talk with her. John Jay was the first project that came to mind which only led his thinking back to how Viv was not speaking to him. Although he was in 'control' of things now, there was nothing he could do to get her to respond to him. Finding John Jay was the only olive branch or bait that he could think of. He had, more than once, thought to just out Lourdes, and her affair with the man, in order to redirect Viv's shunning energies from off him and get her to focus her attention on the pending trouble. But people had an uncanny way of shooting the messenger and he was sure as the sun was shining that Viv would murder him for telling her that truth.

His anxiety over the woman all seemed silly and desperate which only made him pace his room in a fit of anger before the music began. Had this been happening with the slave-woman, he would have gotten her straight real quick. She knew better than to ignore him, but Viv wasn't the slave-woman, and he certainly didn't hold that kind of sway over her even though she had developed a strange hold over him. All of it made him want to scream; not knowing what kind of threat John Jay was, not having all the information he felt he needed to pursue his hunt. There were too many variables that exceeded his expertise.

What he did know was that surveillance specialists, like Viv, were called into time Fields to survey events that had influenced major shifts within the fabric of time and humanity. Magnus Sanderson had been sent to survey them, and even though that was a great nugget of knowledge, it still wasn't much to go on. He tried to cheat by peeking ahead into the future but his intermediate knowledge of nexus study only led him into black holes in time. Nothing gave a hint as to what he was truly up against.

Taking full advantage of his freedom, he decided to take a walk and clear his head when the calming effect of the music had faded. He needed a new course of action. His failed plan to get Viv and Lourdes under his boot had derailed him and left him worse off than he had been before. Revenge was no longer a plan, Lourdes aside. Getting free was pointless since he had no place to go as of yet, and finding John Jay was proving easier said than done if he couldn't figure out how the boy had managed to disappear without a trace. Even the nexus gate couldn't find him.

Tucker John knew he could employ his skills as a bounty hunter and tracker to find his trail somehow but he needed information to do that and Viv's mouth was sealed shut like a fresh caught clam's, which only dropped him back at square one.

She'd told him a few short details about how John Jay disappeared, that according to her, the nexus gate wasn't working properly because it needed nanoids from 6037. She said they had ordered them from the Cleric's Office but they still hadn't arrived. He decided he would start with investigating the nexus gate and nanoids, since John Jay was the one responsible for its upkeep.

It took him nearly three hours to reach the Cleric's Office since he really had no idea where exactly it was located. What he did know was it was in town and had a specific clock face with a symbol of an hourglass on its exterior. He also had to attribute the length of his journey to the surrounding distractions of the world outside of Viv's property and Balm Hill. He'd learned about the use of modern farming equipment; harvesters, sowers, tillers, all of them computerized and only used for greater farming jobs. He'd not had to use any of them for Viv's property, at least not yet, but seeing them hover across fields, directed by men and women in conical hats certainly struck a picture against the serene and simplistic landscape.

Besides all of that, walking to town was seemingly uneventful. As Viv had told him, little in the way of scenery had changed much since his era or rather much of it had been recreated. Central Georgia, as the capital city was called, made him feel, not so much like he'd stepped back into 1837 Georgia, but that he had gone straight home to South Carolina, back to his boyhood. The city center reminded him of Charleston's French Quarter, the only difference being that most of the buildings were the golden color of sand; few of them had the soft blush of pastel hues brushed into their facades. All of them were capped with copper roofing that shone in the sun like gold. The streets were cobbled or paved. Modern lights hung in place of those he was familiar with.

Several triangular floral and fruit gardens with central fountains pointed in the direction of Main Street, which was at the center of town, guiding denizens into its hub like a compass. Large palms, benches, and light posts stood sentry along the walking paths with an inviting allure that drew a soul into its heart.

The city was exquisite.

What struck him was the integration of dark and light skin, the seeming equality that threaded throughout the community. Black folks worked alongside white folks and even had the shameless gall to look them in the eye or touch them. The first time he bore witness to a black man touch a white woman, he felt his ire rise, only for it to rise higher when he heard his conscience question his primary response.

That was another 'something' he had to pin on Viv. He'd all but concluded he had no conscience until the day she'd given him his first *Spadds* treatment. His conscience's recent resurrection had nearly driven him mad. More so than anything, he reckoned his mama's God was doing a work on him, work he had given Him leave to do since he'd bargained with his freedom.

Then there was the coloring of a majority of the people around him. Like the buildings of Central Georgia, no matter the person's eye color, hair texture, rounded features or otherwise, most of them had a distinctively golden skin tone. *Mullatos*, he'd whispered under his breath, remembering what Viv had told him. From the late 3000's into the 4000's, the world, especially in the Americas was experiencing what they called the 'New Golden Age.' Viv hadn't gone into depth about it, assuming that the *Spadds* had given him all the information that he needed about that era. It was evident, now, what the term meant.

Cursing under his breath, he batted stinging sweat from his eyes. For the first time since being out, he regretted not grabbing the silly looking conical hat from the coat hooks by the door. He knew better. The Georgia sun was fierce, and his exposed and pampered skin was paying for it. Mostly, he wanted the horrid thing so that he could hide his eyes as he watched the golden natives of the land milling about; buying and selling their wares in the open street markets, enjoying meals at cafes. He wanted to know what made them tick.

Mullatos of his day and age had a hard and vicious go of life. It didn't seem so now. Now, everyone was truly equal, equally broken and subject to death at any show of too much emotion. But none of that mattered as long as they all had the same golden color. He gave a mocking and derisive snort. It was all fool's gold.

Catching what he was certain was the Cleric's Office a few blocks ahead he directed his steps toward it, drawn by the unmistakable emblem of the Ministry of Time, pressed into the stones just below the clock face. The large spire and columns that lined the lower level of the structure reminded him of St. Philip's church in Charleston. It was a chilling likeness, a monument from his past, and yet a perfect deception hidden in plain sight. *Just like the nexus gates.*

He took his time walking up the steps toward the main entrance, the feel of trepidation slowing his strides. What he was about to do was risky, beyond any danger he'd faced in his day, but it was necessary. The possible risks he was putting himself and Viv under by his present choice was equally as weighty as the risk of John Jay. At least with this he knew that he was walking into a potential battlefield, but he also knew things could simply work in his favor. They had thus far.

Standing at the threshold, he fingered the smaller marking for the Ministry with a tentative touch before pushing through the heavy doors. Cold air met his perspiring skin when he finally passed the threshold which brought him some much-needed relief along with a temporary air of confusion. Had he not just touched the emblem outside the doors, he would have thought he stepped into the wrong building.

Rather than entering directly into the Cleric's Office, he'd entered into a library and shop filled with a massive array of clocks and literature. The space smelled sweet and heady like bergamot and leather. The gentle tick of the clocks along with the sound of trickling water had an instantly calming effect.

He took slow and careful appraisal of the store's sanctuary-like space, glancing over the pews, tables, and noting the other exits. Force of habit. At least twenty other people sat in the pews that faced a large and intricate stained glass window, reading, or meditating. Not a single one looked his direction.

He continued his perusal, his eyes gliding over the gilded bindings of age-old tomes, his fingers tinkering with the array of clocks and watches before his eyes landed on the familiar emblem again right on the entrance of a doored corridor. The words 'Specialist Entry' were chiseled into the stone beneath the Ministry of Time's emblem.

Emboldened, he followed the long path down the narrow hallway until it deadened into a wall of black doors. There were at least twelve of them; all of them with the same, matte finishes, no handles. He selected the seventh and pushed against it only for it to slide away at his touch. Stepping beyond the threshold he found himself face to face with yet another door, this one like frosted glass. The black matte door slid closed behind him making his fist clench. A band of green light lined the bottom casing of the enclosure he was now trapped in and slowly ran up and down his body before shifting to blue and fading into a dim yellow.

With quick eyes, he surveyed the small enclosure. He wasn't claustrophobic but he didn't shine one bit to being boxed in. Deciding he wasn't in any immediate harm—but almost certain he was now being watched—he calmed himself and took another step forward. He'd come this far. There was no turning back. The moment he did so the words 'confirmed' flashed across the frosted pane of the door before him.

Confirmed? Confirmed, what? He flexed his fingers again; a holographic image of a thumb signature box drew itself upon the glass at his chest level. The thing was similar to the one that he'd touched in order to unlock the missive Magnus Sanderson had sent him. Clearly, the Cleric's Office wasn't just going to let any old Jo walk in off the street. He should have considered that before coming, giving thought to the security measures they would employ. He and John Jay sharing the same face was one thing. Him walking into the Cleric's Office as the man wasn't proving to be as easy as he'd thought.

Again, he had thought of the risk he would be causing himself and Viv before he'd made it into Central Georgia, he'd also considered the risk he would be taking if he left everything to chance and didn't investigate what he needed to know about the nexus gate. The only thing standing between him and the potential answers was a signature scanner and another step forward. Thus far, he'd been confirmed; twice if he included Magnus'. There was no reason for his signature to be rejected now.

"Thirds a charm," he mumbled.

Holding his breath he pressed his thumb against the glass shield and stepped back as the door slid open. The instant shift from the warm dark woods of the store, the cavernous dark of the hallway, the pale yet muted glow of the enclosure, to bright sterile whites, made his eyes ache, and his adrenaline rush in his ears. Blessedly, just like Viv's nexus gate, the whole of the Cleric's Office and their systems had indeed believed him to be John Jay and welcomed him with open arms.

"John Jay, it's been a while!"

Tucker John shifted his gaze to see the cleric behind the massive desk. He quickly stepped into character, bringing to memory some of John Jay's vocal recordings. He hadn't had the chance to really practice them on anyone until that moment, besides Viv. *No better time than the present.*

Plastering on a smile he approached the counter. "It certainly has been."

The man nodded, inputted information in the desk's computer, and then responded again. "Yeah, I hear you and Vivian are really busy up at the house. You must be close to some fantastic verification."

"We've been working hard. We've had a few hiccups, though."

The man looked up, a curious expression on his face. Tucker John didn't know if the expression was because of suspicion with Tucker John's under-practiced accent or something else. He was relieved to find out it was something else.

"Hiccups? Vivian was in here a few hours ago. She kicked up a bit of dust over some T.R she thought was scheduled but wasn't. Lourdes was in before that and said she hadn't heard anything about the Review, but said Vivian was locking herself up and taking a ton of *Paz*." The man spoke with an easy conversational tone. Still, Tucker John heard the slight mark of concern that accented each word.

He fixed his expression but his ears burned a shade redder and it wasn't because of sunburn. Lourdes knew full well a Review had been scheduled! What was she playing at telling that lie? He said, "You know how Lourdes is, she must've forgotten with all that we've been working on. She's been a busy girl herself. Obviously, it slipped her mind."

The cleric raised his brow. "That's bizarre because we looked and have no record of a Review. Sorry to say it, but a bit of chatter had been going about because of Vivian calling so much in regard to the situation. You know it can be very inconvenient when people talk in 4037."

Tucker John shook his head. "I don't know what happened. I just know Viv, uh," he cleared his throat covering up his use of her shortened name. "Vivian overslept the day of her Cleric's Assessment and her conversation with the Chief didn't go so well. Chief Quinn said she was scheduling a Team Review." He could have kissed the feet of Jesus for allowing him to remember the woman's name from the comfort basket note Viv had dropped outside her bedroom door in her haste to get away from him.

The cleric stood straighter, his shoulders back. "Oh, now it's starting to make sense. That must have been the day Chief Quinn was reprimanding just about everyone in her path. Her hormone levels had been much compromised by her pregnancy. I think she had twins. No wonder the comfort basket was sent. I'm sure everything will be put back in order as soon as she returns to active duty."

Tucker John nodded. "That's good news. I was beginning to think the unrecorded T.R was a result of a system malfunction." He threw in the words, hoping to sound as modern as John Jay.

"What do you mean? The systems have never had a malfunction."

He took that moment to segue into a conversation about the nexus gate. "Well, you know our nexus gate is having problems. I figured the system might have been having a similar problem."

Someone approached and handed the cleric a clipboard. "Excuse me, Evan, can you double check the verification markers in this clipboard before we send the information to 2024?" They smiled at Tucker John. "Hey, John Jay."

Tucker John smiled back. Evan took the clipboard and turned his attention back to Tucker John. "Sorry about that. Now, what were we talking about? Oh yes, malfunctions." He fiddled with the clipboard in his hands and then set it down on the desk. "Your gate needed a nanoid upgrade and replacement. That problem is rare as far as replacements go." He furrowed his brow. "I know it's been nearly a year since we had this conversation, but I figured you would remember with all the notes you took on the nanoid replacement processes. I mean come on, you're like the resident expert with nexus gates."

Evan shook his head and laughed before he connected the clipboard with his main desk for the marker verification. The familiar ball of yellow light encapsulated the clipboard, enabling it to hover. Evan manipulated several strands of the light orb before disconnecting it from the desk again.

Tucker John's ears perked. The conversation was getting more interesting by the minute. "Evan, about those nanoids, did our order for the replacement parts come in yet?"

Evan raised a finger and moved some things around on his desk screen. Another curious expression appeared on his face. "It says here that you picked those up yourself three days after they were ordered."

A strange silence filled the air. Tucker John refused to tense with the information. What he was learning about John Jay was only going from bad to worse. If John Jay picked up the replacement nanoids three days after they were ordered then what in the world was he doing making Viv believe they didn't have them? He already knew the answer. John Jay had not gotten lost. He had indeed planned this charade. But why?

Evan sighed. "By the looks on your face, you don't know what you did with them."

Tucker John played into Evan's suspicions and wiped his hands down his face. "No, don't mind me." He shook his head and laughed. "I know where they are, and all this time I thought I didn't pick them up. Verifications like this one can derail you a bit."

Evan didn't laugh. He leaned forward and waved Tucker John forward. Tucker John offered Evan his ear but was ready to strike him and run if he had to.

Evan's voice was a low whisper. "Listen, I get that you and Vivian might be on to something amazing, and by the way she looked and sounded today when she came in, it is clearly taking up a lot more time than you or she bargained for. And that's fine. I admire your dedication, but Lourdes also said she is taking a lot of Paz. Is that true? Did she get a prescription from the pharmacy?"

Tucker John considered how to answer the question. He obviously took too long. Evan read into the silence.

"I'll take that as a yes. Are you taking them too?" There was a tinge of urgency in Evan's voice.

Tucker John leaned back and studied his eyes. His gaze was sincere. "No, Evan. I am not."

Evan moved more things around on the desk. "Let me check something else. We usually don't tap into the systems of our host lines, but with so many locals being a part of the Ministry of Time, we need to at times. They're a different sort of people here." His gaze darkened. "Says here that a large order for *Paz* was placed at the pharmacy and picked up six weeks ago. Lourdes signed for them."

"Lourdes may have needed them."

"Or she got them as Vivian's proxy." Evan winced.

Tucker John frowned. "I don't know anything about that."

Evan grimaced. "I'm sorry to pry and apologize for overstepping but listen. I know I'm not directly in the Field right now, and that working behind this desk doesn't put me in the way of the same challenges that you face once you walk out those doors. It's tough here. We've had that conversation before, but as a friend, and a fellow traveler from the 6030's, I feel it is my responsibility to say something.

"Vivian is your wife, she is an admirable woman, dedicated, and reliable, but she is very ambitious. I know you can't go into detail about what you guys are verifying just yet, but she needs to be careful with the *Paz*. I personally don't believe anything in the past is worth jeopardizing our health and future. Just ask Yasmina Flytch. You know, the Surveillance Specialist who pushed for permission to do a triple-double? She hasn't been in her new Field for a complete month and already her team may be pulled." He shook his head before meeting Tucker John's gaze again. "Anyhow, Vivian ought to know how addictive *Paz* can be and mentally paralyzing."

Tucker John lowered his head and thought about all the times he had seen her pop the pills in her mouth as if they were nothing more than sunflower seeds.

"You two just be careful with those. Tell her to take an *XBalance* and detoxify before she gets herself in trouble with those things. Actually," he raised his finger again and left from behind the counter, went into one of the back rooms, and returned with a tiny black package. He handed it to Tucker John. "She can still use the *XBalance*, but tell her to take these first. They'll flush all traces of the Paz out of her system. If she's already addicted, the *XBalance* will curb that."

He stared at the small package in his hands. There were three tiny pills inside. Evan reached forward and squeezed Tucker John's shoulder, pulling him out of the pool of thoughts he had plunged into.

Tucker John looked up, curious as to the man's sincere care for a woman that was not even his. "Why are you doing this for her, Evan?" he asked. He truly wanted to know. What was it about Viv that possessed this man, Evan, to go out on a limb for her? Maybe his explanation would shed some light on why Tucker John was just about doing the same thing.

Evan gave a wan smile. "You know why. If it weren't for her I wouldn't even have this job. She's helped me get where I am, saw potential in me when no one else did, even when I screwed up. I get to be reinstated as a Field Officer in a few months' time and that's all due to her recommendation. She's a great woman. You're lucky to have her, so take care of her. Give her those on my behalf."

Tucker John tucked the package in his pocket next to Lourdes' earring. He wrapped up the niceties with Evan and began his trek back to Viv's property.

He found himself walking even faster back to the manor. He didn't know what he was going to tell Viv, not just yet. The situation was proving to be far more tangled than he had previously imagined. Ruminating on it made his blood boil with the taste for the hunt.

John Jay had picked up the nanoids for the gate three days after they were ordered. He was an expert on nexus gates. He was having an affair with Lourdes, and right in Lourdes' dead mama's basement was a homemade nexus gate that had most likely been built with the very nanoids that John Jay had ordered. And for Lourdes to be the mistress she seemed awfully smug and at ease with John Jay being gone, like she knew something. The only thing that seemed to burn her goat was the fact that Tucker John was present and alive.

Then there were the lies about going to see her mama when Alba Berry was long dead. There was no reason under the sun, that the girl didn't tell Viv that her mama had been euthanized unless she had ulterior motives. Building an unauthorized nexus gate in her basement was definitely a motivation for silence, especially if the gate in question was constructed from Viv's stolen nanoids.

He still couldn't prove anything, not as far as the boy having planned what he'd done along with Lourdes. In his own reckoning of things, he was completely convinced. But he knew Viv would be a harder sell.

Worse, he couldn't figure out why they had dragged him into it, all the way from 1837, in the first place, and as sure as his name was 'Tucker' John Josephus Spruce, there was a reason for him being present. There was going to be hell to pay, whatever their reasons were. Tucker John didn't cotton to being fooled with.

CHAPTER 38

<u>(6037)</u>

Emlen Spruce smiled as she read her monthly letter from John Jay. She still found it very amusing to be reading something that was written a couple thousand years ago by her very own son who had probably dictated the messages just moments before she received them. She was glad to have received the letter. She had been battling a small case of loneliness as of late, and John Jay's letters always brought her peace and hope for the future, even though all messages were completely one-sided.

Oh, she could respond to the messages quarterly at the Cleric's Office, where an hour was granted for families to catch up beyond the boundaries of time; something she looked forward to doing. But it certainly wasn't enough for a woman missing her small family.

Emlen was a recent retiree and a seasoned widow though she was reasonably young for a woman in transition in the 6030's. She had just turned fifty-six and John Jay had remembered her birthday. Most women her age were in the process of life reinvention, finding newer careers that were less demanding and more adventurous. She had no desire for a new career. She had a few profitable hobbies but she was more ready than anything to become a grandmother. She had deduced that her loneliness was really a case of lonely arms. It had been nearly thirty-six years since she had smelled and held a baby of her own.

Marcus and Collins had been generous with their babies and brought them over at least once a week to see her. But those little rascals were getting big and at the end of the day, they were not hers.

She found herself wondering what John Jay and Vivian's firstborn would look like. She had already decided that the baby would be the most beautiful baby ever since he or she would be her grandchild. Even though she spent much of her time imagining their child, Emlen had not initially given John Jay her blessing on marrying Vivian.

Vivian was too ambitious in her estimation. Emlen respected and even admired women who had solid career goals and managed to meet each and every one of them head-on. She really appreciated the ones who could do that and balance a family. Family was most important after all, and even though Vivian was very well integrated with her family she didn't give Emlen the impression that she had any desire to have a child in the near future. She had actually gone as far to say that she had no desire to raise a family, at least not until after she and John Jay had wrapped up their surveillance work, which could be anywhere from ten to fifteen years.

Emlen shook her head and began to put John Jay's message away. She needed to get the house in order. Marcus and Collins were dropping the children off for a few hours while they spent some alone time. As it stood, Marcus suddenly had to do more surveillance monitoring than usual. Several of the teams sent out into the Field were experiencing troubles in their assigned eras. None of the teams were his but the Cleric's Office was short staffed in regard to the recent demand and needed help. That meant he was going to have to spend more time away from home than usual.

She felt sorry for Collins and the children having to miss Marcus so much. She was going to miss him too, but such was the life of the men and women who'd taken up the mantle as Ministers of Time. She comforted herself with the knowledge that at least John Jay and Vivian were alright within their Field assignment. The letter was proof of that. She wished them the best with their work, although she shamefully admitted to herself that she wouldn't mind them coming home a little bit early.

***

<u>*(4037)*</u>

For the martyred we march on lest the living die. The words suddenly sprang into Vivian's mind and, for the first time in her life, she was beginning to think of those words as nothing more than a cattle prod—they didn't inspire her to move forward anymore, they shoved her forward with violent and threatening force. Somewhere within the last several weeks, those words had spit in her face. Who was she marching on for? Who was in danger of dying if she didn't?

At first, she had believed Tucker John to be the source of her decided march but now she saw him as the very force that was shoving her. If she stopped marching, if she stopped looking for John Jay, she would die, even if it was because of failed hope. She wouldn't allow Tucker John to kill her although she was very certain of the pending threat despite the fact he seemed focused on other things. Nevertheless, he had sworn that he would kill her and was very adamant about the fact that he was a man of his word, the negative ones more likely.

He had failed to keep his bargain with her in regards to his freedom, so she couldn't really put much stock in his integrity. Why had she done so in the first place? She knew by the way he called her 'negress' that he didn't count her worthy of any real honor. A man kept his promises with other men and even women. Tucker John viewed her as subhuman—part of the class of the missing link.

Nevertheless, she had decided she would put a bullet in him from his very own rifle if he tried to harm her. She also decided she would die the very day she did so, even if it weren't a physical death.

His rifle, a *Winchester Model 94. 30-30 Lever Action Rifle,* still held intrigue all its own. Vivian wasn't much of an expert on the invention of firearms and rifles, but she was well versed enough in history to know that rifles with the ability to fire more than one bullet without having to immediately reload were not a convenience in the 1830's. The model number itself told that it was created well after Tucker John's day. That had been one of the reasons she'd been so confused about who Tucker John was. Still, she had no answers, no real ones. How had he gotten his hand on something that was not of his timeline before he came into contact with her? All she knew was that he was not John Jay and that she was growing more fearful of the pending truth with each quandary that she faced.

All seemed at a complete loss. Her searching was still very inconclusive, both for John Jay and the strange substance that had begun to grow on her faulty nexus gate. She was beyond melancholy but she couldn't shake her own natural tenacity. She would keep searching until she found something.

She finished the cold meat sandwich she had thrown together and pushed the plate aside. If anything had blossomed in her favor it was the fact that she was no longer feeling nauseous as she had been before.

She flinched at the sound of heavy footfalls echoing in the house. It amazed her how, even with soft soled shoes, Tucker John managed to be heard as if he had on boots, but then, that was only when he wanted to. She had lost count of all the times he'd suddenly appeared out of nowhere.

She quickly moved toward the lab door and made sure it was sealed tight. If all else failed, she could use her emergency exit and take the hidden staircase all the way up to her room without him ever knowing she had been there. She'd been using that very stairwell to avoid Lourdes. Lourdes had no knowledge of it either. No one but Vivian knew about it.

Both Lourdes and Tucker John had almost completely embittered her view of humanity. At least she was right in her initial estimation of both their characters—they were indeed cut from the same selfish cloth that was devoid of any regard for the lives of others.

She made a guttural sound and shook her head. She didn't have time to spare on them anymore. She redirected her thoughts back to her research. Inputting a few codes into her computer, she waited for the test results for the strange substance to come up. She had tried conventional testing methods to find out more about the substance, but now she was employing something more organic, she was allowing the computer to describe the substance on its own.

Its description would give her a few stepping stones in regards to the rusty bloom. She was at a loss for any appropriate adjectives to describe it herself and 'glitter' certainly wasn't an option.

Several words projected themselves from the computer; *Capability, prospect, eventuality, probability, possibility, potentiality, chance, opportunity.*

She had several thousand words to weed through but they were all nearly the same thing. To sum them up, 'interrupted inertia' or better put, 'static potentiality' were the words the computer used most to identify the substance. Vivian's heart was pounding and her head grew foggy. This was big, big enough to distract her from the war zone that had become her life, and the dangerous, inexplicable curiosity of 'Tucker' John Josephus Spruce.

She made several recorded notes of what the computer had said about the substance but what had made her heart race the most was not the words 'static potentiality' nor *hazard, risk* or *accident*. Those perfectly described what she and John Jay were experiencing, and if this 'static potentiality' had anything to do with him disappearing then she would have to agree with them.

It was the last two descriptions that somehow didn't seem to fit with the others. These seemed to pock at her ribs, more so than any of the findings she'd ever unearthed about the end of the New Golden Age and the start of the Silent Revolution. These words jumped out at her and made her legs grow numb: *déjà vu* and *jamais vu*, literally 'already seen' and 'never seen'.

Those, coupled with 'static potentiality' or 'interrupted inertia,' spelled out the words 'very bad news' when it came to dealing with time travel in Vivian's estimation, and John Jay disappearing into thin air and lost in time and space was proof positive of that.

Tucker John and Lourdes suddenly became the least of Vivian's concerns. If she couldn't figure out what it was that she was dealing with, what it was that was pouring out of her nexus gate like molasses, then she was never going to see John Jay again. It would be like he had never existed; seen and yet never seen...again.

***

John Jay's heart was beating at an irregular rate. His mind was flashing with broken memories. He felt his insides convulsing as if to purge them but nothing came forth. He was losing himself.

He felt his legs being pulled in opposite directions, drawn onto competing timelines, one reality, one a possibility. The face of Tara, the pleading of Lourdes, came at him with abrasive force.

"Don't do this, John Jay!" Vivian's voice screamed forth from a pulsating time thread. John Jay cupped his ears and still, he heard her screaming. Gulping, he pulled his legs free from the confusion of the static and hurled himself into the vein of another nexus gate, buying himself a momentary pause as he fought to get back to 4037.

He shuddered from the icy prick of regret. He'd only looked back a few times at the mess he was making upon his timeline. None of it would matter in the end. The Cleric's Office would sort it all out somehow. He just needed to get back to Lourdes. This was all for her. He'd have to blame the mess on the static, just as much as he would Vivian. They both, formally appearing to be his salvation, were proving to be his ruin.

***

Clarence watched as another tear in the timeline pulsed like an infected wound before drawing closed over the body of another of John Jay's time-wraiths. There were still several more to be born and then hunted before Clarence was to dispose of them, tossing them back into the static from which they'd abominably come.

This one was far more aggressive than the other he'd hunted, the one that had stalked Tucker John through the night upon his first visit to Balm Hill. Still, it met its end and was cut off, along with the perversion of time it bred like cancer.

CHAPTER 39

Vivian had finally struck a golden vein within the mountain that had been standing in her path for the last several weeks. She paced the floor and spoke into the air allowing the computer to record her findings. She had been at it for the last thirteen hours and still was going. She knew that she was running off nothing but adrenaline fumes but she couldn't stop and risk losing her momentum. Rest would come once she was finished recording. She would resume work later on in the day.

Sleep was indeed a necessary evil.

"The static," Vivian had decided to call the substance 'static' instead of 'static potentiality' or 'interrupted inertia.' The single word fit perfectly and flowed off the tongue. "…has a similar quality to the static electricity that is around us. It attracts, while also carrying with it the ability to repel. It has potential to cause lasting damage to the tangible and intangible—including time—if it is made to move away from its natural flow, hence the applied words 'interrupted inertia'. However, this static differs from static electricity, as it is not charged like static electricity. But it is always present, like electricity, hovering in the atmosphere around us."

She yawned, pressing shut her heavy eyelids. She was suddenly losing her drive. Had her fumes been sapped so quickly? She rushed to finish her dictation. "My belief is that this static is a form of creative matter that deals with time itself. If time was a series of residential roads all leading to different places, then static is like the residential cul-de-sacs, branching off those roads. The static-cul-de-sac is a pocket of energy that moves in a loop that ultimately leads nowhere unless something breaks into it. It—like the other roads of time—has growth, but unlike the other roads, its growth is contained and instead of being verifiable it is 'probable,' similar to nutrient-rich soil.

"If the cul-de-sac's loop is broken into, then it opens up new pathways to places that were normally not accessible or even imagined, hence the potentiality. Imagine a growing source of condensed energy flowing in an unbroken circular motion. That sudden release of energy once interrupted, could be positive or negative. The reaction is similar to a liquid that is heated beyond its boiling point without having the chance to create proper air bubbles for the energy to radiate outward evenly. When the liquid is disrupted, one large bubble rapidly forms, causing an explosion. This is not always the case,"

She yawned again. Her eyelids felt like they had lead weights hanging from them. "Pause dictation." She moaned. There was so much more she wanted to say. She would give herself a few hours of rest and then go over her notes. She grabbed a few bedlinens from the cabinet and put them on the examination bed. Crawling onto it, she pulled them up to her chin and made herself relax. She would compile her findings sometime within the next few days and then take them to the Cleric's Office for a report. She had to report this.

Her discovery of the static was too big for her to sit on. This was bigger than her or John Jay. It could change time as the world had come to know it, and probably already had. She could even use its discovery as a segue to help her confess the mess she'd already made with John Jay missing and Tucker John's presence.

***

Tucker John carefully studied the inner belly of Lourdes and John Jay's nexus gate. He cracked his tightening neck and again skimmed over the information about nexus gates and nanoids. Nanoids were not visible to the naked eye. They required certain equipment and lenses to view. What could be seen, however, were the results of nanoids, especially nanoid-upgrades and replacements. He took a risk by scraping away some of the gold mess that had grown on the inner parts of the gate, but it was a risk well taken. The evidence of an upgrade was right there, plain as the nose on his face.

"Well, there are those replacement and upgrading nanoids you ordered, Johnny-boy." His discovery was bittersweet. Every shred of evidence he uncovered was not only making Lourdes look more dangerous but John Jay as well. John Jay was indeed hiding somewhere, somewhere in time where Viv couldn't find him, and Lourdes most assuredly knew where. Disgustingly enough, this was all for one reason, for John Jay to get to have Lourdes without Viv's interference, which didn't make sense.

For one, the imbecile could have just given Viv her walking papers and been done with her. For two, same race coupling was against the law in that era and Lourdes was just as lily white as John Jay.

Nevertheless, the slick-willy, John Jay, had certainly made a trade down, in Tucker John's mind by choosing Lourdes over Viv. He'd done a bit of reading up on Viv. The woman was beyond impressive. Some of the things he learned about her made him whistle through his teeth. The discoveries she had made, the programs she had initiated, the lives she had ultimately changed, because of her Field studies and work were monumental. She had earned enough rewards from her work in surveillance within her thirteen-year career to cover the manor walls like a good paint job.

Her record was pristine. He especially liked that. It reminded him of himself. His records in his fields were pristine as well. Didn't matter what he was doing, it all came down to one thing, being thorough and worth your salt, the best there was. Viv was worth her salt. The woman had proven to be finer than frog's hair. She was the total package.

The newfound knowledge brought a wrinkle of shame in his belly. Viv was many things but a lady-dandy she was not. With all that she had achieved she had the right to be nasty and high-minded, even so much so to look down on him with disdain. But she hadn't done any of that until he had stabbed her right in the very center of her chest.

At the end of the day, it really didn't matter how he had betrayed her. Her own husband had done so and in the worst of ways. If Viv thought of Tucker John as a liar, if her countenance had deflated with him, a man she hardly knew, because he had lied to her, what would become of her when she found out that John Jay had lied to her and betrayed her by bedding down with Lourdes and scaring her out of her wits by pretending to be lost?

Her spark and fire would either fizzle or rage until it engulfed everyone and everything. Tucker John couldn't help that. All he could think about was the waste of her spirit that was going to take place once the truth came to light.

His gaze eased toward the side window. The sun was stirring and preparing to wake a new day. It was best he be found at Viv's manor when it did. He grabbed his things and headed back home removing every shred of evidence that he had even been at Balm Hill. Tomorrow he'd have to do a bit more following of Lourdes. She'd been doing an awful lot of circling Viv's property. He needed to know why.

CHAPTER 40

Hours turned into days and days turned into weeks, three weeks to be exact. Tucker John still hadn't gotten the chance to talk with Viv and, with each hardnosed rejection, even when he caught her unawares, he felt his resolve toughening. He still had the pills Evan had given him for her in his pant pocket. He knew full well Viv was still taking Paz and as long as she was steering clear of him, the harder it was going to be for him to get her to detoxify.

The last thing he needed was for Viv to lose her mind completely because of an overdose on *Paz* and actually turn into the enemy he'd previously been imagining her to be. He needed her mind clear, but he didn't know how to make that happen without reasoning with her. Forcing her would only make her fear him, which used to be what he wanted, once upon a time. Now he needed her full trust but he didn't know how to attain it. He still had no olive branch to offer. All the information he'd gathered against their enemies had been won by means of his lying to her.

He felt like he was in the path of a tornado. Everything had grown uncomfortably still around him. The manor was like a hollow, cold cave. Things were far too quiet. Something was getting ready to happen. Silence, stillness, and the deceitful play of peace in the atmosphere were the telltale signs of pending destruction.

Sitting at the dining table, he took a slow, cool, gulp of fresh milk and licked the cream from his upper lip. Lourdes shifted in her seat. It surprised him how every day, even amid Viv's absences, she showed up to the table. She kept with the rhythm of his and Viv's former agreement as if she was ignorant of it being broken. Each meal with her was just as cold and quiet as the house, riddled with oppressive and yet welcomed silence, only giving room for the sounds of silverware scraping against the bone china they ate from.

Their menus were vastly different. Lourdes kept to her orphan-diet while Tucker John had taken it upon himself to pick and slaughter his own food, not daring to give Lourdes the chance at poisoning him. Today it was yard-bird even though he'd done some real hunting out on Viv's land. The hunting made him feel himself again, kept his skills sharp as he cornered his kill. Sure, he'd grown to love the recoil of his rifle whenever he'd used it in the past. It was quick and efficient, but nothing could compare to the rush he felt when he earned his game with his bare hands and blade.

It was amazing how the brutality of his childhood had birthed in him a skill of beauty. It had become his way of doing things, only donning his boots and over clothes for his 'fancy' high dollar hunts. But tracking a slave, catching his fouler bounties, he kept to his basics, especially when he was about to strike. All he needed then was his suspended trousers, and a length of rope, one to keep his long hair back and another to drag in his prize. It made him harder to see and harder to hear, being barefoot. He moved faster as well.

It did something to his blood each time he stripped down to nothing but his trousers, before he covered himself from head to toe in red clay, letting the scent of the earth conceal him. It rooted him to his environment, left him unseen by his prey even as he drew but a few feet away from them right before he spilled their blood.

Runways always kept their eyes open for a white man on horseback, clothed and clad to the teeth with a pack of yapping dogs. They never suspected a bare chest, barefoot white man covered in earth to come after them. The only slave he ever went after in his boots was Vivian.

After only a couple of weeks, he had three deer hanging up in Viv's smoker, evidence of hardy runs on her property. He had no bow and arrow only stealth, patience, and an exacting aim each time he let the cold metal in his hand soar at his targets.

Learning to listen, waiting for the attack of Ash had trained him to master silence, only allowing himself to be heard when he wanted to be. What had once been his response for having been prey had turned into the fire of a predator. Runaway slave, bounty in the wind, deer meat for his table...John Jay and Lourdes Berry, they were his prey and he would see their blood run.

If Magnus Sanderson had come back in time to verify whatever was about to happen involving the folks at Viv's manor, then Tucker John was going to give him a right good show.

Chewing his yard-bird supper, he took the time to study his target, each cut of his knife a hopeful prelude to what he planned to do to Lourdes' belly. He learned in those three weeks that Lourdes' fingertips had grown a deep shade of pink as if they were raw. Even with the conical hat her hands and face had abandoned its once creamy hue and adopted a more honey color. She had been spending a lot of time in the sun, work for the co-op aside. She also had obtained a distinctive odor that he was certain she hadn't noticed herself. The scent was that of the blood from a specific weed that he'd seen further out on Viv's property.

Within the span of the first week, he had counted the scent as being far from coincidence and decided to investigate. The weed she stank of grew in a strange pattern, outlining the very edges of Viv's property. The pattern sandwiched the perimeter fence. There was a furrow in between the two rows of weeds that was eighteen inches across. It took him a great amount of digging through files to find out what the perimeter fence was since Viv had gone to even greater lengths to keep him ignorant about it. It was one of her safety measures. He understood that now. People had a way of putting up secret safety nets. He had developed his own over the last near thirty-six years. Of course, Viv's were far more subtle than his and certainly less volatile.

Lourdes, however, was not very good at hiding her measures in anything. She wore her emotions on her face, her intentions in her eyes, and in every single shift of her mannerisms. The way she sat at the dining table had gone from tense to leisurely, to down-right snooty. How she handled her knife and fork, and cut each boiled pea in half before carefully placing it in her mouth spoke volumes. She was taking her time. Whatever she and John Jay had cooked up for Viv and him was just about ready to come out of the oven. Lourdes behaved just like she had a gun to his head with her finger on the trigger, and there was nothing to keep her from pulling it outside of her own amusement.

He would've been lying to himself if he didn't admit that the joy in her face didn't chafe him a little. She practically floated on air whenever she passed him, giving him that if-you-only-knew-what-you-got-coming-to-you look. It was that look, and his knowledge of what was lurking behind it, that made him put down his utensils, pick up his fried chicken, and ravenously tear into before sucking the meat and grease off the bones, and his fingers with an air of ease. Lourdes couldn't see through his poker face. His ignorance at her schemes was nothing but a ruse.

He'd gathered a pretty good hand of cards set up against her and John Jay. When it came to cards, figurative or literal, he'd lost only a few hands in his lifetime, and had one win that he should have disputed. Had he not won that pretty rifle Viv kept hidden from him, and learned how to make some fine bullets to fit it, he would've brought the man he'd played for it to task. Nevertheless, his lust for the rifle had gotten the best of him and made him go on as if he knew nothing about how the game had been fixed in his favor. Nobody he knew had a rapid-fire rifle.

But things weren't fixed in his favor now. He truly had to earn his supper, but he was already aching for the hunt. Trial and error had cost him a bit of time, but he'd learned the rules of his new engagement, having jury-rigged his own golden bowl with the grainy matter inside of it, just like Lourdes'.

He'd spent enough nights watching Lourdes in the basement of Balm Hill, speaking into her bowl, and quietly sitting before speaking again, to know that she must have been hearing something during her silent pauses.

So he'd started eavesdropping.

The ability to do so had turned out to be a happy accident. Before, he'd tried to imitate Lourdes' set up by way of a tin cup with a pair of forks welded to it. In no way was it a golden bowl but hell, he was desperate. He'd even tried to make it fancy by using bits of gold lining he'd found stashed away at Balm Hill.

He tried connecting his instrument to Lourdes' nexus gate, following the same steps he'd seen her go through. His goal was to be able to later attach the contraption to Viv's gate and listen in from there. It was a good plan. The results of his efforts, however, proved far different from what he was aiming for. What he'd gotten, after at least ten trials was nothing but a cup filled with frustration and touches of the gold matter blooming in its seams.

He disconnected the instrument from Lourdes' gate and reconnected her bowl just moments before the golden grains within it started dancing. Sure enough, sound was coming out of it. The grey-blue smoke that wisped up and away from the prongs on the golden bowl seemed to direct themselves toward the forks that jutted out of Tucker John's tin cup, setting the insides of the tin to glow with an eerie light, and sounds of grinding metal to vibrate from within it.

No, he hadn't been successful in his attempts to mimic what Lourdes and John Jay had created, but what he had stumbled upon was just as good, maybe even better. He could hardly make out what was being said through the instrument the first few nights he'd set out to use it, but at least he was on the right track. What he was able to do with it was take note of when Lourdes was having chat with, who his gut told him, was Johnny-boy. Even from Viv's manor the welded forks still picked up traces of nexus smoke produced whenever Lourdes was having her secret meetings. The trail that had once been invisible came alive in the presence of the instrument he'd made.

The smoky path reminded him of an ant trail. His little instrument had created such a path with Lourdes' gate, leading back to it. That was good. It kept him better informed of her movements. Still, he needed more. He needed a bowl like hers to hear with greater clarity what his true enemies were actually planning.

To buy himself the much needed time, he rose each day a few hours earlier than his chores required, making quick work of them before hunting down the tools he needed to create a proper listening and speaking bowl of his own. Providence had been on his side. Seemed Lourdes' mama had a matching set of those gold bowls just in her kitchen, tucked deep within the bottom cupboard.

Having one of those bowls made it a million times easier to mimic Lourdes' and John Jay's design. He prayed that his most recent efforts would yield him worthy fruit. He was going to take a risk with it and try it out the next time Lourdes made her escape and Viv made herself ghost. The potential of getting caught would surely prove worth the risk if his construction actually worked. Hopefully, he'd get his chance to do so tonight.

He watched Lourdes dancing in her chair the way she did each time she went on her night adventures. He would leave his instrument outside in the smoke path while he employed the use of the bowl.

He hoped to God what he was planning would work. He hoped he would be able to hear everything that they were up to. Nothing was better than having a one-up on your bounty, especially when they had lost wind of wise caution, and had grown too confident in their own infallibility.

He glanced over at Lourdes as she took one last sliced pea and plopped it in her mouth with a sense of exaggerated delight. He had to fight off a smile. The cocky little harpy was playing herself and she didn't even know it. Besides that, no pea in the whole of creation tasted that good.

CHAPTER 41

Vivian finally managed to pry herself from the call screen. She'd been listening to dead air for nearly five minutes. Chief Quinn had made a quick return to the Cleric's Office in preparation for her official return to work. There were still a couple more weeks left before she was able to take on any heavy responsibilities, but she was deemed fit enough to call in a private meeting with Vivian. She had actually requested it. It wasn't just a private meeting; it was an urgent private meeting, scheduled for 6:30 that evening. The lateness of the call and the meeting made Vivian's anxiety and worry resurface with a vengeance.

She eased down into her armchair and tried to calm her heartbeat. Had she sent herself to the guillotine with her recent request for a verification? No, she hadn't! It didn't matter that her daily calls to the Cleric's Office were inconvenient, what she had to share about the static took precedence over any so-called inconveniences. But even with that truth she still couldn't shake the anxiety that was overtaking her.

She pulled out her refill of *Paz* and dropped several of them underneath her tongue. She had long since lost count of how many she was taking in order to stay grounded. The knowledge of her blind dosage somehow didn't matter. The Paz was hardly bringing on the desired effect and it certainly wasn't knocking her out like it had done before.

Resting her head back she let the tiny pills dissolve into her bloodstream. She relaxed even more as the river of numbness washed over her. Casually pulling herself up from the chair she headed to her desk in her bedroom. She had been organizing her findings on the static ever since she had discovered it having completely abandoned her and John Jay's original research. She was anxious to share what she had found with the Chief. She wondered if she would ever get back to her former research again. It wasn't likely, especially if John Jay was never recovered.

Pushing the thought away with a cold shiver she turned on the Tracker that she had been keeping with her. It was 5:30 in the evening, an hour before she had to be at the Cleric's Office, but she didn't want to run into either of her housemates on her way. Lucky for her, Lourdes was no longer on the property and Tucker John was heading off it in the direction of Balm Hill.

Taking her opportunity to leave without being cornered by him, she quickly freshened up, gathered her clipboard, and headed for her sled.

***

Tucker John gave the instrument a once over on the path he had placed it. It was only a couple hundred yards from Viv's property line. It was close enough to Balm Hill for him to hopefully pick up Lourdes' voice—he had been measuring safe sound distances over the last week and a half—and it was close enough to Viv's for him to retrieve it before Lourdes came over the hill when she was headed home.

That leg of his experiment was in order. The only problem he now faced was in how to find a way to keep Viv out of the nexus room during the early evening. He couldn't help but offer up a 'Thank You, Jesus!' the moment he returned to the manor and found her gone. He couldn't imagine where she had run off to at that hour, but at least now he didn't have to blockade her in her bedroom somehow. He figured, if he did, then he could fake a rescue afterward and get her to talk with him. He had already determined if his golden bowl worked like Lourdes' he wasn't going to hear anything good come out of the conversation. In the event that he was right in his reckoning, he would have earned the chance to finally talk to Viv and lay his case before her.

He gave the house a once over, locked up the doors good and tight, rigging them to make a loud enough noise to alert him when Viv was back. Then he headed to the nexus room to get his equipment set up.

***

Vivian was having an out-of-body experience. It was as if her entire being was rebelling, and all her basic faculties had forgotten how to work. She couldn't think, she couldn't speak, she didn't know if she should scream. She was blank.

All of her gusto and fight had fled. Even after the impassioned argument and the strain of her raised voice, Chief Quinn didn't seem to be holding any grudges. Instead, she was showing a great deal of compassion, a tenderness that was really putting Vivian off and making her want to scream all the more. All Quinn cared about was being right, and she had proven twice in less than two hours how right she was. The blood sample that had been taken the day that Vivian requested her team activity log had born witness to that.

Quinn really hadn't even heard a word that Vivian had said about the static, let alone her weak attempts at a confession of absolute wrongs. She brushed it all aside in order to make her point, no matter how earth-shattering it was to Vivian. Vivian didn't need this. She felt helpless, gutted. The only thing that might have strengthened her case was to force out the truth that John Jay was missing and that the static was probably responsible. But her mouth refused to budge. Her brain was stuck in a loop.

"I know this is hard," Quinn said. The warmth of her hand on Vivian's shoulder irritated Vivian's skin. "But this is the reality. It's the hard truth and you need to accept it." There was a hint of sternness laced in her tone.

Quinn continued. "I really wish John Jay were here. I should've called him in with you, but I felt it best to confront you with this in private before bringing him in. I think, in light of the circumstances, this is something that you need to talk to him about as his wife and as his Team Lead, and you need to do it soon. We do have aid for cases like this but if aid is not a conducive alternative, going back to your timeline may be the,"

Vivian finally exhaled. Silent, hot tears streamed from her eyes.

Quinn noticed them. "Vivian, this isn't the end of the world or your career. It happens. None of us are impervious to this. Sure, this isn't what we plan for in the Field. We take the mantle of Ministers of Time to make a difference, and you've made many. Honestly, I don't know why you didn't apply for a Chief Cleric position a long while ago. Believe it or not, they are less stressful than being directly in the Field." She shook her finger as if chastising herself. "No, I do know why you stay in the Field. You're ambitious. But ambition comes at a cost most people don't realize they're paying. Count yourself blessed."

Vivian pressed her lips together. She couldn't move. Quinn had made it sound so blasé. What had her exact words been? *"Many within the Cleric's Office were beginning to question your mental state. At least now we have an explanation for why you were behaving so out of character."*

Is that what this was? A simple, understandable reason for why they thought she was acting strangely? No! This was life altering! Looking at the evidence before her she still couldn't bring her mind to accept it. She would focus on why she had come in the first place; shove this revelation aside as if she hadn't heard it.

She said, her voice hitching, "What about the static? There's more I need to tell you,"

Quinn gazed at her empathetically. With a pitying sigh, she leaned over Vivian and gave her a tight, informal but most sincere hug. "Don't bother with that—"

"But did you hear what I said about it? Did you even look at my data?" Vivian pulled away from her. "I need to tell you something, Quinn. I-John Jay—"

Quinn nodded her head. "Vivian, I'll look at what you brought me, but I need you to look at what I've shown you. You need to make some decisions about your life, big ones. Whatever it is that you've collected really is not as important as your health. John Jay will understand that. Trust me on this. This has gone unchecked for far too long—"

Vivian finally sat up. If she lay on that bed any longer she was going to melt right into it and disappear. "But this is just as important!"

Quinn closed her eyes and raised a hand. "Vivian! You're deflecting from the facts right now. And it's because you're afraid, but what's done is done!" Vivian tried to speak again but the Chief cut her off. "You need to own this. That's where you start. There's no blame-game going on here but you did this. You, so own it, accept it, and then figure out what your next step is going to be. We're here to help you. I have a specialist waiting in the other room to counsel you, do the necessary labs to prepare you for what's ahead when we're done here."

She touched Vivian's shoulder again, this time she took hold of both of them, giving them a gentle squeeze and an even gentler shake. "Here's the first step. I had to do it myself years ago. It helped me get past the first hurdle. So let me hear you say it. I'm actually not going to let you leave until you do." She shook her again.

Vivian took a shuddered breath and more tears fell. It didn't matter. She was going to make the confession, tell the specialist what they needed to hear, and then run home as fast as she could, and hide away in her room. She lifted her red eyes to the Chief, her voice distant in her own ears. "I'm Vivian Leona, and I'm thirteen weeks pregnant."

CHAPTER 42

Tucker John was very short on patience. He'd already used a few choice words to express his irritation. He'd been so wrapped up in his short-lived tirade that he hadn't even heard the rigging on the door pop when Viv came into the house. Lourdes had been gone for nearly three hours, and if she and John Jay had been talking about anything, he had certainly missed it thanks to faulty construction.

His makeshift bowl plugged into Viv's nexus gate had not worked.

He raked his fingers through his hair, took a step back from the nexus table, and blew out a few breaths before looking at the bowl again. He had one more ace up his sleeve. If this configuration didn't work, he didn't know what he was going to do. Refocusing, he disconnected the bowl and reconnected it again. He realized one good thing at the very last minute. He made sure the bowl was devoid of any of the grainy matter. If Lourdes could talk into it and be heard it was probable that he would be heard too if this worked.

It took him a few short seconds to get every piece in place before he sat down and waited right on the very edge of disaster or triumph. Seconds passed and then minutes without hearing a sound. He felt his shoulders sinking and then drawing taut again when he heard an echoic voice resonating in the base of the bowl.

His ace had worked. He could hear them!

He shot to his feet and gave an elated hoot before reining in his excitement. He could celebrate his engineering victory later. Right now he needed to feed his suspicions.

Anger suddenly crawled up his spine when Lourdes' voice quieted only to be met by a masculine voice, one he'd grown quite familiar with—John Jay's.

The words of Magnus, the question he'd posed Tucker John, had its answer. John Jay wasn't lost at all and Viv was none the wiser, thinking all along that she was at fault. It was because of that misguided thought that Tucker John had unwittingly stepped through time, evading a supposed watery grave, but plunging into something just as deadly.

He felt the ire in his belly rise. "John Jay, you sorry piece of—"

"What are you *doing*?" Viv's voice filled the room with such force that it pulled Tucker John from his seat, his mouth open, and his eyes wide like a child that had been caught in the act of something improper.

He turned toward her just as she stormed in his direction, her face twisted with rage, and her fist balled.

"I told you not to touch the gate!" She roared. "I told you, no! What have you done to it?" Her eyes ran over the disarray he had caused with disgust. Her teeth clenched. Lunging forward, she reached for the bowl and the wires.

"No!" Tucker John shouted, grabbing her arm, yanking her away from it. Viv swung around on him and caught him with a cuff clean across his face. She startled at striking him before she went in for another hit. This time Tucker John stopped her.

"Stop it, Viv!" he hissed, his ear still ringing from the blow. He tried to hold onto her, tried to get a steady grip, but doing so was like trying to hug a wolverine, and all the while Lourdes and John Jay spoke on, their voices overshadowed by Viv's ranting.

He shouted at her again before finally pulling her down to the floor, her back against him and her arms straining for the cords he'd attached to the gate. He wrapped her legs in a vice grip with his own and braced one of his arms around hers before covering her mouth with his free hand.

Vivian's guttural battle cries instantly turned into panicked squeals when she realized in just an instant Tucker John had overpowered her. He wasn't drunk and weak like he had been in the thicket. This time she couldn't break free of him, and if she didn't get loose there was no telling what he would do to her. She thought about what he had done to the slave-woman and screamed even louder.

The sounds of distant voices moving around her only made her resist all the more. She prayed they would hear her even if it was someone from the Cleric's Office. Tucker John pressed his hand harder against her mouth.

"*Shut up!* Shut. Up!" He barked the order several times in her ears, but she refused him. Her nails broke into his skin, and he growled. It was when John Jay's voice and the sound of her name registered in her ears that she suddenly stopped, slapped frozen by confusion.

"*They think Vivian has gone crazy? You were able to get them to think that?*" John Jay. His tone was notably delighted.

Lourdes' voice responded. "*You told me to do something. I did. Really, she did it to herself. The Animal helped. I just—*"

Vivian struggled again. Tucker John jerked her body. "Shut up, Viv, and listen! *Listen!*"

John Jay answered whatever it was that Lourdes had said. "*...the perimeter fence, baby! We're still going to have to get rid of Vivian, which bothers me. I'm not going to lie. I-I figured out how to do it, though, how to e-euthanize her,*" he stuttered.

"*I thought we were going to make it look like she hangs herself, kind of like how we did with the other Vivian?*"

"*No, it needs to look like the Animal hangs her. It fits his nature. It'll get rid of her and him at the same time, justify us putting him down.*"

Vivian went ramrod straight. Had she heard correctly? Even Tucker John froze still.

John Jay continued. *"Euthanizing Tucker's the easy part. Dealing with Vivian's body is...I don't even want to really think about it."*

"Well, you have to, Johnny. It's been three years with her between us, and I'm tired of being away from you. This is your time for glory, for your name to be first, to take the Lead. You discovered the static, not Vivian. This is your moment. You promised me, you promised us!"

"I know," John Jay's voice wavered before silence filled the air.

Vivian felt Tucker John carefully ease his fingers from over her mouth as the wetness of her tears poured from her eyes and onto his calloused hand. She pressed her lips closed, tried to keep herself from making a sound, but the trembling in her body resisted her efforts.

"I miss you so much, Johnny. I love you."

"I love you too, Lourdes. I loved you since the day I met you."

Vivian's heart all but stopped beating.

CHAPTER 43

The dampness from Tucker John's sweaty chest began to saturate the back of Vivian's tunic. The seeping heat of it was just another intrusion that she couldn't handle, not amid everything else. He was one of them! He was just as deceitful as Lourdes and…and John Jay. He was sleeping with Lourdes just like John Jay!

Wrestling her body away from his, she let out an ear-piercing shrill from within her belly, screaming for help until she tasted blood in her throat, knowing full well no one would hear her.

Tucker John didn't try to stop her, instead, he watched, seemingly stunned. Scurrying away from his grasp she narrowed her eyes. "You're with them!" she accused. She eased up from the ground, her eyes locked on him, watching his every move. Her every fiber trembled. "You stay away from me,"

"What? Didn't you hear anything they said? *Your* John Jay has plans on killing me too! How in *hell* do you think I'm with them?" Tucker John rose up from the ground but kept his distance.

Vivian shook her head, her weeping eyes darting around the room searching for a weapon. He had her cornered, standing in the path of both exits. "I heard everything they said," God had she wished she hadn't. She couldn't process it, not this, not any of it. What had become of her life? She felt as if she were suffocating, like the rope they planned to use on her was already wrapped around her neck, tightening with every breath she took.

Tucker John's blood set his skin ablaze. How had Viv accused him with the likes of Lourdes and John Jay? "You heard what they said," he repeated. "Clearly, you missed the part about

Johnny-boy 'euthanizing' me." He managed a step toward her but stopped when she cried out again. Bristling, he stayed in his place. He needed Viv to listen to him. He wouldn't be able to navigate through that era without her and she wouldn't be able to navigate past Lourdes and John Jay without him. "Viv, I am not with them. I've been trying to talk to you for weeks *about* them,"

Viv shook her head. "No, I know about you and Lourdes! I watched you leave with her all those nights. Just-just," she paced helplessly in the tight corner she was in, her voice dropping into a whisper. "John Jay wants to kill me? He loves Lourdes." She let out a moan before turning her rage back on Tucker John. "Just leave me alone! Why are you trying to kill me? Why?!"

He took another step forward. She lashed out at him with wild kicks and even used the chair as a barricade as if he couldn't move it.

"I'm not trying to kill you, woman! I'm trying to reason with you, and where did you get the idea that I was sleeping with Lourdes?" He forced himself to stay still. Viv was reasonably on edge. Everything was happening so fast. "Them nights you saw me leaving I was following her cause I was spying on her just like now—"

"No!"

He nodded his head. "Yes!"

"No, I don't believe you," she took a few deep breaths, wiped her face and slowly shook her head. Tucker John knew those signs. She was resigning to believe the lie she was building in her head, rather than dance with the bloody truth. "No. None of this is real. You and Lourdes set this up," she pointed at the bowl. "You're trying to trick me, make me look crazy, and make me doubt John Jay."

Tucker John chewed back a nasty retort. He'd known she wouldn't be easily convinced. Calling her out as the fool she was acting wouldn't get her any closer to the side of truth. He asked, "What do I have to gain by making you look crazy, Viv?"

"Freedom—"

"Got that. So how am I profiting by bringing you down? How do I benefit by making you think your husband wants you dead? And why in hell would I bed down with that nasty, sneaking, cockroach Lourdes? She has done nothing but poison me in your eyes since I been here. You said yourself she has tried to get you to put me down like I was some lame animal. *He* called me an animal!" He pointed at the bowl. "You just need to accept the truth, just like I had to." Her wide eyes met his. "You're not my enemy, same as I'm not yours. Like it or no, we need each other."

"No, you made this up. You're only admitting what I've been working to convince you of, finally accepting things now that you've been caught messing with the nexus gate." She shook her head again. "You want to take John Jay's place—"

"You asked me to!" He bristled. He wanted to shake her. Her faulty reasoning had put more starch in her stance. It was more palatable for her than what she had just heard. She ceased to crumble under the burden of truth, and instead challenged the very person who had made her hear it, him.

"You want me to look crazy so you can be rid of me, and you can have Lourdes and then, then you two will be able to be together, and-and you'll never have to go back to 1837! This is about your need for control. You two have been planning this all along. This is why she didn't want me to contact the Cleric's Office when John Jay first went missing. It was all about you! It's always been about you!"

Tucker John roared with laughter before finally shouting. "Are you hearing yourself?"

"This is all some scheme you've concocted so you can have Lourdes and stay here with her! The only way for you to stay is if John Jay never comes back. That's why you made me listen to that," she accused. "You wanted me to believe my husband is a liar, like you!"

"He's worse than a liar, Viv,"

"This isn't going to work. I'll bring you and Lourdes down before I let you do this to me! Or John Jay," she stared at him as if she were a lioness ready to pounce on her prey. "What have you two done with him?"

Tucker John ran his hands down his face and took in several breaths. Vivian Leona was no fool, but she was human and had been struck with an awful revelation regarding the man she loved. Disillusionment—shock—had that effect on the best of people. But they were short on time. They needed to be on a united front. He needed to dangle his bate, get her to bite the line of pure, hard, truth if he was going to be able to reel her in. Both of them would be good as dead if he didn't.

"Viv, you know better than what you're saying to me. You know better." Her eyes bored into his. He matched her gaze. "After what happened between you and me in my room, do you really think I would have to sneak around if I wanted Lourdes? Hell, I ain't afeared of you. If I wanted to I could'a laid with her in your bed, and you couldn't of stopped me."

She flinched and stepped back at his words. He pressed on, "But see, this ain't about her. This is about you and me, and the fact your husband and his whore want both of us dead. They used us—"

Viv shook her head vigorously. "No! You planned this,"

"What did I plan? You say I wanted you to hear that? How could I have possibly known that you were even here? You left! I took an opportunity to use your gate. That's all. I didn't *plan* anything. I'm making plans now, but they ain't against you! Not no more, anyhow."

Viv remained still. Tucker John continued. "And your accusation doesn't even make sense. Why would I go through all this trouble to be with Lourdes if in 4037, me being white I can't even have a white woman? Why? Why would I draw unwanted attention to myself? That's the last thing I'd do. And why would I leave my timeline where I was successful to come here to be with a bunch of crazy folks who'll hang they own mama if she sheds one too many tears? I wouldn't!"

Viv scowled, but her scowl broke into something else. Tucker John couldn't decipher it. He didn't waste time trying to. He spoke on finally pulling the red bobble earring from his pocket. "You see this?" He tossed it at her but she let it fall to the ground. Clenching his jaw he reigned in his irritation. "If you pick that up you'll see I'm not lying to you. If you hold that bobble up to the light you'll see your husband's face and a message about 'being worth it'. I found that in Lourdes' room when I was searching it.

"That gal has hated me from the beginning, but she really hasn't cottoned to me since I called her out about bedding down with your husband." Viv lurched but caught herself. Tucker John didn't let up. "I'll admit Viv," he stalled, and his jaw worked left to right. He had to speak the words through clenched teeth. He hated apologizing. "I'll admit I was wrong about you. What I done to you was wrong. Lying to you and, and breaking our agreement. But I'm not lying to you now. And I don't want to kill you. If I did, we wouldn't even be having this conversation. You know that. I could've snapped your neck right there on the ground, and been done with it if that is what I wanted. But that ain't what I want."

Tucker John's gunmetal-gray eyes seemed to darken. Vivian's sparked with resignation at what he was saying. He could have done whatever he wanted after their showdown in his room, and he could have killed her moments ago. The iron grip he'd had on her was just a preview of his strength. But he had let her go. Not because she had snatched from his grasp, but because he chose to.

Her head was swimming. It was like she had been punched repeatedly in the forehead, and was defenseless to stop the blows. Tucker John called her name but she couldn't move her tongue.

She wanted to run away again. She felt like she was drowning, or worse like her body was being turned inside out. She *had* heard John Jay say what he had said. Her imagining that Tucker John was the culprit didn't change the facts. What was becoming of her life?

Without a second thought, she bulldozed from the corner, shoving her way passed him. He stumbled before calling her name and chasing after her.

Vivian's body shook. She couldn't catch her bearings, the horrid conversation was playing itself over and over again in her head. She couldn't make Lourdes and John Jay's voices stop. She couldn't make Quinn's voice stop. She couldn't do anything but take her own pain away even if it were for a brief moment.

She had come to the 4030's to save her marriage, give John Jay what he wanted, but what he wanted wasn't her. His resentment of her was far more bitter than he'd let on. It had turned deadly, murderous. She'd been killing herself over losing him in the nexus of time when all the while he'd planned it, planned it as he asked for one last kiss that had led to far more than that, only to dive between the folds of time waiting for the right moment to steal her life.

Choking on nauseous tears, she thrust her hand into her pocket, fumbling with the bottle of *Paz*. Before she could remove the lid, Tucker John yanked her arm, spinning her around like a rag doll. It was only his tight hold on her arm that kept her standing. Instinct instantly kicked in, adrenaline driving her fist as she punched him several times with her free hand clipping him only once in the lip, drawing blood.

He staggered back, cursed, but he didn't release her, nor did he strike her like she had expected. Instead, he tore the bottle of *Paz* from her hand and flung her away from him with a stream of curses through clenched teeth. Turning on his heels he stormed toward the kitchen.

Vivian hurried after him. "Give them back!" She hollered. Desperation climbed up her throat and poured out in her voice.

She grabbed his arm and pulled at him like he had done her, reaching for the bottle that he kept out of her grasp. "Tucker John! Give that to me,"

He yanked away from her and turned on the kitchen faucet. Vivian swung at him again, beat at his back with her fist, but he didn't yield. "Give them to me!" She tugged at his tunic, pulled at it until the black fabric burned across his neck, and tore open over his arm. Blinded by desperation, she sunk her teeth into his flesh.

He cursed again and shoved her down to the ground with one arm before she could draw blood. He assessed his arm before turning back toward the sink. "It's for your own good, Viv," he hollered, popping open the bottle and dumping the contents down the drain.

Horrified, she clamored to her feet reaching for the sink basin. Catching her in his grasps, pinning her arms to her waist, he tugged her back just before she could reach it. Again he applied his iron grip and held her back until the last of the *Paz* had washed away.

"It's for your own good," he said again, holding her about her waist with one arm and cuffing her wrists together with his free hand. "Those things are ruining your mind! And right now we need to think!" He finally let her go and turned off the faucet. His face burned and his neck and back ached from Viv's fired attempts to fight him. He could already feel a bruise growing where she'd sunk her teeth into him.

Oh, how he had changed. He'd never let a woman beat up on him like Viv just had. He leaned over the counter and tried to calm himself. He turned when he heard her stumbling out of the kitchen and toward the stairs. He quickly took after her. He didn't know if she had a hidden stash of *Paz* in her room. If she did, he wasn't going to let her have it. She needed to be sober.

He met her slamming bedroom door with his forearm and hip and kept it from closing. He pressed his weight against it until Viv ceased to push it from her side although he could have easily forced it open.

Having lost the strength to keep him out, she finally let him in, her face twisted in grief, and her eyes running with new tears. She wasted no time attacking him. She was angry, and hurt, and scared out of her mind. Someone had to pay. Again, he was to be the scapegoat. She hurled reviling words and accusations at him as if they were fists full of sharp gravel, intent on drawing blood.

He pressed his lips together and chewed on each cutting response that his mind told him to scream back. Viv's eyes brimming with wounded tears from the crushing betrayal kept him silent. Her body curving in on itself, as if she would collapse, made him reach for her. She had just had her heart ripped out by the one she loved, and everything she valued had been stolen away from her. Ashford Junior had done that to him when he took his siblings away. He was familiar with a similar pain. That pain had shaped him into the man he was, the 'Animal' called 'Tucker' that so many feared.

"Viv," he touched her arm only to be shoved away, his sudden worried gaze met with one of pure hostility. He should have expected it. The truth of her beloved was a lie. It didn't help him at all that he and the man wore the same face or that he had hurt her himself with a betrayal of his own. But he wasn't the one that caused this storm in her life. He was an unwitting victim just like she was.

He took a step back from her and stood ramrod straight. "I ain't the one that done this to you. I ain't gon' let you punish me for his crime, or hers. But we do need a plan if we aim to survive. We're running out of time, but I'll give you a bit to get your mind straightened out. You deserve that much." He backed toward the door.

Viv finally collapsed to the ground and cried out. She covered her mouth with her hands, pressing hard against her lips as she tried to keep the wailing inside of her. Tucker John stopped only a few steps away from the door. He was angry.

Every muscle in his body was tense. The friction burn on his neck was irritating him along with the bite on his arm, and his lip was throbbing from where she'd struck him.

Even though she was the one who had done these things to him her pitiful sounding-offs were like pricks to his heart, a heart that had been long dead until she took to fiddling with it. He turned away only to go back her, several curses slipping from his lips.

"What did I do wrong?" she asked him.

He didn't answer.

Viv's posture was no longer volatile. Now she was worn. "What did I do? Why doesn't he love me?" Her shoulders shook with sobs. "I've worked hard, I've been faithful. I loved him with every fiber of my being. I came here for him," she tugged on her clothes, her teeth clenched. "I trusted him and he betrayed me. Why?" she shouted.

He shook his head. "I don't know, Viv."

She forced a tear-soaked smile as she looked up at him. "You're probably thinking that I deserve this. What right did I—an 'uppity *negress*'—have being with a white man? Who did I think I was?" She was mocking him.

He wouldn't take the bait. "I wasn't thinking that at all, actually." And that was the truth. The thought hadn't even crossed his mind, at least it hadn't in a long while. How much he had changed. The realization startled him.

Viv's mouth turned downward and released another painful wail. "I loved him, Tucker John!" She buried her face in her hands and sobbed for several moments before lifting her head in anger. Again she pulled at her clothing, this time she touched her abdomen and screamed. "I'm pregnant with his *child* and he wants to kill me!" She sobbed again.

Tucker John flinched. Viv was pregnant? That certainly complicated things.

"I don't deserve this! I've been faithful to him. I gave him everything that I had and still, that wasn't enough. He just threw me away...he threw me away."

She turned her eyes to him. "My own husband wants to kill me. Do you understand that? He's been planning to kill me for years. I've been searching for my own murderer, and now there's a baby," she took in air like the wind had been snatched from her lungs. "I don't want to feel this. I just don't want to feel this...."

She wrapped her arms around her body and rocked on her knees. "Why did you destroy my *Paz*? I don't want to feel any of this," she gasped.

Tucker John pushed himself toward her. He'd never been the comforting type, not since his baby siblings and the slave-child, Luckette. After them, he'd thrown his heart away, and exchanged it for iron and stone. But Viv was aching just like he had been when he was lost in the thicket of her property. He was hurting from his need for alcohol. He knew that now. He was lost, wounded, confused, and scared out of his mind. The shoe was on Viv's foot now.

Like him, she had once had everything in order, under control, and within a matter of well-played moments all of that control was gone, and she was sucking from a bottle of pills to help her cope the same way he had taken to liquor.

He did his best to be gentle even though his touch was tempered with anger of his own. His want to kill John Jay and Lourdes had amplified. He pulled Viv up from the ground with a firm hand and pressed her close to him. She protested in his embrace like a ranting child. She behaved as if someone had died, and that someone was John Jay.

Tucker John didn't let her go. He held firm to her like she had held onto him even though she hadn't asked him to. She, finally resting her hands on his chest and leaning into him instead of away, let him know that she needed him there. Her tightly wrapping her arms around his middle and holding on to him as if he were the only thing keeping her from drowning, drove the point home.

Startled by the strange urge that welled inside him, but refusing to resist it, he tightened his embrace, resting his cheek on her crown, stroking the woolen lochs of her head.

***

Magnus made it home just as the sun was winking over the horizon. He'd done a good night's work of surveillance and verification so why did he feel like, when he was verifying what he overheard from outside of Vivian Leona's manor, that he was doing little more than eavesdropping? The poor woman couldn't catch a single break, which was a shame since she was such an elegant person in his estimation.

Nevertheless, he was glad that it was the dawn of a new day. After verifying that John Joseph 'Jay' Spruce and Lourdes Berry were indeed planning to kill Vivian Leona and 'Tucker' John Josephus Spruce, he just couldn't bring himself to relax. The wickedness that sprung from Lourdes Berry's heart made his skin itch. He thought about her feigned innocence a few weeks ago when she had convinced many of the clerics that Vivian was on the verge of losing her mind. He was glad that Clarence had called his name or else he might have done something dreadful to the woman.

How he despised liars.

John Jay's behavior certainly rendered him speechless. It baffled him to no end, and he really didn't have the stomach to try and figure things out about him. At least he didn't have to figure out the whys of what was happening. He simply had to verify what had actually happened. History tended to be very murky waters, and the case of Vivian Leona was almost like peering into a settling mud puddle—there was what seemed to be clarity on the surface, but there were plenty of fearsome uncertainties hidden beneath, swirling about in a dense veil of earth and water.

There was still so much yet to be seen.

CHAPTER 44

Vivian slowly blinked into the brightness of the sunlight. She didn't remember falling asleep or even getting in bed for that matter. Tucker John must have put her there. She startled and sat up on her side when she heard her bedroom door opening, her lead-nerves suddenly shooting upward.

Tucker John entered carrying a small tray of food in hand. Vivian kept her wary eyes on him as he neared her bedside. The smell of hot buttered biscuits, spoon-grits, and scrambled eggs almost had her hypnotized like a snake to a charmer's tune. She had worked up quite the appetite last night from crying. Even still, she dared not touch the food.

He poured up a glass of water from a pitcher, and then reached into his pocket, pulling out a tiny black pouch. He tore it open, dumping three tiny pills into the palm of his hand. He turned to her. They stared at each other for a moment before he eased the glass and the pills in her direction. Vivian's eyes narrowed.

"Take 'em," he said. "They'll help you detoxify from the *Paz*."

Her mouth bobbed open, the vision of him washing her *Paz* down the drain came back to mind. She instantly remembered how she had violently pounded on him with her fist. It only took a quick, shameful, glance at him to see his split lip and the screaming red traction burn that ran awkwardly along his neck. His back was probably just as marked, never mind the teeth marks that were probably a garish purple-blue from where she'd sunk her teeth into him. Still, she didn't budge.

Neither did Tucker John. "Evan at the Cleric's Office told me to give these to you." The mention of Evan's name broke her icy stillness. "He said you're probably addicted to *Paz*, that it's dangerous. Furthermore, you should've known better than to have taken 'em in the first place. He said they're known to make folks lose their right way of thinking. He also told me that he owed you, so now he is paying up. Honor the man and take 'em." He pushed his open palm closer to her.

Vivian pulled her eyes from the glass, and the pills, and glanced at Tucker John. His southern drawl had returned again even though it was tempered with less broken words. Pale, blond bristles had already begun to push from his bronzed face, evidence of the beard he was growing. He was done playing the part of John Jay.

Good. She understood that all too well. Tucker John wearing the soiled clothing of his own actions was one thing. Having to be clothed in someone else's was another. What she couldn't understand was the absence of hostility in his eyes, although there was a grave seriousness deep within them.

She slowly took the pills from his palm and placed them one by one beneath her tongue. Then she drank down the water. Had Tucker John not mentioned Evan she wouldn't have taken either of them from him. Aside from what she'd heard last night, he had still betrayed her trust and made it very clear where she stood with him. It didn't matter that he'd said he had no intentions of killing her, she was still too raw to see him any differently than she had begun to. She couldn't afford to trust anyone.

"You're going to have to use some *XBalance* along with those he said."

Vivian nodded. The shame and realization that she had become an addict was just another weight to put on her scale. Even now, her skin burned for *Paz*. She clenched her jaw and refused to cry again. Hadn't she done enough of that?

"I made you some breakfast. Your eggs are runny like you like 'em." He scratched the back of his head and grabbed her desk chair. Dragging it outward he sat down and stretched out his legs, crossing his bare feet at the ankles, folding his arms across his chest. "Didn't know if you shined to buttermilk biscuits, but I wanted some and figured to share. You don't have to eat them if you don't want to. But that baby is gone need," Vivian stiffened, bringing his words to a halt. She didn't want to hear about John Jay's seed growing inside of her. She didn't want to remember any of it.

Tucker John caught Viv wince at the word 'baby'. He didn't push the issue of the child. He could tell she was taking the news of being pregnant just as well as she was the news of John Jay. The thought of his own mama came to mind with the memory of her bitterness every time his daddy filled her belly with baby, and Ash had never planned to kill her, even though he had threatened to on several occasions, and had done so by given her a sickness.

He changed the subject. "Anyhow, they're might good biscuits if I do say so myself. So I wouldn't waste them."

Vivian glared at him. The sudden change in positions, the burning ache in her heart and soul, the knowledge that she had hit a wall and the only help she had for support was the very man who was the catalyst for her downward spiral, infuriated her. She did her best to hold down her voice. She couldn't stop her mouth from dipping in an angry scowl. "What is it that you want, Tucker John?" Her words were clipped, gravelly.

He didn't seem phased at all. "In light of everything that has transpired, I want to have a word with you, as I've been saying for quite some time. We need to figure out what we're going to do. We need a plan. I have my own ideas, but I wanted to run them by you first. Mind you, this is not my general modus operandi, but I'm on foreign ground."

Vivian shook her head. "*We* don't need a plan. There is no 'we'. *We* tried that once, remember? And I certainly don't trust you, not after what you've done."

His eye ticked. "That was then. Things have changed. New cards and new players are at the table."

Vivian huffed. "This isn't a game. This is my life! My hus—" she turned away and choked down the tears with a hard swallow as if she had tossed back a strong shot of liquor. It burned the same. She cleared her throat. But she couldn't manage any words.

Tucker John reached for his clipboard. He had placed it on her desk earlier that morning. "It's my life too, Viv. And if I reckon correctly, I never asked to be here."

"But you refuse to leave!"

"Anybody not willing to die a fool's death would do the same as me. As I said before, if you ain't got nothing, you take what you can get your hands on. I'm taking this opportunity to live and have a better life for myself. I aim to make the best out of this timeline, or another. I need your help to do that," Viv's mouth drew open with a contradiction, Tucker John spoke over her. "...just as you need me to survive whatever attack that's coming our way. I don't expect you to trust me right off, especially not under our circumstances. That's why I'm going to share everything that I know with you. Consider this my olive branch."

He passed her his clipboard. "Careful of that grainy bloom,"

"Static," she said taking the clipboard in hand. "I've unofficially named it static."

"Yeah, well, careful of it. I got my clipboard infected with it when I connected it with Lourdes and John Jay's nexus gate at Balm Hill." He purposefully stopped talking. He knew Viv needed a moment to absorb what he'd just said. She couldn't even mask the horror in her eyes.

He continued. "I'd been noticing Lourdes leaving the house late at night. I realized that the little harpy was leaving on the nights she'd caused friction between you and me,"

Viv's brow came together.

"I know it seems like a stretch, but she was, and I played into her hand just to learn her ways."

"And mine." Her eyes were a dark fire staring into his.

"And yours. Anyhow, the night I removed the intermezzo sensor from my leg, I followed her."

"And she didn't know?" Viv looked at him still suspicious of what he was saying.

"No, she didn't. I know how to track folks, Viv. I've done it for years. It isn't wise to get seen before you're ready to collect your bounty. I made certain to keep out of sight. The first night I went to her mama's house, I saw her in the basement talking into a golden bowl, like the one I put on your gate. When she finished up, I broke into the house and took a look around. I didn't know what the bowl was all about, but I could tell that rickety thing she had in the basement was a nexus gate. It's nowhere near the size of yours but it is a gate. She and Johnny-boy made it."

Viv raised her hand. "You broke into Alba Berry's house?"

He nodded.

"And what did Alba Berry do in response?" She stared him down waiting for him to stumble over his words.

"We'll get to Alba Berry in a minute," Viv protested but he cut her off again. "In a minute. I'm not trying to pull the wool over your eyes."

"Fine, so you saw the nexus gate and then what?" She was less than convinced.

Tucker John pushed passed it. He dove right in, explaining how he'd searched the house and found it empty. Then he told her about how he'd examined the nexus gate at Balm Hill, saw the static all over it, but still connected his clipboard to it.

They both agreed that his clipboard was what had infected her gate with the static. He then told her that John Jay had received the nanoids for her gate three days after they had been ordered that he had picked them up himself and that the homemade gate showed evidence of the nanoid upgrading.

He finally got to Alba Berry. "There isn't much to say about her, but, there's a copy of her euthanasia certificate on my clipboard."

Viv's jaw dropped. "What? Alba...Alba Berry's dead? Since when?" She scrolled through his clipboard and found the certificate and the report with very little trouble. "Oh, my goodness,"

Tucker John snorted. "Why are you surprised, Viv?"

She looked at him, her face still frozen in shock. "She had her mother euthanized. What do you mean why am I surprised?" She sat the clipboard on the bed and buried her face in her hands. "Alba Berry didn't deserve that,"

Tucker John helped himself to one of the biscuits. Steam swirled up from it. It was still a little warm in the middle. He spread freshly churned butter on it. His mouth was half full when he responded. "Maybe not, but then neither do you."

There was a silence that filled the room when their eyes met. It had been a while since they had shared the strange gaze, peering at each other over the invisible line. Viv was the first to break free from it. She reached over and took a biscuit herself, skipping passed the butter she bit into it. Her brow rose.

His lips parted in a half smile, exposing some of his teeth. "Told you they're good."

"You did. Is there anything else you want to tell me?" She dipped the biscuit in the buttery grits and took a bite of the eggs.

He scratched the stubble on his chin. The first thing to come to mind was his encounter with the wiry man called Magnus. It was his letter that had tipped him off concerning the bad they were in. It was also his letter that had caused the ruckus between him and Viv. He decided not to tell her about him in the end. Magnus had already said he couldn't help them, and to forget about him. He told her about the perimeter fence instead.

"What do you think she's done to it?" he asked, wiping crumbs from his tunic.

"I honestly couldn't say. I would have to look at its current configuration."

"Well, can you at least tell me how it is they're supposed to be together? This whole stupid affair has got me beyond curious." He knew the question was piercing, but it had been beating around in his mind like a moth to a flame. He couldn't resist.

"What do you mean how? I certainly don't know how two people can break someone's heart and not care—"

He shook his head. "No, that ain't what I meant. You said last night that you thought Lourdes and I were trying to be together, get rid of you and John Jay to do so. How does that make any sense if in 4037 white folks can't pair up just like black folks can't, so on and so forth? What do you suppose they're aiming at with this?"

Vivian considered his face. For a second she thought he was just being his old hateful self, trying to wound her with questions she didn't want to answer, but the innocent curiosity in his eyes convinced her of his sincerity. "You really don't know?"

He shook his head and waited for her to give him the answer.

"You should know. You received all of your *Spadds* treatments. The basic information was in them."

"I missed a few actually. As I recall you dropped one on my skin, and most of that dissolved before I could take it. The one following that treatment ended up smashed to Lourdes' heel, so I got a few gaps in time up here." He tapped his temple with his finger.

Vivian winced at his confession.

"Why do you think I demanded that you let me give myself the treatments? I didn't want any more mishaps. It's water under the bridge now. So, what information am I missing?"

Vivian sighed. "With advancements in genomics, specific markers were developed to determine the 'ethnicity' of each person. Just looking at a person's outward appearance as a determining factor was no longer considered proof of anything, especially if the Government was doing all it could to create the perfect ethnically ambiguous society; the Golden Ones, pure caste race, hence the name The New Golden Age. To ensure the success of the program the Governing forces made certain not to leave room for such errors as visual ethnic classification.

"You're well aware of black people passing for white in your time. Well, that's not the case anymore. Each ethnic group is given a genetic number code, determined by these markers. In Lourdes' case, her markers fit within the African or black group. She is not considered white, therefore hypothetically, she and... ...they could be together without any legal issues. Their coupling would continue the genetic ambiguity that is desired in this era." She rushed the ending of her explanation.

Tucker John's eyes were wide. He shook his head before diving back to his original point. "Well, I don't expect you to just fall in line with me and trust me right out anymore. I reckon I'm going to have to further earn that, but I'm being honest with you now. The fact is I need your help and cooperation to survive whatever them two have planned, same as you need mine. No tricks up my sleeve. You tore one of those off last night so I am sure you know that already." Vivian didn't laugh at his crude joke.

Instead, she countered with a question of her own, a hint of suspicion riding her gut like a rollercoaster. "You sure you're being honest with me?" She let her gaze linger against his. His expression was blank. "What about the letter; the one written to John Jay that somehow accepted you're DNA signature? How do you explain that?" She allowed a few silent moments to pass before chuckling. "I suppose you can't, and yet you want me to trust you."

The muscles around Tucker John's eyes seemed to tighten, a sign he was either caught in a lie or simply considering what it was worth to keep her in the dark. His lips parted. The front door swung open and closed, drawing both their gazes toward the exit of Vivian's room. Lourdes was back. They both stood as the doorbell rang.

Vivian's teeth bared, instant anger surged through her. Tucker John caught her by the crook of her arm. "Don't," he whispered.

Vivian tried to snatch away. She hissed back. "Don't what? Rip her heart out and force it down her lying throat! Or maybe yours! You still haven't explained the letter, Tucker John. Call me a fool for being overly suspicious, but from here you're not in the clear with me. As a matter of fact, your reluctance to answer only makes you look guiltier. You can't be trusted." She pulled toward the door.

Tucker John grabbed her other arm and made her face him.

"Let me go!" She felt his grip tighten. Panic licked up her spine.

The front door opened again and the familiar jovial tenor of the cleric at the door carried upstairs. Tucker John held her gaze. Vivian sucked in a breath aimed to holler. He clamped a hand over her mouth, his eyes icy and hard. "Don't make me kill that man, Viv. I swear 'for god, I'll kill him if you draw his attention. His blood will be on you, not me."

His cold threatening stare made her eyes brim with tears. He'd promised he'd make her pay. He promised he would be in control and now he was. If she screamed, if she managed to gain the cleric's attention, Tucker John would kill not only her but him as well. She could stomach him doing Lourdes in, but an innocent young man....

"I'll be quiet just let me go!" Her words trembled. She yanked her arm again wanting nothing more than to be far from him.

He drew her nearer. "Then be still and listen," he hissed, so close to her face that she felt the moisture of his breath settling on her skin. "I ain't going to hurt you none, and I ain't trying to trick you. Hell, I'll even tell you about the letter just—"

"When?" She countered with false courage, anything to make him believe she wasn't as terrified as she actually was.

"In due time. When John Jay and that gal is dealt with, to be precise. But right now it won't do us one lick of good if you get that cleric killed, and have Lourdes running off somewhere when she is the only one that knows where John Jay is. We need her alive, and we need her close by. That means you let me handle this." He gave her a stern look and slowly released her arms.

Vivian quickly took hold of the places his hands had been, replacing the searing heat of his touch with her on. Her eyes, of their own volition, quickly glanced at the door. Tucker John stepped closer to her, his face only inches from hers again, "I'm out of warnings, Viv." She stilled under his gaze. "Now, I'll tell you about the letter soon enough, and I'll prove my salt to you, but I need you to stay put, and stay quiet. Now."

Nostrils flaring, she stepped away from the door and further out of his reach. She had no chips with which to bargain. Her brain seemed muddled with a thousand 'what if's' all of them pointing toward deadly chaos. She pressed her lips closed.

Tucker John shot her one more warning glance before rushing from the room and down the stairs.

CHAPTER 45

Lourdes hung up her conical hat and smoothed down her hair before opening the door. A smiling cleric greeted her. She offered him a cordial welcome. He responded in turn.

"Well hello! I say this is the third time I've come to this residence in a month and a half, and I have to tell you it's been all great news!" He laughed to himself. "You all must be some very special surveyors."

Lourdes held on to the door and smiled again as she looked at the large box the young man had on the back of his sled.

"I would imagine that since I've had the pleasure of meeting with Vivian and John Jay that you must be Lourdes, their assistant?"

She nodded. "I am. Is that for me?" She pointed at the box.

The cleric shook his head. "Oh no! That's for Vivian and John Jay. It's a congratulatory gift since congratulations are in order!" He chuckled, turned back toward his sled, and unloaded the large box.

Lourdes gave a confused smile. She had no idea what was going on. She'd been so busy with her preparations that she had not given much attention to Vivian besides that of making sure she was losing her grip. The thought that maybe she'd discovered the static and took credit for it herself made her blood run cold. *What about Johnny?* "Congratulations?"

The cleric noticed her expression. "It's for the baby! It's the end of their first trimester!" He handed the box to Lourdes. The color drained from her face. The news and the box nearly knocked her flat. "The baby? Oh…yes, the baby!" She forced a laugh, but could feel her lips curling into a snarl. Her legs felt numb with the same assaulting quickness that dizziness was having upon her head.

Vivian was pregnant? Johnny couldn't have! But the cleric had said it was the end of their first trimester. That was thirteen weeks! "Do I need to sign for this?" She said a bit too quickly but covered it with another forced smile. She hadn't even heard Tucker John come down the stairs.

The cleric nodded and smiled. "Yes actually, if you don't mind." He placed a signing screen on the box and held onto the box while Lourdes gave her thumbprint. She slid the screen to him and shut the door in his face just as he was waving and saying hello to Tucker John, congratulating him and Vivian on completing their first trimester.

Lourdes turned to find Tucker John right behind her. She didn't try to mask her hatred of him. Tucker John gave her a wicked smile, snatching the box from her faulty grasp with such force that she stumbled forward and nearly fell to her knees.

"I believe this belongs to Viv since she is the one with child." He said the words with an air that was akin to massaging salt crystals into a fresh wound, slowly and methodically. "No need in leaving her parcel in your care so you can do like all dim-witted, conniving, Jezebels tend to do, and destroy it in your jealousy. I intend to save you the trouble of all that anxiety and tantrum throwing."

He went for the stairs but Lourdes rushed to block his path, her fist balled. "Vivian is none of your concern. That *box* is none of your concern! The *baby* isn't yours! So what's it to you?"

"It's everything to me just to see your wicked heart bleed. Seeing that pain in your devil-eyes knowing that *your Johnny* has been planting his seed in someone else's garden, brings me much joy. And knowing that you don't get to put your greedy hands on this box to damage it, seeing that helpless lust in your eyes to do so, just warms me on the inside." He flashed a smile. Sunlight sliced through his eyes making them appear pale and piercing.

Lourdes' muscles tensed. Her lip drew over her teeth. She wanted to claw his eyes out. She was still too winded by the news to think clearly.

He strolled toward the stairs again. "Thirteen weeks," he whistled. "That boy sure knew how to handle his business, didn't he? Made sure to sire a child before he died."

Lourdes blocked him once more, pushing against the box and stopping him in his tracks. "Johnny isn't dead!"

Tucker John looked at Lourdes' hand and then at her face. He flashed another smile. He'd riled her alright. "Now, see that is a matter of opinion depending on your reckoning of time isn't it? Is he alive or is he dead? Will he die soon?" *He won't live past 6037 if I have anything to say about it.* As far as he was concerned, John Jay was a dead man, but then so was Lourdes.

Lourdes snarled and grabbed the box from the other end, her chin raised so that she could look down her nose at him. "If I go and tell Vivian that you have her box," she slapped her own cheek so fiercely that the sound of skin on skin echoed up the stairwell. Tucker John cocked a brow. "If I tell her you hit me," she snarled again. "She *will* kill you. She'll listen to me, especially after what you've done to her!"

He tilted his head. "Viv isn't in a friendly mood right now. Wouldn't be wise for you to go bounding up them stairs only to end up tumbling right back down on your hind parts. But you aren't very good at doing what is wise now, are you? Why don't you turn that other cheek toward me so I can even you out, knock a little sense into your empty, scheming, head."

Her eyes grew wide. "You're nothing but a dirty *animal* on borrowed time! A dead man walking! You had better—"

Tucker John leaned closer to her. The fire in his eyes made all the ice in her melt into a puddle. "You had better get your hands off this box, and get out of my way, Lourdes, before I lose my temper. It would be a shame if Viv, in her state, couldn't come and rescue you from me like she has all them other times."

He waited until she fully deflated and pulled her hands away before brushing past her, taking to the stairs.

"Thirteen weeks," his voice boomed up and through the stairwell. "I wonder are they having a boy or girl. What you think, Lourdes? Think the little whelp will look like Johnny? I reckon so." He glanced back down at her and then laughed at her pallid snarl that contrasted the ridiculous, screaming red handprint on her cheek, before ascending out of her sight.

He walked passed Viv's room, making sure not to make eye contact as he rounded the corner and headed the flight of stairs to his room. He placed the box on his bed, popped it open, and took a quick look inside. A sizable white oval contraption, at least two feet long and two feet high, was inside, nestled in between diapers, socks, gowns, and other items a mama and baby would need. Etched into the oval's satin finish was the words 'birthing center.'

Not bothering to figure out how an oversized egg was a birthing center, he closed the lid and slid it out of sight. He didn't believe Lourdes to be gutsy enough to enter his room, but he knew that Viv was, and he certainly didn't need her to see the box and have another breakdown.

He closed the door to his room and went back to Viv's. She was angrily twirling the red earring in front of her tear-stained face, a wounded look in her eyes as she stared at her husband's image, and the inscription he had penned for another. She touched the white obsidian pendant at her neck before yanking it free with one quick tug. She threw it and the earring in the direction of the door with a growl.

Tucker John scooped them up.

Viv startled, "I didn't see you there," she turned toward the window, brushing a tear from her eye. Tucker John put both the pendant and the earring in his pocket.

"Why was the cleric here?" She turned back around and leaned against her desk. She wore a controlled mask of fixed emotions, but there was that fire again in her eyes, that fire that

Tucker John had first seen all those weeks ago and missed because of the *Paz* that had all but put it out.

He left his hands in his pockets. "Dropping off a package."

Viv folded her arms across her body. She was still so narrow. How was she pregnant? "Was it another secret message for John Jay?" Her scowl was sharp. Her chin trembled. She was feeling trapped, defensive. Pacifying her was not in his nature but clearly, it was necessary to calm her.

Keeping his spot by the door, he answered, "No, it was for you,"

Her eyes flashed. "Then way—"

"It was for the baby, Viv." Her mouth instantly clamped shut. "I put it away so as Lourdes couldn't damage it. Now that she knows about it and the child she is none too pleased." He kept his voice low and eased the door closed behind him.

Viv pinched her eyes closed. "She left again. I just saw her on the path. She's headed to Balm Hill. I thought you said you needed her close by."

"I know the harpy left. And I know where she's off to. It's my job to know these things about my hunt. Makes for a better kill."

She stared at him for a few hard seconds, before sighing and nearly collapsing to the ground. Within a flash, he scooped her into his arms and settled her on her bed. Beads of sweat peppered her brow and upper lip. "Viv?" His hand wiped the moisture from her face of its own volition, startling him. In the same instance, Viv's eyes, churning with fear, fluttered and snapped open, right before she scooted away from him.

Once upon a time, he would have savored that look, basked in it as if it was the sweetest of sunshine. For some reason foreign to him, it now gnawed at his gut and struck him with resentment.

Rising away from her he growled, "What's wrong with you? Is it the baby?"

"No!" Her quick response only made him scowl at her. "I'm achy. Whatever Evan gave me is working, I need to take the *XBalance* soon or else I'll be completely bed-ridden for days. And I can't have that not with," she stopped her mindless rambling, and let her head drop against her pillows.

Tucker John finished her sentence. "Not with the lingering threats over your head?" He moved toward the window. "I promise on my mama, and I don't ever do that, but I promise on my mama you will be in no harm from me, Viv. I can't give you no more than my word on that. Just as I didn't have much of a choice but to trust you, now you got to trust me."

She shook her head. "But you never trusted me. So why in the world would you expect me to trust you now?"

"Cause I don't expect you to play the part of a fool. I made my mistake. You bore witness to it. Why would you repeat it?" She didn't respond to his query, didn't even move. He didn't need her to. "I'm going to go and see I if I can hear anything through the static? You called it static, right?"

She nodded.

He headed back to the door. "You might want to get a head start on your other treatment while she's away, then. And Viv, do me a favor,"

She opened her eyes and looked over at him, her hand gripping the back of her neck.

"Whatever you do, don't let on to Lourdes that you know anything about what's going on between her and John Jay. Don't strike at her yet. Promise me that."

Her stoic expression crumbled. "I can't do that."

"I'm asking you to try."

"Or else you'll kill innocent people and make me live with it?" She didn't attempt to mask the mocking tone in her voice.

Tucker John held his ground. "It doesn't have to come to that. I don't want it to."

Her jaw clenched. "I refuse to believe someone like you is asking me to turn the other cheek and pretend nothing has happened like I didn't just find out that my husband is planning to kill me so that he can live happily-ever-after with our assistant!"

Tucker John considered his words. "If you really knew a person like me, Viv, then you would know I'm not asking you to do that at all. What I'm asking you to do is give me time."

She huffed. "Time for what?"

"To set a trap of my own, get us out of this mess."

He watched Viv's eyes slide closed again. She clearly didn't believe he could do it. He shouldn't have cared one iota about her opinion of him, but he did. With long strides, he was back at her side. He said to her, leaning over her on the bed, ignoring the startled look in her tired eyes, "Ain't no place in time that boy can hide from me. I *will* bring John Jay back quicker than you can blink! I'll deal with him and that cockroach, Lourdes. And I'll make sure you and I are left to tell the tale about it. I swear 'for god I will!'"

CHAPTER 46

John Jay's vision blurred. His organs shook like jelly. He wasn't well. He needed out, out of the static. He felt trapped, thrown into the heart of a maze whose pathways not only yielded no exit but seemed to shift and turn; throwing him into confusion right when he'd begun to believe that he'd found his bearings. Where he'd once felt confident and in control, he now felt like a lost, battered child being hunted down by the things of nightmares.

Several times he'd felt as if he'd been drawn and quartered, parts of him splitting and sliding into the black nothing of the static with rippling echoes of his voice screaming outward. The feeling had come upon him at least three times. The last time had knocked him unconscious. He experienced the horrifying splitting and tearing sensation whenever he forced his way through paths in time that had once had an exit but had suddenly closed up. Fear and desperation drove him to break through the blockades. The brain-numbing pain was the consequence.

The splitting had just happened again. John Jay let out a dreadful echoing roar that sent him into a violent spiral before the sound of it descended into silent nothing only to open up to another cacophony of voices.

"Lourdes?" he called out, but he could no longer hear her beyond the shouting that beat at his ears, the sound screaming out of a static-path that had appeared out of nowhere, just like so many others. Vivian was shouting now, too. Angry panic made him curse. This was all her fault; the confusion, the pain, the barricades. Vivian was the barricade!

Drawing himself upward, he followed the sound of her voice into the Static path that had just been born. Light shone upon it from the mouth of a nexus gate, but the image was all wrong, the house was wrong, Vivian was wrong.

Her hair was short. Her stomach was massive with child. John Jay ground his teeth. The child wasn't his! "It's not mine, Lourdes!" He shouted toward the gate, lunging for its opening when he saw the glint of a knife being thrust into Vivian's middle by Lourdes' hand.

"No!" He screamed. "Not like that! Not like that," but it was too late. The light died away. The path of the gate died into darkness. Lourdes and Vivian were no longer in his path.

It had already happened this way three times before, maybe four; the static-path, the mouth of the nexus gate, Lourdes somehow killing Vivian. He'd interfered once, stepped through the gate and yanked from Lourdes' hand the strange weapon she'd used to stop Vivian's heart. He'd never seen anything like it. He still had it with him in a white-knuckled hold. He'd taken it when he'd fled out of that gate path. Rubbing his raw hand down his worn face he collapsed in the dark.

He was so exhausted. He hadn't heard from Lourdes in so long…he didn't know how long. But he knew if he didn't get out of the static soon, he was going to lose his mind. He shuddered, realizing that he'd probably had already.

***

Tucker John forced a smile as he cinched tight the tie of the burlap sack, and handed it to the golden woman on the other side of the counter. She smiled in turn and waved him off same as she had done for the last couple of weeks. Viv's business with the co-op was finished. Her share of goods had been delivered in exchange for what she would need for the winter and early spring.

"How'd I do this time?" he asked Viv once they'd walked a good distance away from the thicker part of the crowd, the sea of conical hats dwindling down, as a less congested cobblestone path became clear.

Viv gave him a resentful look from beneath her hat's brim. "Believable enough."

It had been nigh on four weeks since they'd found out about the baby. That long since he'd sworn to her that he would find John Jay and bring him back dead as a hollow oak. Yet, he'd come up short. He hadn't even caught the foul man's scent, but he had seen Viv sour even more towards him if that were even possible.

As frustrated as he was, he'd cut himself some slack, at least as it pertained to hunting John Jay. He wasn't hunting the fiend through God's earth. John Jay had taken his scent into places no man's feet should ever tread. The near-impossible circumstances didn't make him end his search. Tucker John had a taste for his blood. He still looked for him, mostly he prepared for his pending return.

He'd gotten so focused on his prey that he could have sworn 'for god he'd seen John Jay's ragged form slinking through the house on occasion, or hearing his voice shouting out at him in the woods at least a few times over the past few weeks.

That too was a recent occurrence. He reckoned his preoccupation in thinking about John Jay was causing his mind to paint the coward just about everywhere he'd turned, especially when he was tired. Even Viv had confessed to having frights concerning her murderous husband.

The way Tucker John saw it, regardless of Viv's reluctance or resentment, the sooner John Jay was toes up underground the better. Getting rid of him needed to be quick and as cleanly done as possible, nothing to make anyone question him or Viv later.

His plan was simple although Viv was none too pleased with it. But what choice did she have but to comply? From her perspective, Tucker John had forced her hand. She could think that was the case all she wanted, no matter how deadly wrong she was.

Yes, he'd forced her to his way of things, but this way wasn't what he'd originally had in mind. Truth be told, it wasn't as if it was the most convenient option for him either, even if the prospect of killing John Jay was absolutely gratifying. Hell, the promise of doing so was probably the reason why visions of John Jay seemed to be haunting him in the first place; appearing like a ghost in the shadows, then disappearing.

The last thing Tucker John wanted was to be stuck with Vivian Leona for any longer than necessary, but since killing John Jay was the only solution to their deadly problem, taking on John Jay's identity within the timeline was the hateful consequence.

He'd been comforting himself, especially in the face of Viv's moods, that this solution was a temporary fix to a present danger. He and Viv would have six years to work out a more palatable alternative, one where both of them went their separate ways.

The other token of comfort that came to him was that of eventually reporting Lourdes to her government for having lost her mind, and then being able to bear witness to her euthanasia. It was far less hands-on than he was used to when it came to dealing with his marks, but he was going to have to take what he could get and so was Viv. Neither of them had made the mess they were in, but if they intended to live beyond it, they were going to have to clean it up.

"I'm hungry. I want to get something to eat before heading back to the manor." Viv's voice broke into his thoughts. He studied the grim line of her mouth. The woman was growing more hostile by the day. He understood. Feeling like someone's prisoner had that effect on a body.

Pushing deeper into the crowd, Tucker John gently eased his hand around her bicep and leaned down toward her ear. "We can grab you some vittles, but you're gon' have to fix your face." He pulled away and gave her a smile. Contradicting the resentful glint her eyes had shown him, she smiled back and caressed his face as if she were indeed the doting wife, before shifting completely out of his grasp, and moving a few paces ahead of him.

He let her have her space. It was funny how the tables had turned; the one on the leash, and the holding it, changing hands. Viv had brought it up a few nights ago over supper, pointing out the hateful exchange with such bitterness that it made Tucker John's meal taste like gravel. He wasn't bothered by her attitude or the fact that he had the control he'd prayed for. On the contrary, as far as he was concerned, he was right where a man was meant to be, at the head of his own life.

The ruining of the savor of his meal came with the whispered reminder to his spirit. He'd promised the Good Lord that once he got control of his life back, shimmied his way out from under Viv's slippered foot, he'd turn it over to Him. Tucker John was a man of his word, and God had proven His end of the exchange. That truth had worn on him. It made his insides quiver. Trusting Him as his mama did, trusting His way to be right for him, was the hard part.

Flinching, he narrowed his eyes against the harsh rays of the sun. His mind must have been playing with him again, or maybe he was as hungry as Viv was, hungrier since he was doing all the heavy lifting. He could've sworn he saw a raggedy John Jay running headlong across his path before turning tail and disappearing into the unusually bright sunlight of the October sun. He was certain that he saw the boney man called Magnus, staring in Viv's direction, watching her with hawk eyes.

A territorial growl rumbled in Tucker John's chest. He couldn't fight the fire of it nor keep himself from purposefully standing in Magnus's line of sight, giving him a sharp but meaningful stare down. He didn't care who Magnus said he was or what he was doing. He didn't cotton to the way he was watching Viv like he was stalking her.

As if it were possible, Magnus' face went a shade whiter before rising with a heated red. With just as much ire, he returned Tucker John's scowl, pulled his long coat tight around himself before moving through the crowd, and out of Tucker John's sight.

Shaking his head Tucker John joined Viv at a food cart, instinctively placing his hand on the small of her back before ordering himself a double portion of what she was having.

***

Clarence stood at a distance, watching Magnus weave through the crowd away from the threatening stare of Tucker John. Mr. Spruce had keenly sharp eyes, so keen that Clarence was certain he'd seen the wraith of John Jay break through the timeline before disappearing again into the maze of the static. Clarence wasn't worried about the wraith. His employers had assured him it would appear again a little after midnight a few miles northeast of town. Clarence would deal with it then. Nevertheless, he was concerned about being seen by Tucker John. Not leaving room for a potential confrontation, he pushed himself further into the shadows before following after Magnus.

It was a wild thread of hunt and prey he'd been walking upon. The outcome of the game should have been easily set. But threads in time had been knotted by John Jay's stumbling feet, his wraiths and perverted timelines he'd unwittingly born, had caused things to get...complicated.

Clarence was good at complicated. His life's breath was spent dealing with such things. His true employers appreciated that most about him. That was why they'd allowed him to be snared by Aiden Schulsler. When he'd first contacted Mr. Lemon—one of his true employers—about the Schulsler predicament, Mr. Lemon simply told him that they needed him in close proximity to the man. Ultimately, they would need his services in 4037 where certain happenings had gotten very problematical. Things were only going to get worse with several yellow flags of unverifiable moments showing themselves within the log of time, but Clarence was ready, even if others were not.

He was a hunter and fixer after all. His tactics were far less visceral than Tucker John's but no less thorough. He, too, watched, waited, and then struck at his hunt with exacting precision.

He'd already destroyed three of John Jay's static-born copies, each of them appearing upon the mother-timeline of 4037. He needed to handle this last wraith, wait until after the mother-timeline had been securely anchored and set again, then he would handle the next phase of his assignment, the mission Mr. Lemon and the others were most concerned about. He just needed Magnus to make his move and Aiden Schulsler to sign off on what was necessary to be done.

CHAPTER 47

Vivian smoothed the dark fabric down over her midsection and took in her reflection with a scrutinizing eye. With a great deal of emotional and mental turbulence, she'd managed to enter her seventeenth week of pregnancy, and yet she hardly had much of a belly to show for it. If anything, she looked as if she were bloated or just full, but not pregnant, and certainly not by Tucker John. The hateful thought made her stomach roil as if her meal at the food cart hadn't been enough. Remembering the heat of his hand at the small of her back nearly made her vomit.

He was clearly getting very comfortable with becoming John Jay. *'We ain't got no other option, Viv!'* he'd argued. But he'd also argued that he didn't want to do so. *'It ain't like I wanna spend the rest of my life playing the part of a fool, hogtied to you either. If I wanted me a wife I woulda' got me one. I sho'nough wouldn't be plotting to kill nobody to take theirs. You can bet your hide on that.'*

But the way he was falling into his role, even when eyes weren't looking, made her leery of his argument. She was wise to not trust him. John Jay had fooled her, taken from her, and then turned on her with a deadly vengeance. It was only a matter of time before Tucker John did the same.

She let the fabric relax again against her stomach and pinched the bridge of her nose. Tears clogged her throat. She recalled the day that life had taken root inside of her. John Jay had said 'one last kiss' but it had certainly been more than that, much more. Why had he played over her? Why hadn't he just insisted that they'd divorced before they came all this way back in time? Why?

"Because you would have fought him to stay with you, that's why." She hiccupped angry tears and swallowed them down. She wouldn't keep crying. Tears wouldn't get her out of Tucker John's reach. They wouldn't save her from John Jay. They could do nothing. They certainly couldn't heal this suffering.

What she was suffering was far more than the sting of rejection. She wasn't the first woman to feel that. Women throughout history had been used, abandoned, and left filled with just as much bitterness and hardness of heart as their bellies were of baby, by selfish boys parading as men. She only hated that she had joined them in their ranks. But worse than the abandonment was the fact her husband wanted to kill her...and his seed.

Part of her wanted to dive through the static, hunt him down, and drive a stake through his heart. He was like a vampire; a devil that sucked the lives out of their victims. For weeks she'd ruminated upon that truth. And felt it sting even harder when Raul had contacted her, inviting her and her team in to speak to him. He'd wanted to apologize for the confusion caused with the Cleric's Office. He seemed to be the only one who remembered the pending T.R that never happened, and had no record of ever having been scheduled. He'd also been the only one in the room to question John Jay's absence even though Lourdes was present.

He's sick, was what Vivian had told him, not wanting Tucker John to make an official public debut at that time. She'd simply lied and said John Jay was sick.

"He's beyond sick..." she whispered as if she'd stumbled upon a thread of enlightenment.

Marcus had warned her to leave John Jay alone, said he was still broken, had alluded to something more by the strained looks he gave her when he lacked words during their confrontation. Vivian hadn't listened. Was it pride that kept her from doing so? She hadn't loved John Jay then, so it had to have been pride. She'd never come against a mountain she couldn't climb or a puzzle she couldn't solve. She must not have thought John Jay to be any different.

She should have known better, would have even done better had she been conscious of her fallacy, and arrogance. Human hearts were not puzzles made for men to solve. Hearts were the Lord's territory, and she had trespassed on sacred ground and was now paying a price she didn't have the means to pay. There would be no reward for her haughtiness this time. No badge of honor, no mark of mastery to go down in the annals of the Ministry of Time. Instead, she was losing everything—most of which was her mind—and being left with two reminders of what she'd done; a baby she'd never wanted, and Tucker John, a man who'd bound her for life.

How in the world was she going to survive living with the heavy shadow of the lies she was prepping to tell once John Jay was gone...dead? She couldn't. She couldn't do that, and stay sane. She couldn't raise an unwanted child who would one day ask about their father only for her to respond with fiction. She already figured Tucker John would find some way to leave her, leave them, and live a new life as a consolation prize for his time and inconvenience. She couldn't then sit at Emlen Spruce's table and tell her simply that John Jay—Tucker John—had abandoned her, and their child when the whole truth was far more nefarious than that. The man who would one day abandon his life and family was not even her son. That man would have murdered her son.

That truth would eat her alive. It already was!

As fragile and cracked as she felt, she was certain that if no one saw through her and Tucker John's tale, Marcus Taylor would. He would drill her down to her marrow and force the truth out of her if it was the last thing he ever did that side of Heaven. He would blame her.

"But aren't I to blame?" Conflicted, she wrapped her arms around her middle, and let her mind drift. She was running in aimless circles while John Jay and Lourdes plotted against her, while Tucker John did plotting of his own. She really had no plan of action to lean on, no matter how many nights she spent trying to construct one. All she could do was force smiles, biding her time as she was dragged along by Tucker John.

Her hands had become just as tied as they were idle. She had only done one follow up call with the Cleric's Office in regard to her report on finding the static, only to be treated yet again like a loopy pariah worthy of nothing more than congratulations for her pregnancy. Quinn Ellington was gone again, had not kept her word regarding Vivian's report, and another Chief was about to be promoted up the ranks, while Raul instructed her to just let it go, and move forward with her surveillance. *"For the martyred we march on lest the living die."*

Yet again, Vivian was left with the appearance of a person on the edge of having a mental time-break. If Quinn hadn't shared the news of her pregnancy before she'd gone off duty, taking a fulltime Chief Cleric's position in her proper timeline, Vivian was certain everyone would have already concluded that she was mentally gone. If she told the truth about John Jay and Tucker John…and Lourdes…they would definitely have her removed from the Ministry, and swiftly 'cleared' of all broken consciousness.

"That would work to Tucker John's favor at least," she tried not to think about it any further. She didn't want to think about anything she had found out over the last weeks or so; not the baby, not Alba, not the affair, and certainly not how she was her own husband's target.

Doing what she knew would soothe her, she dropped down upon the leather folds of her armchair, and turned on the tunes of Tom Dorsey, allowing him to sing her soul to meditative silence.

CHAPTER 48

Clouds covered the light of the moon like a veil drawn over the face of the dead, professing the extinguishing of life's light. The wraith's eyelids mimicked the movement of the clouds as death overtook it in the shrouded fields in 4037, Georgia.

The deed was done, although it wasn't an easy task. The static-copy of John Jay had nearly been intercepted several times by Tucker John. Clarence had to laugh. The man was indeed a bloodhound. Tucker John had tracked this wraith, caught sight of it while he stalked Lourdes. If it wasn't for the fact the being weaved in and out of the static-membrane, back and forth through the threads of time, Tucker John would have surely caught and killed him before Clarence was able to do so.

Luckily, Clarence got to it first. Had things gone in the opposite direction, Tucker John and Vivian would have been sitting ducks, living off of false assurance, ill-prepared for when the true John Jay made his appearance. None of that was a concern now. All the pieces were now properly set. The wraiths were gone and with them, their timelines.

With quick movements, Clarence moved the body and positioned it for the last time the static would open up upon the mother-timeline in that hour. He stared unblinkingly and watched through his periphery as movement and threads of static and time pulled apart. Stifling a grunt, he unfolded John Jay's wraith into the opening and watched it dissolve as if eaten by acid.

Static was very aggressive with disposing of ideas that had been aborted from time. It left no evidence of it ever having been born.

The static opening upon true time wasn't all that a bizarre occurrence, although most had very little knowledge of it happening. As far as they were concerned those moments were nothing short of déjà vu.

Whatever made people sleep easier at night. Holding his hand up to the side of his face, assured all evidence of his violent act had left no traces of ever having happened, he whispered, "It's done. Please inform Mr. Lemon. We'll be back on track as soon as the real John Joseph Spruce makes his appearance upon the mother-timeline. I'll be able to retrieve the rapier from him then." The rapier—the single trace of the last ill-born reality that John Jay had snatched into the static with him.

The nearly inaudible voice of Mr. Lemon's assistant whispered back, "Excellent work, Mr. Mantov. Please await your final instructions. Your assignment within this timeline is nearly complete."

Clarence nodded and disconnected from the call. Glancing up at the shrouded moon, he dashed deeper into the darkness.

***

Lourdes was certain that she'd heard Johnny whispering to her three nights ago. She could have sworn that she felt his lips upon hers, and his hands against her skin. He'd told her not to kill Vivian, not yet. That confused her. Why would she kill Vivian now, and why wouldn't he just come home already?

She knew the answer to that. He'd told her when they'd last spoke a few weeks ago that shifting the future—his present— was much harder than manipulating the past. She just hoped he'd be back before the colder weather set in. She hoped she'd be done with her tasks as well. She still hadn't gotten everything on her end completely ready, but she was close.

Sweat dripped into her eyes and stung them as she forcibly realigned the cells within one of the final joints of the perimeter fence. It was a cool day, but reinforcing the fence, exactly as

Johnny had told her, was back-breaking work. Her fingertips throbbed from the vibrations of the cells that drummed against them. She wasn't a Tech, so it took her longer to manipulate the core spacers of each joint that held the fence together, but she'd get it done. She'd do anything for Johnny.

Wiping her sleeve against her brow, she sat back on her haunches and let the wind blow her face dry. She took a scan of the property line, comforting herself with the knowledge that she had only a few yards left of fencing to reinforce. She'd already sent Johnny a message through the static telling him so. She hoped he'd gotten it.

She needed his reassurance more than anything. She needed to know he loved her like she loved him. Circumstances and time had caused her to question everything. Although he'd promised her that the baby in Vivian's womb wasn't his, she was finding it hard to believe, even though she desperately wanted to believe Vivian had been intimate with the Animal. Worse, now that the rest of the Cleric's Office was aware of Vivian's pregnancy, they were giving her grace for her prior questionable behavior.

"If they don't think she's having a time-break then they won't believe she kills herself later." But what did that matter? Now it was supposed to look like Tucker John killed her. The plan was changing as much as the shifting circumstances. First, it was Tucker John, and now a baby.

Irritated, Lourdes slapped her thigh but then smiled remembering what Johnny had told her about Vivian not wanting to have a family yet; that she believed a child would derail their current career success.

Johnny's child or not, this unplanned pregnancy could work in their favor. They could even say the pregnancy was what pushed Vivian over the edge, that maybe it was, in fact, the Animal's after all, that that revelation put them at each other's throats. And then there was the argument that Vivian had with Tucker John a few mornings ago. Lourdes had caught the tail end of Vivian's shouting and Tucker John's hissing, but she couldn't make out what had been said. What she did know was that Vivian's attitude had set a heat off in the house that had lingered clear into that afternoon.

No, things weren't as bad as they seemed. Circumstances had changed but they were still right on track.

With a new found confidence she applied the last level of coding to the cell core of the joint she was working on and giggled as she watched the changes take root. Smiling, she plucked a strand of grass from the ground and twirled it between her red fingers. "Things are going to be just fine. All of this will be over soon."

***

That was at least five yellow markers in one day that Magnus had come across. His surveillance of Vivian's case had been running so smoothly, with only one yellow marker rearing its head. Now there were five, five!

He read through his logs again, and the case file he'd received from Schulsler from 6039. According to the file, they were only days from the major storm hitting. The anticipation and the warning glare Tucker John had given him at the market was only making the acid in his stomach churn. The man was an absolute ingrate. Magnus was tempted to just tell Vivian the truth about everything, and be done with it. Her life had become nothing short of a nuisance for him, that, and the static.

He stared down at the container of static he'd collected. The sudden urge to use it to erase Vivian Leona, and everyone connected to her pricked his skin. "Better yet, I should use it on Schulsler."

That made him laugh. He doubted that static could actually erase a person, but he couldn't be certain that it couldn't prevent them from ever existing in the first place. He stared more intently at the golden matter. He'd only been toying with the notions of erasing people out of frustration, but maybe the notion wasn't so unreasonable after all.

"Stop it, Magnus!" he rebuked himself, pushing away from his desk and staring out his window. The leaves had long since faded from green and burned with fiery colors. The world in 4037 was indeed about to catch fire. It was better he do what he was there for, watch it all burn to the ground, verify it's happening so that he could be done with Aiden Schulsler for good.

CHAPTER 49

"Did you practice what I told you, today? It's important you get this right, Viv." Tucker John was referring to the recent amendments he'd made to their original plan. It especially affected Lourdes. Euthanasia was no longer an option.

Viv had been riled up ever since he'd told her that he intended to read Lourdes her last rights, same as John Jay. He didn't want to leave room for backlash from the Government or the clerics. Viv had shouted over the change, kept insisting she wasn't a murderer and didn't want more blood on her hands. After nearly an hour of shouting, he'd eventually gotten her to heel...mostly. Viv was as hardheaded as females came, but he was just going to have to take what he could get.

Some strange things had happened over the last few days, things he couldn't ignore. First, he was hearing Johnny-boy running through the house. Then he was sure he'd seen him. He'd even tracked him three nights ago before his trail ran cold, disappearing as if into thin air. Even the things he'd heard Lourdes talking about, while in her mama's house, came off as odd even for a murderous wench. She too had been seeing him.

The games needed to end. John Jay needed to meet his Maker as soon as possible, and leaving the little Jezebel to get euthanized was too much of a risk. She'd sing like a canary first chance she got, get them all killed. As he'd heard her say, her life was nothing without Johnny and that boy was already on his way to the noose. The girl had to go too.

He glanced at Viv before taking a cut of the tender baby lamb. He soaked gravy onto a roll and plopped it into his mouth waiting for her answer.

Viv cleared her throat shooting him a scathing look and a clipped 'yes.' She turned her churning brown eyes back to her plate and continued to saw at her meat. Very little of what she cut actually made it to her mouth.

"Well, let's hear it." He prodded.

Viv clenched her knife and fork but didn't look at him. It had been less than a week since she'd become jittery around him like she thought he'd strike her or worse. Their last argument had done that. She didn't say so, but she was afraid of him now, afraid he'd come up with some reason to kill her too. That, she had said.

Killing her wasn't what he wanted, not anymore, but her misunderstanding him served its purpose. She was finally minding him, still only mostly. "Come on, Viv. We're losing daylight," he knocked his knuckles on the table.

Viv dropped her fork and folded her arms across her chest, her eyes suddenly burning red. "Can we just eat and not do this right now?"

Tucker John leaned back and stared at her down his nose. "Ain't like you eating none. Might as well do something constructive besides ruining that lamb." She scowled at him. *That's right. Get angry.* It was better to have her angry than cowering. He didn't need Lourdes suspecting a thing. He was certain she'd heard them arguing a few mornings ago. He prayed she hadn't heard what it was about. By her continuous smug posture, it was becoming more and more evident that she hadn't.

"Fine." She shoved her plate away. Her dictation began. "I don't know what happened to her. I don't know when Lourdes became obsessed with my husband. I don't know the extent of her obsession, and I don't want to. I can't tell you what happened last night, not really. It's all a blur," her chin trembled and she angrily gnawed her lower lip until the quivering ceased.

Her voice cracked when she started again, her agitation with him colored her tone. Tucker John kept eating. "I heard screaming. It woke me up. I looked out the window and saw that she'd hanged herself. She tried to kill John Jay, but couldn't, so she killed herself instead." Sighing, she swiped the water from her eyes, picked up her fork and knife, and resumed the senseless sawing of her meat.

He snorted. "Really, Viv?" his lip curled with a disgusted snarl. "You done left out just about every part of the tale! Never mind the fact you don't sound anywhere near believable. What about John Jay starting to sleep on the third floor 'cause you been working late? What about how the rope got there in the first place? What about—"

"I don't want to go over this right now! What about, this is all making me crazy, and I just want to have a moment to get my head together." Her eyes were angry but pleading. "I'm sure once everyone is dead I'll be believable enough when I finally have to tell the Cleric's Office what happened. And so what if I miss a few details like bed linen ropes or where John Jay had been sleeping. You'll be right there to fill in any gaps I may leave out so what's the problem? You're John Jay now, right? That's the plan, to become him? You can explain your own behavior when the clerics start asking. They already think I've lost my mind due to pregnancy hormones so they'll most likely defer to you anyway." A tone of resentment laced her words. It always did when the baby was brought up.

She finally said, "I won't mention your real name to anyone if that's your concern. I won't blow your cover. So stop worrying. Lourdes will kill herself in a fit of rage. The end. You have nothing to worry about so just leave it for now. Please." Another tear slid down her cheek. She brushed it away before drawing her plate closer to her. This time she did take a bite.

The conversation dropped into an oppressive silence, one Vivian's nerves couldn't bear. Mostly it was the discomfort that came from being under Tucker John's gaze. He watched her so much now, more than he had before. It unnerved her.

She forced herself to speak again, hoping to do anything to shift his gaze and concentration on something else. "What've you been up to today? I noticed you got the chores done early. How's the new calf?" She didn't care about the calf in the least. She just wanted to think about something else, something other than how she was being made to plot her husband's death, and now his mistress', all in an attempt not to get killed herself. All of this, while allowing her accomplice to take her adulterous husband's place in time. No, she'd rather think about the calf. At least two had been born.

Tucker John cocked his brow, huffed a laugh, and then answered. "The calves are fine. There were a few piglets that got sick. I had to get rid of 'em, but that was easy enough. I was at Balm Hill most of the morning though, had to wait until the harpy came back here first. She's fiddling with the perimeter fence again. She's just about been around the whole circle of it." He took a gulp of milk. Some of it clung in the short hairs of his growing beard.

Vivian stared at it. She was glad that he hadn't taken the care of shaving or trimming his hair. Even the little bit of growth he had acquired made him at least tolerable to look at. He appeared as a different man than John Jay, more like himself. "What were you doing at Balm Hill?" She winced, suddenly wishing she hadn't asked.

He wiped his mouth. "A little remodeling. Setting a good stage for when I poke the bear and folks get to investigating." He gave her a look. He'd only hinted to how he'd intended to rattle Lourdes enough to get her to run off, calling John Jay back to 4037. "As I said before, it may be best you don't know everything, fewer facts to keep track of, and less cause for suspicion. No offense, but you ain't that good with acting,"

"Lying, you mean?" She took a bite of the lamb.

"Nothing but semantics, Viv. And still, you stink at it. But as I recall, the plan is that you only just find out about Lourdes' obsession with Johnny-boy when everyone else does. The point is things will fall right into place once I set the ball rolling."

He belched and gave a weak 'pardon me' before continuing. "I have the mind to get this over with as soon as possible. It's already been weeks, and I just ain't comfortable with letting more time pass with this. Ain't no telling what that boy's been up to while he's been lurking in the static. If I had my way, I'd deal with the both of them before week's end. Hell, I'd even do it tonight."

He leaned back in his chair and considered her again. "I know you ain't got a mind to talk about the finality of these things, but do you think you can handle it if he were to come, say, tonight?" Plucking meat from between his teeth he added, "I can't promise nothing, but..."

Vivian stopped chewing and forced down a bite of lamb. It was the second bite she'd taken and now it was clawing back up her throat. "I don't think I have much of a choice in the matter. You'll do what you want."

Again he stared at her. She shifted under his gaze. "We all have choices, Viv. Just do as I told you and things should go fine. At least I reckon they will." His brow lowered, "And stop acting like I'm the one that's done turned you into a victim. I'm trying to help you stay alive, woman!" He snatched up his glass of milk, downed it before taking hold of the pitcher and pouring another glass full.

Vivian's voice lowered. "You keep saying that but the truth remains that I am right where you've always wanted me, and I refuse to pretend that I trust you, that you aren't just biding more time before you turn on me just like they have. In fact, you have already." She looked over at him. Her nostrils flared as she fought back tears.

Tucker John stared at her over the rim of his glass before setting it back down on the table. "I recommend you not think on those things. As I've said a thousand times already, I have no intention of harming you, Viv. I gave you my word and I asked you to allow me to prove my salt to you. I can't do that if you don't keep up your end of things, get your story straight.

"I reckon this is hard for you, having to trust someone else's lead. Hell, you probably ain't killed a thing in your life. The good thing is, you don't have to kill nothing or nobody now. I'll handle that part of the damage, and when it's all done you'll know you can trust me."

Vivian pressed her lips together. All she had to do was trust him? She couldn't. She couldn't even stomach the lie he was grooming her to tell. As far as she could see she was as good and dead as the sliced lamb on her plate, and all she could do was follow along, doing what he'd instructed her to do.

She'd rehearsed the lines he'd fed her over and over again as evidence of that fact. She knew the story he'd rewritten a few days ago. He put the tale together so nicely, she almost believed it herself. She just didn't want to keep going over it. Lourdes had become obsessed with John Jay. That was a fact. Her mother, Alba, had found out about it but Lourdes had her euthanized. That was a fact. Lourdes, being rejected by John Jay, trying to kill him in his third-floor bedroom, but only kills herself when she is unsuccessful, was so far from the truth that Vivian could've retched right there at the table.

Still, she could tack a nice 'the end' to the woven lies and truths, just like Tucker John wanted her to. The only problem was, it wouldn't be the end. In fact, it would only be a prelude to the beginning of another nightmare that she was going to have to live through. It scared her near beyond death.

Staring forward, her fingers tightened around the knife and fork in her hands. There were so many thin lines in life, thin lines between genius and insanity, peace and war, love and hate. She felt like she had crossed over all three of them. She definitely had stepped into insanity. Tucker John had hinted at them having time to figure out their next steps over the next seven years they'd have together. Basically, he was formulating his escape plan, how to detach himself from all of what was happening, and start his own life, away from her. She would be left holding the bag of her life's broken bones as well as a child born from the fire and ashes.

The insanity was that she was actually feeling more afraid of facing the aftermath without Tucker John than anything else. She was afraid of him staying, and yet she was terrified of him leaving. She was terrified of him sitting so close to her without a means to protect herself should he turn on her, and afraid he would simply turn away from her, leaving her alone with the monsters that were lurking in the shadows along with a baby, and a life she would no longer be able to make sense of.

More silence blanketed the table until he spoke again. "Can you tell me anything about what Lourdes has been doing with the fence? That might be useful to know right about now. I've been waiting for your response on this for almost a month already."

Vivian snapped out of her daze and cut another piece of meat. She moved it around her plate with her fork. "She's reinforced it somehow. I don't know how, but the fence is denser."

"That's not all bad in and of itself is it?"

"I suppose not. If worse comes to worse, we can activate it to keep ourselves alive, sho-should things not go as planned." Why had she said that? They looked at each other but said nothing else.

The sound of the front door opening and shutting again brought an instant silence over the dining room. Lourdes was back. She'd clearly been out at the property line again. Her hands were that familiar screaming red color.

Vivian tensed. Tucker John lightly placed his bare foot on top of hers. *'Keep it calm'*, his eyes said. Vivian let out a trembling breath and forced food into her mouth.

Sitting down across from her, Lourdes pulled out a plate and loaded it with potatoes and mixed vegetables. Her eyes were chilly when she looked at Tucker John but quickly, falsely, warmed when they turned toward Vivian.

"Vivian, it's been a while. You've been hiding in your room for nearly a month. I was beginning to think you were ill. I suppose the pregnancy has had that effect." She smirked. "Don't worry though. I've been covering for you at the Cleric's Office. I've told them that you've been working on things that have taken up a lot of your time. I didn't want anyone suspicious of you and us. It seems there was little to no need for me to say anything at all considering your condition. Imagine all of our shock when we found out you were pregnant, and right in the middle of your surveillance." Her smirk deepened.

Vivian glared at her.

CHAPTER 50

The look on Lourdes' face made it clear she'd taken Viv's glare as a welcome challenge. She calmly bowed her head in a show of piety before taking a bite of potatoes. It amazed Tucker John how much a woman could say without saying anything at all.

Lourdes said, "What I don't understand is why you would keep that news from me. I mean, we've worked together for three years. Not to mention you've known about this for over a month and still failed to tell me yourself. The only reason I know is because of the cleric who delivered your care package," she let her fork hover in the air. "Don't you trust me anymore? I image not since he showed up." She shifted her eyes in Tucker John's direction before taking a bite of potatoes.

Shifting in her seat, she poured gravy over her plate and took another bite, sucking the potatoes down her throat. "I honestly don't understand why I've been getting shut out, Vivian." She made her voice tremble as if she were fighting back tears. "I apologize for this emotion. I know I need to vaccinate but I can't help it. This has been extremely hard on me. I think I might have even infected my mother. She's gotten worse over the past few weeks."

Lourdes touched her lips as if to still them. Ducking her head she pierced Tucker John with another glare before turning her attention back to Viv. "If I had any other chance to do so, I would've talked to you about this without him present but what choice do I have? Even with my own family struggles, I'm concerned for you, but you don't seem to care."

Viv's mouth cracked open. Tucker John added more pressure to her foot. She clamped her lips shut again, letting a tempered breath flow from her nostrils.

Lourdes dropped her cutlery. She looked between Tucker John and Viv. "Oh, I see what's happening here." Her eyes narrowed and a crocodile tear slid down her cheek. "You two have formed some kind of alliance against me! What have I done to you? I've supported you in this. I've supported John Jay and you..." She shook her head and made as if to choke on tears.

Viv leaned back in her seat and stared hard at her. Tucker John was amazed that she hadn't leaped across the table and smothered her with her napkin. By the glint in her stormy eyes, she had certainly imagined doing something of the sort in her head.

Lourdes continued. "That's it, isn't it? That's why you've stopped looking for John Jay. That's why you've been hiding in your room for nearly an entire month! You haven't eaten with me or talked with me, but somehow you're able to share the table with him. You even let him get your deliveries for you too." She was referring to the baby care package.

She leaned forward. Her grey eyes narrowed into razor slits. "What else have you shared with him, Vivian? I mean, he looks a lot like John Jay. I can imagine he could act as a great stand-in. That was your idea in the first place, wasn't it?"

Tucker John watched as the color drained from Viv's face. In his periphery, he was certain he saw a flash of a smile slip across Lourdes' face. "I'll take your hiding and your silence as the answer." Another tear fell from Lourdes' eye. Shaking her head, she even peppered her performance with the sounds of weeping. "Is the child even John Jay's? Is that why you've stopped looking for him like you were before? Is that why you've been hiding away?"

Viv took in a sharp breath. Lourdes pulled her napkin from her lap and cried into it. Viv yanked her foot from beneath Tucker John's. Her chair made a distressed screeching sound when it shot out behind her. Throwing down her napkin she exited the dining room without a single word. Tucker John let her go.

Only a few seconds passed before Lourdes peaked from behind her napkin, her eyes full of laughter even though she continued to make the sounds of bitter weeping.

Tucker John chewed his food slowly and watched Viv leave the room. Lourdes didn't wait very long before she dropped her napkin and began to drip more venom from her lips. She loaded up her fork again, her voice a fiery whisper. "See how easy that was?" She turned her attention to him now. "It's not looking good for Vivian is it, Tucker John? Which means it isn't looking very good for you either. She's clearly showing signs of aggression and depression. I think she might be coming down with some kind of condition. That can be a dangerous thing around here. I don't know what the Cleric's Office will do but the Government has euthanized for lesser offenses than tha—"

Swift as lighting, Tucker John grabbed Lourdes by the wrist, his movements so quick that the crystal on the table hardly had time to move. Lourdes dropped her fork, her mouth cracking open with the intent to let loose a cry when the tip of his steak knife caught her beneath the chin, drawing the slightest trace of blood.

"I swear fo' god if you holla' I'll gut you like the pig you are! I'll slit you from navel to nose." His southern drawl was as thick as the first day she'd heard him speak. "Be a good gal, shut your trap." He whispered tightening his grip on her arm as if to crush the bones with his large hand.

Lourdes let out a squeal but quickly cut it off. Her mouth clamped shut but trembled uncontrollably. Sudden fear radiated throughout her body. Tucker John pulled the knife from her chin but he kept it in her line of sight. He still hadn't let go of her wrist.

"What are you going to do?" She questioned. She drew in a breath and held it in her chest, too afraid to let it out. She'd expected him to react, but not like this. He'd always had reins on him before, always threatened but never put a hand to her.

"I'm going to kill you, Lourdes." He said the words with such ease. The sound was no different than if he were telling her he was going to bed or going to take a walk. It made her stomach clench.

"Then why don't you do it now? What are you waiting for?" She asked preparing herself for the inevitable.

Tucker John tightened his grip again. Lourdes writhed in her chair and reached for her wrist, real tears pressing from her eyes. "Matter of convenience," he said.

Stuttering to breathe, she searched his eyes before scowling. She would call his bluff. "No, you won't! You won't kill me. You want to live. If you kill me, they'll kill you. So I suggest you let—"

Tucker John cut her off, his face drew into a hard snarl. He angrily hocked spit onto her dinner plate, his face washing nearly as red as her hands. "A dead man walking don't give a witch's cold titty bout' dying! Way I see it, I been dead some two-thousand years. I'm already on borrowed time I can't pay back, so *I* suggest you tread lightly.

"You been running 'round here scheming, you and that *boy*. You two are the worst kind of selfish sons of b*%$^es! You sitting up here telling me how bad a person I was for what I done, called me an animal," he spat the word out like a dragon would fire. A throbbing vein pushed forward from his forehead. His face was florid. "...and the whole time you was setting Viv up to be dropped right in my care so you could bed down and be her husband's whore. You was going to send her back to 1837 and keep my Vivian here. You were sentencing both of them to death! Hell, I don't even have a future past my first day here. So you was intending to kill me too,"

"You weren't meant to be here!"

Tucker John made her wince again. She would have a nasty bruise by the time he let her loose if he let her loose.

Lourdes' eyes darted throughout the dining room. Who would help her? She took in another deep breath preparing to scream. She prayed it would draw Vivian. No matter how she'd goaded her, Vivian still wouldn't let him kill her. She couldn't.

Tucker John put the knife to her throat once more. "Scream and I'll kill you now."

Desperate, Lourdes drew at weak straws. Her heart racing out of control. She'd broken out in a nervous sweat. She'd never felt pain or fear like this before. "I-I was trying to help her,"

He growled. "You wasn't trying to help no d@#$ body but yourself,"

"No! I was helping the slave-woman! Vivian Leona has done nothing but ruin everything for her and John Jay. She has ruined your life too! She doesn't deserve what she has. Your Vivian would've had a better life here had Vivian not interfered. That was the plan. I swear! D-Don't you love your Vivian?"

"Ain't nobody said a d@^# thing about love! And on her having a better life here, Bull$%^&! The Governors would'a had her put down for being out of place, just like they will me. Never mind the fact she was feebleminded. You two was killing three people so you could have a good time under some sheets. I'm sorry, make that four people since your mama done gone and met her Maker on account of finding out about you and Johnny-boy."

Lourdes' eyes widened with shock and then darkened at the mention of her mama. How did he know?

Tucker John continued "And since your original plan fell to scraps now you wanna give me some cheap song and dance that Viv is to blame for all of this? Hell no! You done messed up, Lourdes. You messed with the wrong one this time."

Lourdes groaned, the pain of her wrist snaking up her arm. She tried to pull free to no avail. She would stop pretending. "What? So you're feeling noble now? Your hands too dirty with innocent blood and you think by playing hero to Vivian Leona you can win some brownie points?" She gave a derisive laugh.

Tucker John bent her hand backward bringing her to her knees. She panted from the fire that shot through her joints.

"This ain't about being no hero and it sure as shooting ain't about points either," he leaned into her face speaking through clenched teeth. Spittle mixed with chewed lamb peppered her check. She gaged. "This is about you done screwed with me, and I don't take kindly to being screwed with!"

Fire burned hot in his eyes. The Animal, the one she and John Jay had come to despise, had finally come to the stage. He said, "I *promise* you, Lourdes, I'm going to get you and that ignorant boy of yours who had the nerve to call me 'animal.'" He bent her arm again and pressed the knife deeper into her ashen skin. "I swear fo'god before all this is said and done, you gon' find out why they give me the name *Tucka'*!"

He shoved her away from him, and rose from the table, heading out of the dining room. Lourdes clumsily pulled herself to her chair, cradling her arm. Before the tears could flow evenly and her face could turn a deeper shade of red Tucker John had returned, startling her with a mocking warning.

Whispering in her ear, he grabbed her by the nape of her neck and gave her a gentle but firm shake. "Mind me, gal. Fix your face and make yourself presentable. You wouldn't want folks around here thinking you had some kind of sad disease. I hear that can be a deadly thing in these here parts."

Lourdes's shoulders rose to her ears.

"One more thing, be sure to give Johnny-boy my regards." With that he was gone, whistling through his teeth a tune that matched the jazzy music Vivian had begun to play from her office.

CHAPTER 51

Lourdes didn't bother grabbing her coat or closing the door behind her. Instead, she bolted down the path tripping several times as she headed toward Balm Hill. She took the shorter path home, cutting off two miles by heading for the graveled forest path. She gave little care to the risk she was taking, running like a mad woman in the bright of day. Anyone in their backfields, which butted against Vivian's property line, could have seen her and reported her immediately to the Governing forces.

They would have thought she was infected. *Tristitiahiemsmultum—Winter sadness*. It claimed lives every year. But she couldn't stop her feet from moving. She couldn't shake the fear biting at her heels.

Twice the speed of her legs overtook her and she fell to the ground, each time tears sprung from her eyes like water being rung from a soggy dishcloth. The tiny cut beneath her chin, where the tip of Tucker John's steak knife had clipped her, was throbbing, her chest and heart constricting. *I'll gut you like the pig you are*. His raspy threat overtook her thoughts.

The Animal was going to kill her!

She needed Johnny to protect her. He'd told her that he was coming back, was closer than he'd been before, and they would make an end of the hell they'd been living apart. And she believed him, even though there was a ring of uncertainty to his voice. She'd asked him about it but he'd only told her not to worry, to keep to the plan, keep the Animal on edge and Vivian looking suspicious. That had been weeks ago.

Now she felt helpless like a bloody bird in the mouth of a hungry fox. She felt more helpless than she had when she told Johnny that Vivian was pregnant. She was trying to trust what he'd said, trying to trust they'd overcome the growing threat, but fear was poisoning her strides. She needed him to come back, now.

She didn't believe that she would last much longer if he didn't. Either the Animal would kill her or emotional sickness would consume her and she'd be euthanized. The best she could think to do was to retreat and pass a few days at Balm Hill but there was no telling how long it would be before Tucker John came for her there. She knew his history. He loved to play cat-and-mouse with his prey, loved to build their fear before he devoured them.

The very thought that he was able to even do so was Vivian's fault! She had let him loose, bargained with the fair-haired devil, and now he was out to kill.

The thought of getting help from the Cleric's Office skirted across her mind but she quickly shook it away. Everything was risky as it was, but involving the clerics would only ruin things for her and Johnny. She couldn't take the chance. She'd rather die trying to be with Johnny than die because she'd failed to hold her ground.

Her thighs burned as her feet rounded the steep hill to her mother's home. She slowed her pace and whimpered barreling into the front door. She clumsily swung it open and slammed it shut behind her, securing it with lock and key. A false sense of safety washed over her with the familiar hum of the nexus gate vibrating through the floorboards. Groaning, she rested her forehead on the old wood of the door and finally gave way to a good cry as she pounded the door with her fist.

"Stupid! *Stupid!*" She rebuked herself. Why had she baited Vivian in front of Tucker John? Why had she not left things alone? She just needed to get that one last jibe, hadn't she? She couldn't let the bitterness of uncertainty, and sheer jealousy concerning the baby go. Now she was paying for it. Her wrist was swelling by the second, her chin was wounded, and her level of fear had reached a height she had never experienced before.

Legs like jelly, she slowly dragged her feet toward the basement door, her heart aching to call out to Johnny through the static. The sole of her shoe catching momentarily upon the smooth wood floor gave her pause. She took several more steps only to feel her shoe snag again.

Stopping completely, she turned her attention to the floor. Quarter-sized dark puddles connected by a chain of tinier droplets led to the basement door, but the trail, nearly invisible, began elsewhere. Nerves sloshed violently in the well of her belly. Someone had been in her house!

Greater fear told her to run from Balm Hill the same way she'd run from Vivian's manor, but the thought of all that was at stake kept her in place. She couldn't run. Where would she go? Stilling her nerves and summoning false courage, she backpedaled away from the basement door, her eyes taking in with exacting scrutiny her surroundings, her mind doing its best to discern the familiar from the foreign. She was very conscious not to intercept the dark trail, only recognizing the deep, blackening red of its color the closer she got to the staircase leading to the second floor.

Scurrying to the kitchen she grabbed the longest knife she could find, another whimper squeezing from her throat. Johnny had promised her that he'd take care of Vivian, that he'd take care of the Animal. The thought of drawing human blood made her own curdle in her veins. This wasn't like euthanasia. This was savage.

"But this is for Johnny." No one could know about the nexus gate, and if they'd been in her mother's home, they likely knew about it already.

Licking her fevered lips, she slid from the kitchen, her body pressed against the wall and the bread knife she'd chosen held out in front of her like a sword. Sweat tickled the back of her neck and made the pearl handle of the knife falter in her grasp. She steadied it once she made it to the bottom stair leading to the second floor. Another dark droplet sat mockingly on the second stair tread, two others taunted her from the fourth and fifth. Keeping to the wall as best she could, she eased her way upstairs.

From all she could see, things looked normal, untouched, just like her mother had liked them, except for the tiny dark red droplets. Bracing herself, she thrust open the first bedroom door to her right. There were no droplets anywhere around. Nothing was out of place, not even the linens on the bed. She repeated her search with the remaining rooms and found them in the same condition; absent of the dotted trail and pristine, aside from the stale scent of disuse.

Feeling more frustrated than the fool, she shook her head. The trail was a dead end. She let her head fall back against her shoulders, her eyes rolling over the ceiling before sliding shut only to snap open again. A tiny corner of dark fabric peeked out from the seams of the attic door. A slice of cold terror ripped through her.

Stumbling away from the door the knife tumbled from her hand, clanging against the wood planks of the floor. She cried out before covering her mouth and falling back against the wall, forcing herself to speak.

"I know you're up there! I-I've contacted the Peace Officers," she lied, fumbling for the knife. She cowered just below the attic door, pinned in place by a tiny swatch of fabric, and what or who it was connected to. Several minutes passed with nothing happening, not even a sound from above. Batting her eyes, now dry from staring almost without blinking, she forced herself to move closer to the attic door.

She reached upward for the drawstring and held her knife at the ready. Tugging down the door and the fold-down stairs she let out a battle cry that was so shrill she was left seeing stars. The fabric fell free and covered her face. She screamed even louder swinging the knife wildly, tripping over the unfolded attic stairs. The knife tumbled from her hands. She flailed against her attacker, tears bursting from her eyes with the same force as the urine that poured from between her legs.

But no one was on top of her, no one fighting with her, there was only a torn tunic, now tangled about her bruising legs. Catching her bearings, sitting in the puddle she'd made, she cupped her face, and cried in her hands, the names of a thousand different emotional diseases running through her mind. Although she was relieved there was no intruder and shamed for having wet herself, there was still the question of the droplets that led her upstairs.

She angrily swiped tears from her eyes and snatched up the fabric that had caused her to fall. Her eyes narrowed and her heart beat with a wild tattoo. The tunic was Johnny's but why was it in the attic?

Staring into the dim light of the third floor she pressed the fabric to her lips. She'd need to clean herself, take several vaccinations for her emotional trauma, but not before she was certain no one was hiding above her head. With new found courage, but a greater respect for caution, she picked up the knife and slowly edged her way up the attic stairs.

A strange odor hit her nose the moment her head crested the threshold. A horrified gasp escaped her lips. She turned around and took in the sight before her. Dust motes swirled in the dim light of the desecrated room. What had once been a place of storage now looked like a treehouse shrine. Drapes and bed lines, all from her bedroom down below, were spun around the room. An old Oriental rug that Mother only used during the winter months was spread out and stained with more red droplets. Some areas were darkened by puddles. Just below the window sat a baby doll crib, stuffed with bundles that were cloaked in the shadow of the sunlight. To the other side of that was a long table, decorated with welled candles and other items.

The once pristine white of her mother's attic was painted red with hateful phrases. *'There will be no child,'* dripped from the wall adjacent to the crib, but *'I love you Johnny,'* was scrolled on the wall where the shrine had been placed. With rapid breaths and shaky legs, Lourdes drew closer to it. Several of Johnny's personal items had been positioned with hers; shirts, shoes, even his undergarments. At the center of the shrine was a wooden jewelry box Mother had given her. It always sat in her bedroom, right on her nightstand, but now it was there in the attic, on a shrine she had not made.

She back away from the display, and turned toward the crib. Foolishly she drew back the folds of the blankets only to back away from what had been bundled within it. Tiny bodies of headless piglets tumbled free from the fabric and onto the floor. Scrambling away from them she knocked against the shrine, tipping over most of what was on the table. The lid to the wooden box flew open letting out a voice recording of Johnny's laughter.

Overcome by the mental assault, the iron smell of pig's blood and dust, Lourdes released the bile that rose from her stomach and splattered on the already soiled attic rug. *I will gut you like the pig you are.* Tucker John's words sounded off in her head again, echoing over and over.

"Tucker John," he had been in her mother's house!

Lourdes' hackles rose. She hated him! She screamed from her gut this time, her muscles straining as she clawed her way up from the floor. Enraged, she tipped over the already disturbed shrine and tore down the drapes and sheets that clung to the attic ceiling and walls.

Her heart sank and her head felt like it was going to explode. He'd been in her house. The Animal had been in her house. He'd done this. Taunted her, toyed with her, poisoned her emotions. "No!" Her vision blurred as she took to the attic stairs, nearly tumbling down them in her haste.

She tore down the main stairs of the house and all but leaped down the basement stairs, rushing for the nexus gate. She tripped at the bottom step, and could hardly rise from the weight that held her down. Three piglet heads sat just in front of the bowl of Static, right where Tucker John had set them.

I will gut you like the pig you are. She heard his warning again.

"No! No, no, no!" He'd known everything! He'd seen everything long before she'd goaded him and Vivian at the dinner table. He'd just used that as an excuse to attack her. He was a ruthless beast, a filthy animal. She would be glad when she was rid of him.

Her stomach roiled violently with each tiny head she moved from her nexus table. Hands pressed against her tightening chest she plopped down in the chair in front of the static and screamed again, tugging at her short hairs. This time she called out Johnny's name.

The static gurgled back in response, something it hadn't done in weeks. "Lourdes?"

Johnny's voice made her heart skip. Relief washed over her with a wave so fierce she nearly fainted. Gripping the edge of the table with white knuckles she cried, "He's going to kill me, Johnny!" She choked past tears. "You have to come now! The Animal is going to kill me! He knows everything!"

CHAPTER 52

The man crooned the lovesick lyrics, words urging lovers to leave candles burning for their desired mates who got away from them, pleading that they say a prayer for them, asking angels to watch over them. It was melodic torture, one that seemed to twist Vivian's heartstrings into a completely different key. She didn't want to pray for John Jay and yet she found her heart doing so.

She sat, her head tilted toward the window. The gentle breeze made the trees sway in perfect rhythm with the song. If she allowed her imagination to take over, she would almost say they were dancing.

Tucker John rapped his knuckle on the doorframe. Vivian startled and looked his direction. He took that as permission to enter. "What's that you're listening to?"

Frowning, she turned off the music. "It's Tom Dorsey. I listen to him when I need to calm down."

Tucker John frowned in turn. "I noticed that much a while back. Why'd you turn it off?" He pointed at her desk.

Vivian shrugged her shoulders. "Force of habit I suppose. John Jay never liked Tom Dorsey. He actually hated his music or anything that came from the 1930's and 40's. When I saw you I just assumed…" Her words trailed off into silence.

Tucker John approached her desk. "I ain't him." He stared into her eyes for a long while before he spoke again. "I actually really like those tunes, Viv. I wouldn't mind listening a bit more."

She considered him before giving a slow acquiescing nod. It was easier to catch flies with honey, and if she wanted Tucker John to give her anything at all she was going to have to play nice. The music came on again filling the entire room. The song was *Will You still be Mine?* Tucker John's face eased into a smile. He offered Vivian his hand.

Vivian shrank away from his hand as if it were a snake waiting to bite her. She was so overwhelmed with misplaced emotions. She hardly knew where her head was. What she did know was that it was nowhere near dancing, least of all with Tucker John. She didn't want him to touch her at all. Shaking her head, she pressed deeper into her chair as if to escape. "No, I'm not dancing with you." She said the words with finality and prayed he'd heed them.

The seriousness in Viv's eyes could have made any flame turn tail and freeze up into ice, but Tucker John brushed right passed it. He wanted to dance. Things were playing right into his hand which was a cause for celebration. He took hold of her hand and tugged gently against her, plying her from her leather chair and onto her feet.

"Tucker John, I said I don't want to dance!" She was scowling now and her tone was sharp. The tiniest tremble radiated from her fingers against his palm.

Although his heart went tender over her fear of him, he didn't ease his grip. "But I do. I know you're fired up about what happened at dinner."

Viv seemed to deflate recalling the hateful moment. He took that as his chance to reel her into his embrace. Before she could protest, he was dancing with her, not with any real form, just swaying with the tune. He smiled into her frown and moved her beyond her stiffness. He almost blushed realizing he was holding her closer than the propriety of his era would have allowed. Almost.

"Lourdes is gone again," he said.

Viv looked away from him, her jaw set. "Good."

"It is indeed. We had somewhat of an exchange after you excused yourself. It played quite well in our favor." He couldn't help but smile.

Vivian turned her eyes back to his but quickly turned away again. It was a prick to her, hearing him use 'our' as if they were a team warring against another—her husband and his mistress. Had his solid arm not been so locked behind her back she would have jerked out of his grasp.

"I won't lie to you. I shook her up a bit." He said. The rumble of his low-spoken words reverberated in her chest. They were so close, too close.

She tried to remain stoic although her rapid pulse betrayed her. She pressed her eyes closed and steadied her breath. He was her enemy, the wolf that hunted her, the fire that had burned her world to cinders, and yet, she somehow felt a strange need to be close, not necessarily to him, but to someone. The corners of her mouth dipped down with the hateful revelation.

Tucker John misread the meaning of her frown. "Viv, I know how you feel about that, menfolk being rough with the weaker sex. You never said so, but I can tell." She opened her eyes and he gazed into them, his expression gentle, too gentle for her to manage. She turned her head away.

Tucker John continued. "Point is, Lourdes went running off to Balm Hill. I'm certain she'll call out to Johnny-boy, tell him to come on home and quick. If she was battling any doubts on doing so from here to there, the message I left her will aid in her decision making." He twirled her and then brought her back to him. His grip wasn't as firm but they were still just as close.

Vivian chewed her bottom lip. Part of her wanted to hear about how he'd shaken Lourdes up, but he was right about her constitution concerning such acts. She cringed at the thought of a man abusing a woman, even a deadly black widow like Lourdes. For the first time, she thought euthanasia was a reasonable option.

"What did you do?" She finally asked.

"I told you, a bit of remodeling. Don't ask though."

She let out a long breath, Tucker John twirled her again. "And since I'm certain she'll call John Jay and he'll come running sooner rather than later, I'm going to need my rifle and satchel back from you. I know you kept it with all the questions you was asking about it when this all started a little while ago."

Trouble flashed across her face but she quickly concealed it. The rigidity that took over her body again gave her away. She tried to concentrate on the sounds of the song and allow Tucker John's moving of her to envelope her mind completely rather than acknowledge what he had just said. But she had wondered about the rifle, the relic that was created some sixty years after his death, yet was in his possession when he came through from 1837.

She asked, "Tucker John, where exactly did you get that rifle?" She chanced a look into his eyes as if that would expose any lie he might throw her way.

He didn't break his gaze. "I won it in a card game. Technically, the game was fixed. I should'a lost but that thing was so pretty I just went on and took it. Why?"

She swallowed and shook her head. "No reason. Don't worry about it."

She felt his hand on her waist grow tighter. "What ain't you telling?"

She considered her answer before finally saying, "We'll throw all our cards on the table when this is over. You'll tell me about the letter you got from the Cleric's Office and I'll tell you what has me bothered about your rifle." She swallowed down the dry knot that had suddenly tangled her throat.

Tucker John tipped his head to the side and stared at her with hooded lids. "Fair enough." The look on his face gave little away but she was almost completely certain, that if he had more time, he would go and research the rifle himself.

They danced in silence for the duration of the song. When it was finally over and Tucker John ceased to sway was when she spoke again. She peered up at him, still in his arms, as if they had only paused and were waiting for the next selection to begin. "I know you're set in your plans against John Jay and Lourdes, and that you need me to trust you, leave things to your will. But I can't." She waited for him to say something, but he didn't. He only stared down at her. "I don't expect you to understand my position, not in the least. Truth is, I don't understand it, not completely." She pressed her eyes closed as if that would clear away her confliction.

And the moment was going so well. Tucker John gave an exhausted sigh. "What are you saying? Go on and spit it out."

Viv bit deep into her bottom lip. Its color was a deep shade of red when she finally released it. Tucker John's belly did a wild flop. It had been a long time since he had kissed a woman, held her so close that her warmth and scent clung to him. His stomach flopped again when he realized how distracted just the shade of Viv's bottom lip had made him. Their lives were in jeopardy and he was thinking about stealing a kiss. He took a half step away from her but still kept her in his grasp.

"John Jay is sick—"

"That's a bit of an understatement!" Lightning fast, his brow darkened, the distraction gone.

Viv's face contorted as if wounded. She was. "He needs help. He needs treatment, Tucker John. I," she stumbled over her words. "I know none of this is making sense, but I'm just trying to figure out how we can do this without having to kill him. How we can get you in a safe place where you can live and, and, so can he, without anybody knowing about any of this,"

Tucker John shook his head, the muscles in his jaw contracting and releasing.

She whispered, "He needs treatment."

"Viv don't be foolish! You can't treat what he's got. Bottom line is when he comes, and that boy is coming, we need to be prepared. I need my gun for that. After what he's done, that's the best treatment I can give him! That's the only treatment he deserves."

Viv shook her head. "I can't give you the gun,"

Sudden irritation helped him to release her. "Are you being serious right now? After what you heard from his own mouth? After all the plotting and trickery, you can stand here and just say 'he needs help,' and you can't give me my gun?"

Viv gripped his shoulders and kept him facing her. "I know I agreed to your plans, but you've changed them. I need to change them now. This is my life, too. This isn't easy for me! He may be able to sit around and plan my death, but I'm not wired like that. I don't want to be!"

He tried to increase the distance between them. Viv took a desperate hold of his forearm. "I don't know what your exact plan is, besides killing him, and taking his place in the timeline, but I, I-I can't agree to that. I shouldn't have. Giving you that gun to shoot him...I might as well keep it with me and put a bullet in him myself. God knows I didn't want any of this to happen, and I'm trying to find a way to make things right for everyone involved."

Tucker John rotated his head around his shoulders, kneading away the growing tension. "Get to your point, Viv."

She squeezed his arm. "I don't want you to kill him, Tucker John."

Stifling his anger, he slowly pulled his arm from the choke hold she had put on it and raked his fingers through his hair. "That's. Madness."

"More plotting and killing isn't going to fix this situation!"

"You just don't want to see what's in front of you, Viv—"

"I took oaths when I took this job. I made pledges to the people of the future. I made promises to myself to be a certain kind of person—" Her voice rose.

"That's all well and good but that boy and his mistress is fixing to kill you and me! I am thirty-five years old. I plan on seeing my thirty-sixth birthd—"

"I know I sound ridiculous!"

"You're darn right!"

"I don't want to die either!"

"I can't tell,"

"I know I agreed to it, but planning to kill him or Lourdes isn't a decision easily made,"

"It is when it's you or them that's gotta' die!"

"He's my *husband*!" She finally shouted. Tucker John didn't offer a rebuttal. Viv managed to calm herself but she couldn't hold back the tears. "He's my husband. We've been married for ten years. That is a *long* time. He is the only man I've ever loved. And I take responsibility for not seeing his illness before. That's my fault. For that reason, it's a bit hard for me to decide in the span of a few weeks to kill him and actually commit to it."

Tucker John glowered. "Are you telling me you still love that dog and his flea?" Her silent affirmation riled him. "Viv!"

"Love isn't a faucet that you can just turn on and off! If it's that easy for a person to just stop loving another, then they never loved them in the first place. I can't speak for John Jay, but I can speak for myself, and yes, I loved him, I still love him. I came here because I loved him and I want, I wanted to fix us."

The defeat in her voice, the simple seed of revelation she'd given him made his jaw clench even tighter.

"But I *hate* him just as much. And all of this is tearing me apart," Her chin trembled. She closed her eyes and took several deep breaths.

Tucker John stared at the ground considering her words. He was careful with his response. "Viv, no woman should ever have to make the decision you're making, but the reality is many do and have, not because they've turned ugly in heart or abandoned their principles." He was thinking of his mama. "Sometimes, it's just a choice they have to make, not for themselves but for others."

She eyes were troubled, her expression wrestling with a scowl. "You want me to kill my husband for you? Is that what you are asking me to do, step aside so you can kill him, and then stay silent while you take his place?"

Tucker John shook his head and pointed at her belly. "I'm telling you to make the right decision for that child you're carrying."

Viv groaned and moved around her desk dropping her weight in the desk chair. She looked as if she was going to be sick. "That's your reality, Viv. It's John Jay or that baby. It's you or John Jay. And I'm going to just be frank with you, I don't give a mind what your opinion is about Lourdes. That girl has got to go and I don't need my gun for that." He blew out a deep breath. "I will, however, offer you this much in exchange."

"Exchange? Exchange what? For what? You have everything. What else could I possibly give you?" Her tearful eyes bored deep into his.

"I want you to look the other way, and let me go and make a new life of my own, without your interference, once this is done."

She jerked as if stung even though she'd suggested the same thing.

"I'm accepting your offer. I'll do my best to apprehend your sick Johnny, even though I warn you that trying to do so is like trudging blindfolded through gator-infested waters. It plain ain't wise. Hell, doing it with your eyes opened is foolish. But I'll try, although I can promise you nothing in the process. It's his life for mine. Contrary to your accounting of things, I'm not trying to bully you or back you into a corner, but what you're asking is costly for all three of us." He nodded towards her belly again.

"I'll consider your silence to mean we have reached an agreement." The glow of victory had dimmed since coming to talk to Viv.

Viv remained silent at first. It was only when he turned and said goodnight that she called out to him.

"Tucker John?" The look in her eyes was beyond pitiful. "Thank you."

Holding her gaze he shook his head slowly. "Don't thank me yet, Viv. Save that till after the smokes cleared." He exited

the room and closed the door behind him. Viv turned back on
Tom Dorsey.

CHAPTER 53

John Jay's muscles ached from the force that he excreted against the static. Hearing Lourdes cry, the sound of her fear, tasting it as if it had coated his tongue, had given him a surge of purpose, one he'd nearly lost each time he felt his body tear in two. The tearing hadn't happened in a long while, the false paths through the static taunting him with twisted realities. Now he was back on track.

Lourdes' cries had led him back to the true path on the timeline like a beacon piercing through the darkness. Even still, even though he was indeed in 4037, not some strange apparition of that time or the people therein, he still struggled to break through completely. Threads of the static seemed to split at the oddest moments, causing him to drop through, into the timeline, the same way he had when he'd hanged the slave-woman, or when he'd given his silent goodbyes to his family in 6037. He was there but he was hollow, mostly invisible to the naked eye.

Now, that gift, slipping through the treads of the static, had become an enraging nuisance. It was as if the spirit of time had given him all he'd ever wanted but now mocked him by holding it just out of his grasp.

Clenching his teeth, he ran headlong against the flow of the static only to find himself dropping back onto the timeline as nothing more than a mirage. Still, he kept running, his direction set on the nexus gate at Balm Hill. He'd told Lourdes to be there, that he was coming. He laughed and pumped his legs harder as another opening in the threads of the timeline sighed open. With undeniable purpose, John Jay leaped through it back into the static, closer to Balm Hill and reality, closer to the end of the Animal.

***

Magnus removed his overcoat and dabbed the perspiration from his brow. It was definitely Fall, but an aggressive heatwave had come upon them with stifling humidity. Now there was a storm brewing. Of course, on the worst day recorded in the notes that he was sent to verify, did it rain terribly. It was as if the sky was mourning what was getting ready to take place in Vivian Leona's home.

He shook his head, pitying her over himself. Heavy rain dripped into his eyes and slid down his back quickly bringing him back to focusing on his own discomfort. "First hot, now wet!" At least tomorrow would have blue skies. He nestled in deep at the base of a tree just outside Vivian's perimeter fence and listened in via the static that had been born from her nexus gate.

***

Tucker John's eyes snapped closed from the sudden rain and the almost blinding flash of lightning. The thunder overhead crashed violently and blue light flashed again blinding him just before he saw the demon-black figure of a man, dashing for the front door of Balm Hill.

It had appeared out of nowhere and seemed to disappear into nothing, just like other times he'd seen it. Even then, he wasn't sure that he'd seen it, but he'd heard what he'd thought was the muffled sound of Lourdes screaming, but the sound had been drowned out by the crashing drum of thunder.

Forcing his eyes to focus through the rain, grateful for the recent heatwave that allowed him to hunt true to his form, he drew closer to Balm Hill, slowly placing one bare foot ahead of the other, focusing his hearing beyond the crashes and cries of nature.

He didn't hear anything else, but an uneasy feeling had settled on him. His instincts told him what his ears couldn't hear but had indeed heard already. His mama would've crossed herself and told him it was a devil that had run before his eyes, that the cry was from it, running from its own hellfire and torment. Tucker John wouldn't argue with that, he'd only give the imp he'd seen a name, John Jay.

He'd seen his figure running several times before that night, had hunted it nearly a week ago. He'd heard his voice calling out then too, but Lourdes hollering just seconds after he'd seen the shadowed form run by and into the door of Balm Hill confirmed it was indeed John Jay. He couldn't explain how John Jay was doing it any more than he could explain the static that he'd hidden in.

Before Tucker John had thought he was losing his mind, seeing the man's figure running in and out of his sight, but his instincts told him better, same as they'd told him to camp out in the darkness outside of Balm Hill and wait for the fiend to show himself once again. Lourdes hadn't come back to the manor that evening, just as he'd expected she wouldn't, not after their encounter at the dining table, and especially not after finding the shrine he'd built for her. The girl was too dumb and too darn nosey not to follow the little, dotted trail he'd left for her.

The traps had been set, now all that was left was for him to go and catch his prizes.

Magnus Sanderson had warned him about the ways of that time, their ability to track a murderer. That fact raised several concerns in the face of what he'd been planning to do, but there was nothing else to be done. He and Viv would have to deal with the mess of suspicion if and when its stink began to rise. If he'd played his hand just right, there would be no need for anyone to question anything.

He eased closer to the house in the direction of the window he'd rigged for his silent entries. He pulled himself inside and slid down to the floor, careful not to make a sound. The familiar hum of the homemade nexus gate vibrated through the pads of his feet as he took careful steps away from the window, consciously keeping to the indigo shadows. He drew one of the several knives he'd taken from Viv's kitchen and held it at the ready. If the demon Lourdes had sold her soul to came across his line of sight, he'd impale him with one flick of his wrist just as sure as his name was 'Tucker' John Josephus Spruce. Lourdes, he'd just have to catch. The rope was where she'd meet her end.

More lightning flashed blue through the windows causing dark shadows to dance upon the white walls. Tucker John held his footing. He calmed himself sending out the feelers of his sixth sense. No one was nearby, but he did hear Lourdes and an all too familiar voice whispering beneath his feet.

His pulse sped just as it did whenever his prey was just within reach. Like a wolf on the prowl, he crept toward the cellar door. The lust for John Jay's blood was so strong that he could almost taste it.

"I won't fit in there with you, Johnny! I don't want to go," Lourdes' voice rang with better clarity. "Johnny, please don't make me,"

"Lourdes—"

"And you're hurt. You're bleeding," Lourdes whimpered.

"Don't worry about that now! I can't leave you here. The Animal could be out there, now. If I left you here and he still got to you...getting rid of Vivian wouldn't even matter. Please, Lourdes. Get in the gate with me. This'll be over soon. I promise."

"But the static—"

"Won't hurt you since you aren't moving it. We're just going to the manor, I'll deal with Vivian and then—"

Tucker John couldn't hear anymore. He didn't know if it was because of the high volume thrum of the nexus gate kicking into gear or the blood hammering in his ears. They were going to sweep through time and in a matter of seconds be where it would take him at least twenty minutes running in the rain!

His heart skipped a beat and his jaw clenched. He burst through the cellar door, praying the sound of the door crashing against the wall and his feet pounding on the floor as he jumped down several stairs would gain him the element of surprise.

It hadn't. He was too late!

Snarling, he launched the first of three knives at the glass coffin connected to the nexus gate. John Jay's crazed eyes locked on his as the glass of the gate cracked and shook, right before he and Lourdes disappeared through time.

CHAPTER 54

The crash of lightning startled Vivian awake. How she managed to sleep in the first place was beyond her. Maybe the weight of stress had held her down and drawn her eyelids closed. Nevertheless, she was awake now. Thirst made her rise up from her pillows and reach for her nightstand.

She sighed remembering that she'd set the water pitcher and glass on the dresser. She moved to place her foot on the ground when she heard a floorboard creak. She froze. Swallowing down the knot that tangled her throat she quietly set her feet down. More flashes of lightning crashed and wind beat against the house making her door creak. Her head snapped toward it. It was closed just as she'd left it, and securely locked.

She was being paranoid, but with good reason. She finally rose and headed to her dresser, comforting herself with the thought of security. Tucker John would've warned her if something was wrong. He'd made it very clear earlier that evening that she was his ticket to freedom. It would do him no good to let anything happen to her.

She should have felt safe with his admission. Instead, she felt like the prize pig on a pig hunt. Everyone was out to catch her. Her value was of little more than what she would produce once she was had.

Wood creaked and moaned again just as she reached for the water pitcher. Her hand stopped mid-air. She turned toward her door again. *Still closed.* She let out a stuttered breath and closed her eyes, opening them just as lightning struck. The flash illuminated the room enough to cast her reflection in the mirror before her and the dark figure that stood in the frame of her open door!

She turned back in the direction of the door that again had been closed. What was she going to do? Tucker John's rifle was stashed under the floorboard in front of her bed. She wouldn't get to it in time. But she could scream for him and pray he reached her before it was too late. She filled her lungs with a deep breath and—

Cold, calloused fingers clamped against her mouth. A clammy forearm wrapped around her waist, pressing her back against a solid chest. Vivian gave a sharp squeal before her voice was completely cut off.

"Quiet, Viv! It's me! Tucker," Tucker John hissed but he didn't move his hand from her mouth nor loosen his hold on her. "Don't make a sound," one by one he removed his fingers from over her mouth. "John Jay's here. I just saw him—"

"What?" Her voice was shrill.

Tucker John covered her mouth again even as she struggled. He'd nearly collapsed when he saw her standing at her nightstand, breathing, untouched. He'd thought for sure he'd been too late, that Lourdes and John Jay had already gotten to her. God had answered his prayers. Now he just needed to get her secured.

"I said, quiet, Viv!" He pulled her closer to his chest. Her hands took a firm hold around his wrists. He still had no idea where John Jay was, or why he hadn't taken Viv already. If his senses didn't assure him that no one else was around he would have thought for certain that he'd walked into a trap.

He whispered in her ear. "Listen carefully, plans changed again. John Jay and Lourdes are somewhere close by. I meant to deal with them at Balm Hill, but they got in their nexus gate and headed here before I could," he pulled his hand away from her mouth and gripped her fingers, pulling her toward the bedroom door.

He tilted his head and listened, closing his eyes, letting himself feel the atmosphere. Still, there was no one but him and

Viv. He quietly opened the door, drawing Viv in the direction of Lourdes' bedroom. She grabbed his arm again.

"How'd you get in my room? Where are you taking me?"

"I picked the lock! What'd you expect me to do, knock? Now I'm hiding you," he kept dragging her along.

"Wha-where?"

He held up a finger and shushed her before easing into Lourdes's bedroom. He gave a quick once over before pulling Viv inside.

"Why are we in Lourdes' room?"

"Cause they gone know you're hiding. Folks generally hide where they feel safe. You hate Lourdes. This is the last place they'll check."

Viv rubbed her arms and shivered. "I don't want to hide. This is my house. I want to help. Maybe I can reason with him—"

"Don't be foolish! You ain't see 'em, Viv. Ain't no reasoning with him."

"But you said you wouldn't kill him, you said you would try," her voice clogged with tears. She was panicking.

He growled, giving her a quick shake. "I aim to keep my word but I can't do that if your safety is a distraction. The best help you are to me is staying out of the way and staying alive."

Viv stared at him, her eyes searching his face in the dark. "I don't want to hide in here!"

"See your way of thinking? You don't wanna be here and they suspect as much. I promise you they on the same page as you. They won't look for you here." He dug into Lourdes' closet, sliding the chest of drawers she had tucked inside of it over to the center, leaving enough room for Viv to shimmy inside the small alcove he'd made and squat in the corner, hidden from sight. Safe...he hoped. He prayed.

"What about your room?" She grabbed his arm, "There are more places there to hide and—"

Viv's head snapped back toward the door. Tucker John's tensed. The low thrum of the nexus gate vibrated through the house. He tore himself free of Viv's grasp only to grab hold of her arm instead, propelling her into the closet. Viv's mouth flew open, her eyes so wide that, even in the dark, he could see the fear in them. He took her face in his hands, drawing her so close that he could feel his breaths bouncing off her skin as he stared hard into her eyes.

"Do not move from this place, do you understand me?" Viv hesitated but finally nodded. "You stay here until I fetch you. I mean it, Viv. I need you to mind me on this."

"But what if,"

Tucker John shoved her back and slid the dresser over as if it was nothing. "Ain't no 'what-if.' Stay put! Wait till I fetch you!" He drew out a knife and grabbed the closet door, closing it in her face.

Fire burned in his chest. He should have demanded his rifle. That would have made things go by much quicker, but now he was out of time. He could already feel the enemy's presence moving through the house.

***

The pain of stepping out of the static only to step back into it was numbed over by the realization that he had lost precious time. That infuriated John Jay. The Animal was to blame. The cracks he'd made in the glass of the nexus gate with each knife he'd thrown had distorted the flow of time. What should have taken a matter of seconds at best had in fact taken several long minutes, almost thirty to be exact, each one a reminder of what he was truly up against.

Finally, he'd locked eyes with the Animal, seen the hell in them. The man deserved the moniker he'd been given by his own father and even the slaves and bounties he'd hunted. Tonight he'd die true to that name.

"Johnny?" Lourdes' voice echoed through the static.

He silenced her with a wave of his hand. The effect of seeing her alongside him in the static was bizarre. Violent ripples of vibration waved all around her like a halo. They were on him too. They were the treads of true time trying to latch onto them, trying to pull them back unto the timeline.

Not yet. The static was the best place to hide Lourdes while he hunted down Tucker John. As much as he hated the pain the static had caused him, he wouldn't risk coming at his imposter face to face without it. No, he'd been raised with civility while brutality was the only language the Animal spoke. Hiding in plain sight was the only thing he could use to level their battlefield.

Lourdes said his name again. He smiled at her. Tears pooled her eyes and spilled over her cheeks. It broke his heart.

"I need you to stay in the static, babe,"

Lourdes' lips fell open but she quickly clamped them shut, her eyes appraising him with what he could only guess was fear. Manipulating the static had wounded him, rubbed him raw. He had no idea how badly he'd been assaulted by it. Even now, as he looked at his hands, all he saw were blurred nubs of red. Yes, all of his limbs were still firmly intact, but they burned and ached like vinegar in open wounds.

He swallowed away the anxiety that made his bones shake. He'd deal with the damage he'd endured when this night was over. Again he met Lourdes' gaze. "I promise that you won't be in this long enough for it to harm you, but it's the only way that he can't see you, not easily at least."

Lourdes nodded and touched his face.

"As soon as I've gotten rid of him you can come out."

"And Vivian?"

He let out a long breath through flared nostrils. *This was all her fault.* "We'll get her too," he kissed her. "And then, then it's just me and you, just like it was always meant to be."

Lourdes kissed him again, this time she smiled right before activating the perimeter fence.

***

Tucker John could feel him in the room, smell the iron scent of his blood and the strange nodes of static electricity pulsing from him with every breath he took, but he couldn't see him and it had nothing to do with the darkness. John Jay was there in the manor same as he'd been present all the other times Tucker John had thought he'd seen him, but he was somehow not there at the same time, leaving himself visible only through periphery.

Tucker John stayed in the shadows blanketed in the darkness. His heartbeat slow and steady as he waited, feeling John Jay with all his senses except his sight. He heard the sound of his footfalls trying with failed stealth to creep through the front of the house. They'd been stalking each other with a wild dance for the better part of twenty minutes. Unlike John Jay, Tucker John was learning his prey. He had to keep him in his periphery if he was to see him. He had to stay in the dark if he was to remain unseen himself.

He'd thought to make his way to the power hub of the home, dismantle the electricity just until he'd finished his kill or capture, but his path was cut off by the presence of another. He figured it was Lourdes. He could have easily been rid of her but he had to be careful. He couldn't just snap her neck and leave her lying in the static. Viv would need Lourdes' body for when the clerics were finally involved. How exactly she'd explain John Jay was another matter altogether.

He wanted to keep his word to her, try and capture her insane husband without killing him, but he was already holding that promise with a loose hand. Instinct told him that it wasn't an option. The bloodlust he'd seen in his eyes back at Balm Hill told him that. Tucker John had seen that look more times than he could count and knew better than to fight his bounties on it. John

Jay was willing to die for what he wanted. Tucker John would oblige him.

He slowed his breathing, feeling the man just on the other side of the dining room wall. If he'd had his gun he would have put a shot straight through his skull, filled it up with plaster and lead. Instead, he positioned the knife in his hand readying it to land the first kill blow to John Jay's side.

Measuring the sound of John Jay's falls, he matched his pace and moved as if in a tandem toward the nearest opening of the dining room. They'd crest the opening of the room at the same time and then he'd plunge the sharp steel into the soft tissue of his belly right before driving it into his chest. Then he'd go after Lourdes.

Five feet.

His hearing heightened, funneling with accuracy until John Jay's breathing through the wall crescendoed over the howling wind and rain that beat against the house.

Four feet.

His vision focused outward, not steadying on any particular object but seeing everything in one frame.

Three feet.

The smoothness of the knife's hilt melded with the curve of his palm making it one with him.

Two feet.

Another presence trespassed upon the threads of their battleground! A curse shouted in his mind. *Lourdes.* He caught only a glimpse of her through his periphery before she rushed forward from the other entrance of the dining room.

John Jay's shoulder crested the opening of the dining room right where Tucker John stood waiting.

"Johnny!" Lourdes screamed just as Tucker John drove the knife toward John Jay's middle. The blade met with flesh and drew out a howling cry that matched the wind as whatever John Jay held in his hands as a weapon fell to the ground with an erratic clatter and a flash of light against the floor. John Jay fell away from the entrance of the room, the sound of his scrambling almost lost in Lourdes' cries. Lourdes screamed again, this time turning on the lights to the dining room, exposing Tucker John. He should have turned off the power!

Growling, he flicked one knife from his wrist and cut through the cords of the dining room chandelier. The large light snapped back to black as orange sparks of electricity sputtered like blood from its severed cords just before it crashed to the dining room table with a spray of splintered wood and broken crystal.

Lourdes tumbled in and out of Tucker John's sight right before the sudden flash of the chandelier's light blinded him.

"Run, Lourdes! Get away from him. Aghh," John Jay hollered as he scrambled further away from Tucker John and up the stairs. Tucker John pulled out another blade and drew back into the shadows but carefully followed John Jay up the stairs at a slower pace than he'd have liked. He'd cut the man deep, not sure where exactly, but John Jay was bleeding like the pig he was. Only the blood that he spilled was just as lost outside of Tucker John's periphery as the man himself. Slipping up the stairs, tripped by splashes of blood had proven that.

"Stay away, Lourdes!" John Jay cried out.

"But, Johnny—" Lourdes' voice cried back from down the stairs.

"I said stay back!"

Tucker John felt Lourdes at his back, her breathing giving away her position. She was a flight down, still standing in the foyer, the stink of her fear radiating clear up to his nostrils. He tilted his head in the darkness, his eyes had already adjusted to the absence of light once again. With one hand, John Jay held the flesh just at his hip where the knife had cut through. With the other, he held a weapon of his own—a long thin object that, in the shade of the dark and the blur of periphery, appeared to be a rapier. If it weren't for the dull currents of light undulating around it, Tucker John would have thought it to be so.

John Jay stared down at him, a black shadow against the smoky grey of the stormy night, unmoving as if he thought that was enough to keep him hidden from Tucker John's sight as if he was waiting for Tucker John to walk blindly into the line of danger he'd set for him.

Keeping his vision so that the devil remained in the sideline of his sight, Tucker John obliged him, following up the flight of stairs as if he had no idea where his prey stood.

Lourdes had disappeared.

CHAPTER 55

Without the aid of a nexus gate, the threads of time splintered, breaking open at his command. Clarence stepped through and waited in the shadows of Tucker John's room. Soon he and John Jay would arrive, bringing their fight there.

There was to be very little interface on Clarence's end. He wasn't even to be seen. All that was left for him to do at this juncture, was to retrieve the rapier John Jay had snatched from the perverted timeline, copy its structure, send its data to Mr. Lemon's assistant, and then return it to the static for its complete disposal and any evidence hinting to its timeline.

He'd already memorized the steps of the brawl that was about to unfold in just a few short moments. Disarming John Jay would be relatively simple. Doing so, while keeping his presence unknown to Tucker John, was the difficult part. John Jay was bound to be oblivious to him. Furthermore, he wouldn't even be able to see Clarence.

There were layers to static, those less volatile than the one that John Jay had discovered. But even without sight, Tucker John would feel him there. That distraction could pose a slight problem, one that could potentially cause the man's death.

He had to be careful. Too much was at stake.

***

"Show yourself, boy. I know you're here, hiding like the coward you are." Tucker John eased up several more steps.

With each step he took, John Jay drew back. Warm blood seeped from the wound at his side and through the cracks of his raw fingers. The fact that he was still standing was a good sign.

The Animal had struck him, drawn first blood, but he had not made a death blow as he'd intended. At least he had hoped he hadn't. There was only so much blood he could lose. The fact that he hadn't swooned from dizziness, or felt himself grow weak, only bolstered his courage. Fate was on his side. He'd come too far to die and not take hold of his prize.

With his free hand, he tightened his hold upon the baton he'd taken from the static. The other Lourdes had stabbed Vivian in the chest with it. She hadn't broken her skin but had somehow sent enough voltage through her to stop her heart. Vivian wilted to the ground instantly and didn't get up. The look in her open eyes as they stared outward reflected nothing but death.

John Jay had acted on impulse, pulling the baton from Lourdes' grasp but then he fell through the opening of time again and was back in the static. The shocked Lourdes and the lifeless body of the short-haired Vivian were gone but the baton remained intact. It was just as firm and real as his desire to kill the filthy man that Vivian had pulled through time and now stalked him up the stairs.

His back against Tucker John's door, he slowly lifted the baton aiming it at his bare chest.

***

Johnny had told her to stay back, told her to get as far away from the Animal as she could, and she had. She'd retreated back to the dining room where she fought to catch her breath. It was a fruitless attempt. Even in the dark, she could see the destruction Tucker John caused with just one flick of his wrist. Vivian's dining table bore the wounds of the shattered chandelier. The floor was littered with broken shards of crystal.

All with one blow...

Her throat tightened with a greater stroke of fear. She couldn't leave Johnny alone with him, even if he was in the static. She knew better than he did what kind of a monster he was up against. Johnny wouldn't stand a chance on his own, especially not bleeding the way he was! And what about Vivian? What if they teamed up against him? Lourdes had to help him.

Squatting downward she stifled a scream as her fingers met with the biting edge of broken crystal. Grimacing, she fished through the debris until she found the knife that Tucker John had thrown. They'd come too far for her to wait in the darkness, cowering in the corner until Tucker John murdered Johnny and then came for her. No. They would deal with the Animal together. She'd kill him herself if she had to, and Vivian too.

Swallowing the bile and the dizziness that assaulted her at the thought of drawing their blood, she white-knuckled the knife in her hand and forced herself back up the stairs just as she heard John Jay cry out.

***

The rapier in John Jay's hand made an upward arc against the darkness just as Tucker John lunged at him. The sweep of his knife caught nothing but air before plunging deep into the wood of the door frame to his room. John Jay fell backward the moment he touched the door tumbling against the stairs that led to Tucker John's room and nearly out of Tucker John's sight. Catching the dull glint of light of the rapier, Tucker John leaped upon him, although he could no longer see him, leaving his knife impaled in the wood.

He swung wildly with his fist, making contact with John Jay's ribs and even his bleeding side. John Jay howled from the pain but quickly lost his sound to the connecting blow of Tucker Johns knuckles against the breadth of his nose. Again Tucker John struck him, feeling the cartilage of John Jay's nose crumble on impact, but not before the rapier grazed the side of his head.

A jolt of electricity knocked him to the side wall, causing him to lose his grip and advantage. He heard the man scurrying up the flight of stairs and further out of his reach, heard him tumble to the ground as if caught in a struggle with someone else just above his head.

Viv!

Tucker John cursed and pushed himself back up from the ground, his vision crossing from the aftershock of the electric blow to his skull. He clawed his way up the final flight of stairs, his head twisting to the side as he fought to shake off the dizziness. He'd just made it to the top of the stairs when fire sliced down the flesh of his back. He swung his arm back like a club, felt his forearm connect with the side of Lourdes' head just before he heard her tumble down the stairs and land with a satisfying thud just below.

"No!" John Jay roared. The impact of his body, barreling into Tucker John's, sent them hurtling toward the window near his bed.

Glass shattered at their impact. Wind and rain whipped at Tucker John's face just as he felt himself free falling outdoors, his desperate hands gaining purchase on the bedlinen rope tucked in the sill, drawing it outside with him just as he fell toward the ground.

CHAPTER 56

Lourdes forced herself away from the stairs the moment she heard the window above breaking and Johnny roaring. The shrill sound of his cry only convinced her of the worst. The Animal had gotten him. For all she knew, Johnny was lying in a bloody heap just below Vivian's window. Gulping on tears she forced herself upward and away from Tucker John's door.

Retreat was the only thing she could think to do. Her stunt with the knife was what had probably gotten Johnny killed. The cut she'd carved into Tucker John's back had only angered him. She limped down the hallway, pain eating at her heart the same way it was devouring her hip joint. She'd fallen hard down the single flight of stairs, catching most of the impact of her tumble against her left side even though both sides of her head were throbbing from Tucker John's forearm and the wall.

In her retreat, she'd managed to gain the knife again. She'd need it the moment Tucker John came for her. This time she'd thrust into his black heart! She'd kill him, but she'd kill Vivian first if she could.

She only had a few moments before Tucker John came for her. She'd use the guise of the static to get Vivian. "He's dead because of you!" She hissed under her breath, the image of Vivian's face flashing across her mind. The door to Vivian's room was slightly ajar. Flashes of lightning made shadows creep through the crack and dance against the floorboards. Wincing, she eased it open. It wasn't likely that Vivian was out in the open. At best she was hiding somewhere within. She'd definitely heard the screaming, heard the brawl and the window shattering above her head.

Knife in the air, she hobbled toward Vivian's bed, driving it down several times into the heap of fabric. She was finished overestimating Vivian's intelligence. The woman had welcomed Tucker John to her table. She'd invited him to kill her Johnny. If she was foolish enough to do that, then it stood to reason she would trust bedlinens to protect her.

The swipe of taut fabric brushing against the window drew her attention from the bed. Catching her breath, giving the room a quick glance, she drew near the water-slick window. Her heart leaped into her throat at the way the rope-like material kicked back and forth like a pendulum.

Noose. It's like a noose. The realization nearly knocked her to the ground. She dropped the knife in her hand and opened the window, pushing the screen free and down to the grass below. "Oh Johnny, I'm sorry," she'd just managed to squeeze the words out when her vision cleared enough for the figure below to come into clearer view.

Tucker John dangled mid-air nearly two stories up from the ground, the sodden folds of the sheet-rope wrapped around his arms. Blood dripped down his back like a wash of paint and fell from him with the rain. The flashes of lightning ahead highlighted his paling skin a deathly shade of blue.

His grey eyes flashed with the lightning the moment he looked up, almost as if he'd seen her. A painful grimace creased his face and made the already tight cords of his muscles contract even more. Was he afraid?

Staring down at him, a strange euphoria washed over her. *Jucondo Perversa; illness of perverted delight.* Murder was no man's business. Delighting in it was disgustingly archaic, but she was going to delight in finally killing him.

"I hate you!" She screamed down at him before retrieving the knife she had dropped from her hands, the thought of killing Vivian all but gone from her mind. She grabbed the wet linens with one hand and with the other began to saw through the strained threads.

Tucker John glanced over his shoulder and felt the torn flesh at his back protest. The wind whipped around him making him sway mid-air before smacking his body mercilessly against the side of the house again. He felt his hold slip by a fraction but quickly tightened his grip on the linen rope. The ground was too far away. He couldn't jump, not from that high, and survive. He was still disoriented from the shock of electricity that had rattled his brain. The first impact he felt when he fell through the window and collided with the side of the house, had him dangling from the tangled rope like a fish on a line. Catching hold of the linen rope was just by the grace of God. The thing had tangled around him before he had gotten a grip on it and had all but wrenched his arm out of socket. Still, he managed to hold on.

But now he purposefully loosened his grip. Balancing his feet against the wall, clawing at the stucco with his bare toes, he began to clumsily slide down to the ground, quickening his descent before Lourdes had her way and sent him to his death. He'd seen her through his periphery. With each foot down, the harpy took another bite out of his rope.

He had closed most of the distance between himself and the ground but he still had a healthy distance to go before he could attempt a safe leap. He felt the linen begin to give way above him. The wind blew at him, twisting the rope around, causing him to lose his footing against the wall. With bared teeth, he chanced another look upward just in time to see the smile on Lourdes' face through his periphery.

He narrowed his eyes and worked with painfully awkward movements to get the last few knives free from his belt, tossing them out of his fall radius. He grunted through the pain that burned through the muscles and tendons in his shoulder and slid down several more feet before bracing himself and letting go of the rope just as the linen broke free beneath Lourdes' hand.

***

Vivian gave the dresser one more shove before it finally moved enough for her to come out of the closet. She'd promised Tucker John that she would stay hidden, that she would wait until he came for her, but from the sounds and shouts, the breaking glass and the way Lourdes' voice echoed triumphantly through the hall, it was apparent that moment was not likely to happen.

She forced her mind from the thought that she was to blame for Tucker John's death. Had she not brought him forward through time, had she not hidden him from the Cleric's Office, had she just given him his rifle....

His rifle! It was still beneath her floorboards just in front of her bed. She'd get it and she'd...she'd what? She pressed her hand against her chest and pinched her eyes closed. Hot, stinging tears escaped from the corners of her eyes. She was afraid, terrified, but she would do what she had to do. She owed Tucker John that much.

"Lord Jesus, help me," she whispered forcing one foot in front of the other, out of the suffocating safety of Lourdes' room and in the direction of her own. She'd do what she had to do and deal with the consequences when the smoke cleared.

She crept into her room but quickly slid into the black that covered the wall. She could hear Lourdes' voice, could hear the sound of her taking in deep ragged breaths but she couldn't see her. She did see one of her paperweights lift into the air and launch itself out the window!

Vivian bit the inside of her cheek and dug her nails into the palms of her hands to keep from crying out in panic. Everything she was seeing and yet not seeing defied logic and pushed her near over her mental limits. Her eyes, wide, searched the dark of her room, fighting desperately to see something. She looked past her open window only for a shadowy figure, small and feminine to appear in her periphery. Her eyes snapped back toward the window but saw nothing.

Again she let her eyes wander, and again she saw the figure, Lourdes, in her periphery, but only there. *The static!* She angled her head just enough to keep Lourdes in sight even as she searched for a weapon, anything to use against her. She took the risk and tip-toed to her dresser. The water pitcher was the first weapon to come to mind. She'd knock her unconscious with it and then get the rifle.

Lourdes' face was soaked with rain droplets. Her chest rose and fell with a rush of adrenaline. She didn't know if murdering Tucker John had made her feel ill or exhilarated as she looked at his body lying motionless in the grass atop a bed of broken glass. The Animal had dropped a good twenty feet or so. The distance to the ground, however, was not a guarantee that he was dead. She dropped several large objects from the window. None of them hit him, unfortunately, but they all made a deep sound on impact with the ground.

He still didn't move.

The former pain that had made her head pound when it had collided with the wall suddenly came back upon her and made her body tremble. She didn't like adrenaline. She dropped her head between her knees and waited until the sensation had gone. Then she looked back out the window. He was still there. He had to be dead. There was a decent amount of blood that shown around him when the lightning struck, darkening the broken glass at his back.

She backed away from the window, only to scream as the sound of a water pitcher shattering against the floor and Vivian screaming, drew her out of her oblivious state. Johnny had taken hold of Vivian from behind, pinning her arms to her sides. Vivian screamed again, and fought against him, hitting him in his bloodied side. Pain made him strike her, his large, raw hand cupped across Vivian's face, drawing blood from her mouth and nose.

Vivian crumpled from the blow, her mouth open and her eyes searching her surroundings as if from confusion. But she wasn't confused, only stalling. Her hand slid across the wet wood planks of her floor and grabbed hold of the nearest piece of broken glass. "John Jay," she slurred his name.

"Get up, Vivian!" He ordered her, his voice clogged from his broken nose and tears. "Look what you've made me do. Look what you've done to me!"

"Johnny," Lourdes took a step toward him.

"Stay back, Lourdes!"

Vivian flipped over on her back and pushed further away from them. John Jay grabbed her by the collar of her nightgown. Vivian screamed. Flailing and kicking she stabbed at his forearm and made him release her.

"Tucker John!" She screamed running for the door only to trip over John Jay's outstretched arm.

John Jay straddled her, prying the glass from her hand and tossing it across the room.

"Tucker John!"

"He's dead! He fell from the window," Lourdes screamed. She limped to stand over her, now pinned to the ground. "And you're going to die for what you've done to us, for what you've done to Johnny."

"Vivian shook her head against the floor and tried to break free to no avail. She cried out Tucker John's name one more time before her voice was cut off by hands covering her mouth.

"Get out of the static, Lourdes. And wait for me in the den. I don-I don't want you to see this. I'll finish this."

"No!" Vivian shoved his hand from her mouth and screamed again. John Jay towed her up from the ground with a painful grunt. Vivian screamed Tucker John's name one last time before he wrapped his hands around her throat and lifted her to her toes.

"Get out of here, Lourdes and wait for me. Please! Please?" His whimpered. Without another look back, Lourdes hurried from the room. Vivian began to see stars.

***

Clarence had purchased them some time. Opening the door behind John Jay, causing him to stumble back against Tucker John's stairs, had brought the timeline back in order. The presence of the rapier would have devastated each thread thereafter, had it been used at full voltage against Tucker John's chest. It had grazed the man's head but he had survived the blow.

But Clarence butting John Jay with its hilt behind his head was all that was needed to allow for Tucker John's fall and Vivian's capture. Mr. Lemon would be pleased. More than that, Clarence was pleased. There was too much at stake for him not to be.

CHAPTER 57

Tucker John jerked on the bed of glass. The sound of his name as if being called from a dream pulled his eyes open. He sucked in a staggered and pained breath. The wind and the consciousness had been knocked clean out of him. He gritted his teeth and pinched his eyes shut. Everything was blurry at first. Glass crunched as he rolled to his side and fire burned up his back and arms. Even his head was stinging. There was a great deal of blood pouring from his back, scalp, and arms. The broken windowpane had done a nasty job breaking his fall, most of the shock was born in his feet but the slick grass made him fall backward with great force. The linen rope had lessened some of the edge from the glass but hadn't formed the best of barriers.

He lay on his side and slowly pulled fragments of glass from his back and arms and other tiny pieces from the back of his head.

The sound of breaking glass and another muffled cry came from the house. Viv called out his name, again. Hers was the voice that had called him to consciousness. A surge of panic shot through him driving him on all fours. He quickly looked for the knives he'd tossed and then forced himself to his feet. His adrenaline kicked in and the pain suddenly ebbed into intermission. He knew it was only a matter of time before the adrenaline subsided and the pain and bruised ribs he knew he had, reminded him of their presence. He couldn't dwell on it now. At that moment all he had was tunnel vision.

He cut off a wad of linen rope and pressed it against the back of his head to stop his scalp from bleeding, ignoring the wounds that seeped blood. Then as fast as he could, he rushed toward the nearest window and back into the house, his knife angled at the ready.

***

Nothing Vivian had tried to do was prevailing against John Jay. She couldn't break free of his hold no matter how much she bucked and flailed. His arms remained strongly braced around her ribcage as he dragged her into the nexus room. She had gotten free of him once but he'd struck her in the chin with his fist and she'd nearly blacked out. He'd never hit her before but then he had never tried to kill her either.

Tucker John had been right. There was no reasoning with him although that didn't keep her from trying. She couldn't even bring herself to cease calling out Tucker John's name. She jerked her body and kicked at the shelving on the wall, doing anything possible to get free. Several vases fell to the ground and shattered. John Jay tightened his hold on her. The pressure made her holler.

"Vivian, please don't make this any harder than it already is!" His voice was pitiful, whiny, jumping from remorse to rage. She feared his sound and was grateful she couldn't see him.

She took in a deep breath and screamed Tucker John's name at the top of her lungs again. John Jay's hand clamped tight over her mouth and nose, cutting off her air. He held his hand there until she'd nearly gone unconscious. The slickness of his raw, bloody skin stained her face. "Were you calling that *Animal*? that racist, sack of flesh!" He jerked her hard, and pain shot up her neck and down her back.

She tried to pry away his hands but she couldn't gain purchase against the slickness. She was beginning to lose consciousness again. The irony of it all crashed down on her. Not so long ago she had been careful of Tucker John and praying for the protection of her husband. Now, rendered helpless, she was crying out for the very man she had blamed for her misfortune. Why didn't he come? She couldn't believe he was dead.

As if he'd heard her thoughts, John Jay answered. "I threw him from the window, Vivian, just like the trash he was, just like you should've done a long time ago! How could you live with that *thing* in this house? After all the lives he destroyed!"

Fatigued from resisting him, Vivian sank into his grasp. John Jay dropped her to the ground, his handling of her devoid of any mercy. If she survived the night she would have several friction bruises and a swollen lip, eye and nose to attest to his brutality. He treated her as if she were a hated dog that he was putting down.

She found it hard to keep her eyes open. He'd cut off her oxygen so many times. Even out of his grasp she was very unsteady. She focused long enough to see him step through the nexus gate and then back again, his mask of invisibility completely gone. His bloodied broken state finally revealed.

Vivian's heart nearly stopped at the sight of him. He looked as if he'd been left in the desert sun for days and then had his skin peeled until his hands and arms cracked and ran with blood. His face was badly bruised and his nose swollen and askew from his brawl with Tucker John.

Staring down at her, tears rolled out from his swollen eyes. "Do you see what you've done to me?"

She shook her head. "I didn't do that, John Jay—"

"Yes, you did! You did this,"

"You're sick," her voice cracked. "You need help. You need to stop this,"

He shook his head and turned toward the nexus table. "I'm not sick, Vivian. If I am then you're the virus and being rid of you is the only cure."

"No,"

"Yes. This is your fault. You take credit for everything else, take credit for this. Own it!" He uploaded a foreign command that made the gate moan and hiss. Static poured out from it like fluid from a festering wound. Vivian had crawled only a few feet out of the nexus room by the time he turned to face her.

With new found rage, he was upon her again.

"Stop fighting, Vivian, please! The sooner this is over the sooner the pain will end. I don't want to hurt you, but you've left me no choice!" He turned her to face him, cupping her face in his hands. There were more tears in his eyes. What had happened to him?

Vivian cried and tried to pull free. "Let me go, John Jay!"

He shook his head. "I can't. I wish you'd just shut up. I wish I still had the baton. If I had that, this could've been done already," He raked his raw fingers through his damp hair. "But it disappeared upstairs, just like someone snatched it from my hand." His voice trailed off with a faraway look in his swollen eyes.

Vivian stayed as still as she could. John Jay wasn't making any sense. He was beyond sick, beyond broken by time.

Focusing again, he said, "Had you just gone easily none of this would be happening. Had you just listened to Lourdes and sent him back to 1837 or-or euthanized him," his mouth dipped at the corners and his bruised face blotched red with tears. "But he has infected you and we can't turn back now. I'm sorry. This isn't what I wanted for you, not like this." He took her by the arm and dragged her through the house and down into the lab.

He shoved her down to the ground and grabbed the rope that draped over the lab desk. Realization punched like a fist to her temple. He was going to hang her. "No!" She kicked at him and managed to create space between them. Snarling, John Jay closed the distance and reached for her, the noose in hand.

Aiming for his bloodied side she kicked him in his wound and brought him down to his knees. Again she scrambled up to stand but was yanked down by her ponytail. His arm clamped underneath her chin. Gagging, she fought to reason with him. "I'll leave! I swear! John Jay, please! Think about what you're about to do!"

"I have! This isn't what I wanted!" He tightened his grip. "This decision has been eating at me, Vivian. I've been thinking about it for a long time—"

"No, you haven't! You can't turn back if you go through with this. This is murder. I'm your wife. You're murdering your wife!"

He shook his head. "Don't say that," he bristled and shoved her beneath him, pinning her down with his weight.

Vivian raised a trembling hand. "Okay! Okay...Just think, please. There's still a chance to get you help. No one else has to die—"

He yanked her upward by her wrist, bringing her nose to nose with him. "This is the only way! And I'm not the one who's sick. I wrote several letters to my mom and Marcus telling them how you've been acting strange."

He pulled a container of Static from his pocket and poured it on the floor. The Static pooled and spread. Viciously he dragged Vivian's exposed flesh against it until her skin began to chafe and bleed.

She let out a cry of pain and managed to break free of his grasp. John Jay didn't resist her but he kept his weight on her. "You're the one that found the static," he pointed at the puddle.

"Tucker John!" she cried out again to no avail.

"You're the one that got me lost inside it and then got obsessed with the Animal! Then you broke the nexus gate. You let too much static out and it ate you up. That's why your arms are bleeding so badly, and you tried to cover your tracks by killing the Animal, then you hanged yourself because you lost it! But Lourdes, Lourdes saved me."

"John Jay, please," Vivian hit at him, struck him with all her might. He took hold of a fistful of her hair and yanked her head back down. Vivian hollered. "Don't kill us, John Jay, please!"

John Jay seethed through his teeth. "I told you he's dead!" He pulled her from the ground by her hair. He was going to hang her there in the lab.

"No, John Jay, our baby, not Tucker John. Our child. Don't kill us, please. Please?"

He froze still, his gaze icier than any winter she'd ever lived through. Vivian turned and tried to get to her feet but was knocked back down by his boot to her backside. Weeping, John Jay took a hold of her hair again and straddled her back. He held her like that for a few short seconds. Silence crept into the room with a deathly chill. Vivian felt the tension in John Jay's fist ease upon her scalp only to feel the burn of a rope tighten around her throat.

"No, Vivian. You had an affair with that Animal. That baby isn't mine! It's not mine!"

CHAPTER 58

Tucker John was having trouble moving his right shoulder. He reckoned he'd done it a lot of damage in the fall. At least he couldn't feel it as intensely as he had before. Either way, it was a bad mark against him. He'd given John Jay a good working with his fist, but fighting an invisible man came with its own set of challenges, that and John Jay hadn't been pushed out of a window.

It was going to be a hard-won war, trying to best the man without his rifle. Shooting him left winged would be just as hard. If Tucker John had been in the same level of health as he was before his fall or the jolt of electricity to his head, it would've been a different story. But with his vision crossing and his body trembling with dull pain and bleeding, he wasn't so sure. He was certain that he was going to give the bastard, and his whore, a filthy fight to the death, even if he ended up being the one to meet his Maker.

"Johnny?"

He stilled, hearing the hateful whisper of Lourdes call to him from behind.

"Johnny, is it over?" She paused, softening her tone. "Did you get rid of her already? I know this is hard for you, but we have to. And you need to be taken care of. Your arms are still bleeding, you're bleeding all over," her voice hitched.

Tucker John felt her move closer to him.

"Did she hurt you more than you already were?" She reached out and touched his shoulder. "Oh, Johnny,"

Tucker John turned around and caught her wrist, squeezing it until she growled with guttural pain. "Not like I'm about to hurt you, Lourdes."

Her face drained of color. She called for John Jay right before catching a fist to the stomach, its force so fierce it lifted her off her feet. She buckled to the ground, heaving the contents of her belly.

Still twisting her wrist he said, "I wouldn't normally punch a female, but since you dropped me from almost two stories high, I figured I had the right to, being that you're in the murdering way and all." He yanked her up by the arm. "Where's Viv, Lourdes?" He hissed into her ear.

Lourdes held her belly, gasping for air. Tucker John hooked her under the chin with the blade and took a slice out of her chin. She cried out, her hands grabbing the wound, her eyes wide with shock.

"That's for my back." He cut her across the breadth of her stomach, only deep enough to make her buckle in pain, then he twisted her back to him hooking his forearm under her bleeding chin, giving her only enough room to breathe, enough room to answer.

"That's for dropping out of the window. Now that we're working toward even, where's Viv?"

Lourdes began to stutter, her slippered feet, kicking as she fought for more air. The point of Tucker John's blade sliced down her cheek. Her body arced with resistance.

"If she dies because of your stalling—"

"The lab!" She coughed out with tears. She took several breaths and sobbed as the tightness eased from around her throat. "Johnny's going to kill you! He's going to kill both of you for hurting me," she cried.

Tucker John gripped her by the nape of her neck and shoved her forward.

***

"You made me do this!" John Jay cried. He pulled on the rope's two ends with trembling hands. Vivian forced her fingers underneath the cord and fought with all her might to keep from strangling.

"Johnny!" Lourdes gagged out his name and cried out as the knife in Tucker John's hand dragged across her collarbone.

John Jay ceased to tug the ropes around Vivian's neck but held her to the ground. The sight of Lourdes caught in Tucker John's hands made his entire body shake with tremors. He couldn't move.

"You're a dead man,"

Tucker John narrowed his eyes. "Get yo' a$$ off of her. Now boy! Turn her loose!" Tucker John shouted. The veins in his neck and chest bulged. John Jay didn't budge. Tucker John yanked at Lourdes' hair and dragged the knife down her collarbone a second time, making her cry out again.

John Jay screamed. Tucker John had his attention.

Color seeping from his bruised skin, John Jay dropped one end of the rope around Viv's neck. She collapsed onto the floor and gasped for air, pulling the rope from around her.

"Don't you hurt her!" John Jay called out pointing a trembling raw finger.

"Are you crying, Johnny-boy?" Tucker John laughed. He tugged Lourdes' head back again and took a limping step deeper into the lab. "Lourdes, you gone through all this trouble to swipe a tear-soaked man from underneath his wife?" He laughed again and tugged at her hair even harder, giving her head a violent shake. "A man that cry more than a female ain't worth a slop pot."

John Jay shifted his weight from on top of Viv. He hadn't even noticed he was doing it, but she had. The more Tucker John bated him, the more he loosed her. All he could focus on was Lourdes and the pained look in her eyes. Viv carefully crawled out of his reach sparing a glance a Tucker John. He took another step forward with Lourdes.

John Jay hollered. "Get your hands off her! Lourdes, baby, it's going to be okay," he fixed his gaze on Tucker John. "I'll give Vivian to you if you let her go. You want her too, don't you, Animal?" Vivian was too numb to feel the ache of John Jay's exchange of her.

She watched as he reached down with a searching hand for the other end of the rope only to find that the rope was completely slack and she out of his grasp.

Her eyes met his one final time before she scurried to her feet and toward the back wall in the lab, opening up the secret door to the stairwell that led to her bedroom.

John Jay clumsily stood but Viv was gone, taking the stairs two at a time upward.

Thucrump!

John Jay's head swung from Viv's direction back to Lourdes and Tucker John. The sound of breaking breastbone and the punctured flesh giving way to the knife in Tucker John's bloodied hand pulled at him like a marionette string in the hand of a puppeteer.

Lourdes grey eyes were round, blood poured from her lips. Her hands felt the hilt of the blade, still in Tucker John's hands protruding from her chest.

Tucker John kept his eyes locked on John Jay as he spoke in her ear, but loud enough for John Jay to hear, "I told you I was gon' gut you," he tore the blade free from her breast and drove it into her again, this time right into her naval and upward before he slung her body away from his. "Pig!"

Her body was still mid-motion when John Jay leaped on him. Tucker John lost hold of the knife, his body ramming into the wall. John Jay's fist collided with his chin. The shelf rocked behind them and several glass beakers crashed to the floor.

Tucker John used his left elbow and drove it hard into John Jay's jaw, then steadied himself as dizziness overtook him. John Jay slacked at the knees but didn't lose his grip on Tucker John. With a guttural roar, Tucker John landed a solid fist against John Jay's temple, breaking his hold. He landed another against his jaw. John Jay finally made contact with the ground, his body arced as the glass pieces bit into him.

Tucker John forced him harder against the cutting glass, landing several more punches to his face. Fueled with hellfire and a surge of energy, John Jay growled from within. He'd lost everything, and the look in his eye said he intended to make Tucker John pay.

John Jay blocked the impact of another punch and managed to land one of his own, the force of it so on target that Tucker John's teeth chattered. His eyesight darkened and he staggered to his knee. Forgetting the strain on his wounded side, John Jay foolishly kicked at him, the heel of his foot pushing hard against Tucker John's abdomen. Both men crumpled to the ground.

Winded, Tucker John fell over, this time on his back. John Jay was up on his feet again. He'd managed to get hold of one of Tucker John's knives, raising it above his head, ready to drive it into Tucker John's chest the same way he'd done Lourdes. Rushing forward, his foot kicked the broken neck of a beaker into Tucker John's reach and with a swift upward movement, Tucker John ferociously ripped through his belly and then across his face.

John Jay's lungs emptied with a horrified roar, dropping the knife as he examined the damage done to him. The side of his mouth flapped open awkwardly and drained of blood and saliva. The jagged edge of the beaker had torn his face open, exposing his teeth and gums.

Tucker John knew he hadn't cut the man deep enough in his stomach to kill him, but it had given him enough time to climb to his feet, an effort that cost him too much energy and left him very little to do anything else besides fight off fainting. Black splotches began to pepper his vision giving John Jay the opening he needed to ram his shoulder into his stomach and drive upward.

He felt his body lifting from the ground and his teeth chattering as his back slammed down into the lab counter with a force that rocked the walls and sent a nasty echo resonating throughout the lab.

His neck whipped brutally on impact. The sudden jarring force shook his brain again and his eyes went black for a few seconds too long. John Jay took hold of his throat, straddling him on the lab counter, shrieking as if he were on fire, blood pouring from the flap of his cheek like lava.

"You murdered her!" His bloody words slurred as he wept. He jerked at Tucker John as if he were trying to ring the head off of a chicken.

Tucker John tried to break his lock on his throat, to no avail. Mustering strength, he caught John Jay one good time in the eye with his fist. He briefly released him just long enough for Tucker John's vision to clear, only to blur again from the blow to the eye and cheekbone that John Jay landed him.

His hands too heavy to lift to punch, he thrust his clawing fingers into John Jay's hip wound and tore at the flesh. An animal-like cry rose from John Jay's belly right before he slammed his forehead into Tucker John's jaw.

That was enough to knock the wind out of Tucker John's sails completely. That blow, coupled with the slam against the countertop, the fall from the window, and the loss of blood, made his arms sprawl outward. His body wanted to slide from the lab counter like spilled liquid. It could give no more, and his head could take no more. He'd given a good effort but he was finished. Still, his soul cursed and fought within him, urging him to keep fighting back, but he couldn't move.

"I'm going to kill you!" John Jay slurred. More blood slid down the side of his face and neck and sputtered from his lips. His bloody, trembling hands squeezed Tucker John's throat again.

Tucker John managed a smile before his oxygen was closed off. He may not have killed John Jay but he had ruined him. He tried to rise up, fight for his last breath, but his body felt like lead. He was done for. At least he'd finished off Lourdes like he'd planned. He just prayed he'd bought Viv enough time to have gotten away or at least called the Cleric's Office for help.

Hope. That and prayer were all he had left. *Jesus, please help her.* He felt his puffy eyes close of their own volition, the sounds of John Jay's ranting ebbing into the background of his descent into unconsciousness.

Click-click BOOM!

Tucker John's eyes snapped open with a jarring start. His eyes focused just as John Jay's body flew back and away from his, his head blown wide open by the familiar drum of his rifle. Trembling with a moan, Tucker John lifted his head long enough to register what had happened before he dropped his head back down on the counter and looked upside down at Viv. She didn't look back at him. Instead, she stood staring blankly outward, tears streaming down the bruises of her face, the rifle still raised at her shoulder and smoke streaming upward from its barrel.

The image nearly made his heart stop. He was grateful for her kill-shot that saved his life, but he couldn't keep his heart from sinking down into his bare feet, not just for Viv, but for himself.

Just like that, with the sound of the shot and shattering skull, he'd been jettisoned back into the past, back into the Spruce cabin when he was fifteen years old. Viv had done just like his mama. She had killed the man she'd once loved right before he could kill Tucker John.

She had saved his life at the cost of her own.

CHAPTER 59

(Three Months Later)

Drinking down a cold glass of water, Tucker John stared at Viv through the kitchen window. She stood alone outside, in her thin slippers, on top of the shallow graves he'd dug for Lourdes and John Jay. Viv had said the heavy winter boots made her swelling feet ache all the more. But right now she just needed a little more time to think. She was still stuck in the 'why's' and 'good-byes' of her life, trying to make sense of things that had no answers within reach.

He understood. He understood her struggle, just the same as he understood why she'd taken to just calling him Tucker, omitting his given name of John. She couldn't cope with doing so, not yet anyhow. It would take longer than three months to heal from the wounds she had received. It was that, and the mounting questions that still remained without answers, especially those concerning how and why their lives had collided that made her toss and turn with fitful sleep at night.

Those questions came to light again the very week he was able to stand on his own two feet and start living again, living really for the first time. He'd mustered the courage to ask Viv for his rifle. Since the night she'd blown John Jay to kingdom come, it had gone missing again. She paled and trembled at the mention of it, tried to deflect the issue of it by asking him about the mysterious note he'd received from the Cleric's Office, the one postmarked to John Jay.

"I met a man the first night I followed Lourdes and found the gate she had in her mama's basement. I meant to kill him but he convinced me not to, said he was in surveillance, same as you, that he was here surveying us, actually." He watched Viv stiffen, her eyes glaze over as she shrank back into her dark thoughts. Touching her hand he'd pulled her back into their present.

"He told me that night you weren't my enemy, that John Jay was, and that I needed to be very careful of him. That's when I started looking at you and everything from a different perspective. The man, Magnus, sent me the note as a sign of good faith, a way of proving who he was."

Viv had flinched when she'd heard Magnus' name. "Magnus Sanderson sent you the letter?"

Tucker John had simply nodded.

Viv took in a stuttering breath, her brow pulled tight together. "He's the acting Chief in rotation, brought in on a special assignment that no one knew about. He was brought here because of us." It had been a statement, not a question. Before he could say anything else, Viv had left the room only to return with his rifle. Fear made her dark eyes glassy with unshed tears.

She said, "Can you tell me what you know about this rifle and how you got it?"

He told her the truth, same as he had the first time she'd asked. "I won it in a rigged card game a while back. A fella' wearing glasses surrendered it to me. Even taught me how to make bullets for it. I knew he'd fixed the game to my favor but this automatic firing makes life a whole lot easier and hell, I just wanted the dang thing. Didn't bother asking him too much about it in the way of details you're looking for."

Viv pressed her eyes shut and pointed an accusing finger at the rifle. "Tucker, that rifle is a *Winchester Model 94. 30-30 Lever Action Rifle*, a repeat fire rifle, which isn't even invented until 1894." She opened her eyes and stared at him, her lips pressed into a grim line while she'd let him do the math. "Someone tampered with the timeline, orchestrated all of this, chose you, chose me and…" Tears had fallen from her eyes. She'd given into faint and would have fallen to the ground had he not caught her.

He had to admit that his stomach sank when she gave him the revelation. He didn't know what to think. Why would anyone go through such trouble for him? His heart gave a wild but peculiar kick in his chest. Viv had gone through a heap of trouble for him and by the way things where sounding with the rifle and the mess they were in, there was only more trouble to come. It only made him do as much learning about time, surveillance and the static as he could, when he could. He hated being out of his depth. It was a deadly thing.

Nevertheless, Viv seemed to be doing her best to survive. A lot had happened since the night that John Jay had come back through the nexus gate, and she was fighting hard against the weight of it all. He admired how strong she was. The woman had grit that was for sure.

She did have a slight breakdown and a fit of tears that morning, which in his estimation, was at least a sign that she was processing some of her emotions. She was feeling them and not letting them fester. He had worried she would become like his mama after she had shot his daddy, or worse yet, his old self after his family had been taken away from him. She hadn't, but she had tried to avoid confronting much of what had taken place.

He woke up that morning to the sound of her beating against the nexus gate. He took another drink of cold water and replayed the ordeal in his mind.

Viv was on her knees, crying with frustration and mumbling to herself as she tried to fix whatever it was that John Jay had done to the nexus gate on the night of his death. Lourdes had activated the perimeter fence so they were stuck inside with no way out especially since the nexus gate was disabled and the perimeter fence reinforced in a way that went beyond Viv's understanding.

When Tucker John drew closer to her he realized she was more beating the gate than fixing it.

"Viv! Stop that," he caught her arm in mid-strike and pulled the mallet from her hands. The wood of the nexus table and the doorframe was badly dented. "What in Sam Hill are you doing?"

Her red eyes narrowed. "What does it look like? I'm trying to fix this! I can't figure out what he did to it." She stood, fist balled, and hollered out the window in the direction of John Jay's grave. "What did you do?"

Tucker John sighed. "Viv, come on now, calm down," his voice was gentle.

She spun on him. "Calm down? How? The Cleric's Office thinks I'm a rebel now and the Governing forces have started to gather."

He nodded. He didn't mind the Governing forces gathering. They'd become a captive audience with which he could take up his soapbox. He intended to go to the property's edge later on that day and give whoever was there a good talking to on Viv's behalf. It had become part of his daily routine since he'd been able to move about on his own.

Viv continued. "We're stuck here. We can't get out. They trapped us in here!" She pointed behind her with a stiff arm.

"But they can't get in so that's a good thing. And we have more than enough food to last us several long years. Rain still gets through the perimeter fence, so we are just fine on that front."

Viv's brow twisted. His words didn't placate her one bit. "The nexus gate still isn't working!"

He nodded. "I know that,"

"Then how are you telling me to calm down?"

"Because I know, as well as you do, that being stuck in here was their plan, and far as I can tell they didn't mean to be trapped in here forever. They just wanted time alone."

Viv's jaw set. She folded her arms across her chest and turned away from him, shaking her head. Then she started in on the nexus gate again, this time kicking it.

Tucker John grabbed hold of her elbow. "Stop it before you go and hurt yourself over nothing."

"You think this is nothing?"

He kept his tone calm, but sighed, taking a quick second to buffer his response. "That ain't what I meant. What I meant was, you can't fix it right now so don't get riled up. That's all. It'll work when it's supposed to, all in good time. For now, we'll just make the best of things."

"I can't, Tucker," her chest swelled, more tears were on their way. Pregnancy had certainly given her a full supply of those. "I can't get you home if I stop," her voice cracked.

He gave her a look. "You already know where I stand on that, Viv."

"But it's not right that you are stuck in here. I should at least be able to get you out! He was my problem! This is my problem. You shouldn't have to pay for it." The tears overflowed from her eyes.

Tucker John finally pulled her into his embrace. She was stiff against him like all the other times when he decided to comfort her. "That's enough, now. Go on and calm yourself."

She finally rested her head on his shoulder and turned her face toward his neck. The warmth of her breath tickled his skin. "I just want to go home," she whispered.

"I know," he rested his chin on her crown.

Now the wind blew and tugged at her dark tunic. The silhouette of her body enhanced. He rubbed the spot on his belly where hers had pressed against his and little feet kicked against him. The baby was growing so fast. Viv still looked very tiny in comparison to other pregnant women he'd seen in his life, but she was growing and sooner than they knew it, the baby would be born.

He walked away from the kitchen window and gave Viv some privacy. He had some thinking of his own to do. He'd actually been doing it ever since time had sucked him up and dropped him in 4037.

Despite Viv's insistence upon getting him home, he'd already told her several times that he wasn't going back to his timeline. It didn't make sense for him to return back to 1837, pending death aside. What man in his right mind would do such a thing? That period in history, even for him, a half Irish, white man, born at the very bottom of the barrel to a Catholic woman, and a poor, whore-mongering drunk, was a scraping, uphill battle.

Sure he had a name and a level of status, but he had earned his position by bringing others down to their knees. It was a vicious survival of the fittest battleground dressed in over-starched clothes. And even then he still wasn't good enough to be invited to eat at the master's table or even his own brother's.

He would always be the blight, the mar in the room, the 'necessary evil' he had once heard the mistress of a plantation refer to him as. History may have recorded him as dead in 1837 but he had died the day his daddy came home and took shots to his head from his mama's rifle. Life had closed his coffin right in that very instant. Ashford Junior drove in each and every nail not long after.

Beyond that, he was thirty-five years old, way past the age a decent man took a wife and had little ones. He now realized that the reputation he'd once hid behind with a false air of pride was nothing more than a millstone around his neck. No respectable woman in 1837 would have him.

He honestly hadn't even considered taking a wife before or ever being in the family way after the demise of his family. Whites worth their salt would shun him as a mate for their daughters and having a black woman wasn't even heard of. Sure he'd had his fair share of black skin in his bed to sate his manly appetite, but he'd never once thought about taking one to wife. The thought would've been absurd.

It wasn't like that in 4037. There was nothing absurd about it. It was the natural thing in that timeline. After being forced into the chokehold of Vivian Leona, being made to listen to her, and learn her, the darkness inside of her and the light, to him having any other woman for a wife *but* that woman was the absurdity. That woman had put a bullet in her own husband to spare his life. Even with her own bruises and wounds she still made time thereafter to tend to him. She bandaged his cuts and his bruises, and she certainly didn't have to. She could have left him to die from his own wounds, but she didn't.

In the following weeks, when they both had healed up enough to sleep in their own beds, he found himself being woken up by her asking to lie next to him. It was nothing intimate. She never touched him and he fought hard not to touch her. She was just too afraid to sleep alone, to be alone. But she took comfort in his presence, which only made him warm to her all the more. She needed him, although she hadn't said so. It was troubling to think what level of fear ruled her nights to the point she would find comfort in the very man she had so adamantly feared. But he was just as adamant in making her never fear him like that again. He was determined to get her to love him.

He still wasn't much on godly things, though he'd kept his promise and had made it a point to seek his Lord, but he did know the parable of the man who had found a priceless pearl and sold all he had to obtain it. Funny, he felt like that man in regards to Viv.

By no means was *The New Golden Age* golden, no matter the façade the natives of that time put up. Tucker John still knew better. Life without feeling was nothing but death. He'd been the walking dead long enough to know that. This was his chance to start over, live again. Live for the first time. Why shouldn't he?

He was determined to have what he had the right by God to have and no one was going to stop him. He was even going to have him a good woman to raise up a family with, a woman to love and to be loved by.

Viv had locked her heart up tight and made no signs of warming to him in that way but Tucker John banked on the time alone that they had trapped on her property to work in his favor.

He would court her somehow, win her before it was all said and done. No longer was he going to be the lone Spruce in a dead forest. He was going to have a family with the best woman he could find, with the best woman who'd found him and snatched him several millennia through time.

It truly didn't make him any difference what color her skin was. She had the golden heart of a lioness and a fire that drew him like no other. He had found what he wanted, found what he needed, and he wasn't going to let her go and no amount of time could make him.

Dear Reader,

I do hope you enjoyed this time-twisting tale of suspense and thrills. Tucker John and Vivian's story has only just begun and only time will tell where they will end up. Thank you for joining me with the start of their story. Book two, Nexus Gate 4037: The Mystery coming soon! If you would consider posting a review for Nexus Gate 4037: The Animal at your online retailer that would be most appreciated. Review NEXUS GATE 4037: THE ANIMAL

In the meantime, enjoy this teaser from my next novel and Sci-Fi adventure, WARDEN, coming Spring/Summer 2019.

For promotions and new releases, be sure to subscribe to Candice Coates' mailing list: www.candicecoateswrites.com

WARDEN

Ever since the bizarre death of her grandmother, Maeve Grandie has made it her sole purpose to be reliable, even if that means living a dreadfully predictable life. The only sense of adventure Maeve experiences is in her dreams. The only problem is her strange hereditary condition that gives her rashes on her hands and arms, turning the veins of her arms a screaming azurite blue, causes her to not only have fantastical REM experiences but sleepwalk as well.

But what would happen if those dreams that carry her into a peculiar land where people can cause their hands to ignite with blue flames and tear open the sky with their bare hands is not really a dream at all?

What if the dream world, Maeve finds herself suddenly trapped in, is actually a true world of wonder but one she is somehow destroying just by being there?

Ward, watch, guard, preserve, protect. Wardens. Senior Warden Vincent Jasper of Trident finds himself facing that very real and immeasurable danger when a young woman in the ugly pink night gown interferes with an arrest right before disappearing through an Unzoned Door in the Universe causing the very threads of the Cluster and Realms to ripple and stretch, putting it and the lives of all who live within it in grave danger. Not only is the woman unknown but she keeps opening Doors and is somehow hiding right underneath his nose.

Can Jasper and his team along with the rest of Trident, apprehend this villainous threat clad in garish pink flannel and ruffles? Or will they find out that she is not the threat at all but the weapon of someone else, all before their side of the Universe collapses?

CHAPTER 1

Maeve turned over onto her back. Her heart raced and her ears drummed from the rapid blood flow coursing through her. She sucked in a sharp breath, held it in her chest for a few moments—just long enough for the pressure to begin to hurt— and then she let it slip slowly from her puckered lips.

She'd had the dream again.

In all honesty, she didn't know if she should call what she was seeing while asleep a dream. It wasn't like the other strange dreams she'd been having lately. Those she knew the instant they began were not real. They had a different feel to them altogether. She felt like she was in a foreign place entirely. This dream, however, this was her reliving a memory. With staunch detail and vivid imagery the events of the day her grandmother died played over and over again as if on repeat the moment she laid her head down to rest.

She was fifteen, nearly sixteen when it happened. It was late spring. The sun was shining but the sky was a deep threatening gray, the kind that makes the trees and grass look far more bright green than they are with a blue backdrop and sunlight. Her grandmother had warned her to come inside, said there was a tornado coming. Maeve ignored her. The trees were still rustling in the wind and had not stopped for nearly an hour. She knew the signs of a coming tornado and this was not it.

She'd hoped it would be one of her favorite spring storms; a dry storm with loud, rumbling thunder and lightning but had no rain to go with it, just sound and lights and gloriously thick, chilled wind. Or a warm spring shower with big, lazy raindrops that soaked clear down to the bones.

This storm was neither of the two.

441

Maeve couldn't see her grandmother, not in the night memory and not on that day. She could only hear her yelling from the house, calling her name as only agitated grandmothers could. "Maeve! MAEVE! Come now! I NEED YOU!" Her grandmother had called her before with the same urgency each time a storm like this brewed.

Obediently, Maeve had gone to her but soon came to know her grandmother to be just like the-boy-who-cried-wolf. As soon as the rain would fall or the lightning would crack the sky, her grandmother would pat her shoulders, smile and say, "I just didn't want you electrocuted, darlin', or sucked up like Dorothy in one of those nasty spinners. Come now, I put the kettle on some time ago and your tea's fixing to catcha' chill." Then she would walk away, her chin up in the air as if nothing had happened, like she had gained some kind of victory.

That was Catherine Much, her grandmother, fighting against the storms in her own mind.

It was the same song and dance over and over again until Maeve began to ignore her grandmother, take her time in going to her, if she even went at all.

She remembered sighing this particular day, yelling back at the house with enough sass to make her tremble with the thought of her grandmother's retribution, had the woman heard her above the rustling wind. She remembered the smell of the soil as the grass tore open. She'd slipped when she went to stand and pulled the turf away with the toe of her sneaker. It reminded her of a sore. More so than anything, more than the smell and the heat, or the moisture on her backside from sitting on the ground too long, she remembered the sound.

What was that sound?

Even after reliving it once again, and hundreds of times before, Maeve could not describe it with due justice. She had told the authorities that it sounded like the sky was being ripped in two, like boulders were being hurled together at incredible speed, like lightning had ripped right inside her inner ear. That

442

sound had shaken her to the ground. The reverberation made her cover her ears and scream, her body pressed down in the grass. And although the sound was incredible and had shaken her until her teeth chattered even into the following day, there surprisingly was no pain.

But she had seen lights following that sound. She lay in the grass, struggling to catch her breath, struggling to make her heart stop racing, her hands still pressing into her ears when she gazed up at the sky. In the east, just above the tree line, the sky drew together in a knot like crumpled black paper, angry and ruined. Then the lights came, jettisoned from the center of the dark space in three unison lines of electric blue.

Time seemed to slow down in that moment and all Maeve could do was stare in fearful wonder. Were they shooting stars? Their tails of light were too perfect to be lightning. Lightning was erratic and unpredictable. It came in one line and then in an instant branched out in several. These three lights did not move erratically. They moved with singular purpose as if they were sent, the center light pulling in front of the others creating a triangular formation, aimed directly for her house, and her grandmother!

Maeve dumbly watched as the lights overtook her home. The stab of instant regret and the sound of her shouting out her grandmother's name were swallowed up by the shock of impact that came at her like a wave the moment the stars made impact. It hit her with such force that she fell backward, knocking her head hard against the ground. A rush of what she thought was electricity broke forth in and around her. She screamed as it streamed out from her hands, covering them like gloves, with a strange sensation akin to a dull itchy rash.

The feeling reminded her of the rashes she'd started to get when she turned twelve, but much more intense. As a younger child, the rashes would cover her hands and wrist like gloves, turning her peanut butter brown skin a nasty shade of red. The veins in her hands and arms, clear to her elbows, would peek past her melanin in strong shades of blue like someone had traced them with azurite-blue oil pastel.

Her hands would throb and tingle and grow numb, and stay that way until the red died or the throbbing in her chest and head ceased. The blue of her veins never faded completely although the intensity of the blue did lessen when she wasn't having flare-ups.

As a child, the doctors never said anything about the rashes or the blue because she never got to see any doctors about it. Her grandmother assured her that there was no need to 'cause bills over something harmless and hereditary.' Maeve just had thin skin, she'd said. What she had was 'the same as when someone got eczema or allergies to eggs—hereditary.' After all, her rashes were not damaging to her health, they were just a minor irritant.

How were throbbing red rashes, crazy blue veins, and a strange pulsing in her head and chest minor?

Maeve couldn't recall anything else about that peculiar stormy day except for finding her house completely empty with an ash gray triangle where her grandmother must have been standing when the shooting stars hit. She also had the lingering curiosity of whether or not shooting stars could vaporize a person.

That was nearly eight years ago to the day.

Her hands still flared up with itchy rashes and screaming blue veins.

*   *   *

"Maeve, are you sure you don't want to go?" Lyrice called out from her bathroom ensuite with a whine. Maeve lay on her stomach across Lyrice's bed, her eyes widening as she read some of the price tags still attached to Lyrice's new clothing.

"Yes, I am sure. I told you I have to work."

Lyrice poked her head out the door and gave Maeve a look.

"It's the truth. Some of us have bills to pay." She flicked the clothing tags out of her sight. The way Lyrice spent money made her head hurt.

"You also need a vacation. Come on, it's Sky Caribbean. It's just ten days—"

"Ten days?" Maeve croaked.

"It's going to be amazing! And you are going to miss it just like always."

Maeve sat up. "That's not true—"

"Yes it is." Lyrice finally came out of her ensuite, pushing a post on the back of her earring. She was getting dressed for the sky cruise flight like she was going to a dinner party; short navy blue cocktail dress, flashy makeup and jewelry. And maybe she was going to a dinner party. Sky Caribbean promised your vacation would begin from the moment you boarded their space craft.

Lyrice said, "You have gone to a total of zero of the events that I have invited you to in the last three years," she made a circle with her hands and peeked through it. "You have missed every date that I have set you up with. Where are my shoes?"

Maeve rubbed her hands together; they were tingling, turning red. She grimaced. She always had crazy dreams when her hands tingled, crazy apart from the night memory about her grandmother. "I don't have the money for a vacation right now."

"I find that hard to believe with all the overtime that you put in." The two stared at each other. "I also told you that I would pay your way and then you could pay me back later, offer is still on the table." Shoving her hand beneath the bed, Lyrice grunted, pulling her heels out from where she had absentmindedly kicked them.

"Debt makes me uncomfortable. You know that."

"I'm like your sister, Maeve. So it's not real debt." Lyrice snorted and shook her head. She was like Maeve's sister. They had been friends since the first grade, when Maeve came to live with her grandmother after her parent's died in Kentucky, and then Lyrice's parents became her guardians after Maeve's grandmother was shooting-star-vaporized. She and Lyrice had been inseparable ever since.

"Lyrice I don't have time to pack my things—"

"I have already packed for you." Cheeky smile painted across her face, Lyrice pointed to a bag in the corner.

Maeve felt her collar tighten. "My passport has expired and there is no time to renew it. The carrier leaves for the cruise in less than three hours."

Exasperation poured from Lyrice's response. "How is it you can come up with a thousand reasons why you can't have a life, but not a one when it comes to going to work, finishing school, paying bills fifteen days before they are due? It's like you are glued to routine. Or you're just scared to have a good time."

Maeve stood up. She was going to leave the room. She hated arguing with Lyrice or anyone for that matter. "I am not scared, I am responsible. I rely on being reliable. People rely on reliable people. If it weren't for someone like me, someone like you would not have the ability to take a space cruise. You need a reliable person to coordinate the cruise and—"

"Maeve Grandie! You live in a bubble, and it's a boring bubble. But fine, don't come. Unpack your bag and continue to be dull and alone. My goodness girl you are going to fade away and it's going to be slow and uneventful. And that makes me sad. Hmmm I am forgetting something . . . " Lyrice did a twirl, patting her body down as if she had pockets. She finally stopped when she touched her hair. "Oh! My hair! How did you let me forget to do my hair?" Her broad shoulders slouched and her knees slightly buckled, bringing Lyrice down to Maeve's height; five foot six to Lyrice's solid five eleven barefoot.

She hurried back to the ensuite tugging at her short, black; pixie cut hair, all drama. The style didn't suit her long narrow face and square jaw at all in Maeve's opinion, which only made Maeve feel guilty. Maeve's hair was similar in style to hers except she had tighter curls. Her face was also a bit rounder with a delicate chin so the hairstyle worked for her. She should have known better than to suggest, or rather allow Lyrice to bully her into suggesting that she get the same look. Twenty times Lyrice had asked if she should and Maeve had, in a roundabout way, told her no. By the eighteenth query Maeve had given in and said Lyrice should go for it. Times nineteen and twenty she had even insisted.

Although Lyrice loved her bad hair, she had decided that she was going to wear it long and colorful for the cruise. Men loved long hair, she'd said.

Silently, Maeve followed Lyrice into the ensuite and watched as she wrapped and attached threads of Super Tracks to her head. She was always amazed at how fast the synthetic hairs grew from the threads, and even more surprised with the different textures and colors that Lyrice chose. They all looked so real and yet none of them matched Lyrice's face, which was a shame because she was actually very beautiful in Maeve's opinion.

"Oh! Oh! Oh! That's long enough." Lyrice stopped the growth of her Super Tracks with her longest layer at her waist. Then she massaged in the desired color scheme; red hair for the top layer, honey blonde of the middle layer, and platinum for the longest layer.

The color combination made Maeve wince. It was a tragic attempt at ombre.

Catching Maeve's reaction in her periphery Lyrice scowled. "I shouldn't even let you see my hair since you aren't coming along." Her shoulders slouched again. "Pleeeeassse, Maeve. I need—"

Maeve's back went rigid. "Please don't do that, Lyrice." A tension-filled silence bloomed between them.

Feeling the chilly edge, Lyrice shifted uncomfortably. "Fine, I apologize." She leaned over and kissed Maeve's cheek. She'd intended to push Maeve's "I need you" button, one she knew would throw Maeve into a guilt trip of quick surrender.

Maeve had been that way ever since her grandmother passed away, moved by guilt because of someone else's need for her. Saying she was needed was like a hateful puppet's string.

She had been boring and square with an overly compulsive way of being "responsibly reliable" because of it. She knew Lyrice loved her anyway. But she also knew Lyrice realized she was not playing fair. The resigned look in her eyes indicated that she was going to leave Maeve alone.

"But I am going to miss you, a lot." She added.

"Me too," Maeve whispered. "Enjoy yourself and stay out of trouble."

"I make no promises. But I will take lots of pictures and maybe even get myself a husband," she made praying hands and mouthed "please, Jesus" as she looked heavenward, before looking back at Maeve. "In which case, you, my dear are going to have to find a new place to stay." She winked.

Maeve hugged her before helping her get her bags downstairs and into the taxi, even though the concierge had offered his assistance. Maeve had to be downstairs anyway so it was no problem. She had to go to work after all.

* * *

Maeve made it home a quarter after one in the morning. Second shift was not her favorite, but it gave her a few extra dollars in pay since nobody else wanted to work the shift. She felt that was a decent exchange. Museum security was certainly not for the faint of heart, especially on a Friday night. Or maybe it was not for those who had healthy social lives.

She made quick work of dinner, smelling the two-day old carton of Szechuan Chicken before warming it up and washing it down with flat Ginger Ale. She needed to go grocery shopping. Lyrice was supposed to. She must have really thought I was going to go on that cruise. Sighing, she shook her head before preparing for bed.

She let herself enjoy the heat of a shower, getting out only after her fingers had pruned and her body was warm to the bones. Lately, whenever she had an outbreak, her body would catch a chill. She massaged cooling cream into her hands to soothe the increasing throb, and pulled on her long, bright pink, checkered, flannel nightdress with the tiny pink and white flowers. Lyrice told her that she was going to burn the thing when Maeve wasn't looking. Maeve didn't care about the unflattering nightdress's appearance. She was only concerned with not being cold throughout the night.

She pulled the covers up to her head and went to sleep expecting to have another one of her crazy dreams . . . her hands had broken out completely by the time she'd closed her eyes.

*   *   *

Maeve struggled to open her eyes. Wind was rushing at her face terribly fast and whipping past her ears with the same sound that vehicles make when they pass each other at high speeds. Her feet were also freezing. Whatever she was standing on rocked and she lost her balance, hitting her knees hard on the cold surface.

She opened her eyes jolted by the loss of balance and the clanging of the metal underneath her. She was on top of a fast moving train! She fought to take a breath and would have completely lost herself in the panic of the dream had it not been for the sounds coming from the top of the train that raced beside her.

Two women were fighting on top of it. Teeth were bared and faces were twisted in angry determined scowls. Language that Maeve preferred not to hear was being exchanged between the two. She must have fallen asleep with the television on and something less than wholesome was playing while she slept . . . had she even turned the television on?

She eased her knees in between the ridges on the top of the train, finding just the slightest bit of security in her not-so-secure grip. She hated to fall in dreams. She always had a sour stomach the following day from her swimming equilibrium.

The two women continued to tussle. The one on top, the one with the black leather jacket, short-cut sandy hair and elfish eyes, reached for her hip, grabbing for her weapon. It's a gun. Maeve thought. It's always a gun. Except for it wasn't a gun. Maeve

449

couldn't tell what it was that the woman was wielding and she didn't get the chance to figure it out. The woman that had been losing the fight somehow managed to gain the upper hand.

Maeve's knee's had also slipped from their position. She grabbed at the air and took hold of the train again, just in time to see the armed woman lose her weapon and then her footing before flying awkwardly from atop the train and out of sight into the pearlescent purple nothing that the trains were traveling through.

Maeve's heart leapt in her chest. She flinched at the sudden burning sensation that assaulted her hands and arms and the pain that pulsated at her temples. Even in the dreams she felt the dull, familiar pain. Bellowing with laughter the other woman managed to stand, not caring at all about what had become of her adversary. She held her belly and chuckled considerably hard after having knocked another person to their death. Then she turned to Maeve, her smile suddenly fading and her hands rising in fear as if she was trying to block Maeve from coming at her with trembling hands, all the while repeating, "No, please, no!"

Maeve only stared harder, her unattractive flannel gown pulling in the wind, snagging on a sharp metal edge of the train top, the lace ruffled neckline scratching her beneath her chin. Then she saw it, a black angry hole breaking open in the sky behind the woman and a streak of blue light arching in lightning speed in her direction. It was just like when her grandmother died!

Her stomach roiled. She had not had a dream like this before.

"Look out!" She warned but her words were for naught. The blue light hit the woman from behind, knocking her almost completely from the train as well, her head snapping back like a ragdoll's. She should have fallen off the train top and been crushed to death but a man had taken hold of her. He was suddenly there right where the light had hit, his face angry. With what seemed like very little effort he yanked the woman back on the train's top, slamming her down hard. The woman gagged. The man straddled her, pinning her shoulders down with his hands that burned with blue flames.

He stared down hard at the woman, and said something to her that Maeve could not hear. The woman responded in turn, but pointed a sharp arm in Maeve's direction. The man turned his head Maeve's direction, his face flickering with shock for just a second before it fell into a dark, and threatening, scowl.

There were a number of things that should have gone through Maeve's mind at the sight of him and the danger he imposed. Thinking that he was the most handsome Black-ginger she'd ever laid her eyes on was not one of them.

He glowered at her through the most amazing molasses eyes. His honey-brown skin began to burn red, giving his complexion an attractive allure. The color in his cheeks only drew out the copper shade of his short-trimmed goatee and mustache that followed a well tapered line into a head of low-cut copper waves that fluttered against the wind.

Stomach quivering, Maeve's eyes slid down to his lips. They were pinched tight but seemed deliciously formed. Although they looked a bit too small in her estimation, she was certain they would be great for a kiss or two . . . or three. But who would keep count kissing that guy. He probably smelled good too.

She paid no attention to the death stare that he was giving her, but she did notice the blue flames in his hands amplifying with intensity right before the oddest thing happened. Her arms erupted with similar fire and light!

Panicked, she tore her eyes from his and stared at her hands and arms. They were fully engulfed in star-dusty, blue fire, the flames of them licking up at her face.

Screaming until she near fainted, Maeve slammed her eyes shut, and swung her arms with all her might, anything to put out the fire, anything to wake up from the dream.

The unforgiving contact of her knuckles smacking hard against the countertop in the kitchen, snatched her out of her dream and back into reality. Her knuckles were bruised now, and she had been sleepwalking...again. That was another "minor irritant" associated with her hereditary disorder, hence the need for the long flannel nightdress. There was nothing more frightening then wandering out in public with your undergarments exposed while asleep. That had yet to happen to her but Maeve wasn't taking any chances.

She rubbed her knuckles and sucked them until the pain had completely ebbed away. Then she made her way back to her bedroom and threw herself on the bed, glancing at her clock. It was 4:40am. She only had two more hours to sleep before she had to get ready for her other job. The crazy dream and the sleepwalking had left her feeling even more exhausted than she had been before she'd even gotten into the bed a few hours ago. At least she got to dream about a handsome man. That was well worth it, bruised knuckles and all.

A smile crept across her face at the thought of the leather-clad, dreamy, Black-ginger. She figured had she not woken up, the two of them could have really had something. He was eating her up with his eyes even if it was in a death-stare. She giggled as embarrassed heat warmed the apples of her cheeks. She hoped she'd dream of him again.

Sadly she didn't, nor did she notice the fresh tear at the hem of her nightdress.

CHAPTER 2

"What was that? Somebody open up Magen Satellite, I need to connect! Did you see that? Did anyone see her?" Senior Warden Vincent Jasper rushed through the command room of Trident headquarters, urgency in his heels. The glass windows of the Trident building reflected the silent lightning flashes that cut through the continuous black of the sky around them—black accept for the azurite blue hue of light that shined down from Magen Satellite.

Jasper kept the image of the young woman firmly on his mind; Black, medium height, brown skin, short black curls, dark brown eyes, ugly nightdress.

Two Deputies and one Junior Deputy slid open the upper window to Magen Satellite. The black triangular tabletop of the viewing bay beneath it began to break apart like a puzzle, pulled upward by a magnet. The smallest center triangle ascended three-hundred feet upward, with the middle triangle one-hundred feet below it, and the largest at equal distance from that. The three tiered triangles hovered in place as the harnessed energy of the powerful wormhole—Magen Satellite—streamed down into the center of the viewing bay painting the black of it radiant blue.

Magen Satellite. It was Trident's heartbeat. It was the very essence and energy of each and every Warden and Deputy. It was also the very substance that had built and held the whole of the Cluster and Realms together.

Senior Warden Jasper tapped into it like he'd done numerous times before. He needed the others to see what he'd seen. He waited until the center tier spun with such speed that it appeared as an orb and burned white. Then as the energy poured in a column through the center of the larger and second triangle ring, Jasper slid his hands underneath the third and largest, resting his hand upon the surface of the viewing bay that was one hundred and fifty feet around. Instantly Magen adapted to his pulse, pulling white threads of his energy upward into its core, connecting with his memory, taking the very image that Jasper wanted exposed.

More azurite blue energy radiated downward, coursing through the seemingly random cracks and grooves of the viewing bay's surface and Trident's flooring, projecting the image Jasper had given into the minds of each Warden on call and even a few of the Deputies that were due for promotion.

Everyone saw the blurry image of the woman in the garish pink flannel nightdress. They saw her energy, felt its pulse and the wildness within it. They saw her scream and disappear, and then use a Door, an Unauthorized Door! They also saw the ripple that broke forth when she did.

This was beyond bad news. Opening an Unauthorized Doors or Unmarked Doors was like weakening threads of a delicate fabric. A rippling Door was a sign that it was Unzoned altogether and there was no telling what the consequences of using one of those could be. Several Wardens rushed to the edges of the room and stared through the large glass wall out into the Realm of Trident.

Nothing outside had changed. The tinted-glass office building still stood sentry. The orange clay earth was still fractured and dead with the impossibility of life every growing there. The sky was still ebony black and cracked with streaks of continuous lightning and burst of deep purple like bruises. The golden train car, the very needle that had knit together the threads of the Cluster, remained in its place, with its continuous humming vibrating outward. It had been vibrating since the very day it ceased to move, the day the Cluster had fully formed. But it had continued to vibrate as if it still had somewhere to go after all these millennia, as if it had one more song of creation to play. But it had not budged nor played a single song in all that time. Instead, it sat at the kissing edge of the Darkest Star like the needle of a record player against an old vinyl record just waiting to play one last tune.

The Darkest Star had not budged either. Its pulse remained consistent and even, its menacing black depth well under control. A black hole, flattened and devouring, but only with a controlled appetite, controlled by Magen itself, and the infrastructure of Trident.

The Wardens stepped away from the windows. "Nothing's changed out there," Warden Eli Fossi remarked, his near black eyes shined, reflecting the flashes of the lighting outdoors.

His mouth was turned slightly down at the corners, making his once round dimples look like elongated wrinkles against his pale skin. He was stating the obvious, however. Even the Junior Deputies would have felt a change in the Realm if one had taken place. It was still comforting to all of them to hear the words. Most everyone went back to their prospective post. Those Wardens and Deputies that had seen Jasper's memory stayed put.

Jasper turned to Eli. "Nothing yet. But you know what could potentially happen when an Unauthorized Door is used. We all know what's at stake. Unfortunately, that Door was Unzoned. Furthermore, who the heck was that?"

*　　*　　*

The train pulled into station just as if nothing had happened. And for most of the passengers nothing had happened. Everyone knew that the crime rate in Bigsby was on the rise. Bigsby was a Passage Station that led to Authorized Doors to other Realms. Unlawful Pulsars were bound to be around, and unpleasant encounters with Wardens were equally expected to happen. So no one paid any attention to the clanging above their heads, or the beams of Warden light that often reflected light against their windows during Warden-Pulsar altercations. It was a usual occurrence upon an arrest.

But someone had noticed. They had watched with careful eyes everything that had happened. They had not paid much attention to the Wardens or the Pulsar they had apprehended. Who they had noticed was the woman in the pink checkered flannel nightdress, the one who beamed with wild energy, and then disappeared through an Unzoned Door. Hardly anyone knew how to access those Doors or even how to use them. But she had. She was impressive.

"Passage to Iotona, please." The woman handed her passageport to the Station Warden and waited her turn to pass through to her desired District, all the while thinking about the woman in the nightdress and all the possibilities that she could bring, would bring when she saw her again. And she would see her again. She had lassoed the woman in the nightdress' pulse.

CHAPTER 3

Maeve rolled her head around her shoulders and yawned again. She was so tired from the night before she could hardly keep her eyes opened. It didn't help at all that she was at the Library on a sunny Saturday afternoon. It was too quiet and too predictable. The most excitement that had taken place that morning was someone returning a movie in the audio return slot of the Library memory bank. Other than that, it was nothing but white noise.

She stood up several times and stretched her legs hoping that would get her blood flowing, but it wasn't helping. All she needed was two more minutes and then she would take a quick nap in the restroom lounge area.

Her break finally came, bringing with it a wave of relief. She was feeling terribly strange, apart from being sleepy, like something was squeezing her middle. Moaning, she loosened up her belt and ran her thumbs in between her pants and stomach. The synching feeling didn't go away. With another groan, she settled on ignoring it, deciding it was probably a side effect of eating two-day-old Chinese food even though she didn't have any urges to heed any calls of nature.

She checked each stall in the restroom before turning on the "out of order" sign and locking the door behind her, only to suddenly grip her head, a wave of lightheadedness hit her hard making her feel weightless. She mustered all of her strength and staggered to the nearby lounging couch, gripping its arm for support. Food poisoning, it had to be food poisoning. She took several breaths fighting against the urge to faint. The tightness around her waist only increased. Unable to stand any longer, Maeve finally sat down letting her head dangle in between her legs, hoping that would help with the dizziness and the tightness.

Taking a deep breath she pulled her head from between her knees and leaned back into the support of the couch cushions, except her head never touched the back of the couch. She hadn't even touched the wall. No, Maeve was falling, tumbling fast and backward into black nothing!

Darkness engulfed her like someone had placed a bag over her head. Her lungs constricted against the rush. No matter how hard she struggled to take a deep breath she couldn't. Panic tugged at her just as firmly as the pressure around her waist. Now she felt like a noose was dragging her, not at all like food poisoning.

She reached her arms out, swinging them wildly, snatching at the open air, hoping to catch hold of something to stop her fall. She was alone, and in the dark, and she needed something firm to hold onto, something reliable! One thing was for sure she was never eating Szechuan Chicken again.

Smack!

Maeve landed hard on her back, forcing what little breath she had from her already strained lungs. She clinched her fist and tightened her jaw muscles, grinding her teeth as she focused to breathe.

Within seconds her lungs inflated like balloons, giving way to the oxygen they so desperately sought. Her back and head ceased to scream at her and her eyes, even behind pinched lids, began to register the light above them. Sound slowly flooded her ears with the whooshing sound of moving trains and dripping water.

Trains? Dripping water? Maeve sprung up from the ground, tiny pebbles of gravel stuck to her hands leaving pink and white dimples in her palms. Spinning around, she brushed the pebbles off on her pant legs as if they were some sort of frightful bug, her eyes widening almost as much as her mouth. Where was she? Had she fallen asleep and slept walked? She knew she sleepwalked, that was one of the reasons why she locked the bathroom door. But she had never walked this far. She didn't even remember falling asleep!

"Don't panic, Maeve. Stay. Calm." She whispered to herself hoping that the sound of her own voice would be enough to settle her nerves. Her equilibrium was still swimming, keeping her off balance. She stumbled to a rusted support poll that was nearest to her and held on to it for balance.

As quickly as her mind could, she began to take in her surroundings. She was under an overpass. There were several train lines overhead. She was standing in gravel, leaning against a rusty poll.

"Okay, you are clearly not at home," she grimaced, her eyes burning with tears. She blinked her vision clear and massaged her forehead with the heel of her hand. A hot tear ran down her face. "Maeve, what did you dooooo?" She pushed away from the rusted pole and tried to decide which way to go. She obviously needed to go to the doctor over this. Her grandmother was absolutely wrong. Her condition was far more than a minor irritant. This, whatever it was that she had, was absolutely frightening.

Balance having been restored, she convinced herself to move. Standing there alone in the shadows of a train overpass was not going to help her find out where she was, let alone get her back home. She was definitely no longer in any area of Cincinnati, Ohio that she was familiar with.

And why had none of the people she worked with stopped her, asked her where she was going, woken her up? Sure she only worked with two other librarians but one of them could have said something. Karen was always so attentive.

Taking careful and timid steps, she eased herself into the sunlight. Sunlight? There was indeed light and it was warm, but there was no sun. At least Maeve couldn't see it. The sky wasn't even blue but more a sallow shade of buff, or was it grayish-white?

"Watch it!"

Maeve staggered backward almost falling. The passerby who'd shoved her away from his path shook his head at her with an irritated grumble. She hadn't seen his face, only caught a subtle whiff of his sweat as he shoved past her.

"S-sorry," her throat was suddenly constricting and dry. She felt like a lost, abused puppy, a wet, lost and abused puppy, because being wet made her more pathetic. Here she was in the middle of somewhere foreign, hopefully a bad dream—it had to be a bad dream—and she had no idea how to wake up or where to go. The only thing that she could think to do was to follow the direction of the crowd.

That bit of logic was flawed since there was no crowd to follow, only the path of the rude man who'd nearly knocked her over. But she would follow him. What choice did she have?

There was also the squeezing tug at her waist, the same sensation that she'd felt before her horrible dream began. And that is what she was going to believe it was, a horrible, bizarre dream, empty of people—except one rude one—and full of rust, and trains, and a pitifully colored buff sky.

*　　　*　　　*

Maeve had been walking for hours seeing nothing but the field of gravel beneath her feet and hearing little besides it crunching and shifting with each step she took. She had long since lost the person she was following as if that were possible in a sea of gravel. But they were indeed gone nonetheless. At least three hours had to have passed. She was certain of it even though she could not tell by her watch since it had broken in her fall, ceasing to tick, and she couldn't tell by the sun since there clearly wasn't a sun. But she could sense that it had been three hours. She knew because she always grew hungry two hours before her shift at the library ended. And she was hungry.

She startled. How was she going to eat? She didn't have her wallet. She had left that in her locker back at work. But if this was a terrible dream then someone would feed her, hopefully.

Maybe it would be that handsome Black-ginger she saw on top of the train last night in the other dream. She hoped so.

She found herself smiling and a nervous giggle released from her throat at the thought of him. Her smile quickly faded. Goodness, Lyrice was right. My life is so boring I am fantasizing about a man from my dreams taking me to lunch!

She kept walking. Within twenty minutes sounds of life began to call to her. She could hear people and birds although she failed to see evidence of either of them. Still, she quickened her pace, moving at a slow jog, her heart jumping higher in her throat with each stride she took. She slowly came to a stop at the threshold of what had to be a town.

"Welcome to the Iotona", a sign read aloud in English before making other audible sounds she couldn't place.

"Iotona?" Her face twisted. Where on Earth was Iotona? She'd certainly never heard of it and she'd heard of lots of places. She was a librarian for goodness sakes, apart from being a museum security guard by night.

Pssss! Maeve startled at the sound. Fast gusts of air blew past her from the columns that flanked the large Welcome to the Iotona sign. There were twelve columns in all standing at least one hundred feet high. Each of them had digital images of trees blowing in the wind. Even birds flew across the pictures, soaring from one digital tree column to the next.

"That's where the bird sounds are coming from?" After walking in miles and miles of gravel and not recalling having seen one bird she was convinced that the sound came from the columns.

Shaking her head and staring at the columns with absolute wonderment, Maeve took her first official steps into the Iotona.

*　　*　　*

(Day 1 of Sky Caribbean Vacation)

The shuttle gave another violent jerk, knocking Lyrice off her balance and nearly out of her seat. Face scrunched in an irate pucker, she flipped up her sleeping mask and unfrosted her carriage window just in time to see an explosion.

Before the question of what had happened could be pushed from her grape colored lips, a holograph of a pilot appeared in her carriage. "Please excuse the disruption."

"The second disruption you mean." She rolled her eyes.

The holograph continued. "Sky Caribbean has experienced a bit of turbulence. Pressure levels in all carriages have been cleared at maximum function. Please continue to remain calm and enjoy your flight."

The holograph was gone just as a fiery explosion let off several miles out, leaving a flash on Lyrice's eyes. She waited for the holograph to reappear with an explanation, but realizing it wasn't going to, she phoned the stewardess.

"This is Jessica," the smiling brunette said. "How can I assist you?"

Lyrice leaned forward and thumbed out her window. "There was a flash of fire out there right after the turbulence. It looked like a chunk of the ship."

Jessica's smile fell but suddenly reappeared. "It is nothing to worry about, Ma'am. We've, unfortunately, encountered a bit of turbulence that claimed our lesser baggage unit. Anyone who is missing luggage will be fully compensated. But for safety measures, our anti-debris shields have been enforced. Will there be anything else; warm towel, cocktail? We are serving lobster." Her smile was far more forced than before.

Lyrice cocked an eyebrow and shook her head. "No. Thank you, Jessica. How long until we reach the dock?"

Jessica made several lines of information flash upon Lyrice's screen. "We will reach dock in twenty minutes, at which time you will board either the Single's Cruise or the Couples." Another smile.

"Thank you." Lyrice broke contact. Twenty minutes; that was sure to be enough time to get herself freshened up for all those delicious single men who were waiting for her picking.

"Maeve, you have no idea what you are missing. Oh!" A large piece of chard luggage slammed into the anti-debris shield at Lyrice's window before sliding off into space.

Lyrice watched it, shaking her head, bits of chard intimates and clothes dotted the sky like confetti. "God pity the soul who just lost their underwear." Shrugging she began to fix her hair.

CHAPTER 4

"What do we have on the woman from the train? It's been four days." Senior Warden Jasper swiftly moved through Trident like the wind was on his back. He always moved fast, walking as if he was trying to keep up with something, as if everything he was doing was of the highest priority and urgency.

Out of all the Senior Detective Wardens in the Trident, he was the only one who had managed to solve and close every case that had ever been given to him, every case but one. He seldom thought of that case, and when he did he thought of it in terms of a woman who was right under his nose, one he failed to notice until it was too late. She was gone and never coming back. She was 'the one that got away'. Everyone in Trident knew of the case as The-one-that-got-away, but no one knew what she was about. No one bothered to ask, and Jasper never bothered to tell.

To anyone who did not know him, Senior Warden Vincent Jasper was all seriousness, all work and no play. That was only partly true. Although he saw things in two colors of morality, black and white—right or wrong, he was easy going and did enjoy a joke or two. He just enjoyed them at a faster pace than others, and quickly moved on to the next phase of thought, generally a more serious phase of thought. All he'd been thinking about for nearly a week was the brown-skinned woman in the horrid nightdress, riding atop a train toward Bigsby.

Warden Loomes, the main Warden who kept the viewing bay to Magen, nodded toward his apprentice Deputy, Smith Janks. They'd had a bit of time to do some digging in regard to the woman from the train; the one who'd disappeared through an Unzoned Door.

Ready to answer, Deputy Smith Janks squared his shoulders, clearly wanting to make the best impression on Jasper. Most everyone did. His calm but powerful presence demanded it.

Deputy Janks' voice cracked, his nerves getting the best of him. Jasper could feel it. This was the young man's first time reporting on Magen and out of all the Wardens he had to report to Jasper. Jasper knew it was a tough break.

"Senior Warden Jasper," he swallowed down the cotton that had formed in his mouth.

Jasper remained calm, wide stance, and shoulders square, hands clasped behind his back, and chin slightly lifted. If anyone from the outside was looking on at the exchange, they would have seen Jasper as arrogant and intimidating. But Deputy Smith Janks saw and felt differently, reading the pulse of Jasper's energy. He projected confidence to the Deputy, pulsing his own energy so that Deputy Smith Janks would relax, and feel secure in his place. It was encouragement given without words.

Jasper lifted his brow as if they were hooks, pulling Deputy Smith Janks up and together. It worked. The young man's energy and posture changed.

He cleared his throat one last time. "Senior Warden Jasper, Warden Loomes and I,"

"We, Deputy, always 'we'. Trident is many but one. We are community. Proceed."

All Wardens were to speak using the pronoun 'we'. It spoke of group dependency, removed the bounds of superiority. That was the rule for all Wardens except Senior Wardens. They were the only ones within Trident permitted to use 'I' when addressing a fellow Warden unless context suggested otherwise. They were the only ones with enough energy to singularly sustain Magen Satellite and thusly the Darkest Star. It was that knowledge and that truth that brought meekness and humility.

The Cluster would be completely devoured and all life within it consumed, otherwise.

The Senior Wardens recognized that with one false move they could destroy all of Trident, and their very own existence. All of them recognized their responsibility for what it was—a sacred trust. They were part of the threads that kept their world firmly knitted together.

"Yes, sir." Deputy Smith Janks responded. "We've been successful in isolating a signature read on the woman in question. Although the signature is faint, it should prove to be enough to properly identify her."

Jasper studied the Signature Isolator, taking note of the scarce energy traces that had been captured within it. The main S.I of Trident was only a few yards away from the central viewing bay, erected of the same black-as-sackcloth stone, with a waist high asscher cut surface. The table top was smooth apart from Trident's emblem that was carved in its center. The sides of the structure were etched with similar cracks and grooves as the floors of Trident. Energy from Magen coursed through the crevices like blood through veins, pushing itself upward through the center of the table where everything that had been isolated floated within a blue orb of Magen light.

The energy signature retrieved seemed fragile, like the breath of a whisper against the ear, breaking and fading with the start and end of each word. But it was there and it would have to be enough. Jasper had to take what he could get.

"Can we receive it?" he asked, still staring at the signature, his appetite for it increasing.

Deputy Smith Janks looked to his superior. Loomes nodded again. "Yes sir, Magen is ready whenever we are."

Jasper exposed his wrists and with one slight flinch absorbed what had been gathered of the woman's signature. Instantly he was given access to far more information than the suspect's DNA. Although faint, every aspect of her became exposed, her personality characteristics, dominant emotional patterns, her strengths and weaknesses. The very core of her person was laid out for him to see. Very little was left hidden from that single, fragile reading. Ironically, it failed to give clear details like her name.

As if he were sleeping, Jasper's chin rested against his chest and his eyes closed, his brow just slightly drawn together. He stood for several moments taking in all that he could from the frailty of the absorbed signature, rubbing his fingertips together, massaging the signature into a more firmly rooted memory. The gesture was nothing more than a force of habit.

His head cocked to the side. Well, she certainly isn't a lunatic. That blew that theory out of the water. Other Wardens had suggested that perhaps she, the woman in the ugly nightdress, was one of the Broken, the kind who had to be given over to Magen before they reached complete adulthood. The Broken were far too dangerous otherwise. They were uncontained Magen power with little-to-no concept of reality. The power within them drove them mad, turned them into weapons of mass destruction. They couldn't be reasoned with.

At least that was one concern brushed away. On the contrary, this young lady was very firmly grounded which only troubled Jasper.

What else did he see? What else could he gather? He concentrated deeper, shifting his head at slight angels as if he was trying to hear a very faint voice, and he was. The word, coming forth, translated in a pulse of energy, finally came into focus and held strong long enough for Jasper to receive it and not lose hold of it. Resolute.

He straightened, still gnawing on that single word. That was all he could read from that signature. He had gotten other things from it, things of importance, but lesser importance: things like her physical attributes, her fragrance.

As usual her physical attributes would be taken into consideration with Trident, but they would not be held with the highest of esteem. Attributes like those were seedy. They could be easily mistaken with someone else's. But Signature Traits, like being resolute, were strong and easy to grasp. They were solid—distinct. Everyone had a unique type of resolution. This woman's resolution was specific; it reminded Jasper of his own.

He almost smiled. It wasn't a happy smile, or maybe it was; but it wasn't the kind of happy that this woman would appreciate. No, what it meant was the hunt was on. He felt his own energy rising at that thought.

If you enjoyed the teaser to WARDEN, be sure to subscribe to Candice Coates' mailing list for an official release date as well as promotions and other new releases: www.candicecoateswrites.com

ABOUT THE AUTHOR

Candice Coates is an author, and artist, born and raised in central Ohio. She has always had a love for telling a story and bringing to life the seeds of worlds born in her dreams and imagination, weaving together concepts of struggle, adventure, redemption, and triumph.

Although she studied Advertising and Graphic Design and has a talent for visual arts, and music, her greatest love is found between the marriage of paper and pen, as well as languages.

While she loves to tell a new story, she appreciates and is drawn to the challenge of reforming and exploring different ways to interpret common concepts within her own work especially themes such as time travel, alternate universes, alien encounters, and anti-heroes just to name a few.

Jumping from genres ranging from speculative science fiction, fantasy, action-thrillers and even to comedic contemporary romance, Candice allows her faith in Jesus to kiss each piece with a touch of faith and relatable hope.

When not working on new manuscripts, Candice can be found creating visual art or creating content at her sister site, I came for the soup..., where she encourages other creatives to simply create with courage and faith. She also bakes a mean sugar cookie and other magical treats!

You can also follow her on FACEBOOK, INSTAGRAM, & TWITTER.